W9-ASQ-804

MR. SAMMLER'S PLANET

ALSO BY SAUL BELLOW

Dangling Man

The Victim

The Adventures of Augie March

Seize the Day

Henderson the Rain King

Herzog

The Last Analysis

Mosby's Memoirs and Other Stories

Saul Bellow
Mr. Sammler's Planet

THE VIKING PRESS
NEW YORK

First published in 1970 by The Viking Press, Inc.
625 Madison Avenue, New York, N.Y. 10022

Published simultaneously in Canada by
The Macmillan Company of Canada Limited

SBN 670-33319-0

Library of Congress catalog card number: 74-87248

Printed in U.S.A. by H. Wolff Book Mfg. Co.

Second printing February 1970

This book originally appeared in *Atlantic Monthly*
in a different form.

MR. SAMMLER'S PLANET

Shortly after dawn, or what would have been dawn in a normal sky, Mr. Artur Sammler with his bushy eye took in the books and papers of his West Side bedroom and suspected strongly that they were the wrong books, the wrong papers. In a way it did not matter much to a man of seventy-plus, and at leisure. You had to be a crank to insist on being right. Being right was largely a matter of explanations. Intellectual man had become an explaining creature. Fathers to children, wives to husbands, lecturers to listeners, experts to laymen, colleagues to colleagues, doctors to patients, man to his own soul, explained. The roots of this, the causes of the other, the source of events, the history, the structure, the reasons why. For the most part, in one ear out the other. The soul wanted what it wanted. It had its own natural knowledge. It sat unhappily on superstructures of explanation, poor bird, not knowing which way to fly.

The eye closed briefly. A Dutch drudgery, it occurred to Sammler, pumping and pumping to keep a few acres of dry ground. The invading sea being a metaphor for the multiplication of facts and sensations. The earth being an earth of ideas.

He thought, since he had no job to wake up to, that he might give sleep a second chance to resolve certain difficulties imaginatively for him, and pulled up the disconnected electric blanket with its internal sinews and lumps. The satin binding was nice to the finger tips. He was still drowsy, but not really inclined to sleep. Time to be conscious.

He sat and plugged in the electric coil. Water had been prepared at bedtime. He liked to watch the changes of the ashen wires. They came to life with fury, throwing tiny sparks and sinking into red rigidity under the Pyrex laboratory flask. Deeper. Blenching. He had only one good eye. The left distinguished only light and shade. But the good eye was dark-bright, full of observation through the overhanging hairs of the brow as in some breeds of dog. For his height he had a small face. The combination made him conspicuous.

His conspicuousness was on his mind; it worried him. For several days, Mr. Sammler returning on the customary bus late afternoons from the Forty-second Street Library had been watching a pickpocket at work. The man got on at Columbus Circle. The job, the crime, was done by Seventy-second Street. Mr. Sammler if he had not been a tall straphanger would not with his one good eye have seen these things happening. But now he wondered whether he had not drawn too close, whether he had also been seen seeing. He wore smoked glasses, at all times protecting his vision, but he couldn't be taken for a blind man. He didn't have the white cane, only a furled umbrella, British-style. Moreover, he didn't have the look of blindness. The pickpocket himself wore dark shades. He was a powerful Negro in a camel's-hair coat, dressed with extraordinary elegance, as if by Mr. Fish of the West End, or Turnbull and Asser of Jermyn Street. (Mr. Sammler knew his London.) The Negro's perfect circles of gentian violet banded with lovely gold turned toward Sammler, but the face showed the effrontery of a big animal. Sammler was not timid, but he had had as much trouble in life as he wanted. A good deal of this, waiting for assimilation, would never be accommodated. He suspected the criminal was aware that a tall old white man (passing as blind?) had observed, had seen the minutest details of his crimes. Staring down. As if watching open-heart surgery. And though he dissembled, deciding not to turn aside when the thief looked at him, his elderly, his compact, civilized face colored strongly, the short hairs bristled, the lips and gums were stinging. He felt a constriction, a clutch of sickness at the base of the skull where the nerves, muscles, blood vessels were tightly interlaced. The breath of wartime Poland passing over the damaged tissues—that nerve-spaghetti, as he thought of it.

Buses were bearable, subways were killing. Must he give up the bus? He had not minded his own business as a man of seventy in New York should do. It was always Mr. Sammler's problem that he didn't know his proper age, didn't appreciate his situation, unprotected here by position, by privileges of remoteness made possible by an income of fifty thousand dollars in New York—club membership, taxis, doormen, guarded approaches. For him it was the buses, or the grinding subway, lunch at the automat. No cause for grave complaint, but his years as an "Englishman," two decades in London as correspondent for Warsaw papers and journals, had left him with attitudes not especially useful to a refugee in Manhattan. He had developed expressions suited to an Oxford common room; he had the face of a British Museum reader. Sammler as a schoolboy in Cracow before World War I fell in love with England. Most of that nonsense had been knocked out of him. He had reconsidered the whole question of Anglophilia, thinking skeptically about Salvador de Madariaga, Mario Praz, André Maurois and Colonel Bramble. He knew the phenomenon. Still, confronted by the elegant brute in the bus he had seen picking a purse—the purse still hung open—he adopted an English tone. A dry, a neat, a prim face declared that one had not crossed anyone's boundary; one was satisfied with one's own business. But under the high armpits Mr. Sammler was intensely hot, wet; hanging on his strap, sealed in by bodies, receiving their weight and laying his own on them as the fat tires took the giant curve at Seventy-second Street with a growl of flabby power.

He didn't in fact appear to know his age, or at what point of life he stood. You could see that in his way of walking. On the streets, he was tense, quick, erratically light and reckless, the elderly hair stirring on the back of his head. Crossing, he lifted the rolled umbrella high and pointed to show cars, buses, speeding trucks, and cabs bearing down on him the way he intended to go. They might run him over, but he could not help his style of striding blind.

With the pickpocket we were in an adjoining region of recklessness. He knew the man was working the Riverside bus. He had seen him picking purses, and he had reported it to the police. The police were not greatly interested in the report. It had made Sammler feel like a fool to go immediately to a phone booth on Riverside Drive. Of course the phone was smashed. Most outdoor telephones were smashed, crippled. They were urinals, also. New York was getting worse than Naples or Salonika. It was like an Asian, an African town, from this standpoint. The opulent sections of the city were not immune. You opened a jeweled door into degradation, from hypercivilized Byzantine luxury straight into the state of nature, the barbarous world of color erupting from beneath. It might well be barbarous on either side of the jeweled door. Sexually, for example. The thing evidently, as Mr. Sammler was beginning to grasp, consisted in obtaining the privileges, and the free ways of barbarism, under the protection of civilized order, property rights, refined technological organization, and so on. Yes, that must be it.

Mr. Sammler ground his coffee in a square box, cranking counterclockwise between long knees. To commonplace actions he brought a special pedantic awkwardness. In Poland, France, England, students, young gentlemen of his time, had been unacquainted with kitchens. Now he did things that cooks and maids had once done. He did them with a certain priestly stiffness. Acknowledgment of social descent. Historical ruin. Transformation of society. It was beyond personal humbling. He had gotten over those ideas during the war in Poland—utterly gotten over all that, especially the idiotic pain of losing class privileges. As well as he could with one eye, he darned his own socks, sewed his buttons, scrubbed his own sink, winter-treated his woolens in the spring with a spray can. Of course there were ladies, his daughter, Shula, his niece (by marriage), Margotte Arkin, in whose apartment he lived. They did for him, when they thought of it. Sometimes they did a great deal, but not dependably, routinely. The routines he did himself. It was conceivably even part of his youthfulness—youthfulness sustained with certain tremors. Sammler knew these tremors. It was amusing—Sammler noted in old women wearing textured tights, in old sexual men, this quiver of vivacity with which they obeyed the sovereign youth-style. The powers are the powers—overlords, kings, gods. And of course no one knew when to quit. No one made sober decent terms with death.

The grounds in the little drawer of the mill he held above the flask. The red coil went deeper, whiter, white. The kinks had tantrums. Beads of water flashed up. Individually, the pioneers gracefully went to the surface. Then they all seethed together. He poured in the grounds. In his cup, a lump of sugar, a dusty spoonful of Pream. In the night table he kept a bag of onion rolls from Zabar's. They were in plastic, a transparent uterine bag fastened with a white plastic clip. The night table, copper-lined, formerly a humidor, kept things fresh. It had belonged to Margotte's husband, Ussher Arkin. Arkin, killed three years ago in a plane crash, a good man, was missed, was regretted, mourned by Sammler. When he was invited by the widow to occupy a bedroom in the large apartment on West Ninetieth Street, Sammler asked to have Arkin's humidor in his room. Sentimental herself, Margotte said, "Of course, Uncle. What a nice thought. You did love Ussher." Margotte was German, romantic. Sammler was something else. He was not even her uncle. She was the niece of his wife, who had died in Poland in 1940. His late wife. The widow's late aunt. Wherever you looked, or tried to look, there were the late. It took some getting used to.

Grapefruit juice he drank from a can with two triangular punctures kept on the window sill. The curtain parted as he reached and he looked out. Brownstones, balustrades, bay windows, wrought-iron. Like stamps in an album—the dun rose of buildings canceled by the heavy black of grilles, of corrugated rainspouts. How very heavy human life was here, in forms of bourgeois solidity. Attempted permanence was sad. We were now flying to the moon. Did one have a right to private expectations, being like those bubbles in the flask? But then also people exaggerated the tragic accents of their condition. They stressed too hard the disintegrated assurances; what formerly was believed, trusted, was now bitterly circled in black irony. The rejected bourgeois black of stability thus translated. That too was improper, incorrect. People justifying idleness, silliness, shallowness, distemper, lust—turning former respectability inside out.

Such was Sammler's eastward view, a soft asphalt belly rising, in which lay steaming sewer navels. Spalled sidewalks with clusters of ash cans. Brownstones. The yellow brick of elevator buildings like his own. Little copses of television antennas. Whiplike, graceful thrilling metal dendrites drawing images from the air, bringing brotherhood, communion to immured apartment people. Westward the Hudson came between Sammler and the great Spry industries of New Jersey. These flashed their electric message through intervening night. SPRY. But then he was half blind.

In the bus he had been seeing well enough. He saw a crime committed. He reported it to the cops. They were not greatly shaken. He might then have stayed away from that particular bus, but instead he tried hard to repeat the experience. He went to Columbus Circle and hung about until he saw his man again. Four fascinating times he had watched the thing done, the crime, the first afternoon staring down at the masculine hand that came from behind lifting the clasp and tipping the pocketbook lightly to make it fall open. Sammler saw a polished Negro forefinger without haste, with no criminal tremor, turning aside a plastic folder with Social Security or credit cards, emery sticks, a lipstick capsule, coral paper tissues, nipping open the catch of a change purse—and there lay the green of money. Still at the same rate, the fingers took out the dollars. Then with the touch of a doctor on a patient's belly the Negro moved back the slope leather, turned the gilded scallop catch. Sammler, feeling his head small, shrunk with strain, the teeth tensed, still was looking at the patent-leather bag riding, picked, on the woman's hip, finding that he was irritated with her. That she felt nothing. What an idiot! Going around with some kind of stupid mold in her skull. Zero instincts, no grasp of New York. While the man turned from her, broad-shouldered in the camel's-hair coat. The dark glasses, the original design by Christian Dior, a powerful throat banded by a tab collar and a cherry silk necktie spouting out. Under the African nose, a cropped mustache. Ever so slightly inclining toward him, Sammler believed he could smell French perfume from the breast of the camel's-hair coat. Had the man noticed him then? Had he perhaps followed him home? Of this Sammler was not sure.

He didn't give a damn for the glamour, the style, the art of criminals. They were no social heroes to him. He had had some talks on this very matter with one of his younger relations, Angela Gruner, the daughter of Dr. Arnold Gruner in New Rochelle, who had brought him over to the States in 1947, digging him out of the DP camp in Salzburg. Because Arnold (Elya) Gruner had Old World family feelings. And studying the lists of refugees in the Yiddish papers, he had found the names Artur and Shula Sammler. Angela, who was in Sammler's neighborhood several times a week because her psychiatrist was just around the corner, often stopped in for a visit. She was one of those handsome, passionate, rich girls who were always an important social and human category. A bad education. In literature, mostly French. At Sarah Lawrence College. And Mr. Sammler had to try hard to remember the Balzac he had read in Cracow in 1913. Vautrin the escaped criminal. From the hulks. *Trompe-la-mort.* No, he didn't have much use for the romance of the outlaw. Angela sent money to defense funds for black murderers and rapists. That was her business of course.

However, Mr. Sammler had to admit that once he had seen the pickpocket at work he wanted very much to see the thing again. He didn't know why. It was a powerful event, and illicitly—that is, against his own stable principles—he craved a repetition. One detail of old readings he recalled without effort—the moment in *Crime and Punishment* at which Raskolnikov brought down the ax on the bare head of the old woman, her thin gray-streaked grease-smeared hair, the rat's-tail braid fastened by a broken horn comb on her neck. That is to say that horror, crime, murder, did vivify all the phenomena, the most ordinary details of experience. In evil as in art there was illumination. It was, of course, like the tale by Charles Lamb, burning down a house to roast a pig. Was a general conflagration necessary? All you needed was a controlled fire in the right place. Still, to ask everyone to refrain from setting fires until the thing could be done in the right place, in a higher manner, was possibly too much. And while

Sammler, getting off the bus, intended to phone the police, he nevertheless received from the crime the benefit of an enlarged vision. The air was brighter—late afternoon, daylight-saving time. The world, Riverside Drive, was wickedly lighted up. Wicked because the clear light made all objects so explicit, and this explicitness taunted Mr. Minutely-Observant Artur Sammler. All metaphysicians please note. Here is how it is. You will never see more clearly. And what do you make of it? This phone booth has a metal floor; smooth-hinged the folding green doors, but the floor is smarting with dry urine, the plastic telephone instrument is smashed, and a stump is hanging at the end of the cord.

Not in three blocks did he find a phone he could safely put a dime into, and so he went home. In his lobby the building management had set up a television screen so that the doorman could watch for criminals. But the doorman was always off somewhere. The buzzing rectangle of electronic radiance was vacant. Underfoot was the respectable carpet, brown as gravy. The inner gate of the elevator, supple brass diamonds folding, grimy and gleaming. Sammler went into the apartment and sat on the sofa in the foyer, which Margotte had covered with large squares of Woolworth bandannas, tied at the corners and pinned to the old cushions. He dialed the police and said, "I want to report a crime."

"What kind of crime?"

"A pickpocket."

"Just a minute, I'll connect you."

There was a long buzz. A voice toneless with indifference or fatigue said, "Yes."

Mr. Sammler in his foreign Polish Oxonian English tried to be as compressed, direct, and factual as possible. To save time. To avoid complicated interrogation, needless detail.

"I wish to report a pickpocket on the Riverside bus."

"O.K."

"Sir?"

"O.K. I said O.K., report."

"A Negro, about six feet tall, about two hundred pounds, about thirty-five years old, very good-looking, very well dressed."

"O.K."

"I thought I should call in."

"O.K."

"Are you going to do anything?"

"We're supposed to, aren't we? What's your name?"

"Artur Sammler."

"All right, Art. Where do you live?"

"Dear sir, I will tell you, but I am asking what you intend to do about this man."

"What do you think we should do?"

"Arrest him."

"We have to catch him first."

"You should put a man on the bus."

"We haven't got a man to put on the bus. There are lots of buses, Art, and not enough men. Lots of conventions, banquets, and so on we have to cover, Art. VIPs and Brass. There are lots of ladies shopping at Lord and Taylor, Bonwit's, and Saks', leaving purses on chairs while they go to feel the goods."

"I understand. You don't have the personnel, and there are priorities, political pressures. But I could point out the man."

"Some other time."

"You don't want him pointed out?"

"Sure, but we have a waiting list."

"I have to get on *your* list?"

"That's right, Abe."

"Artur."

"Arthur."

Tensely sitting forward in bright lamplight, Artur Sammler like a motorcyclist who has been struck in the forehead by a pebble from the road, trivially stung, smiled with long lips. America! (he was speaking to himself). Advertised throughout the universe as *the* most desirable, most exemplary of all nations.

"Let me make sure I understand you, officer—mister detective. This man is going to rob more people, but you aren't going to do anything about it. Is that right?"

It was right—confirmed by silence, though no ordinary silence. Mr. Sammler said, "Good-by, sir."

After this, when Sammler should have shunned the bus, he rode it oftener than ever. The thief had a regular route, and he dressed for the ride, for his work. Always gorgeously garbed. Mr. Sammler was struck once, but not astonished, to see that he wore a single gold earring. This was too much to keep to himself, and for the first time he then mentioned to Margotte, his niece and landlady, to Shula, his daughter, that this handsome, this striking, arrogant pickpocket, this African prince or great black beast was seeking whom he might devour between Columbus Circle and Verdi Square.

To Margotte it was fascinating. Anything fascinating she was prepared to discuss all day, from every point of view with full German pedantry. Who was this black? What were his origins, his class or racial attitudes, his psychological views, his true emotions, his aesthetic, his political ideas? Was he a revolutionary? Would he be for black guerrilla warfare? Unless Sammler had private thoughts to occupy him, he couldn't sit through these talks with Margotte. She was sweet but on the theoretical side very tedious, and when she settled down to an earnest theme, one was lost. This was why he ground his own coffee, boiled water in his flask, kept onion rolls in the humidor, even urinated in the washbasin (rising on his toes to a meditation on the inherent melancholy of animal nature, continually in travail, according to Aristotle). Because mornings could disappear while Margotte in her goodness speculated. He had learned his lesson one week when she wished to analyze Hannah Arendt's phrase The Banality of Evil, and kept him in the living room, sitting on a sofa (made of foam rubber, laid on plywood supported by two-inch sections of pipe, backed by trapezoids of cushion all covered in dark-gray denim). He couldn't bring himself to say what he thought. For one thing, she seldom stopped to listen. For another, he doubted that he could make himself clear. Moreover, most of her family had been destroyed by the Nazis like his own, though she herself had gotten out in 1937. Not he. The war had caught him, with Shula and his late wife, in Poland. They had gone there to liquidate his father-in-law's estate. Lawyers should have attended to this, but it was important to Antonina to supervise it in person. She was killed in 1940, and her father's optical-instrument factory (a small one) was dismantled and sent to Austria. No postwar indemnity was paid. Margotte received payment from the West German government for her family's property in Frankfurt. Arkin hadn't left her much; she needed this German money. You didn't argue with people in such circumstances. Of course he had circumstances of his own, as she recognized. He had actually gone through it, lost his wife, lost an eye. Still, on the theoretical side, they could discuss the question. Purely as a question. Uncle Artur, sitting, knees high in the sling chair, his pale-tufted eyes shaded by tinted glasses, the forked veins coming down from the swells of his forehead and the big mouth determined to be silent.

"The idea being," said Margotte, "that here is no great spirit of evil. Those people were too insignificant, Uncle. They were just ordinary lower-class people, administrators, small bureaucrats, or *Lumpenproletariat.* A mass society does not produce great criminals. It's because of the division of labor all over society which broke up the whole idea of general responsibility. Piecework did it. It's like instead of a forest with enormous trees, you have to think of small plants with shallow roots. Modern civilization doesn't create great individual phenomena any more."

The late Arkin, generally affectionate and indulgent, knew how to make Margotte shut up. He was a tall, splendid, half-bald, mustached man with a good subtle brain in his head. Political theory had been his field. He taught at Hunter College—taught women. Charming, idiotic, nonsensical girls, he used to say. Now and then, a powerful female intelligence, but very angry, very complaining, too much sex-ideology, poor things. It was when he was on his way to Cincinnati to lecture at some Hebrew college that his plane crashed. Sammler noticed how his widow tended now to impersonate him. She had become the political theorist. She spoke in his name, as presumably he would have done, and there was no one to protect his ideas. The common fate also of Socrates and Jesus. Up to a point, Arkin had enjoyed Margotte's tormenting conversation, it must be admitted. Her nonsense pleased him, and under the mustache he would grin to himself, long arms reaching to the ends of the trapezoidal cushions, and his stockinged feet set upon each other (he took off his shoes the instant he sat down). But after she had gone on a while, he would say, "Enough, enough of this Weimar *schmaltz.* Cut it, Margotte!" That big virile interruption would never be heard again in this cockeyed living room.

Margotte was short, round, full. Her legs in black net stockings, especially the underthighs, were attractively heavy. Seated, she put out one foot like a dancer, instep curved forward. She set her strong little fist on her haunch. Arkin once said to Uncle Sammler that she was a first-class device as long as someone aimed her in the right direction. She was a good soul, he told him, but the energetic goodness could be tremendously misapplied. Sammler saw this for himself. She couldn't wash a tomato without getting her sleeves wet. The place was burglarized because she raised the window to admire a sunset and forgot to lock it. The burglars entered the dining room from the rooftop just below. The sentimental value of her lockets, chains, rings, heirlooms was not appreciated by the insurance company. The windows were now nailed shut and draped. Meals were eaten by candlelight. Just enough glow to see the framed reproductions from the Museum of Modern Art, and across the table, Margotte serving, spattering the tablecloth; her lovely grin, dark and tender, with clean, imperfect small teeth, and eyes dark blue and devoid of wickedness. A bothersome creature, willing, cheerful, purposeful, maladroit. The cups and tableware were greasy. She forgot to flush the toilet. But all that one could easily live with. It was her earnestness that gave the trouble—considering everything under the sun with such German wrongheadedness. As though to be Jewish weren't trouble enough, the poor woman was German too.

"So. And what is your opinion, dear Uncle Sammler?" At last she asked. "I know you have thought a lot about this. You experienced so much. And you and Ussher had such conversations about that crazy old fellow—King Rumkowski. The man from Lodz. . . . What do you think?"

Uncle Sammler had compact cheeks, his color was good for a man in his seventies, and he was not greatly wrinkled. There were, however, on the left side, the blind side, thin long lines like the lines in a cracked glass or within a cake of ice.

To answer was not useful. It would produce more discussion, more explanation. Nevertheless, he was addressed by another human being. He was old-fashioned. The courtesy of some reply was necessary.

"The idea of making the century's great crime look dull is not banal. Politically, psychologically, the Germans had an idea of genius. The banality was only camouflage. What better way to get the curse out of murder than to make it look ordinary, boring, or trite? With horrible political insight they found a way to disguise the thing. Intellectuals do not understand. They get their notions about matters like this from literature. They expect a wicked hero like Richard III. But do you think the Nazis didn't know what murder was? Everybody (except certain bluestockings) knows what murder is. That is very old human knowledge. The best and purest human beings, from the beginning of time, have understood that life is sacred. To defy that old understanding is not banality. There was a conspiracy against the sacredness of life. Banality is the adopted disguise of a very powerful will to abolish conscience. Is such a project trivial? Only if human life is trivial. This woman professor's enemy is modern civilization itself. She is only using the Germans to attack the twentieth century—to denounce it in terms invented by Germans. Making use of a tragic history to promote the foolish ideas of Weimar intellectuals."

Arguments! Explanations! thought Sammler. All will explain everything to all, until the next, the new common version is ready. This version, a residue of what people for a century or so say to one another, will be, like the old, a fiction. More elements of reality perhaps will be incorporated in the new version. But the important consideration was that life should recover its plenitude, its normal contented turgidity. All the old fusty stuff had to be blown away, of course, so we might be nearer to nature. To be nearer to nature was necessary in order to keep in balance the achievements of modern Method. The Germans had been the giants of this Method in industry and war. To relax from rationality and calculation, machinery, planning, technics, they had romance, mythomania, peculiar aesthetic fanaticism. These, too, were like machines—the aesthetic machine, the philosophic machine, the mythomanic machine, the culture machine. Machines in the sense of being systematic. System demands mediocrity, not greatness. System is based on labor. Labor connected to art is banality. Hence the sensitivity of cultivated Germans to everything banal. It exposed the rule, the might of Method, and their submission to Method. Sammler had it all figured out. Alert to the peril and disgrace of explanations, he was himself no mean explainer. And even in the old days, in the days when he was "British," in the lovely twenties and thirties when he lived in Great Russell Street, when he was acquainted with Maynard Keynes, Lytton Strachey, and H. G. Wells and loved "British" views, before the great squeeze, the human physics of the war, with its volumes, its vacuums, its voids (that period of dynamics and direct action upon the individual, comparable biologically to birth), he had never much trusted his judgment where Germans were concerned. The Weimar Republic was not attractive to him in any way. No, there was an exception—he had admired its Plancks and Einsteins. Hardly anyone else.

In any case, he was not going to be one of those kindly European uncles with whom the Margottes of this world could have day-long high-level discussions. She would have liked him trailing after her through the apartment while, for two hours, she unpacked the groceries, hunting for lunch a salami which was already on the shelf; while she slapped and smoothed the bed with short strong arms (she kept the bedroom piously unchanged, after the death of Ussher—his swivel chair, his footstool, his Hobbes, Vico, Hume, and Marx underlined), discussing things. He found that even if he could get a word in edgewise it was encircled and cut off right away. Margotte swept on, enormously desirous of doing good. And really she was good (that was the point), she was boundlessly, achingly, hopelessly on the right side, the best side, of every big human question: for creativity, for the young, for the black, the poor, the oppressed, for victims, for sinners, for the hungry.

A significant remark by Ussher Arkin, giving much to think of after his death, was that he had learned to do the good thing as if practicing a vice. He must have been thinking of his wife as a sexual partner. She had probably driven him to erotic invention, and made monogamy a fascinating challenge. Margotte, continually recalling Ussher, spoke of him always, Germanically, as her Man. "When my Man was alive . . . my Man used to say." Sammler was sorry for his widowed niece. You could criticize her endlessly. High-minded, she bored you, she made cruel inroads into your time, your thought, your patience. She talked junk, she gathered waste and junk in the flat, she bred junk. Look, for instance, at these plants she was trying to raise. She planted avocado pits, lemon seeds, peas, potatoes. Was there anything ever so mangy, trashy, as these potted objects? Shrubs and vines dragged on the ground, tried to rise on grocer's string hopefully stapled fanwise to the ceiling. The stems of the avocados looked like the sticks of fireworks falling back after the flash, and produced a few rusty, spiky, anthrax-damaged, nitty leaves. This botanical ugliness, the product of so much fork-digging, watering, so much breast and arm, heart and hope, told you something, didn't it? First of all, it told you that the individual facts were filled with messages and meanings, but you couldn't be sure what the messages meant. She wanted a bower in her living room, a screen of glossy leaves, flowers, a garden, blessings of freshness and beauty—something to foster as woman the germinatrix, the matriarch of reservoirs and gardens. Humankind, crazy for symbols, trying to utter what it doesn't know itself. Meantime the spreading fanlike featherless quills: no peacock purple, no sweet blue, no true green, but only spots before your eyes. Redeemed by a feeling of ready and available human warmth? No, you couldn't be sure. The strain of unrelenting analytical effort gave Mr. Sammler a headache. The worst of it was that these frazzled plants would not, could not respond. There was not enough light. Too much clutter.

But when it came to clutter, his daughter, Shula, was much worse. He had lived with Shula for several years, just east of Broadway. She had too many oddities for her old father. She passionately collected things. In plainer words, she was a scavenger. More than once, he had seen her hunting through Broadway trash baskets (or, as he still called them, dustbins). She wasn't old, not bad looking, not even too badly dressed, item by item. The full effect would have been no worse than vulgar if she had not been obviously a nut. She turned up in a miniskirt of billiard-table green, revealing legs sensual in outline but without inner sensuality; at the waist a broad leather belt; over shoulders, bust, a coarse strong Guatemalan embroidered shirt; on her head a wig such as a female impersonator might put on at a convention of salesmen. Her own hair had a small curl, a minute distortion. It put her in a rage. She cried out that it was thin, she had masculine hair. Thin it evidently was, but not the other. She had it straight from Sammler's mother, a hysterical woman, certainly, and anything but masculine. But who knew how many sexual difficulties and complications were associated with Shula's hair? And, from the troubled widow's peak, following an imaginary line of illumination over the nose, originally fine but distorted by restless movement, over the ridiculous comment of the lips (swelling, painted dark red), and down between the breasts to the middle of the body—what problems there must be! Sammler kept hearing how she had taken her wig to a good hairdresser to have it set, and how the hairdresser exclaimed, please! to take the thing away, it was too cheap for him to work on! Sammler did not know whether this was an isolated incident involving one homosexual stylist, or whether it had happened on several separate occasions. He saw many open elements in his daughter. Things that ought but failed actually to connect. Wigs for instance suggested orthodoxy; Shula in fact had Jewish connections. She seemed to know lots of rabbis in famous temples and synagogues on Central Park West and on the East Side. She went to sermons and free lectures everywhere. Where she found the patience for this Sammler could not say. He could bear no lecture for more than ten minutes. But she, with loony, clever, large eyes, the face full of white comment and skin thickened with concentration, sat on her rucked-up skirt, the shopping bag with salvage, loot, coupons, and throwaway literature between her knees. Afterward she was the first to ask questions. She became well acquainted with the rabbi, the rabbi's wife and family—involved in Dadaist discussions about faith, ritual, Zionism, Masada, the Arabs. But she had Christian periods as well. Hidden in a Polish convent for four years, she had been called Slawa, and now there were times when she answered only to that name. Almost always at Easter she was a Catholic. Ash Wednesday was observed, and it was with a smudge between the eyes that she often came into clear focus for the old gentleman. With the little Jewish twists of kinky hair descending from the wig beside the ears and the florid lips dark red, skeptical, accusing, affirming something substantive about her life-claim, her right to be whatever—whatever it all came to. Full of comment always, the mouth completing the premises stated from an insane angle by the merging dark eyes. Not altogether crazy, perhaps. But she would come in saying that she had been run down by mounted policemen in Central Park. They were trying to recapture a deer escaped from the zoo, and she was absorbed, reading an article in *Look,* and they knocked her over. She was, however, quite cheerful. She was far too cheerful for Sammler. At night she typed. She sang at her typewriter. She was employed by cousin Gruner, the doctor, who had this work invented for her. Gruner had saved her (it amounted to that) from her equally crazy husband, Eisen, in Israel, sending Sammler ten years ago to bring Shula-Slawa to New York.

That had been Sammler's first journey to Israel. Brief. On a family matter.

Unusually handsome, brilliant-looking, Eisen had been wounded at Stalingrad. With other mutilated veterans in Rumania, later, he had been thrown from a moving train. Apparently because he was a Jew. Eisen had frozen his feet; his toes were amputated. "Oh, they were drunk," said Eisen in Haifa. "Good fellows—*tovarischni*. But you know what Russians are when they have a few glasses of vodka." He grinned at Sammler. Black curls, a handsome Roman nose, shining sharp senseless saliva-moist teeth. The trouble was that he kicked and beat Shula-Slawa quite often, even as a newlywed. Old Sammler in the cramped, stone-smelling, whitewashed apartment in Haifa considered the palm branches at the window in warm, clear atmosphere. Shula was cooking for them out of a Mexican cookbook, making bitter chocolate sauce, grating coconuts over chicken breasts, complaining that you could not buy chutney in Haifa. "When I was thrown out," said Eisen cheerfully, "I thought I would go and see the Pope. I took a stick and walked to Italy. The stick was my crutch, you see."

"I see."

"I went to Castel Gandolfo. The Pope was very nice to us."

After three days Mr. Sammler saw that he would have to remove his daughter.

He could not stay long in Israel. He was unwilling to spend Elya Gruner's money. But he did visit Nazareth and took a taxi to Galilee, for the historical interest of the thing, as long as he was in the vicinity. On a sandy road, he found a gaucho. Under a platter hat fastened beneath the large chin, in Argentinian bloomers tucked into boots, with a Douglas Fairbanks mustache, he was mixing feed for small creatures racing about him in a chicken-wire enclosure. Water from a hose ran clear and pleasant in the sun over the yellow meal or mash and stained it orange. The little animals though fat were lithe; they were heavy, their coats shone, opulent and dense. These were nutrias. Their fur made hats worn in cold climates. Coats for ladies. Mr. Sammler, feeling red-faced in the Galilean sunlight, interrogated this man. In his bass voice of a distinguished traveler—a cigarette held between his hairy knuckles, smoke escaping past his hairy ears—he put questions to the gaucho. Neither spoke Hebrew. Nor the language of Jesus. Mr. Sammler fell back on Italian, which the nutria breeder in Argentine gloom comprehended, his heavy handsome face considering the greedy beasts about his boots. He was Bessarabian–Syrian–South American—a Spanish-speaking Israeli cowpuncher from the pampas.

Did he butcher the little animals himself? Sammler wished to know. His Italian had never been good. *"Uccidere?" "Ammazzare?"* The gaucho understood. When the time came, he killed them himself. He struck them on the head with a stick.

Didn't he mind doing this to his little flock? Hadn't he known them from infancy—was there no tenderness for individuals—were there no favorites? The gaucho denied it all. He shook his handsome head. He said that nutrias were very stupid.

"Son muy tontos."

"Arrivederci," said Sammler.

"Adios. Shalom."

Mr. Sammler's hired car took him to Capernaum, where Jesus had preached in the synagogue. From afar, he saw the Mount of the Beatitudes. Two eyes would have been inadequate to the heaviness and smoothness of the color, parted with difficulty by fishing boats—the blue water, unusually dense, heavy, seemed sunk under the naked Syrian heights. Mr. Sammler's heart was very much torn by feelings as he stood under the short, leaf-streaming banana trees.

> And did those feet in ancient time
> Walk upon . . .

But those were England's mountains green. The mountains opposite, in serpentine nakedness, were not at all green; they were ruddy, with smoky cavities and mysteries of inhuman power flaming above them.

The many impressions and experiences of life seemed no longer to occur each in its own proper space, in sequence, each with its recognizable religious or aesthetic importance, but human beings suffered the humiliations of inconsequence, of confused styles, of a long life containing several separate lives. In fact the whole experience of mankind was now covering each separate life in its flood. Making all the ages of history simultaneous. Compelling the frail person to receive, to register, depriving him because of volume, of mass, of the power to impart design.

Well, that was Sammler's first visit to the Holy Land. A decade later, for another purpose, he went again.

Shula had returned with Sammler to America. Rescued from Eisen, who walloped her, he said, because she went to Catholic priests, because she was a liar (lies infuriated him; paranoiacs, Sammler concluded, are more passionate for pure truth than other madmen), Shula-Slawa set up housekeeping in New York. Creating, that is, a great clutter-center in the New World. Mr. Sammler, a polite Slim-Jim (the nickname Dr. Gruner had given him), a considerate father, muttering appreciation of each piece of rubbish as presented to him, was in certain moods explosive, under provocation more violent than other people. In fact, his claim for indemnity from the Bonn government was based upon damage to his nervous system as well as his eye. Fits of rage, very rare but shattering, laid him up with intense migraines, put him in a postepileptic condition. Then he lay most of a week in a dark room, rigid, hands gripped on his chest, bruised, aching, incapable of an answer when spoken to. With Shula-Slawa, he had a series of such attacks. First of all, he couldn't bear the building Gruner had put them into, with its stone stoop slumping to one side, into the cellar stairway of the Chinese laundry adjoining. The lobby made him ill, tiles like yellow teeth set in desperate grime, and the stinking elevator shaft. The bathroom where Shula kept an Easter chick from Kresge's until it turned into a hen that squawked on the edge of the tub. The Christmas decorations which lasted into spring. The rooms themselves were like those dusty red paper Christmas bells, folds within folds. The hen with yellow legs in his room on his documents and books was too much one day. He was aware that the sun shone brightly, the sky was blue, but the big swell of the apartment house, heavyweight vaselike baroque, made him feel that the twelfth-story room was like a china cabinet into which he was locked, and the satanic hen-legs of wrinkled yellow clawing his papers made him scream out.

Shula-Slawa then agreed that he should move. She told everyone that her father's lifework, his memoir of H. G. Wells, made him too tense to live with. She had H. G. Wells on the brain, the large formation of a lifetime. H. G. Wells was the most august human being she knew of. She had been a small girl when the Sammlers lived in Woburn Square, Bloomsbury, and with childish genius accurately read the passions of her parents—their pride in high connections, their snobbery, how contented they were with the cultural best of England. Old Sammler thinking of his wife in prewar Bloomsbury days interpreted a certain quiet, bosomful way she had of conveying with a downward stroke of the hand, so delicate you had to know her well to identify it as a vaunting gesture: we have the most distinguished intimacy with the finest people in Britain. A small vice—almost nutritive, digestive—which gave Antonina softer cheeks, smoother hair, deeper color. If a little social-climbing made her handsomer (plumper between the legs—the thought rushed in and Sammler had stopped trying to repel these mental rushes), it had its feminine justification. Love *is* the most potent cosmetic, but there are others. And the little girl may actually have observed that the very mention of Wells had a combined social-erotic influence on her mother. Judging not, and recalling Wells always with respect, Sammler knew that he had been a horny man of labyrinthine extraordinary sensuality. As a biologist, as a social thinker concerned with power and world projects, the molding of a universal order, as a furnisher of interpretation and opinion to the educated masses—as all of these he appeared to need a great amount of copulation. Nowadays Sammler would recall him as a little lower-class Limey, and as an aging man of declining ability and appeal. And in the agony of parting with the breasts, the mouths, and the precious sexual fluids of women, poor Wells, the natural teacher, the sex emancipator, the explainer, the humane blesser of mankind, could in the end only blast and curse everyone. Of course he wrote such things in his final sickness, horribly depressed by World War II.

What Shula-Slawa said came back amusingly to Sammler through Angela Gruner. Shula visited Angela in the East Sixties, where her cousin had the beautiful, free, and wealthy young woman's ideal New York apartment. Shula admired this. Apparently without envy, without self-consciousness, Shula with wig and shopping bag, her white face puckering with continual inspiration (receiving and transmitting wild messages), sat as awkwardly as possible in the super comfort of Angela's upholstery, blobbing china and forks with lipstick. In Shula's version of things her father had had conversations with H. G. Wells lasting several years. He took his notes to Poland in 1939, expecting to have spare time for the memoir. Just then the country exploded. In the geyser that rose a mile or two into the skies were Papa's notes. But (with *his* memory!) he knew it all by heart, and all you had to do was ask what Wells had said to him about Lenin, Stalin, Mussolini, Hitler, world peace, atomic energy, the open conspiracy, the colonization of the planets. Whole passages came back to Papa. He had to concentrate of course. Thus she turned about his moving in with Margotte until it became her idea. He had moved away to concentrate better. He said he didn't have much time left. But obviously he exaggerated. He looked so well. He was such a handsome person. Elderly widows were always asking her about him. The mother of Rabbi Ipsheimer. The grandmother of Ipsheimer, more likely. Anyway (Angela still reporting), Wells had communicated things to Sammler that the world didn't know. When finally published they would astonish everybody. The book would take the form of dialogues like those with A. N. Whitehead which Sammler admired so much.

Low-voiced, husky, a hint of joking brass in her tone, Angela (*just* this side of coarseness, a beautiful woman) said, "Her Wells routine is *so* great. Were you that close to H. G., Uncle?"

"We were well acquainted."

"But chums? Were you bosom buddies?"

"Oh? My dear girl, in spite of my years, I am a man of the modern age. You do not find David and Jonathan, Roland and Olivier bosom buddies in these days. The man's company was very pleasant. He seemed also to enjoy conversation with me. As for his views, he was just a mass of intelligent views. He expressed as many as he could, and at all times. Everything he said I found eventually in written form. He was like Voltaire, a graphomaniac. His mind was unusually active, he thought he should explain everything, and he actually said some things very well. Like 'Science is the mind of the race.' That's true, you know. It's a better thing to emphasize than other collective facts, like disease or sin. And when I see the wing of a jet plane I don't only see metal, but metal tempered by the agreement of many minds which know the pressure and velocity and weight, calculating on their slide rules whether they are Hindus or Chinamen or from the Congo or Brazil. Yes, on the whole he was a sensible intelligent person, certainly on the right side of many questions."

"And you used to be interested."

"Yes, I used to be interested."

"But she says you're composing that great work a mile a minute."

She laughed. Not merely laughed, but laughed brilliantly. In Angela you confronted sensual womanhood without remission. You smelled it, too. She wore the odd stylish things which Sammler noted with detached and purified dryness, as if from a different part of the universe. What were those, white-kid buskins? What were those tights—

sheer, opaque? Where did they lead? That effect of the hair called frosting, that color under the lioness's muzzle, that swagger to enhance the natural power of the bust! Her plastic coat inspired by cubists or Mondrians, geometrical black and white forms; her trousers by Courrèges and Pucci. Sammler followed these jet phenomena in the *Times*, and in the women's magazines sent by Angela herself. Not too closely. He did not read too much of this. Careful to guard his eyesight, he passed pages rapidly back and forth before his eye, the large forehead registering the stimulus to his mind. The damaged left eye seemed to turn in another direction, to be preoccupied separately with different matters. Thus Sammler knew, through many rapid changes, Warhol, Baby Jane Holzer while she lasted, the Living Theater, the outbursts of nude display more and more revolutionary, Dionysus '69, copulation on the stage, the philosophy of the Beatles; and in the art world, electric shows and minimal painting. Angela was in her thirties now, independently wealthy, with ruddy skin, gold-whitish hair, big lips. She was afraid of obesity. She either fasted or ate like a stevedore. She trained in a fashionable gym. He knew her problems—he had to know, for she came and discussed them in detail. She did not know *his* problems. He seldom talked and she seldom asked. Moreover, he and Shula were her father's pensioners, dependents—call it what you like. So after psychiatric sessions, Angela came to Uncle Sammler to hold a seminar and analyze the preceding hour. Thus the old man knew what she did and with whom and how it felt. All that she knew how to say he had to hear. He could not choose but.

Sammler in his *Gymnasium* days once translated from Saint Augustine: "The Devil hath established his cities in the North." He thought of this often. In Cracow before

World War I he had had another version of it—desperate darkness, the dreary liquid yellow mud to a depth of two inches over cobblestones in the Jewish streets. People needed their candles, their lamps and their copper kettles, their slices of lemon in the image of the sun. This was the conquest of grimness with the aid always of Mediterranean symbols. Dark environments overcome by imported religious signs and local domestic amenities. Without the power of the North, its mines, its industries, the world would never have reached its astonishing modern form. And regardless of Augustine, Sammler had always loved his Northern cities, especially London, the blessings of its gloom, of coal smoke, gray rains, and the mental and human opportunities of a dark muffled environment. There one came to terms with obscurity, with low tones, one did not demand full clarity of mind or motive. But now Augustine's odd statement required a new interpretation. Listening to Angela carefully, Sammler perceived different developments. The labor of Puritanism now was ending. The dark satanic mills changing into light satanic mills. The reprobates converted into children of joy, the sexual ways of the seraglio and of the Congo bush adopted by the emancipated masses of New York, Amsterdam, London. Old Sammler with his screwy visions! He saw the increasing triumph of Enlightenment—Liberty, Fraternity, Equality, Adultery! Enlightenment, universal education, universal suffrage, the rights of the majority acknowledged by all governments, the rights of women, the rights of children, the rights of criminals, the unity of the different races affirmed, Social Security, public health, the dignity of the person, the right to justice—the struggles of three revolutionary centuries being won while the feudal bonds of Church and Family weakened and the privileges of aristocracy (without any duties) spread wide, democratized, especially the libidinous privileges, the right to be uninhibited, spontaneous, urinating, defecating, belching, coupling in all positions, tripling, quadrupling, polymorphous, noble in being natural, primitive, combining the leisure and luxurious inventiveness of Versailles with the hibiscus-covered erotic ease of Samoa. Dark romanticism now took hold. As old at least as the strange Orientalism of the Knights Templar, and since then filled up with Lady Stanhopes, Baudelaires, de Nervals, Stevensons, and Gauguins—those South-loving barbarians. Oh yes, the Templars. They had adored the Muslims. One hair from the head of a Saracen was more precious than the whole body of a Christian. Such crazy fervor! And now all the racism, all the strange erotic persuasions, the tourism and local color, the exotics of it had broken up but the mental masses, inheriting everything in a debased state, had formed an idea of the corrupting disease of being white and of the healing power of black. The dreams of nineteenth-century poets polluted the psychic atmosphere of the great boroughs and suburbs of New York. Add to this the dangerous lunging staggering crazy violence of fanatics, and the trouble was very deep. Like many people who had seen the world collapse once, Mr. Sammler entertained the possibility it might collapse twice. He did not agree with refugee friends that this doom was inevitable, but liberal beliefs did not seem capable of self-defense, and you could smell decay. You could see the suicidal impulses of civilization pushing strongly. You wondered whether this Western culture could survive universal dissemination—whether only its science and technology or administrative practices would travel, be adopted by other societies. Or whether the worst enemies of civilization might not prove to be its petted intellectuals who attacked it at its weakest moments—attacked it in the name of proletarian revolution, in the name of reason, and in the name of irrationality, in the name of visceral depth, in the name of sex, in the name of perfect instantaneous freedom. For what it amounted to was limitless demand—insatiability, refusal of the doomed creature (death being sure and final) to go away from this earth unsatisfied. A full bill of demand and complaint was therefore presented by each individual. Non-negotiable. Recognizing no scarcity of supply in any human department. Enlightenment? Marvelous! But out of hand, wasn't it?

Sammler saw this in Shula-Slawa. She came to do his room. He had to sit in his beret and coat, for she needed fresh air. She arrived with cleaning materials in the shopping bag—ammonia, shelf paper, Windex, floor wax, rags. She sat out on the sill to wash the windows, lowering the sash to her thighs. Her little shoe soles were inside the room. On her lips—a burst of crimson asymmetrical skeptical fleshy business-and-dream sensuality—the cigarette scorching away at the tip. There was the wig, too, mixed yak and baboon hair and synthetic fibers. Shula, like all the ladies perhaps, was needy—needed gratification of numerous instincts, needed the warmth and pressure of men, needed a child for sucking and nurture, needed female emancipation, needed the exercise of the mind, needed continuity, needed interest—*interest!*—needed flattery, needed triumph, power, needed rabbis, needed priests, needed fuel for all that was perverse and crazy, needed noble action of the intellect, needed culture, demanded the sublime. No scarcity was acknowledged. If you tried to deal with all these immediate needs you were a lost man. Even to consider it all the way she did, spraying cold froth on the panes, swabbing it away, left-handed with a left-ward swing of the bust (*ohne Büstenhalter*), was neither affection for her, nor preservation for her father. When she arrived and opened windows and doors the personal atmosphere Mr. Sammler had accumulated and stored blew away, it seemed. His back door opened to the service staircase, where a hot smell of incineration rushed from the chute, charred paper, chicken entrails, and burnt feathers. The Puerto Rican sweepers carried transistors playing Latin music. As if supplied with this jazz from a universal unfailing source, like cosmic rays.

"Well, Father, how is it going?"

"What is going?"

"The work. H. G. Wells?"

"As usual."

"People take up too much of your time. You don't get enough reading done. I know you have to protect your eyesight. But is it going all right?"

"Tremendous."

"I wish you wouldn't make jokes about it."

"Why, is it too important for jokes?"

"Well, it is important."

Yes. O.K. He was sipping his morning coffee. Today, this very afternoon, he was going to speak at Columbia University. One of his young Columbia friends had persuaded him. Also, he must call up about his nephew. Dr. Gruner. It seemed the doctor himself was in the hospital. Had had, so Sammler was told, minor surgery. Cutting in the neck. One could do without that seminar today. It was a mistake. Could he back out, beg off? No, probably not.

Shula had hired university students to read to him, to spare his eyes. She herself had tried it, but her voice made him nod off. Half an hour of her reading, and the blood left his brain. She told Angela that her father tried to fence her out of his higher activities. As if they had to be protected from the very person who believed most in them! It was a very sad paradox. But for four or five years she had found student-readers. Some had graduated, now were in professions or business but still came back to visit Sammler. "He is like their guru," said Shula-Slawa. More recent readers were student activists. Mr. Sammler was quite interested in the radical movement. To judge by their reading ability, the young people had had a meager education. Their presence sometimes induced (or deepened) a long, still smile which had the effect more than anything else of blindness. Hairy, dirty, without style, levelers, ignorant. He found after they had read to him for a few hours that he had to teach them the subject, explain the terms, do etymologies for them as though they were twelve-year-olds. "*Janua*—a door. Janitor—one who minds the door." "*Lapis,* a stone. Dilapidate, take apart the stones. One cannot say it of a person." But if one could, one would say it of these young persons. Some of the poor girls had a bad smell. Bohemian protest did them the most harm. It was elementary among the tasks and problems of civilization, thought Mr. Sammler, that some parts of nature demanded more control than others. Females were naturally more prone to grossness, had more smells, needed more washing, clipping, binding, pruning, grooming, perfuming, and training. These poor kids may have resolved to stink together in defiance of a corrupt tradition built on neurosis and falsehood, but Mr. Sammler thought that an unforeseen result of their way of life was loss of femininity, of self-esteem. In their revulsion from authority they would respect no persons. Not even their own persons.

Anyhow, he no longer wanted these readers with the big dirty boots and the helpless vital pathos of young dogs with their first red erections, and pimples sprung to the cheeks from foaming beards, laboring in his room with hard words and thoughts that had to be explained, stumbling through Toynbee, Freud, Burckhardt, Spengler. For he had been reading historians of civilization—Karl Marx, Max Weber, Max Scheler, Franz Oppenheimer. Side excursions into Adorno, Marcuse, Norman O. Brown, whom he found to be worthless fellows. Together with these he took on *Doktor Faustus, Les Noyers d'Altenbourg,* Ortega, Valéry's essays on history and politics. But after four or five years of this diet, he wished to read only certain religious writers of the thirteenth century—Suso, Tauler, and Meister Eckhardt. In his seventies he was interested in little more than Meister Eckhardt and the Bible. For this he needed no readers. He read Eckhardt's Latin at the public library from microfilm. He read the Sermons and the Talks of Instruction—a few sentences at a time—a paragraph of Old German—presented to his good eye at close range. While Margotte ran the carpet sweeper through the rooms. Evidently getting most of the lint on her skirts. And singing. She loved Schubert lieder. Why she had to mingle them with the zoom of the vacuum eluded his powers of explanation. But then he could not explain a liking for certain combinations: for instance, sandwiches of sturgeon, Swiss cheese, tongue, steak tartare, and Russian dressing in layers—such things as one saw on fancy delicatessen menus. Yet customers seemed to order them. No matter where you picked it up, humankind, knotted and tangled, supplied more oddities than you could keep up with.

A combined oddity, for instance, which drew him today into the middle of things: One of his ex-readers, young

Lionel Feffer, had asked him to address a seminar at Columbia University on the British Scene in the Thirties. For some reason this attracted Sammler. He was fond of Feffer. An ingenious operator, less student than promoter. With his florid color, brown beaver beard, long black eyes, big belly, smooth hair, pink awkward large hands, loud interrupting voice, hasty energy, he was charming to Sammler. Not trustworthy. Only charming. That is, it sometimes gave Sammler great pleasure to see Lionel Feffer working out in his peculiar manner, to hear the fizzing of his vital gas, his fuel.

Sammler didn't know what seminar this was. Not always attentive, he failed to understand clearly; perhaps there was nothing clear to understand; but it seemed that he had promised, although he couldn't remember promising. But Feffer confused him. There were so many projects, such cross references, so many confidences and requests for secrecy, so many scandals, frauds, spiritual communications—a continual flow backward, forward, lateral, above, below; like any page of Joyce's *Ulysses*, always *in medias res*. Anyway, Sammler had apparently agreed to give this talk for a student project to help backward black pupils with their reading problems.

"You must come and talk to these fellows, it's of the utmost importance. They have never heard a point of view like yours," said Feffer. The pink oxford-cloth shirt increased the color of his face. The beard, the straight large sensual nose made him look like François Premier. A bustling, affectionate, urgent, eruptive, enterprising character. He had money in the stock market. He was vice-president of a Guatemalan insurance company covering railroad workers. His field at the university was diplomatic history. He belonged to a corresponding society called the Foreign

Ministers' Club. Its members took up a question like the Crimean War or the Boxer Rebellion and did it all again, writing one another letters as the foreign ministers of France, England, Germany, Russia. They obtained very different results. In addition, Feffer was a busy seducer, especially, it seemed, of young wives. But he found time as well to hustle on behalf of handicapped children. He got them free toys and signed photographs of hockey stars; he found time to visit them in the hospital. He "found time." To Sammler this was a highly significant American fact. Feffer led a high-energy American life to the point of anarchy and breakdown. And yet devotedly. And of course he was in psychiatric treatment. They all were. They could always say that they were sick. Nothing was omitted.

"The British Scene in the Thirties—you must. For my seminar."

"*That* old stuff?"

"Exactly. Just what we need."

"Bloomsbury? All of that? But why? And for whom?"

Feffer called for Sammler in a taxi. They went uptown in style. Feffer stressed the style of it. He said the driver must wait while Sammler gave his talk. The driver, a Negro, refused. Feffer raised his voice. He said this was a legal matter. Sammler persuaded him to drop it as he was about to call the police. "There is no need to have a taxi waiting for me," said Sammler.

"Go get lost then," said Feffer to the cabbie. "And no tip."

"Don't abuse him," Sammler said.

"I won't make any distinction because he's black," said Lionel. "I hear from Margotte that you've been running into a black pickpocket, by the way."

"Where do we go, Lionel? Now that I'm about to speak,

I have misgivings. I feel unclear. What, really, am I supposed to say? The topic is so vast."

"You know it better than anyone."

"I know it, yes. But I am uneasy—somewhat shaky."

"You'll be great."

Then Feffer led him into a large room. He had expected a small one, a seminar room. He had come to reminisce, for a handful of interested students, about R. H. Tawney, Harold Laski, John Strachey, George Orwell, H. G. Wells. But this was a mass meeting of some sort. His obstructed vision took in a large, spreading, shaggy, composite human bloom. It was malodorous, peculiarly rancid, sulphurous. The amphitheater was filled. Standing room only. Was Feffer running one of his rackets? Was he going to pocket the admission money? Sammler mastered and dismissed this suspicion, ascribing it to surprise and nervousness. For he was surprised, frightened. But he pulled himself together. He tried to begin humorously by recalling the lecturer who had addressed incurable alcoholics under the impression that they were the Browning Society. But there was no laughter, and he had to remember that Browning Societies had been extinct for a long time. A microphone was hung on his chest. He began to speak of the mental atmosphere of England before the Second World War. The Mussolini adventure in East Africa. Spain in 1936. The Great Purges in Russia. Stalinism in France and Britain. Blum, Daladier, the Peoples' Front, Oswald Mosley. The mood of English intellectuals. For this he needed no notes, he could easily recall what people had said or written.

"I assume," he said, "you are acquainted with the background, the events of nineteen seventeen. You know of the mutinous armies, the February Revolution in Russia, the disasters that befell authority. In all European countries the old leaders were discredited by Verdun, Flanders Field, and Tannenberg. Perhaps I could begin with the fall of Kerensky. Maybe with Brest-Litovsk."

Doubly foreign, Polish-Oxonian, with his outrushing white back hair, the wrinkles streaming below the smoked glasses, he pulled the handkerchief from the breast pocket, unfolded and refolded it, touched his face, wiped his palms with thin elderly delicacy. Without pleasure in performance, without the encouragement of attention (there was a good deal of noise), the little satisfaction he did feel was the meager ghost of the pride he and his wife had once taken in their British successes. In his success, a Polish Jew so well acquainted, so handsomely acknowledged by the nobs, by H. G. Wells. Included, for instance, with Gerald Heard and Olaf Stapledon in the *Cosmopolis* project for a World State, Sammler had written articles for *News of Progress*, for the other publication, *The World Citizen*. As he explained in a voice that still contained Polish sibilants and nasals, though impressively low, the project was based on the propagation of the sciences of biology, history, and sociology and the effective application of scientific principles to the enlargement of human life; the building of a planned, orderly, and beautiful world society: abolishing national sovereignty, outlawing war; subjecting money and credit, production, distribution, transport, population, arms manufacture et cetera to world-wide collective control, offering free universal education, personal freedom (compatible with community welfare) to the utmost degree; a service society based on a rational scientific attitude toward life. Sammler, with growing interest and confidence recalling all this, lectured on *Cosmopolis* for half an hour, feeling what a kind-hearted, ingenuous, stupid scheme it had been. Telling this into the lighted restless hole of the amphitheater with the soiled dome and caged electric fixtures, until he was interrupted by a clear loud voice. He was being questioned. He was being shouted at.

"Hey!"

He tried to continue. "Such attempts to draw intellectuals away from Marxism met with small success. . . ."

A man in Levi's, thick-bearded but possibly young, a figure of compact distortion, was standing shouting at him.

"Hey! Old Man!"

In the silence, Mr. Sammler drew down his tinted spectacles, seeing this person with his effective eye.

"Old Man! You quoted Orwell before."

"Yes?"

"You quoted him to say that British radicals were all protected by the Royal Navy? Did Orwell say that British radicals were protected by the Royal Navy?"

"Yes, I believe he did say that."

"That's a lot of shit."

Sammler could not speak.

"Orwell was a fink. He was a sick counterrevolutionary. It's good he died when he did. And what you are saying is shit." Turning to the audience, extending violent arms and raising his palms like a Greek dancer, he said, "Why do you listen to this effete old shit? What has he got to tell you? His balls are dry. He's dead. He can't come."

Sammler later thought that voices had been raised on his side. Someone had said, "Shame. Exhibitionist."

But no one really tried to defend him. Most of the young people seemed to be against him. The shouting sounded hostile. Feffer was gone, had been called away to the telephone. Sammler, turning from the lectern, found his umbrella, trench coat, and hat behind him and left the platform, guided by a young girl who had rushed up to express indignation and sympathy, saying it was a scandal to break up such a good lecture. She showed him through a door, down several stairs, and he was on Broadway at One hundred-sixteenth Street.

Abruptly out of the university.

Back in the city.

And he was not so much personally offended by the event as struck by the will to offend. What a passion to be *real*. But *real* was also brutal. And the acceptance of excrement as a standard? How extraordinary! Youth? Together with the idea of sexual potency? All this confused sex-excrement-militancy, explosiveness, abusiveness, tooth-showing, Barbary ape howling. Or like the spider monkeys in the trees, as Sammler once had read, defecating into their hands, and shrieking, pelting the explorers below.

He was not sorry to have met the facts, however saddening, regrettable the facts. But the effect was that Mr. Sammler did feel somewhat separated from the rest of his species, if not in some fashion severed—severed not so much by age as by preoccupations too different and remote, disproportionate on the side of the spiritual, Platonic, Augustinian, thirteenth-century. As the traffic poured, the wind poured, and the sun, relatively bright for Manhattan—shining and pouring through openings in his substance, through his gaps. As if he had been cast by Henry Moore. With holes, lacunae. Again, as after seeing the pickpocket, he was obliged to events for a difference, an intensification of vision. A delivery man with a floral cross filling both arms, a bald head dented, seemed to be drunk, fighting the wind, tacking. His dull boots small, and his short wide pants blowing like a woman's skirts. Gardenias, camellias, calla lilies, sailing above him under light transparent plastic. Or at the Riverside bus stop Mr. Sammler noted the proximity of a waiting student, used his eye-power to observe that he wore wide-wale corduroy pants of urinous green, a tweed coat of a carrot color with burls of blue wool; that sideburns stood like powerful bushy pillars to the head; that civilized tortoise-shell shafts intersected these; that he had hair thinning at the front; a Jew nose, a heavy all-savoring, all-rejecting lip. Oh, this was an artistic diversion of the streets for Mr. Sammler when he was roused to it by some shock. He was studious, he was bookish, and had been trained by the best writers to divert himself with perceptions. When he went out, life was not empty. Meanwhile the purposive, aggressive, business-bent, conative people did as mankind normally did. If the majority walked about as if under a spell, sleepwalkers, circumscribed by, in the grip of, minor neurotic trifling aims, individuals like Sammler were only one stage forward, awakened not to purpose but to aesthetic consumption of the environment. Even if insulted, pained, somewhere bleeding, not broadly expressing any anger, not crying out with sadness, but translating heartache into delicate, even piercing observation. Particles in the bright wind, flinging downtown, acted like emery on the face. The sun shone as if there were no death. For a full minute, while the bus approached, squirting air, it was like that. Then Mr. Sammler got on, moving like a good citizen toward the rear, hoping he would not be pushed past the back door, for he had only fifteen blocks to go, and there was a thick crowd. The usual smell of long-seated bottoms, of sour shoes, of tobacco muck, of stogies, cologne, face powder. And yet along the river, early spring, the first khaki—a few weeks of sun, of heat, and Manhattan would (briefly) join the North American continent in a day of old-time green, the plush luxury, the polish of the season, shining, nitid, the dogwood white, pink, blooming crabapple. Then people's feet would swell with the warmth, and at Rockefeller Center strollers would sit on the polished stone slabs beside the planted tulips and tritons and the water, all in a spirit of pregnancy. Human creatures under the warm shadows of skyscrapers feeling the heavy pleasure of their nature, and yielding. Sammler too would enjoy spring—one of those penultimate springs. Of course he was upset. Very. Of course all that stuff about Brest-Litovsk, all that old news about revolutionary intellectuals versus the German brass was in this context downright funny. Inconsequent. Of course those students were comical, too. And what was the worst of it (apart from the rudeness)? There were appropriate ways of putting down an old bore. He might well be, especially in a public manifestation, lecturing on *Cosmopolis,* an old bore. The worst of it, from the point of view of the young people themselves, was that they acted without dignity. They had no view of the nobility of being intellectuals and judges of the social order. What a pity! old Sammler thought. A human being, valuing himself for the right reasons, has and restores order, authority. When the internal parts are in order. They must be in order. But what was it to be arrested in the stage of toilet training! What was it to be entrapped by a psychiatric standard (Sammler blamed the Germans and their psychoanalysis for this)! Who had raised the diaper flag? Who had made shit a sacrament? What literary and psychological movement was that? Mr. Sammler, with bitter angry mind, held the top rail of his jammed bus, riding downtown, a short journey.

He certainly had no thought of his black pickpocket. Him he connected with Columbus Circle. He always went uptown, not down. But at the rear, in his camel's-hair coat, filling up a corner with his huge body, he was standing. Sammler against strong internal resistance saw him. He resisted because at this swaying difficult moment he had no wish to see him. Lord! not now! Inside, Sammler felt an immediate descent; his heart sinking. As sure as fate, as a law of nature, a stone falling, a gas rising. He knew the thief did not ride the bus for transportation. To meet a woman, to go home—however he diverted himself—he unquestionably took cabs. He could afford them. But now Mr. Sammler was looking down at his shoulder, the tallest man in the bus, except for the thief himself. He saw that in the long rear seat he had cornered someone. Powerfully bent, the wide back concealed the victim from the other passengers. Only Sammler, because of his height, could see. Nothing to be grateful to height or vision for. The cornered man was old, was weak; poor eyes, watering with terror; white lashes, red lids, and a sea-mucus blue, his eyes, the mouth open with false teeth dropping from the upper gums. Coat and jacket were open also, the shirt pulled forward like detached green wallpaper, and the lining of the jacket ragged. The thief tugged his clothes like a doctor with a clinic patient. Pushing aside tie and scarf, he took out the wallet. His own homburg he then eased back (an animal movement, simply) slightly from his forehead, furrowed but not with anxiety. The wallet was long—leatherette, plastic. Open, it yielded a few dollar bills. There were cards. The thief put them in his palm. Read them with a tilted head. Let them drop. Examined a green federal-looking check, probably Social Security. Mr. Sammler in his goggles was troubled in focusing. Too much adrenalin was passing with light, thin, frightening rapidity through his heart. He himself was not frightened, but his heart seemed to record fear, it had a seizure. He recognized it—knew what name to apply: tachycardia. Breathing was hard. He could not fetch in enough air. He wondered whether he might not faint away. Whether worse might not happen. The check the black man put into his own pocket. Snapshots like the cards fell from his fingers. Finished, he then dropped the wallet back into the gray, worn, shattered lining, flipped back the old man's muffler. In ironic calm, thumb and forefinger took the knot of the necktie and yanked it approximately, but only approximately, into place. It was at this moment that, in a quick turn of the head, he saw Mr. Sammler. Mr. Sammler seen seeing was still in rapid currents with his heart. Like an escaping creature racing away from him. His throat ached, up to the root of the tongue. There was a pang in the bad eye. But he had some presence of mind. Gripping the overhead chrome rail, he stooped forward as if to see what street was coming up. Ninety-sixth. In other words, he avoided a gaze that might be held, or any interlocking of looks. He acknowledged nothing, and now began to work his way toward the rear exit, gently urgent, stooping doorward. He reached, found the cord, pulled, made it to the step, squeezed through the door, and stood on the sidewalk holding the umbrella by the fabric, at the button.

The tachycardia now running itself out, he was able to walk, though not at the usual rate. His stratagem was to cross Riverside Drive and enter the first building, as if he lived there. He had beaten the pickpocket to the door. Maybe effrontery would dismiss him as too negligible to pursue. The man did not seem to feel threatened by anyone. Took the slackness, the cowardice of the world for granted. Sammler, with effort, opened a big glass black-grilled door and found himself in an empty lobby. Avoiding the elevator, he located the staircase, trudged the first flight, and sat down on the landing. A few minutes of rest, and he recovered his oxygen level, although something within felt attenuated. Simply thinned out. Before returning to the street (there was no rear exit), he took the umbrella inside the coat, hooking it in the armhole and belting it up, more or less securely. He also made an effort to change the shape of his hat, punching it out. He went past West End to Broadway, entering the first hamburger joint, sitting in the rear, and ordering tea. He drank to the bottom of the heavy cup, to the tannic taste, squeezing the sopping bag and asking the counterman for more water, feeling parched. Through the window his thief did not appear. By now Sammler's greatest need was for his bed. But he knew something about lying low. He had learned in Poland, in the war, in forests, cellars, passageways, cemeteries. Things he had passed through once which had abolished a certain margin or leeway ordinarily taken for granted. Taking for granted that one will not be shot stepping into the street, nor clubbed to death as one stoops to relieve oneself, nor hunted in an alley like a rat. This civil margin once removed, Mr. Sammler would never trust the restoration totally. He had had little occasion to practice the arts of hiding and escape in New York. But now, although his bones ached for the bed and his skull was famished for the pillow, he sat at the counter with his tea. He could not use buses any more. From now on it was the subway. The subway was an abomination.

But Mr. Sammler had not shaken the pickpocket. The man obviously could move fast. He might have forced his way out of the bus in midblock and sprinted back, heavy but swift in homburg and camel's-hair coat. Much more likely, the thief had observed him earlier, had once before shadowed him, had followed him home. Yes, that must have been the case. For when Mr. Sammler entered the lobby of his building the man came up behind him quickly, and not simply behind but pressing him bodily, belly to back. He did not lift his hands to Sammler but pushed. There was no building employee. The doormen, also running the elevator, spent much of their time in the cellar.

"What is the matter? What do you want?" said Mr. Sammler.

He was never to hear the black man's voice. He no more spoke than a puma would. What he did was to force Sammler into a corner beside the long blackish carved table, a sort of Renaissance piece, a thing which added to the lobby melancholy, by the buckling canvas of the old wall, by the red-eyed lights of the brass double fixture. There the man held Sammler against the wall with his forearm. The umbrella fell to the floor with a sharp crack of the ferrule on the tile. It was ignored. The pickpocket unbuttoned himself. Sammler heard the zipper descend. Then the smoked glasses were removed from Sammler's face and dropped on the table. He was directed, silently, to look downward. The black man had opened his fly and taken out his penis. It was displayed to Sammler with great oval testicles, a large tan-and-purple uncircumcised thing—a tube, a snake; metallic hairs bristled at the thick base and the tip curled beyond the supporting, demonstrating hand, suggesting the fleshly mobility of an elephant's trunk, though the skin was somewhat iridescent rather than thick or rough. Over the forearm and fist that held him Sammler was required to gaze at this organ. No compulsion would have been necessary. He would in any case have looked.

The interval was long. The man's expression was not

directly menacing but oddly, serenely masterful. The thing was shown with mystifying certitude. Lordliness. Then it was returned to the trousers. *Quod erat demonstrandum.* Sammler was released. The fly was closed, the coat buttoned, the marvelous streaming silk salmon necktie smoothed with a powerful hand on the powerful chest. The black eyes with a light of super candor moved softly, concluding the session, the lesson, the warning, the encounter, the transmission. He picked up Sammler's dark glasses and returned them to his nose. He then unfolded and mounted his own, circular, of gentian violet gently banded with the lovely Dior gold.

Then he departed. The elevator, with a bump, returning from the cellar opened simultaneously with the street door. Retrieving the fallen umbrella, lamely stooping, Sammler rode up. The doorman offered no small talk. For this sad unsociability one was grateful. Better yet, he didn't bump into Margotte. Best of all, he dropped and stretched on his bed, just as he was, with smarting feet, thin respiration, pain at the heart, stunned mind and—oh!—a temporary blankness of spirit. Like the television screen in the lobby, white and gray, buzzing without image. Between head and pillow, a hard rectangle was interposed, the marbled cardboard of a notebook, sea-green. A slip of paper was attached with Scotch tape. Drawing it into light, passing it near the eye, and with lips spelling mutely, bitterly, he forced himself to read the separate letters. The note was from S (either Shula or Slawa).

"Daddy: These lectures on the moon by Doctor V. Govinda Lal are on short loan. They connect with the Memoir." Wells of course, writing on the moon circa 1900. "This is the very latest. Fascinating. Daddy—you have to read it. A must! Eyes or no eyes. And soon, please! as

Doctor Lal is guest-lecturing up at Columbia. He needs it back." Frowning terribly, patience, forbearance all gone, he was filled with revulsion at his daughter's single-minded, persistent, prosecuting, horrible-comical obsession. He drew a long, lung-racking, body-straightening breath.

Then, bending open the notebook, he read, in sepia, in rust-gilt ink, *The Future of the Moon.* "How long," went the first sentence, "will this earth remain the only home of Man?"

How long? Oh, Lord, you bet! Wasn't it the time—the very hour to go? For every purpose under heaven. A time to gather stones together, a time to cast away stones. Considering the earth itself not as a stone cast but as something to cast oneself from—to be divested of. To blow this great blue, white, green planet, or to be blown from it.

The mean radius of the moon, 1737 kilometers; that of the earth, 6371 kilometers. The moon's gravity, 161 cm./sec.^{2}; the earth's, 981 cm./sec.^{2}. Faults and crevices in the lunar bedrock and mountains caused by extremes of temperature. Of course there is no wind. Five billion windless years. Except for solar wind. Stone crumbles but without the usual erosion. The split rock is slow to fall, the gravitational force being lower and the angle of fall correspondingly sharper. Moreover, in the moon's vacuum stones, sand, dust, or explorers' bodies would all have the same rate of fall, so before attempting to climb, it is essential to study the avalanche perils from all sides. Information organs are rapidly developing. Mass spectrometers. Solar batteries. Electricity produced by radioactive isotopes, strontium 90, polonium 210, by thermoelectric energy conversion. Dr. Lal had thoroughly considered telemetry, data transmission. Had he neglected anything? Supplies could be put in orbit and brought down as needed by a braking system. The computers would have to be exceedingly accurate. If you needed a ton of dynamite at point X, you didn't want to bring it down 800 kilometers away. And what if it were essential oxygen? And because of the greater curvature of the moon's surface the horizons are shorter and present apparatus cannot send order signals beyond the horizon. Even more precise coordination will be necessary. For the good of the moon personnel, to increase their inventiveness, and simply as a desirable stimulus to the mind, Dr. Lal recommended the brewing of beer in the pioneer colonies. For beer oxygen is necessary, for oxygen gardens, for gardens hothouses. A brief chapter was devoted to the selection of lunar flora. Well, tough members of the plant kingdom lived in Margotte's parlor. Open two doors, and there they were: potato vines, avocados, rubber plants. Dr. Lal had hops and sugar beets in mind.

Sammler thought, This is not the way to get out of spatial-temporal prison. Distant is still finite. Finite is still feeling through the veil, examining the naked inner reality with a gloved hand. However, one could see the advantage of getting away from here, building plastic igloos in the vacuum, dwelling in quiet colonies, necessarily austere, drinking the fossil waters, considering basic questions only. No question of it. Shula-Slawa had brought him this time a document worth his attention. She was always culling idiotic titles on Fourth Avenue, from sidewalk bins, books with bleached spines and rain spots—England in the twenties and thirties, Bloomsbury, Downing Street, Clare Sheridan. His shelves were stacked with eight-for-a-dollar rubbish bargains hauled in splitting shopping bags.

And even the books he himself had bought were largely superfluous. After you had expended great effort on serious writers you found out little you hadn't known already. So many false starts, blind alleys, postulates which decayed before the end of the argument. Even the ablest thinkers groping as they approached their limits, running out of evidence, running out of certainties. But whether they were optimists or pessimists, whether the final vision was dark or bright, it was generally *terra cognita* to old Sammler. So Dr. Lal had a certain value. He brought news. Of course it should be possible still to follow truth on the inward track, without elaborate preparations, computers, telemetry, all the technological expertise and investment and complex organization required for visiting Mars, Venus, the moon. Nevertheless, it was perhaps for the same human activities that had shut us up like this to let us out again. The powers that had made the earth too small could free us from confinement. By the homeopathic principle. Continuing to the end the course of the Puritan revolution which had forced itself onto the material world, given all power to material processes, translated and exhausted religious feeling in so doing. Or, in the crushing summary of Max Weber, known by heart to Sammler, "Specialists without spirit, sensualists without heart, this nullity imagines that it has attained a level of civilization never before achieved." So conceivably there was no alternative but to push further in the same direction, to wait for a neglected force, left in the rear, to fly forward again and recover ascendancy. Perhaps by a growing agreement among the best minds, not unlike the Open Conspiracy of H. G. Wells. Maybe the old boy (Sammler, himself an old boy, considering this) was right after all.

But he laid aside the sea-textured cardboard notebook, the gilt-ink sentences of V. Govinda Lal written in formal Edwardian pedantic Hindu English to go back—under mental compulsion, in fact—to the pickpocket and the thing he had shown him. What had *that* been about? It had given a shock. Shocks stimulated consciousness. Up to a point, true enough. But what was the object of displaying the genitalia? *Qu'est-ce que cela prouve?* Was it a French mathematician who had asked this after seeing a tragedy of Racine? To the best of Mr. Sammler's recollection. Not that he liked playing the old European culture game. He had had that. Still, unsummoned, sentences came to him in this way. At any rate, there was the man's organ, a huge piece of sex flesh, half-tumescent in its pride and shown in its own right, a prominent and separate object intended to communicate authority. As, within the sex ideology of these days, it well might. It was a symbol of superlegitimacy or sovereignty. It was a mystery. It was unanswerable. The whole explanation. This is the wherefore, the why. See? Oh, the transcending, ultimate, and silencing proof. We hold these things, man, to be self-evident. And yet, such sensitive elongations the anteater had, too, uncomplicated by assertions of power, even over ants. But make Nature your God, elevate creatureliness, and you can count on gross results. Maybe you can count on gross results under any circumstances.

Sammler knew a lot about such superstressed creatureliness without even wanting to know. For singular reasons he was much in demand these days, often visited, often consulted and confessed to. Perhaps it was a matter of sunspots or seasons, something barometric or even astrological. But there was always someone arriving, knocking at the door. As he was thinking of anteaters, of the fact that he had been spotted long ago and shadowed by the black man, there was a knock at his back door.

Who was it? Sammler may have sounded more testy than he felt. What he felt was rather that others had more strength for life than he. This caused secret dismay. And there was an illusion involved, for, given the power of the antagonist, no one had strength enough.

Entering was Walter Bruch, one of the family. Walter, Margotte's cousin, was related also to the Gruners.

Cousin Angela once had taken Sammler to a Rouault exhibition. Beautifully dressed, fragrant, subtly made up, she led Sammler from room to room until it seemed to him that she was a rolling hoop of marvelous gold and gem colors and that he, following her, was an old stick from which she needed only an occasional touch. But then, stopping together before a Rouault portrait, both had had the same association: Walter Bruch. It was a broad, low, heavy, ruddy, thick-featured, wool-haired, staring, bake-faced man, looking bold enough but obviously incapable of bearing his own feelings. The very man. There must be thousands of such men. But this was our Walter. In a black raincoat, in a cap, gray hair bunched before the ears; his reddish-swarthy teapot cheeks; his big mulberry-tinted lips —well, imagine the Other World; imagine souls there by the barrelful; imagine them sent to incarnation and birth with dominant qualities *ab initio*. In Bruch's case the voice would have been significant from the very first. He was a voice-man, from the soul barrels. He sang in choruses, in temple choirs. By profession he was a baritone and musicologist. He found old manuscripts and adapted or arranged them for groups performing ancient and baroque music. His own little racket, he said. He sang well. His singing voice was fine, but his speaking voice gruff, rapid, throaty. He gobbled, he quacked, grunted, swallowed syllables.

Approaching when Sammler was so preoccupied, Bruch, in his idiosyncrasy, got a very special reception. Roughly, this: Things met with in this world are tied to the forms of our perception in space and time and to the forms of our thinking. We see what is before us, the present, the objective. Eternal being makes its temporal appearance in this way. The only way out of captivity in the forms, out of confinement in the prison of projections, the only contact with the eternal, is through freedom. Sammler thought he was Kantian enough to go along with this. And he saw a man like Walter Bruch as wearing out his heart within the forms. This was what he came to Sammler about. This was what his clowning was about, for he was always clowning. Shula-Slawa would tell you how she was run down while absorbed in a *Look* article by mounted policemen pursuing an escaped deer. Bruch might very suddenly begin to sing like the blind man on Seventy-second Street, pulling along the seeing-eye dog, shaking pennies in his cup: "What a friend we have in Jesus—God bless you, sir." He also enjoyed mock funerals with Latin and music, Monteverdi, Pergolesi, the Mozart C Minor Mass; he sang *"Et incarnatus est"* in falsetto. In his early years as a refugee, he and another German Jew, employed in Macy's warehouse, used to hold Masses over each other, one lying down in a packing case with dime-store beads wound about the wrists, the other doing the service. Bruch still enjoyed this, loved playing corpse. Sammler had often enough seen it done. Together with other clown routines. Nazi mass meetings at the Sportspalast. Bruch using an empty pot for sound effects, holding it over his mouth to get the echo, ranting like Hitler and interrupting himself to cry "*Sieg Heil.*" Sammler never enjoyed this fun. It led, soon, to Bruch's Buchenwald reminiscences. All that dreadful, comical, inconsequent senseless stuff. How, suddenly, in 1937, saucepans were offered to the prisoners for sale. Hundreds of thousands, new, from the factory. Why? Bruch bought as many pans as he could. What for? Prisoners tried to sell saucepans to one another. And then a man fell into the latrine trench. No one was allowed to help him, and he was drowned there while the other prisoners were squatting helpless on the planks. Yes, suffocated in the feces!

"Very well, Walter, very well!" Sammler severely would say.

"Yes, I know, I wasn't even there for the worst part, Uncle Sammler. And you were in the middle of the whole war. But I was sitting there with diarrhea and pain. My guts! Bare *arschenloch.*"

"Very well, Walter, don't repeat so much."

Unfortunately, Bruch was obliged to repeat, and Sammler was sorry. He was annoyed and he was sorry. And with Walter, as with so many others, it was always, it was ever and again, it was still, interminably, the sex business. Bruch fell in love with women's arms. They had to be youngish, plump women. Dark as a rule. Often they were Puerto Ricans. And in the summer, above all in the summer, without coats, when women's arms were exposed. He saw them in the subway. He went along to Spanish Harlem. He pressed himself against a metal rod. Way up in Harlem, he was the only white passenger. And the whole thing—the adoration, the disgrace, the danger of swooning when he came! Here, telling this, he began to finger the hairy base of that thick throat of his. Clinical! At the same time, as a rule, he was having a highly idealistic and refined relationship with some lady. Classical! Capable of sympathy, of sacrifice, of love. Even of fidelity, in his own Cynara-Dowson fashion.

At present he was, as he said, "hung up" on the arms of a cashier in the drugstore.

"I go as often as I can."

"Ah, yes," said Sammler.

"It is madness. I have my attaché case under my arm. Very strong. First-class leather. I paid for it thirty-eight fifty at Wilt Luggage on Fifth Avenue. You see?"

"I get the picture."

"I buy something for a quarter, a dime. Gum. A package of Sight-Savers. I give a large bill—a ten, even a twenty. I go in the bank and get fresh money."

"I understand."

"Uncle Sammler, you have no idea what it is for me in that round arm. So dark! So heavy!"

"No, I probably do not."

"I put the attaché case against the counter, and I press myself. While she is making the change, I press."

"All right, Walter, spare me the rest."

"Uncle Sammler, forgive me. What can I do? For me it is the only way."

"Well, that is your business. Why tell me?"

"There is a reason. Why shouldn't I tell you? There must be a reason. Please don't stop me. Be kind."

"You should stop yourself."

"I can't."

"Are you sure?"

"I press. I have a climax. I wet myself."

Sammler raised his voice. "Can't you leave out anything?"

"Uncle Sammler, what shall I do? I am over sixty years old."

Then Bruch raised the backs of his thick short hands to his eyes. His flat nose dilated, his mouth open, he was spurting tears and, apelike, twisting his shoulders, his trunk. And with those touching gaps between his teeth. And when he wept he was not gruff. You heard the musician then.

"My whole life has been like that."

"I'm sorry, Walter."

"I am hooked."

"Well, you haven't harmed anybody. And really people take these things much less seriously than they once did. Couldn't you concentrate more on other interests, Walter? Besides, your plight is so similar to other people's, you are so contemporary, Walter, that it should do something for you. Isn't it a comfort that there is no more isolated Victorian sex suffering? Everybody seems to have these vices, and tells the whole world about them. By now you are even somewhat old-fashioned. Yes, you have an old nineteenth-century Krafft-Ebing trouble."

But Sammler stopped himself, disapproving of the light tone that was creeping into his words of comfort. But as to the past he meant what he said. The sexual perplexities of a man like Bruch originated in the repressions of another time, in images of woman and mother which were disappearing. He himself, born in the old century and in the Austro-Hungarian Empire, could discern these changes. But it also struck him as unfair to lie in bed making such observations. However, the old, the original Cracow Sammler was never especially kind. He was an only son spoiled by a mother who had herself been a spoiled daughter. An amusing recollection: When Sammler was a little boy he had covered his mouth, when he coughed, with the servant's hand, to avoid getting germs on his own hand. A family joke. The servant, grinning, red-faced, kindly, straw-haired, gummy (odd lumps in her gums) Wadja, had allowed little Sammler to borrow the hand. Then, when he was older, his mother herself, not Wadja, used to bring lean, nervous young Sammler his chocolate and croissants as he sat in his room reading Trollope and Bagehot, making an "Englishman" of himself. He and his mother had had a reputation for eccentricity, irritability in those days. Not compassionate people. Not easily pleased. Haughty. Of course all this, for Sammler, had changed considerably in the last thirty years. But then Walter Bruch with his old urchin knuckles in his eyes sat in his room and sobbed, having told on himself. And when was there nothing to tell? There was always something. Bruch told how he bought himself toys. At F. A. O. Schwarz or in antique shops he bought wind-up monkeys who combed their hair in a mirror, who banged cymbals and danced jigs, in little green jackets or red caps. Nigger minstrels had fallen in price. He played in his room with the toys, alone. He also sent denunciatory, insulting letters to musicians. Then he came and confessed and wept. He didn't weep for display. He wept because he felt he had lost his life. Would it have been possible to tell him that he hadn't?

It was easier with a man like Bruch to transfer to broad reflections, to make comparisons, to think of history and themes of general interest. For instance, in the same line of sexual neurosis Bruch was exceeded by individuals like Freud's Rat Man, with his delirium of rats gnawing into the anus, persuaded that the genital also was ratlike, or that he himself was some sort of rat. By comparison an individual like Bruch had a light case of fetishism. If you had the comparative or historical outlook you would want only the most noteworthy, smashing instances. When you had those you could drop, junk and forget the rest, which were only a burden or excess baggage. If you considered what the historical memory of mankind would retain, it would not bother to retain the Bruchs; nor, come to that, the Sammlers. Sammler didn't much mind his oblivion, not with such as would do the remembering, anyway. He thought he had found out the misanthropy of the whole idea of the "most memorable." It was certainly possible that the historical outlook made it easier to dismiss the majority of instances. In other words, to jettison most of us. But here was Walter Bruch, who had come to his room because he felt he could talk to him. And probably Walter, when his crying stopped, would be hurt by the Krafft-Ebing reference, by the assertion that his deviation was not too unusual. Nothing seemed to hurt quite so much as being ravaged by a vice that was not a top vice. And this brought to mind Kierkegaard's comical account of people traveling around the world to see rivers and mountains, new stars, birds of rare plumage, queerly deformed fishes, ridiculous breeds of men—tourists abandoning themselves to the bestial stupor which gapes at existence and thinks it has seen something. This could not interest Kierkegaard. He was looking for the Knight of Faith, the real prodigy. That real prodigy, having set its relations with the infinite, was entirely at home in the finite. Able to carry the jewel of faith, making the motions of the infinite, and as a result needing nothing but the finite and the usual. Whereas others sought the extraordinary in the world. Or wished to be what was gaped at. They themselves wanted to be the birds of rare plumage, the queerly deformed fishes, the ridiculous breeds of men. Only Mr. Sammler, extended, a long old body with brickish cheekbones and the often electrified back hair riding the back of the head—only Mr. Sammler was worried. He was concerned about the test of crime which the Knight of Faith had to meet. Should the Knight of Faith have the strength to break humanly appointed laws in obedience to God? Oh, yes, of course! But maybe Sammler knew things about murder which might make the choices just a little more difficult. He thought often what a tremendous appeal crime had made to the children of bourgeois civilization. Whether as revolutionists, as supermen, as saints, Knights of Faith, even the best teased and tested themselves with thoughts of knife or gun. Lawless. Raskolnikovs. Ah yes . . .

"Walter, I'm sorry—sorry to see you suffer."

The odd things occurring in Sammler's room, with its papers, books, humidor, sink, electric coil, Pyrex flask, documents.

"I'll pray for you, Walter."

Bruch stopped crying, clearly startled.

"What do you mean, Uncle Sammler? You pray?"

The baritone music left his voice, and it was gruff again, and he gruffly gobbled his words.

"Uncle Sammler, I have my arms. You have prayers?" He gave a belly laugh. He laughed and snorted, swinging his trunk comically back and forth, holding both his sides, blindly showing both his nostrils. He was not, however, mocking Sammler. Not really. One had to learn to distinguish. To distinguish and distinguish and distinguish. It was distinguishing, not explanation, that mattered. Explanation was for the mental masses. Adult education. The upswing of general consciousness. A mental level comparable with, say, that of the economic level of the proletariat in 1848. But distinguishing? A higher activity.

"I will pray for you," said Sammler.

After this the conversation sank for a while into mere sociability. Sammler had to look at letters Bruch had sent to the *Post, Newsday,* the *Times,* tangling with their music reviewers. This again was the contentious, ludicrous side of things, the thick-smeared, self-conscious, performing loutish Bruch. Just when Sammler wanted to rest. To recover a little. To put himself in order. And Bruch's rollicking, guttural Dada routine was contagious. Go, Walter, go away so that I can pray for you, Sammler felt like saying, falling into Bruch's style. But then Bruch asked, "And when are you expecting your son-in-law?"

"Who? Eisen?"

"Yes, he's coming. He's maybe here already."

"I didn't know that. He's threatened to come, many times, to set up as an artist in New York. He doesn't want Shula at all."

"I know that," said Bruch. "And she is so afraid of him."

"Certainly it would not work. He is too violent. Yes, she will be frightened. She will also feel flattered, imagining that he has come to win her back. But he's not thinking of wives and marriage. He wants to show his paintings on Madison Avenue."

"He thinks he is that good?"

"He learned printing and engraving in Haifa and I was told in his shop that he was a dependable worker. But then he discovered Art, and began to paint in his spare time and make etchings. Then he sent each member of the family a portrait of himself copied from photographs. Did you see any? They were appalling, Walter. An insane mind and a frightening soul made those paintings. I don't know how he did it, but by using color he robbed every subject of color. Everybody looked like a corpse, with black lips and red eyes, with faces a kind of leftover cooked-liver green. At the same time it was like a little schoolgirl learning to draw pretty people, with cupid mouths and long eyelashes. Frankly, I was stunned when I saw myself like a kewpie doll from the catacombs. In that shiny varnish he uses, I looked really done for. It was as if one death was not enough for me, but I had to have a double death. Well, let him come. His crazy intuition about New York may be right. He is a cheerful maniac. Now so many highbrows have discovered that madness is higher knowledge. If he painted Lyndon Johnson, General Westmoreland, Rusk, Nixon, or Mr. Laird in that style he might become a celebrity of the art world. Power and money of course do drive people crazy. So why shouldn't people also gain power and wealth through being crazy? They should go together."

Sammler had taken off his shoes, and now the long frail feet in brown stockings felt cold and he laid over them the blanket with its frayed silk binding. Bruch took this to mean that he was going to sleep. Or was it that the conversation had taken a turn that didn't interest Sammler? The singer said good-by.

When Bruch bustled out—black coat, short legs, sack-wide bottom, cap tight, bicycle clips at the bottoms of his trousers (the suicidal challenge of cycling in Manhattan)—Sammler was again thinking of the pickpocket, the pressure of his body, the lobby and the hernial canvas walls, the two pairs of dark glasses, the lizard-thick curving tube in the hand, dusty stale pinkish chocolate color and strongly suggesting the infant it was there to beget. Ugly, odious; laughable, but nevertheless important. And Mr. Sammler himself (one of those mental invasions there was no longer any point in attempting to withstand) was accustomed to put his own very different emphasis on things. Of course he and the pickpocket were different. Everything was different. Their mental, characterological, spiritual profiles were miles apart. In the past, Mr. Sammler had thought that in this same biological respect he was comely enough, in his own Jewish way. It had never greatly mattered, and mattered less than ever now, in the seventies. But a sexual madness was overwhelming the Western world. Sammler now even vaguely recalled hearing that a President of the United States was supposed to have shown himself in a similar way to the representatives of the press (asking the ladies to leave), and demanding to know whether a man so well hung could not be trusted to lead his country. The story was apocryphal, naturally, but it was not a flat impossibility, given the President, and what counted was that it should spring up and circulate so widely that it reached even the Sammlers in their West Side bedrooms. Take as another instance the last exhibit of Picasso. Angela had brought him to the opening at the Museum of Modern Art. It was in the strictly sexual sense also an exhibition. Old Picasso was wildly obsessed by sexual fissures, by phalluses. In the frantic and funny pain of his farewell, creating organs by the thousands, perhaps tens of thousands. Lingam and Yoni. Sammler thought it might be enlightening to recall the Sanskrit words. Bring in a little perspective. But it didn't really do much for such a troubled theme. And it was very troubled. He fetched back, for example, a statement by Angela Gruner, blurted out after several drinks when she was laughing, gay, and evidently feeling free (to the point of brutality) with old Uncle Sammler. "A Jew brain, a black cock, a Nordic beauty," she had said, "is what a woman wants." Putting together the ideal man. Well, after all, she had charge accounts at the finest shops in New York, and access to the best of everything in the world. If Pucci didn't have what she wanted, she ordered from Hermès. All that money could buy, luxury could offer, personal beauty could bear upon the person, or that sexual sophistication could reciprocate. If she could find the ideal male, her divine synthesis—well, she was sure she could make it worth his while. The best was not too good for her. There seemed to be no question about that. At moments like this Mr. Sammler was more than ever pleasantly haunted by moon-visions. Artemis—lunar chastity. On the moon people would have to work hard simply to stay alive, to breathe. They would have to keep a strict watch over the gauges of all the devices. Conditions altogether different. Austere technicians—almost a priesthood.

If it wasn't Bruch forcing his way in with confessions, if it wasn't Margotte (for she was now beginning to think about affairs of the heart after three years of decent widowhood—more discussion than prospects, surely: discussion, earnest examination *ad infinitum*), if it wasn't Feffer with his indiscriminate bedroom adventures, it was Angela who came to confide. If confidence was the word for it. Communicating chaos. Getting to be oppressive. Especially since her father had recently been unwell. At this moment actually in the hospital. Sammler had ideas about this chaos—he had his own view of everything, an intensely peculiar one, but what else was there to go by? Of course he made allowances for error. He was a European, and these were American phenomena. Europeans often misunderstood America comically. He could remember that many refugees had packed their bags to take off for Mexico or Japan after Stevenson's first defeat, certain that Ike would bring a military dictatorship. Certain European importations were remarkably successful in the United States—psychoanalysis, existentialism. Both related to the sexual revolution.

In any case, a mass of sadness had been waiting for free, lovely, rich, ever-so-slightly coarse Angela Gruner, and she was now flying under thick clouds. For one thing she was having trouble with Wharton Horricker. She was fond of, she liked, probably she loved, Wharton Horricker. In the last two years Sammler had heard of few other men. Fidelity, strict and literal, was not Angela's dish, but she had an old-fashioned need for Horricker. He was from Madison Avenue, some sort of market-research expert and statistical wizard. He was younger than Angela. A physical culturist (tennis, weight lifting). Tall, from California, marvelous teeth. There was gymnastic apparatus in his house. Angela described the slanted board with footstraps for sit-ups, the steel bar in the doorway for chinning. And the chrome-metal, cold marble furniture, the leather straps and British folding officers' chairs, the op and pop *objets d'art,* the indirect lighting, and the prevalence of mirrors. Horricker was handsome. Sammler agreed. Cheerful, somewhat unformed as yet, Horricker was perhaps intended by nature to be rascally (what was all that muscle for? Health? Not banditry?). "And what a dresser!" said Angela with husky, comedienne's delight. With long California legs, small hips, crisp long hair with a darling curl at the back, he was a mod dandy. Extremely critical of other people's clothes. Even Angela had to submit to West Point inspection. Once when he thought her improperly dressed, he abandoned her on the street. He crossed to the other side. Custom-made shirts, shoes, sweaters were continually arriving from London and Milan. You could play sacred music while he had his hair cut (no, "styled!"), said Angela. He went to a Greek on East Fifty-sixth Street. Yes, Sammler knew a good deal about Wharton Horricker. His health foods. Horricker had even brought him bottles of yeast powder. Sammler found the yeast beneficial. Then there was the matter of neckties. Horricker's collection of beautiful neckties! By now the comparison with his own black pickpocket was unavoidable. This cult of masculine elegance must be thought about. Something important, still nebulous, about Solomon in all his glory versus the lilies of the field. We would see. Still, despite his self-pampering fastidiousness, his intolerance of badly clothed people, despite his dressy third-generation-Jew name, Wharton received serious consideration from Sammler. He sympathized with him, understanding the misleading and corrupting power of Angela, insidious without intending to be. What she intended to be was gay, pleasure-giving, exuberant, free, beautiful, healthy. As young Americans (the Pepsi generation, wasn't it?) saw the thing. And she told old Uncle Sammler everything—the honor of her confidences belonged to him. Why? Oh, she thought he was the most understanding, the most European-worldly-wise-nonprovincial-mentally-diversified-intelligent-young-in-heart of old refugees, and really interested in the new phenomena. To deserve this judgment had he perhaps extended himself a little? Hadn't he lent himself, played the game, acted the ripe old refugee? If so, he was offended with himself. And, yes, it was so. If he heard things he didn't want to hear, there was a parallel—on the bus he had seen things he didn't want to see. But hadn't he gone a dozen times to Columbus Circle to look for the black thief?

Without restraint, in direct terms, Angela described events to her uncle. Coming into his room, taking off the coat, the head scarf, shaking free the hair with its dyed streaks like raccoon fur, smelling of Arabian musk, an odor which clung afterward to the poor fabrics, seat cushions, to the coverlet, even to the curtains, as stubborn as walnut stain on one's fingers, she sat down in white textured stockings—*bas de poule* as the French called them. Cheeks bursting with color, eyes dark sexual blue, a white vital heat in the flesh of the throat, she carried a great statement to males, the powerful message of gender. In this day and age people felt obliged to temper all such powerful messages with comedy, and she provided that, too. In America certain forms of success required an element of parody, self-mockery, a satire on the-thing-itself. Mae West had this. Senator Dirksen had it. One caught glimpses of the strange mind-revenge on the alleged thing-itself in Angela. She crossed her legs on a chair too fragile to accommodate such thighs, too straight for her hips. She opened her purse for a cigarette, and Sammler offered a light. She loved his manners. The smoke came from her nose, and she looked at him, when she was in good form, cheerfully with a touch of slyness. The beautiful maiden. He was the old hermit. When she became hearty with him and laughed, she turned out to have a big mouth, a large tongue. Inside the elegant woman he saw a coarse one. The lips were red, the tongue was often pale. That tongue, a woman's tongue—evidently it played an astonishing part in her free, luxurious life.

To her first meeting with Wharton Horricker, she had come running uptown from East Village. Something she couldn't get out of. She had used no grass that night, only whisky, she said. Grass didn't turn her on as she best liked turning on. Four telephone calls she made to Wharton from a crowded joint. He said he had to get his sleep;

it was after one a.m.; he was a crank about sleep, health. Finally she burst in on him with a big kiss. She cried, "We're going to fuck all night!" But first she had to have a bath. Because she had been longing all evening for him. "Oh, a woman is a skunk. So many odors, Uncle," she said. Taking off everything, but overlooking the tights, she fell into the tub. Wharton was astonished and sat on the commode cover in his dressing gown while she, so ruddy with whisky, soaped her breasts. Sammler knew quite well how the breasts must look. Little, after all, was concealed by her low-cut dresses. So she was soaped and rinsed, and the wet tights with joyful difficulty were removed, and she was led to the bed by the hand. Or did the leading. For Horricker walked behind her and kissed her on the neck and shoulders. She cried "Oh!" and was mounted.

Mr. Sammler was supposed to listen benevolently to all kinds of intimate reports. Curiously enough, though with more thought and decency, H. G. Wells had also talked to him about sexual passion. From such a superior individual one might have expected views more in line with those of Sophocles in old age. "Most gladly have I escaped the thing of which you speak; I feel as if I had escaped from the hands of a mad and furious master." No such thing. As Sammler remembered it, Wells in his seventies was still obsessed with girls. He had powerful arguments for a total revision of sexual attitudes to accord with the increased life span. When the average individual died at thirty, toil-ruined, ill-fed, sickly mankind was sexually finished before the third decade. Romeo and Juliet were adolescents. But as the civilized life expectancy approaches seventy, the old standards of brutal brevity, early exhaustion, and doom must be set aside. Rancor, and gradually even rage, came over Wells at a certain point as he talked about the powers of the brain, its expansive limits, the ability in old age to take a fresh interest in new events diminishing. Utopian, he didn't even imagine that the hoped-for future would bring excess, pornography, sexual abnormality. Rather, as the old filth and gloomy sickness were cleared away, there would emerge a larger, stronger, older, brainier, better-nourished, better-oxygenated, more vital human type, able to eat and drink sanely, perfectly autonomous and well regulated in desires, going nude while attending tranquilly to duties, performing his fascinating and useful mental work. Yes, gradually the long shudder of mankind at the swift transitoriness of mortal beauty, pleasure, would cease, to be replaced by the wisdom born of prolongation.

Oh, wrinkled faces, gray beards, eyes purging thick amber or gum, a plentiful lack of wit together with weak hams, out of the air, crabwise, into the grave: Hamlet had his own view of it. And Sammler on many occasions, listening to Angela as he lay in bed, considering two sets of problems (at least) with two different-looking eyes, a tense stitch between rib and hip making him draw up one leg for an ease he did not attain, had a slight look of rebuke as well as the look of receptivity. His daily tablespoon of nutritional yeast, a primary product from natural sugars, dissolved and shaken to a pink foam in fruit juice, kept him in fresh color. One result, possibly, of longevity was divine entertainment. You could appreciate God's entertainment from the formation of patterns which needed time for their proper development. Sammler had known Angela's grandparents. They had been Orthodox. This gave a queer edge to his acquaintance with her paganism. Somewhere he doubted the fitness of these Jews for this erotic Roman voodoo primitivism. He questioned whether release from long Jewish mental discipline, hereditary training in lawful control, was obtainable upon individual application. Although claims for erotic leadership had also been made by modern Jewish spiritual and mental doctors, Sammler had his doubts.

Accept and grant that happiness is to do what most other people do. Then you must incarnate what others incarnate. If prejudices, prejudice. If rage, then rage. If sex, then sex. But don't contradict your time. Just don't contradict it, that's all. Unless you happened to be a Sammler and felt that the place of honor was outside. However, what was achieved by remoteness, by being simply a vestige, a visiting consciousness which happened to reside in a West Side bedroom, did not entitle one to the outside honors. Moreover, inside was so roomy and took in so many people that if you were in the West Nineties, if you were in fact here, you *were* an American. And the charm, the ebullient glamour, the almost unbearable agitation that came from being able to describe oneself as a twentieth-century American was available to all. To everyone who had eyes to read the papers or watch the television, to everyone who shared the collective ecstasies of news, crisis, power. To each according to his excitability. But perhaps it was an even deeper thing. Humankind watched and described itself in the very turns of its own destiny. Itself the subject, living or drowning in night, itself the object, seen surviving or succumbing, and feeling in itself the fits of strength and the lapses of paralysis—mankind's own passion simultaneously being mankind's great spectacle, a thing of deep and strange participation, on all levels, from melodrama and mere noise down into the deepest layers of the soul and into the subtlest silences, where undiscovered knowledge is. This sort of experience, in Mr. Sammler's judgment, might bring to some people fascinating opportunities for the mind and the soul, but a man would have to be unusually intelligent to begin with, and in addition unusually nimble and discerning. He didn't even think that he himself qualified by his own standard. Because of the high rate of speed, decades, centuries, epochs condensing into months, weeks, days, even sentences. So that to keep up, you had to run, sprint, waft, fly over shimmering waters, you had to be able to see what was dropping out of human life and what was staying in. You could not be an old-fashioned sitting sage. You must train yourself. You had to be strong enough not to be terrified by local effects of metamorphosis, to live with disintegration, with crazy streets, filthy nightmares, monstrosities come to life, addicts, drunkards, and perverts celebrating their despair openly in midtown. You had to be able to bear the tangles of the soul, the sight of cruel dissolution. You had to be patient with the stupidities of power, with the fraudulence of business. Daily at five or six a.m. Mr. Sammler woke up in Manhattan and tried to get a handle on the situation. He didn't think he could. Nor, if he could, would he be able to convince or convert anyone. He could leave the handle to Shula in his will. She could disclose possession to Rabbi Ipsheimer. She could whisper to Father Robles in the confessional that she had it. What could the main thing be? Consciousness and its pains? The flight from consciousness into the primitive? Liberty? Privilege? Demons? The expulsion of those demons and spirits from the air, where they had always been, by enlightenment and rationalism? And mankind had never lived without its possessing demons and had to have them back! Oh, what a wretched, itching, bleeding, needing, idiot, genius of a creature we were dealing with here! And how queerly it was playing (he, she) with all the strange properties of existence, with all varieties of possibility, with antics of all types, with the soul of the world, with death. Could it be condensed into a statement or two? Humankind could not endure futurelessness. As of now, death was the sole visible future.

A family, a circle of friends, a team of the living got things going, and then death appeared and no one was prepared to acknowledge death. Dr. Gruner, it was given out, had had minor surgery, a little operation. Was it so? An artery to the brain, the carotid, had begun to leak through weak walls. Sammler had been slow, reluctant to grasp what this might mean. He had perhaps a practical reason for such reluctance. Since 1947, he and Shula had been Dr. Gruner's dependents. He paid their rents, invented work for Shula, supplemented the Social Security and German indemnity checks. He was generous. Of course he was rich, but the rich were usually mean. Not able to separate themselves from the practices that had made the money: infighting, habitual fraud, mad agility in compound deceit, the strange conventions of legitimate swindling. To old Sammler, considering, with smallish ruddy face, the filmed bubble of the eye, and slightly cat-whiskered—a meditative island on the island of Manhattan—it was plain that the rich men he knew were winners in struggles of criminality, of permissible criminality. In other words, triumphant in forms of deceit and hardness of heart considered by the political order as a whole to be productive; kinds of cheating or thieving or (at best) wastefulness which on the whole caused the gross national product to increase. Wait a minute, though: Sammler denied himself the privilege of the high-principled intellectual who must always be applying the purest standards and thumping the rest of his species on the head. When he tried to imagine a just social order, he could not do it. A noncorrupt society? He could not do that either. There were no revolutions that he could remember which had not been made for justice, freedom, and pure goodness. Their last state was always more nihilistic than the first. So if Dr. Gruner had been corrupt, one should glance also at the other rich, to see what hearts they had. No question. Dr. Gruner, who had made a great deal of money as a gynecologist and even more, later, in real estate, was on the whole kindly and had a lot of family feeling, far more than Sammler, who in his youth had taken the opposite line, the modern one of Marx-Engels-private-property-the-origins-of-the-state-and-the-family.

Sammler was only six or seven years older than Gruner, his nephew by an amusing technicality. Sammler was the child of a second marriage, born when his father was sixty. (Evidently Sammler's own father had been sexually enterprising.) And Dr. Gruner had longed for a European uncle. He was elaborately deferential, positively Chinese in observing old forms. He had left the old country at the age of ten, he was sentimental about Cracow, and wanted to reminisce about grandparents, aunts, cousins with whom Sammler had never had much to do. He couldn't easily explain that these were people from whom he had thought he must free himself and because of whom he became so absurdly British. But Dr. Gruner himself after fifty years was still something of an immigrant. In spite of the grand Westchester house and the Rolls Royce glittering like a silver tureen, covering his courteous Jewish baldness. Dr. Gruner's wrinkles were mild. They expressed patience and sometimes even delight. He had large, noble lips. Irony and pessimism were also there. It was a pleasant, pleasantly illuminated face.

And Sammler, an uncle through his half-sister—an

uncle really by courtesy, by Gruner's pious antiquarian wish—was seen (tall, elderly, foreign) as the last of a marvelous old generation. Mama's own brother, Uncle Artur, with big pale tufts over the eyes, with thin wrinkles augustly flowing under the big-brimmed perhaps romantically British hat. Sammler understood from his "nephew's" face with the grand smile and conspicuous ears that his historical significance for Gruner was considerable. Also his *experiences* were respected. The war. Holocaust. Suffering.

Because of his high color, Gruner always looked healthy to Sammler. But the doctor one day said, "Hypertension, Uncle, not health."

"Maybe you shouldn't play cards."

Twice a week, at his club, in very long sessions, Gruner played gin rummy or canasta for high stakes. So Angela said, and she was pleased with her father's vice. She had hereditary vices to point to—she and her younger brother, Wallace. Wallace was a born plunger. He had already gone through his first fifty thousand, investing with a Mafia group in Las Vegas. Or perhaps they were only would-be Mafia, for they hadn't made it. Dr. Gruner himself had grown up in a hoodlum neighborhood and sometimes dropped into the hoodlum manner, speaking out of the corner of his mouth. He was a widower. His wife had been a German Jewess, above him socially, so she thought. Her family had been 1848 pioneers. Gruner was an *Ostjude* immigrant. Her job was to refine him, to help him build his practice. The late Mrs. Gruner had been decent, proper, with thin legs, bouffant hair sprayed stiffly, and Peck & Peck outfits, geometrically correct to the millimeter. Gruner had believed in the social superiority of his wife.

"It's not the rummy that aggravates my blood pressure.

If there were no cards, there would still be the stock market, and if there weren't the stock market, there would be the condominium in Florida, there would be the suit with the insurance company, or there would still be Wallace. There would be Angela."

Tempering his great glowing affection, mixing fatherly love with curses, Gruner would mutter "Bitch" when his daughter approached with all her flesh in motion—thighs, hips, bosom displayed with a certain fake innocence. Presumably maddening men and infuriating women. Under his breath, Gruner said "Cow!" or "Sloppy cunt!" Still, he had settled money on her so that she could live handsomely on the income. Millions of corrupt ladies, Sammler saw, had fortunes to live on. Foolish creatures, or worse, squandering the wealth of the land. Gruner would never have been able to bear the details that Sammler heard from Angela. She was always warning him, "Daddy would *die* if he knew this." Sammler did not agree; Elya probably knew plenty. The truth was naturally known by all concerned. It was all in Angela's calves, in the cut of her blouses, in the motions of her finger tips, the musical brass of her whispers.

Dr. Gruner had taken to saying, "Oh, yes, I know that broad. I know my Angela. And Wallace!"

Sammler didn't at first understand what an aneurysm meant; he heard from Angela that Gruner was in the hospital for throat surgery. The day after the pickpocket had cornered him, he went to the East Side to visit Gruner. He found him with a bandaged neck.

"Well, Uncle Sammler?"

"Elya—how are you? You look all right." And the old man, reaching beneath himself with a long arm, smoothing the underside of the trench coat, bending thin legs, sat down. Between the tips of cracked wrinkled black shoes he set the tip of his umbrella and leaned with both palms on the curved handle, stooping toward the bed with Polish-Oxonian politeness. Meticulously, the sickroom caller. Finely, intricately wrinkled, the left side of his face was like the contour map of difficult terrain.

Dr. Gruner sat straight, unsmiling. His expression after a lifetime of good-humored appearance was still mainly pleasant. This was not pertinent at present, merely habitual.

"I am in the middle of something."

"The surgery was successful?"

"There is a gimmick in my throat, Uncle."

"For what?"

"To regulate the flow of blood in the artery—the carotid."

"Is that so? Is it a valve or something?"

"More or less."

"It's supposed to reduce the pressure?"

"Yes, that's the idea."

"Yes. Well, it seems to be working. You look as usual. Normal, Elya."

Evidently there was something which Dr. Gruner had no intention of letting out. His expression was neither dire nor grim. Instead of hardness Mr. Sammler thought he could observe a curious kind of tight lightness. The doctor in the hospital, in pajamas, was a good patient. He said to the nurses, "This is my uncle. Tell him what kind of patient I am."

"Oh, the doctor is a wonderful patient."

Gruner had always insisted on having affectionate endorsements, approbation, the good will of all who drew near.

"I am completely in the surgeon's hands. I do exactly as he says."

"He is a good doctor?"

"Oh, yes. He's a hillbilly. A Georgia red-neck. He was a football star in college. I remember reading about him in the papers. He played for Georgia Tech. But he's professionally very able; and I take orders from him, and I never discuss the case."

"So you're satisfied completely with him?"

"Yesterday the screw was too tight."

"What did that do?"

"Well, my speech got thick. I lost some coordination. You know the brain needs its blood supply. So they had to loosen me up again."

"But you are better today?"

"Oh, yes."

The mail was brought, and Dr. Gruner asked Uncle Sammler to read a few items from the Market Letter. Sammler lifted the paper to his right eye, concentrating window light upon it. "The U.S. Justice Department will file suit to force Ling-Temco-Vought to divest its holdings of Jones and Laughlin Steel. Moving against the huge conglomerate . . ."

"Those conglomerates are soaking up all the business in the country. One of them, I understand, has acquired all the funeral parlors in New York. I hear reports that Campbell, Riverside, have been bought by the same company that publishes *Mad* magazine."

"How curious."

"Youth is big business. Schoolchildren spend fantastic amounts. If enough kids get radical, that's a new mass market, then it's a big operation."

"I have a general idea."

"Very little is holding still. First making your money, then keeping your money from shrinking by inflation. How you invest it, whom you trust—you trust nobody—what you get with it, how you save it from those Federal taxation robbers, the gruesome Revenue Service. And how you leave it . . . wills! Those are the worst problems in life. Excruciating."

Uncle Sammler now understood fully how it was. His nephew Gruner had in his head a great blood vessel, defective from birth, worn thin and frayed with a lifetime of pulsation. A clot had formed from leakage. The whole jelly trembled. One was summoned to the brink of the black. Any beat of the heart might open the artery and spray the brain with blood. These facts shimmered their way into Sammler's mind. Was it the time? *The* time? How terrible! But yes! Elya would die of a hemorrhage. Did he know this? Of course he did. He was a physician, so he must know. But he was human, so he could arrange many things for himself. Both knowing and not knowing—one of the more frequent human arrangements. Then Sammler, making himself intensely observant, concluded after ten or twelve minutes that Gruner definitely knew. He believed that Gruner's moment of honor had come, that moment at which the individual could call upon his best qualities. Mr. Sammler had lived a long time and understood something about these cases of final gallantry. *If* there were time, occasionally good things were done. *If* one had a certain kind of luck.

"Uncle, try some of these fruit jellies. The lime and orange are the best. From Beersheba."

"Aren't you watching your weight, Elya?"

"No, I'm not. They're making terrific stuff in Israel these days." The doctor had been buying Israel bonds and real estate. In Westchester, he served Israeli wine and brandy. He gave away heavily embossed silver ball-point pens, made in Israel. You could sign checks with them. For ordinary purposes they were not useful. And on two occasions Dr. Gruner, as he was picking up his fedora, had said, "I believe I'll go to Jerusalem for a while."

"When are you leaving?"

"Now."

"Right away?"

"Certainly."

"Just as you are?"

"Just as I am. I can buy my toothbrush and razor when I land. I love it there."

He had his chauffeur drive him to Kennedy Airport.

"I'll cable you, Emil, when I'm coming back."

In Jerusalem were more old relatives like Sammler, and Gruner did genealogies with them, one of his favorite pastimes. More than a pastime. He had a passion for kinships. Sammler found this odd, especially in a physician. As one whose prosperity had been founded in the female generative slime, he might have had less specific sentiment about his own tribe. But now, seeing a fatal dryness in the circles under his eyes, Sammler better understood the reason for this. To each according to his intimations. Gruner had not worked in his profession for ten years. He had had a heart attack and retired on insurance. After a year or two of payments, the insurance company insisted that he was well enough to practice, and there had been a lawsuit. Then Dr. Gruner learned that insurance companies kept the finest legal talent in the city on retainer. The best lawyers were tied up, and the courts were deliberately choked with trivial suits by the companies, so that it was years before his case came to trial. But he won. Or was about to win. He had disliked his trade—the knife, blood. He had been conscientious. He had done his duty. But he hadn't liked his trade. He was still, however, fastidiously manicured like a practicing surgeon. Here in the hospital the manicurist was sent for, and during Sammler's visit Gruner's fingers were being soaked in a steel basin. The strange tinge of male fingers in the suds. The woman in her white smock, every single hair of the neckless head the same hue of dyed black, without variation, was gloomy, sloven-footed in orthopedic white shoes. Heavy-shouldered, she bent with instruments over his nails, concentrating on her work. She had quite a wide, tear-pregnant nose. Dr. Gruner had to woo reactions from her. Even from such a dismal creature.

As it might not be many times more (for Elya) the room was filled with sunny light. In which familiar human postures were struck. From which no great results had come in the past. From which little could be expected at this late hour. What if the manicurist were to take a liking to Dr. Gruner? What if she should requite his longing? What was his longing? Mr. Sammler had a thing about these unprofitable instants of clarity. Seeing the singular human creature demand more when the sum of human facts could not yield more. Sammler did not like such instants, but they came nevertheless.

The woman pushed back the cuticle. She would not be tempted up from her own underground galleries. Intimacy was refused.

"Uncle Artur, can you tell me anything about my grandmother's brother in the old country?"

"Who?"

"Hessid was the man's name."

"Hessid? Hessid? Yes, there was a Hessid family."

"He had a mill for cornmeal, and a shop near the Castle. Just a small place with a few barrels."

"You must be mistaken. I remember no one in the family who ground anything. However, you have an excellent memory. Better than mine."

"Hessid. A fine-looking old man with a broad white beard. He wore a derby, and a very fancy vest with watch and chain. Called up often to read from the Torah, though he couldn't have been a heavy contributor to the synagogue."

"Ah, the synagogue. Well, you see, Elya, I didn't have much to do with the synagogue. We were almost freethinkers. Especially my mother. She had a Polish education. She gave me an emancipated name: Artur."

Sammler regretted that he was so poor at family reminiscences. Contemporary contacts being somewhat unsatisfactory, he would gladly have helped Gruner to build up the past.

"I loved old Hessid. You know, I was a very affectionate child."

"I'm sure you were," said Sammler. He could hardly remember Gruner as a boy. Standing, he said, "I won't tire you with a long visit."

"Oh, you aren't tiring me. But you probably have things to do. At the public library. One thing, before you go, Uncle—you're in pretty good shape still. You took that last trip to Israel very well, and that was a tough one. Do you still like to run in Riverside Park, as you used to do?"

"Not lately. I feel too stiff for it."

"I was going to say, it's not safe to run down there. I don't want you mugged. When you're winded from running, some crazy sonofabitch jumps out and cuts your throat! Anyway, if you are too stiff to run you're far from feeble. I know you're not a sickly type, apart from your nervous trouble. You still get that small payment from the West Germans? And the Social Security? Yes, I'm glad we had the lawyer set that up, about the Germans. And I don't want you to worry, Uncle Artur."

"About what?"

"About anything at all. Security in old age. Being in a home. You stay with Margotte. She's a good woman. She'll look after you. I realize Shula is a little too nutty for you. She amuses other people but not her own father. I know how that can be."

"Yes, Margotte is decent. You couldn't ask for better."

"So, remember, Uncle, no worries."

"Thank you, Elya."

A confusing, frowning moment, and, getting into the breast, the head, and even down into the bowels and about the heart, and behind the eyes—something gripping, aching, smarting. The woman was buffing Gruner's nails, and he sat straight in the fully buttoned pajama coat; above it, the bandage hiding the throat with its screw. His large ruddy face was mainly unhandsome, his baldness, his big-eared plainness, the large tip of the nose; Gruner belonged to the common branch of the family. It was, however, a virile face, and, when superficial objections were removed, a kindly face. Sammler knew the defects of his man. Saw them as dust and pebbles, as rubble on a mosaic which might be swept away. Underneath, a fine, noble expression. A dependable man—a man who took thought for others.

"You've been good to Shula and me, Elya."

Gruner neither acknowledged nor denied this. Perhaps by the rigidity of his posture he fended off gratitude he did not deserve in full.

In short, if the earth deserves to be abandoned, if we are now to be driven streaming into other worlds, starting with the moon, it is not because of the likes of you, Sammler would have said. He put it more briefly, "I'm grateful."

"You're a gentleman, Uncle Artur."

"I'll be in touch."

"Yes, come back. It does me good."

Sammler, outside the rubber-silenced door, put on his Augustus John hat. A hat from the Soho that was. He went down the corridor in his usual quick way, favoring the sightful side slightly, putting forward the right leg and the right shoulder. When he came to the anteroom, a sunny bay with soft plastic orange furniture, he found Wallace Gruner there with a doctor in a white coat. This was Elya's surgeon.

"My dad's uncle—Dr. Cosbie."

"How do you do, Dr. Cosbie." The conceivably wasted fragrance of Mr. Sammler's manners. Who was there now to be aware of such Old World stuff! Here and there perhaps a woman might appreciate his style of greeting. But not a Doctor Cosbie. The ex-football star, famous in Georgia, struck Sammler as a sort of human wall. High and flat. His face was mysteriously silent, and very white. The upper lip was steep and prominent. The mouth itself thin and straight. Somewhat unapproachable, he kept his hands behind his back. He had the air of a general whose mind is on battalions in a bloody struggle, just out of sight over a hill. To a civilian pest who came up to him at that moment he had nothing to say.

"How is Dr. Gruner?"

"Makin' good progress, suh. A very fine patient."

Dr. Gruner was being seen as he wished to be seen. Every occasion had its propaganda. Democracy was propaganda. From government, propaganda entered every aspect of life. You had a desire, a view, a line, and you disseminated it. It took, everyone spoke of the event in the appropriate way, under your influence. In this case Elya, a doctor, a patient, made it known that he was the patient of patients. An allowable foible; boyish, but what of it? It had a certain interest.

Faced with a doctor, Sammler had his own foible, for he often wanted to ask about his symptoms. This was repressed of course. But the impulse was there. He wanted to mention that he woke up with a noise inside his head, that his good eye built up a speck at the corner which he couldn't scratch out, it stuck in the fold, that his feet burned intolerably at night, that he suffered from *pruritis ani.* Doctors loathed laymen with medical phrases. All, naturally, was censored. The tachycardia last of all. Nothing was shown to Cosbie but a certain cool, elderly rosiness. A winter apple. A busy-minded old man. Colored specs. A wide wrinkled hat brim. An umbrella on a sunny day—inconsequent. Long narrow shoes, cracked but highly polished.

Was he cold-hearted about Elya? No, he was grieving. But what could he do? He went on thinking, and seeing.

As usual, even in the midst of conversation, Wallace with round black eyes was dreaming away. Profoundly dreaming. He also had a very white color. In his late twenties he was still little brother with the curls, the lips of a small boy. A bit careless perhaps in his toilet habits, also like a small boy, he often transmitted to Sammler in warm weather (perhaps Sammler's nose was hypersensitive) a slightly unclean odor from the rear. The merest hint of fecal carelessness. This did not offend his great-uncle. It was simply observed, by a peculiarly delicate recording system. Actually, Sammler rather sympathized with the young man. Wallace fell into the Shula category. There was even a family resemblance, especially in the eyes—round, dark, wide, filling the big bony orbits, capable of seeing all, but adream, dreamy, as if drugged. He was a kinky cat, said Angela. With Dr. Cosbie he was discussing sports. Wallace took no common interest in any subject. With him all interests were uncommon. He caught a tearing fever. Horses, football, hockey, baseball. He knew averages, performance records, statistics. You could test him by the almanac. Dr. Gruner said that he would be up at four a.m. memorizing tables and jotting away left-handed at top speed across the body. With this, the intellectual if slightly pedomorphic forehead, the refinement of the nose, somewhat too small, and the middle of the face, somewhat too concave, and a look of mental power, virility, nobility, all slightly spoiled. Wallace nearly became a physicist, he nearly became a mathematician, nearly a lawyer (he had even passed the bar and opened an office, once), nearly an engineer, nearly a Ph.D. in behavioral science. He was a licensed pilot. Nearly an alcoholic, nearly a homosexual. At present he seemed to be a handicapper. He had yellow pages of legal foolscap covered with team names and ciphers, and he and Dr. Cosbie, who seemed to be a gambler, too, were going over these intricate, many-factored calculations, and plainly the doctor was fascinated, not simply humoring Wallace. Slender Wallace in the dark suit was very handsome. A young man with stunning gifts. It was puzzling.

"You may be out of line on the Rose Bowl," said the doctor.

"Not at all," said Wallace. "Just examine this yardage analysis. I broke down last year's figures and fitted them into my own special equation: Now look . . ."

This was as much of the conversation as Sammler could follow. He waited awhile at the window observing traffic, women with dogs, leashed and unleashed. A vacant building opposite marked for demolition. Large white X's on the windowpanes. On the plate glass of the empty shop were strange figures or nonfigures in thick white. Most scrawls could be ignored. These for some reason caught on with Mr. Sammler as pertinent. Eloquent. Of what? Of future nonbeing. (Elya!) But also of the greatness of eternity which shall lift us from this present shallowness. At this time forces, energies that might carry mankind up carried it down. For finer purposes of life, little was available. Terror of the sublime maddened all minds. Capacities, impressions, visions amassed in human beings from the time of origin, perhaps since matter first glinted with grains of consciousness, were bound up largely with vanities, negations, and revealed only in amorphous hints or ciphers smeared on the windows of condemned shops. All naturally were frightened of the future. Not death. Not that future. Another future in which the full soul concentrated upon eternal being. Mr. Sammler believed this. And in the meantime there was the excuse of madness. A whole nation, all of civilized society, perhaps, seeking the blameless state of madness. The privileged, the almost aristocratic state of madness. Meantime there spoke out those thick loops and open curves across an old tailor-shop window.

It was in Poland, in wartime, particularly during three or four months when Sammler was hidden in a mausoleum, that he first began to turn to the external world for curious ciphers and portents. The dead life of that summer and into autumn when he had been a portent watcher, and very childish, for many larger forms of meaning had been stamped out, and a straw, or a spider thread or a stain, a beetle or a sparrow had to be interpreted. Symbols everywhere, and metaphysical messages. In the tomb of a family called Mezvinski he was, so to speak, a boarder. The peacetime caretaker of the cemetery let him have bread. Water, too. Some days were missed, but not many, and anyway Sammler saved up a small bread reserve and did not starve. Old Cieslakiewicz was dependable. He brought bread in his hat. It smelled of scalp, of head. And during this period there was a yellow tinge to everything, a yellow light in the sky. In this light, bad news for Sammler, bad news for humankind, bad information about the very essence of being was diffused. Something hateful, and at times overwhelming. At its worst it seemed to go something like this: You have been summoned to be. Summoned out of matter. Therefore here you are. And though the vast over-all design may be of the deepest interest, whether originating in a God or in an indeterminate source which should have a different name, you yourself, a finite instance, are obliged to wait, painfully, anxiously, heartachingly, in this yellow despair. And why? But you must! So he lay and waited. There was more to this, when Sammler was boarding in the tomb. No time to be thinking, perhaps, but what else was there to do? There were no events. Events had stopped. There was no news. Cieslakiewicz with hanging mustache, swollen hands, palsy, his ugly blue eyes—Sammler's savior—had no news or would not give it. Cieslakiewicz had risked his life for him. The basis of this fact was a great oddity. They didn't like each other. What had there been to like in Sammler?—half-naked, famished, caked hair and beard, crawling out of the forest. Long experience of the dead, handling of human bones, had perhaps prepared the caretaker for the apparition of Sammler. He had let him into the Mezvinski tomb, brought him some rags for cover. After the war Sammler had sent money, parcels, to Cieslakiewicz. There was correspondence with the family. Then, after some years, the letters began to contain anti-Semitic sentiments. Nothing very vicious. Only a touch of the old stuff. This was no great surprise, or only a brief one. Cieslakiewicz had had his time of honor and charity. He had risked his life to save Sammler. The old Pole was also a hero. But the heroism ended. He was an ordinary human being and wanted again to be himself. Enough was enough. Didn't he have a right to be himself? To relax into old prejudices? It was only the "thoughtful" person with his exceptional demands who went on with self-molestation—responsible to "higher values," to "civilization," pressing forward and so on. It was the Sammlers who kept on vainly trying to perform some kind of symbolic task. The main result of which was unrest, exposure to trouble. Mr. Sammler had a symbolic character. He, personally, was a symbol. His friends and family had made him a judge and a priest. And of what was he a symbol? He didn't even know. Was it because he had survived? He hadn't even done that, since so much of the earlier person had disappeared. It wasn't surviving, it was only lasting. He had lasted. For a time yet he might last. A little longer, evidently, than Elya Gruner with the clamp or screw in his throat. *That* couldn't hold death off very long. A sudden escape of red fluid, and the man was gone. With all his will, purpose, his virtues, his good record as a physician, his enterprises, card games, his loyalty to Israel, dislike of de Gaulle, with all his kindness of heart, greediness of heart, with his mouth making passionate love to the manifest, with his money talk, his Jewish fatherhood, his love and despair over son and daughter. When his life—or this life, that life, the other life—was gone, taken away, there would remain for Sammler, while he lasted, that bad literalness, the yellow light of Polish summer heat behind the mausoleum door. It was the light also of that china-cabinet room in the apartment where he had suffered confinement with Shula-Slawa. Endless literal hours in which one is internally eaten up. Eaten because coherence is lacking. Perhaps as a punishment for having failed to find coherence. Or eaten by a longing for sacredness. Yes, go and find it when everyone is murdering everyone. When Antonina was murdered. When he himself underwent murder beside her. When he and sixty or seventy others, all stripped naked and having dug their own grave, were fired upon and fell in. Bodies upon his own body. Crushing. His dead wife nearby somewhere. Struggling out much later from the weight of corpses, crawling out of the loose soil. Scraping on his belly. Hiding in a shed. Finding a rag to wear. Lying in the woods many days.

Nearly thirty years after which, in April days, sunshine, springtime, another season, the rush and intensity of New York City about to be designated as spring; leaning on a soft, leatherlike orange sofa; feet on an umber Finnish rug with a yellow core or nucleus—with mitotic spindles; looking down to a street; in that street, a tailor's window on which the spirit of the time through the unconscious agency of a boy's hand had scrawled its augury.

Is our species crazy?

Plenty of evidence.

All of course seems man's invention. Including madness. Which may be one more creation of that agonizing inventiveness. At the present level of human evolution propositions were held (and Sammler was partly swayed by them) by which choices were narrowed down to sainthood and madness. We are mad unless we are saintly, saintly only as we soar above madness. The gravitational pull of madness drawing the saint crashwards. A few may comprehend that it is the strength to do one's duty daily and promptly that makes saints and heroes. Not many. Most have fantasies of vaulting into higher states, feeling just mad enough to qualify.

Take someone like Wallace Gruner. The doctor was gone and Wallace, with his yellow papers, was standing gracefully, handsomely, with his long lashes. How much normalcy, what stability was Wallace prepared to sacrifice to obtain the grace of madness?

"Uncle?"

"Ah, yes, Wallace."

Some were eccentric, some were histrionic. Probably Wallace was genuinely loony. For him it required a powerful effort to become interested in common events. This was possibly why sporting statistics cast him into such a fever, why so often he seemed to be in outer space. *Dans la lune*. Well, at least he didn't treat Sammler as a symbol, and he apparently had no use for priests, judges, or confessors. Wallace said that what he appreciated in Uncle Sammler was his wit. Sammler, especially when greatly irritated or provoked, when he felt galled, said witty things. In the old European style. Often these witticisms signaled the approach of a nervous fit.

But Wallace, when he began a conversation with Sammler, was immediately smiling, and sometimes he repeated the punch lines of Sammler's witticisms.

"Not a well-rounded person, Uncle?"

Referring to himself, Sammler once had observed, "I am

more stupid about some things than about others; not equally stupid in all directions; I am not a well-rounded person."

Or else, a recent favorite with Wallace: "The billiard table, Uncle. The billiard table."

This had to do with Angela's trip to Mexico. She and Horricker had had an unhappy Mexican holiday. In January she had had enough of New York and winter. She wanted to go to Mexico, to a hot place, she said, where she could see something green. Then abruptly, before he could check himself, Sammler had said, "Hot? Something green? A billiard table in hell would answer the description."

"Oh, wow! That really cracked me up," said Wallace.

Later he would ask Sammler if he had the exact words. Sammler smiled, his small cheeks began to flush, but he refused to repeat his sayings. Wallace was not witty. He had no such sayings. But he did have experiences, he invented curious projects. Several years ago he flew out to Tangiers with the purpose of buying a horse and visiting Morocco and Tunisia on horseback. Not taking his Honda, he said, because backward people should be seen from a horse. He had borrowed Jacob Burckhardt's *Force and Freedom* from Sammler, and it affected him strongly. He wanted to examine peoples in various stages of development. In Spanish Morocco he was robbed in his hotel. By a man with a gun, hidden in his closet. He then flew on to Turkey and tried again. Somehow he managed to enter Russia on his horse. In Soviet Armenia he was detained by the police. After Gruner had gone five or six times to see Senator Javits, Wallace was released from prison. Then, once again in New York, Wallace, taking a young lady to see the film *The Birth of a Child,* fainted away at the actual moment of birth, struck his head on the back of a seat, and was knocked unconscious. Reviving, he was on the floor. He found that his date had moved away from him in embarrassment, changed her seat. He had a row with her for abandoning him. Wallace, borrowing his father's Rolls, let it somehow get away from him; carelessly parked, it ended up at the bottom of a reservoir somewhere near Croton. He drove a city bus crosstown to pay off debts. The Mafia was after him. His bookie gave him two months to pay. The handicapping hadn't worked. He flew with a friend to Peru to climb in the Andes. Said to be quite a good pilot. He offered to take Sammler into the air ("No, I believe not. Thank you just the same, Wallace"). He volunteered for the domestic Peace Corps. He wanted to be of use to little black children, to be a basketball coach in playgrounds.

"What does this surgeon really think of Elya's chances, Wallace?"

"He's going to take new X rays of his head."

"Are they planning brain surgery now?"

"It depends on whether they can get to the place. They may not be able to reach it. Of course if they can't reach it, they can't reach it."

"To look at him you'd never think . . . He looks so well."

"Oh, yes," said Wallace. "Why not?"

Sammler sighed at this. He guessed how well pleased the late Mrs. Gruner must have been with her Wallace, his shapely head, long neck, crisp hair, and fine eyebrows, the short clean line of the nose, and the neat nakedness of his teeth, the work of skilled orthodontia.

"It's hereditary, having an aneurysm. You happen to be born with a thin wall in an artery. I may have it. Angela may, too, though I'd be surprised if she had a thin place anywhere. But people, young people, too, perfect in every other respect sometimes, drop dead of it. Walking along strong, beautiful, full of beans, when it explodes inside. They die. There's a bubble first. Such as lizards blow from the throat, maybe. Then death. You've lived so long, you've probably come across this before."

"Even for me, there's always something a little new."

"I had a lot of trouble with last week's crossword puzzle, the Sunday one. Did you work on it?"

"No."

"You sometimes do."

"Margotte didn't bring home the *Times*."

"Amazing how you know words."

For some months Wallace had actually practiced law. His father had rented the office; his mother had furnished it, calling in Croze the interior decorator. For six months Wallace rose punctually like any commuter and went to business. But at business it came out that he worked on nothing but crossword puzzles, locking the door, taking the phone off the hook, lying on the leather sofa. That was all. No, one thing more: he unbuttoned the stenographer's dress and examined her breasts. This information came from Angela, who had it from the girl, direct. Why did the girl permit it? Maybe she thought it would lead to marriage. Placing hopes in Wallace? No sane woman would. But his interest in the breasts had evidently been scientific. Something about nipples. Like Jean Jacques Rousseau, who became so engrossed in the breasts of a Venetian whore that she pushed him away and told him to go study mathematics. (More of Uncle Sammler's wide reading, his European culture.)

"I don't like the people who make up the puzzles. They have low-grade minds," said Wallace. "Why should people know so much trash? It's Eastern-Seaboard-educated trash.

Smart-ass Columbia University quiz-kid miscellaneous information. I actually telephoned you about an old English dance. Jig, reel, and hornpipe were all I could come up with. But this one began with an m."

"An m? Might it have been morrice?"

"Oh, damn! Of course it was morrice. Jesus, your mind is in good order. How do you happen to remember?"

"Milton, *Comus*. A wavering morrice to the moon."

"Oh, that's pretty. Oh, that's really lovely, a wavering morrice."

" 'Now to the Moon in wavering Morrice move.' It's the fishes, by the billions, I believe, and the seas themselves, performing the dance."

"Why, that's splendid. You must be living right, to remember such pretty things. Your mind is not devoured by fool business. You're a good old guy, Uncle Artur. I don't like old people. I don't respect many individuals—a few physical scientists. But you—you're very austere in a way, but you have a good sense of humor. The only jokes I tell are the ones I hear from you. By the way, let me make sure I have the de Gaulle joke right. He said he didn't want to be buried under the Arc de Triomphe next to an unknown. *À côté d'un inconnu*. Right?"

"So far."

"My father has it in for de Gaulle because he woos the Arabs. I'm fond of de Gaulle because he's a monument. And he wouldn't go into the Invalides with Napoleon, who was only a lousy corporal."

"Yes."

"But the Israelis wanted to charge him a hundred thousand bucks for space in the Holy Sepulcher."

"That's the joke."

"And de Gaulle said, 'For three days? It's too much

money.' *'Pour trois jours?'* He was going to be resurrected, right? Now that, I think, is very funny." Wallace's grave judgment. "Poles love to tell jokes," he said. He had no sense of humor. Sometimes he had occasion to laugh.

"Conquered people tend to be witty."

"You don't like Poles very much, Uncle."

"I think on the whole I like them better than they liked me. Besides, a Pan once saved my life."

"And Shula in the convent."

"Yes, that too. Nuns hid her."

"I can remember Shula years ago in New Rochelle, coming downstairs in her nightgown, and she was no kid, she must have been twenty-seven or so, kneeling in front of everybody in the parlor and praying. Did she use Latin? Anyway that nightgown was damn flimsy. I thought she was trying to get your goat, with her Christian act. It was a put-down, wasn't it, in a Jewish house? Some Jews, anyhow! Is she still such a Christian?"

"At Christmas and Easter, somewhat."

"And she bugs you about H. G. Wells. But fathers are soft on daughters. Look how Dad favors Angela. He gave her ten times more. Because she reminded him of Mae West. He was always smiling at her boobs. He wasn't aware of it. Mother and I saw it."

"What do you think will happen, Wallace?"

"My dad? He won't make it. He's got about a two percent chance. What good is that screw?"

"He's struggling."

"Any fish will fight. A hook in the gill. It gets jerked into the wrong part of the universe. It must be like drowning in air."

"Ah, that is terrifying," said Sammler.

"Still, to some people death is very welcome. If they've

spoiled their piece of goods, I'm sure many would rather be dead. What I'm finding out is that when the parents are living, they stand between you and death. They have to go first, so you feel pretty safe. But when they die, you're next, and there's nobody ahead of you in line. At the same time I see already that I'm taking the wrong slant emotionally, and I know I'll pay for it later. I'm part of the system, whether I like it or not." Another moment of silent aberrant reflection—Mr. Sammler felt the density and the unruliness of Wallace's thoughts. Then Wallace said, "I wonder why Dr. Cosbie is so keen on football pools."

"Aren't you?"

"Not the way I was. Dad told him how much I know about pro football. College football, too. That's all behind me now. But it was like Dad offering me to the surgeon, so I would do something for him, so that we would all be close and friendly."

"But it's something else you're keen on now?"

"Yes. Feffer and I have a business idea. It's practically all I can think about."

"Ah, Feffer. He abandoned me at Columbia, and I haven't seen him since. I wondered even whether he was trying to make money on me."

"He's a terribly imaginative businessman. He'd con anyone. But maybe not you. Here's what we've come up with, as an enterprise. Aerial photographs of country houses. Then the salesman arrives with the picture—not just contacts but the fully developed picture—and offers you a package deal. We will identify the trees and shrubs on the place and band them handsomely, in Latin and English. People feel ignorant about the plants on their property."

"Does Feffer know trees?"

"In every neighborhood we'd hire a graduate student in

botany. In Dutchess County, for instance, we could get someone from Vassar."

Mr. Sammler could not keep from smiling. "Feffer would seduce her, and also the lady of the house."

"Oh, no. I'd see he didn't get out of hand. I can control that character. He's a top salesman. Spring is a good time to start. Right now. Before the leaves are too thick for aerial photography. In the summer we could work Montauk, Chilmark, Wellfleet, Nantucket from the sea. My father won't give me the money."

"Is it a great deal?"

"A plane and equipment? Yes, it's considerable."

"You intend to buy a plane, not rent one?"

"Rent doesn't make sense. If you buy you get the tax write-off—depreciation. The secret of business is to make the government cover your risk. In Dad's bracket we'd save seventy cents on the dollar. The IRS is murder. He doesn't file a joint return and isn't head of a family since Mother died. He doesn't want to give me another lump sum. It's set up for me in trust so I'll have to live on the income. When I had my chance I dropped fifty thousand in that boutique."

"Gambling, I thought. Las Vegas."

"No, no, it was a motel complex in Vegas, and we had the clothing shop, the men's boutique."

A furious dresser and adorner of men's bodies, Wallace would have been.

"Uncle Artur, I'd like to put you on our payroll. Feffer agrees. Feffer loves you, you know. If you don't want to do it, we'll put Shula on at fifty bucks a week."

"And in return for this? You want me to talk to your father?"

"Use your influence."

"No, Wallace, I'm afraid I couldn't. Why, think what's going on. It's dreadful. I'm terrified."

"You wouldn't upset him. He thinks the same thoughts whether you talk to him or not. Six of one, half a dozen of the other. He's brooding about this anyway."

"No, no."

"Well, that's your decision. There is something else, though. There's money at home, in New Rochelle. In the house."

"Excuse me?" From curiosity, uncertainty, Sammler's voice went up.

"Hidden cash. A large amount. Never declared."

"It can't be, can it?"

"Oh yes it can, Uncle. You're surprised. If the inside of a person were only as simple as a watermelon—red meat, black seeds. Now and then, as a favor to highly placed people, Papa performed operations. Dilatation and curettage. Only when there was a terrific crisis, when some young socialite heiress got knocked up. Top secret. Only out of pity. My dad pitied famous families, and got big gifts of cash."

"Wallace, look. Let's talk straight. Elya is a good man. He stands close to the end. You're his son. You've been brought up to think that for your health you have to throw a father down. You've had a troubled life, I know. But this old-fashioned capitalistic-family-and-psychological struggle has to be given up, finally. I'm telling you this because you're basically intelligent. You've done a lot of peculiar things. No one can call you boring. But you may become boring if you don't stop. You could retire honorably now with plenty of interesting experience to point to. Enough. You should try something different."

"Well, Uncle Sammler, you have good manners. I know

it. In some ways, you're aloof too. Sort of distant from life. But you put up with people's shenanigans and *shtick.* It's just your old-fashioned Polish politeness. All the same, there is also a practical question here. Nothing but practical."

"Practical?"

"My father has X thousands of dollars in the house, and he won't tell where it is. He's sore at us. *He's* in the capitalistic-family-psychology struggle. You're perfectly right—why should a person burn himself out with neurotic fever? There are higher aims in life. I don't think those are shit. Far from it. But you see, Uncle, if I have that plane, I can make a nice income with a few hours of flying. I can spend the rest of my time reading philosophy. I can finish up my Ph.D. in mathematics. Now listen to this. People are like simple whole numbers. Do you see?"

"No, of course not, Wallace."

"Numbers also bear an important relation to people. The series of numbers is like the series of human beings—infinite numbers of individuals. The characteristics of numbers are like the characteristics of matter, otherwise mathematical expressions could not tell us what matter will or may do. Mathematical equations lead us to physical realities. Things not yet seen. Like the turbulence of heated gases. Do you see now?"

"Only in the vaguest way."

"The equations preceded the actual observations. So what we need is a similar system of signs for human beings. In this system, what is One? What is the human integer like? Now you see, you've made me talk seriously to you. But just for a minute or two, I want to go on with that other thing. There is money in the house. I think there are phony pipes through the attic in which he hid the bills.

He borrowed a Mafia plumber once. I know it. You might just slip in a reference to pipes or to attics in your next conversation. See how he reacts. He may decide to tell you. I don't want to have to tear apart the house."

"No, certainly not," said Sammler.

What *is* One?

Homeward.

On Second Avenue the springtime scraping of roller skates was heard on hollow, brittle sidewalks, a soothing harshness. Turning from the new New York of massed apartments into the older New York of brownstone and wrought-iron, Sammler saw through large black circles in a fence daffodils and tulips, the mouths of these flowers open and glowing, but on the pure yellow the fallout of soot already was sprinkled. You might in this city become a flower-washer. There was an additional business opportunity for Wallace and Feffer.

He walked once around Stuyvesant Park, an ellipse within a square with the statue of the peg-legged Dutchman, corners bristling with bushes. Tapping the flagstones with his ferrule every fourth step, Sammler held Dr. Govinda Lal's manuscript under his arm. He had brought it to read on the subway, though he didn't like being conspicuous in public, passing pages back and forth before the eye, pressing back the hat brim and his face intensely concentrated. He seldom did that.

Drop a perpendicular from the moon. Let it intersect a grave. Inside, a man till now tended, kept warm, manicured. Those heavy rainbow colors came. Decay. Mr. Sammler had once been on far more easy terms with death. He had lost ground, regressed. He was very full of his nephew, a man quite different from himself. He admired him, loved him. He could not cope with the full sum of facts about him. Remote considerations seemed to help—the moon, its lifelessness, its deathlessness. A white corroded pearl. By a sole eye, seen as a sole eye.

Sammler had learned to be careful on public paths in New York, invariably dog-fouled. Within the iron-railed plots the green lights of the grass were all but put out, burned by animal excrements. The sycamores, blemished bark, but very nice, brown and white, getting ready to cough up leaves. Red brick, the Friends Seminary, and ruddy coarse warm stone, broad, clumsy, solid, the Episcopal church, St. George's. Sammler had heard that the original J. Pierpont Morgan had been an usher there. In Austro-Hungarian-Polish-Cracovian antiquity old fellows who had read of Morgan in the papers spoke of him with high regard as Piepernotter-Morgan. At St. George's, Sundays, the god of stockbrokers could breathe easy awhile in the riotous city. In thought, Mr. Sammler was testy with White Protestant America for not keeping better order. Cowardly surrender. Not a strong ruling class. Eager in a secret humiliating way to come down and mingle with all the minority mobs, and scream against themselves. And the clergy? Beating swords into plowshares? No, rather converting dog collars into G strings. But this was neither here nor there.

Watching his steps (the dogs), looking for a bench for ten minutes, to think or avoid thinking of Gruner. Perhaps despite great sadness to read a few paragraphs of this fascinating moon manuscript. He noted a female bum drunkenly sleeping like a dugong, a sea cow's belly rising, legs swollen purple; a short dress, a mini-rag. At a corner of the fence, a wino was sullenly pissing on newspapers and old leaves. Cops seldom bothered about these old-fashioned derelicts. Younger people, autochthonous-looking, were also here. Bare feet, the boys like Bombay beggars, beards clotted, breathing rich hair from their nostrils, heads coming through woolen ponchos, somewhat Peruvian. Natives of somewhere. Innocent, devoid of aggression, opting out, much like Ferdinand the Bull. No *corrida* for them; only smelling flowers under the lovely cork tree. How similar also to the Eloi of H. G. Wells' fantasy *The Time Machine*. Lovely young human cattle herded by the cannibalistic Morlocks who lived a subterranean life and feared light and fire. Yes, that tough brave little old fellow Wells had had prophetic visions after all. Shula wasn't altogether wrong to campaign for a memoir. A memoir should be written. Only there was little time left for relaxed narration about this and that, about things fairly curious in themselves, like Wells at seventy-eight still bucking for the Royal Society—his work (on earthworms?) was not acceptable. Not earthworms. "The Quality of Illusion in the Continuity of Individual Life in the Higher Metazoa." They would not make him a Fellow. But to unscramble this would have taken weeks, and there were no free weeks for Sammler. He had other necessities, higher priorities.

He shouldn't even be reading this—this being the pages of Govinda Lal in bronze ink and old-fashioned penmanship. He wrote a Gothic hand. But Mr. Sammler, having seen through so much, had no resistance to real fascination. On page seventy, Lal had begun to speculate on organisms possibly capable of adapting themselves in exposed lunar conditions. Were there no plants which might cover the moon's surface? Water and carbon dioxide would have to be present, extremes of temperature would have to be withstood. Lichens, thought Govinda, possibly could make it. Also certain members of the cactus family. The triumphant plant, a combination of lichen and cactus, certainly would look weird to the eyes of man. But life's capacities are even now inconceivably diverse. What impossibilities has it not faced? Who knows what the depths of the seas may yet yield? Creatures, perhaps even one to a species. A grotesque individual which has found its equilibrium under twenty miles of water. Small wonder, said Govinda, that human beings stress so fiercely the next realizable possibilities and are so eager to bound from the surface of the earth. The imagination is innately a biological power seeking to overcome impossible conditions.

Mr. Sammler raised his face, aware that someone was hastening toward him. He saw Feffer. Always in a rush. Feffer was stout, should have lost weight. He had trouble with his back, and wore at times an elastic orthopedic garment. Large, with fresh color, with the vivid brown François Premier beard and straight nose, Feffer always seemed to demand haste from his body, his legs. An all-but-running urgency. The hands, awkward and pink, were raised as if he feared to collide with another rush like his own. The brown eyes were key-shaped. As he grew older, the corners would be more elaborately notched.

"I *thought* you might stop here a minute," said Feffer. "Wallace said you had just left, so I ran down."

"Indeed? Well, the sun is shining, and I was in no hurry to go down into the subway. I haven't seen you since the lecture."

"That's right. I had to go to the telephone. I understand that you were wonderful. I genuinely apologize for the behavior of the students. That's my generation for you! I don't even know if they were real students or just tough characters—you know, militants, dropouts. It's not the kids who start the trouble. All the leaders are older. But Fanny looked after you, didn't she?"

"The young lady?"

"I didn't just disappear. I assigned a girl to look after you."

"I see. Your wife, by chance?"

"No, no." Feffer quickly smiled, and quickly went on, sitting on the edge of the bench. He wore a dark-blue velvet double-breasted jacket with large pearl buttons. His arm reached the backrest of the bench and lay affectionately near Sammler's shoulder. "Not my wife. Just a girl I fuck now and then, and look after."

"I see. It all seems so rapid. It strikes me that there is something electronic about your contacts. You shouldn't have left. I was your guest. Too late, I suppose, for you to learn manners. Still, she was very nice. She conducted me from the hall. I didn't expect such a large crowd. I thought you might be making money on me."

"I? No. Never. Believe me—no. It was a benefit for black children, just as I said. You must believe me, Mr. Sammler.

I wouldn't put you into a con, I have too much regard for you. You may not know it, or it may not matter to you, but you have a special position with me, which is practically sacred. Your life, your experiences, your character, your views—plus your soul. There are relationships I would do anything to protect. And if I hadn't been called to the phone, I would have blasted that guy. I know that shit. He wrote a book about homosexuals in prison; he's like a poor man's Jean Genet. Buggery behind bars. Or being a pure Christian angel because you commit murder and have beautiful male love affairs. You know how it is."

"I have a general idea. But you misled me, Lionel."

"I didn't mean to. At the last minute a speaker didn't show for another student thing, and some of my graduate-school buddies who were frantic got hold of me. I saw a way to double the take. For the remedial-reading project. I assumed it wouldn't make so much difference to you, you would understand. I made a deal. I got the best of them."

"What was the subject of the missing speaker?"

"Sorel and Modern Violence, I think it was."

"And I talked about Orwell and what a sane person he was."

"Lots of young radicals see Orwell as part of the cold-war anti-Communist gang. You didn't really praise the Royal Navy, did you?"

"Is that what you heard?"

"If it hadn't been such an important call I would never have left. It was a question of buying or not buying a locomotive. The federal government creates these funny situations with tax breaks to encourage investment. Where it thinks dollars ought to go. You can buy a jet plane and lease it to the airlines. You can lease the locomotive to

Penn Central or the B & O. Cattle investments get similar encouragement."

"Are you already making such sums that you need these deductions?"

Sammler didn't want to lead Feffer into dream conversation, exaggeration, fantasy, lying. He didn't know how much the poor young man made up simply to impress, to entertain. Feffer had a strange need to cover himself with the brocade of boasts. Money, brag—Jewish foibles. American too? Being deficient in contemporary American information, Sammler was tentative here. It was, however, no kindness to listen to this big talk. Sammler appreciated the degree of life in young Feffer, the marvelous rich color of his cheeks, the passion-sounds he made. The voice resembling an instrument played with higher and higher intensity but musically hopeless—the undertones appealing really for help.

But sometimes Mr. Sammler felt that the way he saw things could not be right. His experiences had been too peculiar, and he feared that he projected peculiarities onto life. Life was probably not blameless, but he often thought that life was not and could not be what he was seeing. And then again, most powerfully, he occasionally felt on the contrary that he was a million times exceeded in strangeness by the phenomena themselves. What oddities!

"Really, Lionel, you aren't about to buy a whole locomotive."

"Not alone. As part of a group. One hundred thousand dollars a share."

"And what about this other plan, with Wallace? Photographing houses and identifying trees."

"It does sound hokey, but it's really a very good business

idea. I intend to experiment with it personally. I have a great gift for salesmanship, I'll say that for myself. If the thing pans out, I'll organize it nationally, with sales crews in every part of the country. We'll need regional plant specialists. The problems would be different in Portland, Oregon, from Miami Beach or Austin, Texas. 'All men by nature desire to know.' That's the first sentence of Aristotle's *Metaphysics.* I never got much farther, but I figured that the rest must be out of date anyway. However, if they desire to know, it makes them depressed if they can't name the bushes on their own property. They feel like phonies. The bushes belong. They themselves don't. And I'm convinced that knowing the names of things braces people up. I've gone to shrinkers for years, and have they cured me of anything? They have not. They have put labels on my troubles, though, which sound like knowledge. It's a great comfort, and worth the money. You say, 'I'm manic.' Or you say, 'I'm a reactive-depressive.' You say about a social problem, 'It's colonialism.' Then the dullest brain has internal fireworks, and the sparks drive you out of your skull. It's divine. You think you're a new man. Well, the way to wealth and power is to latch on to this. When you set up a new enterprise, you redescribe the phenomena and create a feeling that we're getting somewhere. If people want things named or renamed, you can make dough by becoming a taxonomist. Yes, I definitely intend to try out this idea of Wallace's."

"It's ill-timed. Does he have to have a plane?"

"I can't say if it's essential, but he seems to have a thing about piloting. Well, that's his bag. Other people have other bags."

This last statement about other people was injected with

much significance. Sammler saw what was happening. Feffer was pretending to hold back, out of a delicacy he didn't have, a piece of information he couldn't wait to release. His eagerness shone from his face. In the eyes. Upon the ready lips.

"What are you referring to?"

"I'm really referring to a certain Hindu scientist. I believe that his name is Lal. I think that this Lal is a guest lecturer at Columbia University."

"What about him?"

"Several days ago, after his lecture, a woman approached him. She asked to see his manuscript. He thought she just wanted to glance at something in the text and he let her take it. There was a small crowd of people around. I believe H. G. Wells was mentioned. Then the lady disappeared with the manuscript."

Mr. Sammler removed his hat and placed it on his lap over the sea-marbled cardboard.

"She walked off with it?"

"Disappeared with the only copy of the work."

"Ah. How unfortunate. The only, eh? Quite bad."

"Yes, I thought you might think so. Dr. Lal expected her to come back with it, that she might be just an absent-minded person. He didn't say anything for twenty-four hours. But then he went to the authorities. Is it the department of astronomy? Or some space program Columbia has?"

"How is it that you always have information of this sort, Lionel?"

"I have to have these contacts in my way of life. Naturally I know the security people—the campus cops. Anyway, they weren't equipped to handle this. They had to call in investigators. The Pinkertons. The original Pinkerton was picked by Abraham Lincoln himself to organize the Secret Service, you know. You do know that, don't you?"

"It doesn't seem to me an item of great importance. I suppose these Pinkertons will know how to recover this article. Isn't it stupid to have only one copy? With all these Xeroxes and reproducing machines, and the man *is* a scientist."

"Well, I don't know. There was Carlyle. There was T. E. Lawrence. Brilliant people, weren't they? And they both lost the only copy of a masterpiece."

"Dear, dear."

"By now the campus is covered with posters. Manuscript missing. And there is a description of the lady. Often seen at public lectures. She wears a wig, carries a shopping bag, is associated somehow with H. G. Wells."

"Yes, I see."

"You wouldn't know anything about it, would you, Mr. Sammler? Naturally I want to help."

"I am astonished by the amount of information that sticks to you. You remind me of a frog's tongue. It flips out and comes back covered with gnats."

"I didn't think I was doing any harm. Where you are concerned, Mr. Sammler, I have only one interest, and that is protection. I have a protective instinct toward you. I am aware it might be Oedipal—the names, again—but I have a feeling of veneration toward you. You are the only person in the world with whom I would use a word like veneration. That's the kind of word you write down, not say."

"Yes, I understand that somewhat, Lionel." Mr. Sammler's forehead, grown damp, was itching. He touched it finely with his ironed pocket handkerchief. It was Shula who brought back his handkerchiefs ironed so smooth and flat.

"I know that you are trying to condense what you know, your life experience. Into a Testament."

"How do you know this?"

"You told me."

"Did I? I don't remember ever saying that. It is very private. If I am saying things unaware, it's a bad sign. I certainly never meant to mention it."

"We were standing in front of the Bretton Hall Hotel, that miserable bunch of decay, and you were leaning on the umbrella. And may I say"—there were signs of an upward expansion of feeling—"I may have doubts about other people, whether they're even human, but I love you without reservation. And to relieve your mind, you didn't discuss anything, you only said that you would like to boil down your experience of life to a few statements. Maybe just one single statement."

"Sydney Smith."

"Smith?"

"He said, 'Short views, for God's sake, short views.' An English clergyman."

To hear what Shula-Slawa had done (folly-devotion-to-Papa-comedy-theft) filled oppressively certain spaces for oppression which had opened and widened during the last three decades. Because of Elya, they were all agape today. Before 1939 Sammler could recall no such heaviness and darkness. Was there anywhere in the world a shrinking-tincture that could be prescribed for such openings? Mr. Sammler did try to turn toward the fun of the thing, imagining Shula in space shoes, disorderly crimson on the mouth, coming up like a little demon body from

Grimm's Fairy Tales, making off with the treasure of a Hindu sage. Sammler himself was treated like some sort of Enchanter by Shula. She thought he was Prospero. He could make beautiful culture. Compose a memoir of the highest distinction, so magical that the world would long remember what a superior thing it was to be a Sammler. The answer of private folly to public folly (in an age of overkill) was more distinction, more high accomplishments, more dazzling brilliants strewn before admiring mankind. Pearls before swine? Mr. Sammler, thinking of Rabbi Ipsheimer, whom he had been dragged by Shula to hear, revised the old saying. Artificial pearls before real swine were cast by these jet-set preachers. To have thought this made him more cheerful. His nervously elegant hand made a shaking bridge over the tinted spectacles, adjusting them without need on the nose. Well, he was not what Shula believed him to be. Moreover, he was not what Feffer thought. How could he satisfy the needs of these imaginations? Feffer in the furious whirling of his spirit took him for a fixed point. In such hyperenergetic revolutions you fell in love with ideas of stability, and Sammler was an idea of stability. And how lavishly Feffer flattered him! Sammler was sorry about that. He made sure his large hat was covering the notebook entirely.

"Is there anything you would like me to do?" said Feffer.

"Why yes, Lionel." He rose. "Walk with me to the subway. I'm going to Union Square."

By the wrought-iron gate they left the little park, westward past the Quaker Meeting House, and then the cool sandstone buildings set back among trees. The chained bellies of garbage cans. One of the chains even wore a sheath. And there were dogs, more dogs. Devoted dog-tendance—by schoolchildren, by women in fairly high style, by certain homosexuals. One would have said that only the Eskimos had nearly so much to do with dogs as this local branch of mankind. The veterinarians must be sailing in yachts, surely. Their fees were high.

I shall get hold of Shula right away, Mr. Sammler decided. He hated scenes with his daughter. She might set her teeth, burst into screams. He cared too much for her. He cherished her. And really, his only contribution to the continuation of the species! It filled him with heartache and pity that he and Antonina had not blended better. Since she was a child he had seen, especially in the slenderness of Shula's neck, so vulnerably valved, in the visible glands, and blue veins, in the big bluish eyelids and top-heavy head, a pitiful legacy, loony, frail, touching him with a fear of doom. Well, the Polish nuns had saved her. When he came to the convent to get her, she was already fourteen years old. Now she was over forty, straying about New York with her shopping bags. She would have to return the manuscript immediately. Dr. Govinda Lal would be frantic. Who knew what Asiatic form that man's despair was taking.

Meantime too there was in Sammler's consciousness a red flush. Possibly due to Elya Gruner's condition. This assumed a curious form, that of a vast crimson envelope, a sky-filling silk fabric, the flap fastened by a black button. He asked himself whether this might not be what mystics meant by seeing a mandala, and believed the suggestion might have been implanted by association with Govinda, an Asiatic. But he himself, a Jew, no matter how Britannicized or Americanized, was also an Asian. The last time he was in Israel, and that was very recent, he had wondered how European, after all, Jews were. The crisis he witnessed there had brought out a certain deeper Orientalism. Even in German and Dutch Jewry, he thought. As for the black button, was it an after-image of the white moon?

Through Fifteenth Street ran a warm spring current. Lilacs and sewage. There were as yet no lilacs, but an element of the savage gas was velvety and sweet, reminiscent of blooming lilac. All about was a softness of perhaps dissolved soot, or of air passed through many human breasts, or metabolized in multitudinous brains, or released from as many intestines, and it got to one—oh, deeply, too! Now and then there came an appreciative or fanciful pleasure, apparently inconsequent, suggested by the ruddy dun of sandstone, by cool corners of the warmth. Bliss from his surroundings! For a certain period Mr. Sammler had resisted such physical impressions—being wooed almost comically by momentary and fortuitous sweetness. For quite a long time he had felt that he was not necessarily human. Had no great use, during that time, for most creatures. Very little interest in himself. Cold even to the thought of recovery. What was there to recover? Little regard for earlier forms of himself. Disaffected. His judgment almost blank. But then, ten or twelve years after the war, he became aware that this too was changing. In the human setting, along with everyone else, among particulars of ordinary life he *was* human—and, in short, creatureliness crept in again. Its low tricks, its doggish hind-sniffing charm. So that now, really, Sammler didn't know how to take himself. He wanted, with God, to be free from the bondage of the ordinary and the finite. A soul released from Nature, from impressions, and from everyday life. For this to happen God Himself must be waiting, surely. And a man who has been killed and buried should have no other interest. He should be perfectly disinterested. Eckhardt said in so many words that God loved disinterested purity and unity. God Himself was drawn toward the disinterested soul. What besides the spirit should a man care for who has come back from the grave? However, and mysteriously enough, it happened, as Sammler observed, that one was always, and so powerfully, so persuasively, drawn back to human conditions. So that these flecks within one's substance would always stipple with their reflections all that a man turns toward, all that flows about him. The shadow of his nerves would always cast stripes, like trees on grass, like water over sand, the light-made network. It was a second encounter of the disinterested spirit with fated biological necessities, a return match with the persistent creature.

Therefore, walking toward the BMT, Union Square Station, one hears Feffer explain why it is necessary to purchase a Diesel locomotive. A beautiful stroke of business. So apt! So congruent with spring, death, Oriental mandalas, sewer gas edged with opiate lilac sweetness. Bliss from bricks, from the sky! Bliss and mystic joy!

Mr. Artur Sammler, confidant of New York eccentrics; curate of wild men and progenitor of a wild woman; registrar of madness. Once take a stand, once draw a baseline, and contraries will assail you. Declare for normalcy, and you will be stormed by aberrancies. All postures are mocked by their opposites. This is what happens when the individual begins to be drawn back from disinterestedness to creaturely conditions. Portions or aspects of his earlier self revive. The former character asserts itself, and sometimes disagreeably, weakly, disgracefully. It was the earlier Sammler, the Sammler of London and Cracow, who had gotten off the bus at Columbus Circle foolishly eager to catch sight of a black criminal. He now had to avoid the bus, dreading another encounter. He had been warned, positively instructed, to appear no more.

"Just a minute, now," said Feffer. "I know you hate subways. Isn't there a switch here? I thought you were positively claustrophobic."

Feffer was extremely intelligent. He had been admitted to Columbia without a high-school certificate by obtaining unheard-of marks in the entrance examinations. He was sly, shrewd, meddling, as well as fresh, charming and vigorous. In his eyes a strangely barbed look appeared, a kind of hooking intensity. Sammler, the earlier Sammler, had had little power to resist such looks.

"It isn't because of the crook you saw on the bus, is it?"

"Who told you about him?"

"Your niece, Mrs. Arkin, did. I mentioned that before the lecture."

"So you did. And she told you, eh?"

"Yes, about the fancy dress, the Dior accessories, and all of that. What a terrific gas! So you're afraid of him. Why? Has he spotted you?"

"Something like that."

"Did he speak?"

"Not a word."

"There's something going on, Mr. Sammler. I think you'd better tell me about it. You may not understand the New York idiom. You may be in danger. You should tell a younger person."

"You confuse me, Feffer. There are moments when I am slightly not myself under your influence. I get muddled. You're very noisy, very turbulent."

"The man has done something to you. I just know it. What's he done? He may hurt you. You may be in trouble, and you shouldn't keep it to yourself. You're wise, but not hip, and this cat, Mr. Sammler, sounds like a real tiger. You've seen him in action?"

"Yes."

"And he's seen you looking?"

"That, too."

"That's serious. Now what has he done to scare you off the bus? You told the cops."

"I tried to. Come, Feffer, you're involving me in things I don't like."

"It's being driven from the bus that should bother you, interference with your customs, your habits, and so on. Are you afraid of him?"

"Well, I was aroused. My heart *did* beat awfully hard. The mind is so odd. Objectively I have little use for such experiences, but there is such an absurd craving for actions that connect with other actions, for coherency, for forms, for mysteries or fables. I may have thought that I had no more ordinary human curiosity left, but I was surprisingly wrong. And I don't like it. I don't like any of it."

"When he saw you, did he chase you?" said Feffer.

"He came after me, yes. Now let's drop the matter."

Feffer was unable to do that. His face was flaming. Within the old-fashioned frame of the beard, it prickled with wild modern passions. "He followed you but he didn't say anything? He must have gotten his message through, though. What did he do? He threatened you. Did he pull a switchblade on you?"

"No."

"A gun? Didn't he point a gun at you?"

"No gun." Had Sammler been in good balance he would have been able to resist Feffer. But his balance was not good. Descending to the subway was a trial. The grave, Elya, Death, entombment, the Mezvinski vault.

"But he found out where you live?" said Feffer.

"Yes, Feffer, he tracked me. He must have had an eye on me for some time. He followed me into my lobby."

"But what did he do, Mr. Sammler! For God's sake, why won't you say!"

"What is there to say? It is ludicrous. It is not worth discussing. Simply nonsensical."

"Nonsensical? Are you sure it's nonsense? You'd better let a younger person judge. A different generation. A different . . ."

"Well, perhaps you have a natural claim to these bizarre nonsensical things. Such a hungry curiosity about them. I'll make it brief. The man exhibited himself to me."

"He didn't! That's just wild! To you? That's far out! Did he corner you?"

"Yes."

"In your own lobby, he pulled his thing on you? He flashed it?"

Sammler would say no more about it.

"Stupendous!" said Feffer. "What the devil was it like?" He was also laughing. How marvelous, what a . . . a sudden glory. And if Sammler was any interpreter of laughter, Feffer was dying to see this phenomenon. To protect Sammler, yes. To guide him through the dangers of New York, yes. But to see, to meddle, to intrude, that was Lionel all over. Had to have a piece of the action—Sammler believed that was the current expression. "He yanked out his cock? Didn't say a word? Just flashed? Wow, Mr. Sammler! What the hell did he mean? How big a thing was it? You didn't say. I can imagine. It could be straight out of *Finnegans Wake*. 'Everyone must bare his crotch!' And he operates between Columbus Circle and Seventy-second Street in the rush hours? Well, what does one do about this? New York is really a gas city. And all those guys running for mayor like a bunch of lunatics. And Lindsay, just imagine Lindsay campaigning on his record. His *record,* no less, when they can't even send a cop to arrest a bandit. And the other guys with *their* record! Mr. Sammler, I know a guy at NBC television who has a talk show. It's really Fanny's husband. We ought to put you on that to discuss all this."

"Oh, come, Feffer."

"It would do everyone a hell of a lot of good to hear you. I know, I know, it's as the man said, it's not the mind of the viewer you'll reach but his backsides. You'll tickle his backsides with beautiful feathers of deep thought."

"Absolutely."

"And yet, Mr. Sammler, to have influence and power. Or just confronting the phony with the real thing. You should denounce New York. You should speak like a prophet, like from another world. TV should be used. Used by *us*—and you might like coming out of isolation."

"We did that at Columbia yesterday, Feffer. I came out of isolation. You've already turned me into a performer."

"I'm thinking only of the good you could do."

"You're thinking of the arrangements you could promote, how you could get a finder's fee from Fanny's husband, and how close you could bring together the TV and that person's genitalia." Mr. Sammler was intensely smiling. Another moment, and he would actually have been laughing, drawn out of his preoccupations.

"Very well," said Feffer. "I don't have the same ideals of privacy as you. I'm willing to drop it."

"By all means."

"I'll ride uptown on the bus with you."

"No, thanks."

"To make sure no one bothers you."

"What you want is to have me point him out."

"Really, I know how you dislike, you *hate,* subways."

"It's quite all right."

"Of course you've stirred up my curiosity, why should I deny it? I know you finally told me about him to get rid of me, and here I am pestering you still. You say he wears a camel's-hair coat?"

"I thought it was that."

"A homburg? Dior shades?"

"Homburg I'm certain of. The Dior is a guess."

"You're a good observer, I take your word for it. A mustache, also, fancy shirts and psychedelic neckties. He's a prince of some kind, or thinks he is."

"Yes," said Sammler. "A certain majesty is assumed."

"I have an idea about him."

"Let him be. Leave him alone, I advise you."

"I wouldn't actually tangle with him. I'd never do that. He wouldn't even suspect I was there. But cameras can be introduced anywhere. They even have photos of the child in the womb. Somehow they got a camera in. I just acquired a new Minox which is as small as a cigarette lighter."

"Don't be stupid, Lionel."

"He'd never know. I assure you. Wouldn't be aware. Pictures could be valuable. Catch a criminal, sell the story to *Look.* Do a job on the police at the same time, and on Lindsay, who has no business being mayor while running for president. A triple killing."

The low wall of Union Square, the raised green platform of lawn parted by dry gray pathways, and the fast traffic circling—the foul, reckless, stinking automobiles. Sammler did not need Feffer's hand on his elbow. He drew away.

"I go down here."

"This time of day you can't get a taxi. The shift is changing. I'll ride uptown with you."

Sammler, still holding hat and notebook by his side, the umbrella hooked on his wrist, pursued his way in the half-light of the corridors, in the smoke of grilled sausages. The quick turnstiles metered the tokens with a noise of ratchets. The bison-rumble of trains. Sammler wanted to ride alone. Feffer could not let him go. Feffer could not be quiet. His need was to be perpetually arresting, radiant with fresh interest. And, of course, because he respected Sammler so much he had to make tests or insert small notes or hints of disrespect, a little here, a bit there, liberties, familiarities, insinuations, exploring for spoilage. My dear fellow, why look so hard? There is corruption in many places. I could show you.

"This Fanny—the girl who guided you—she's very willing," said Feffer.

He ran on. "Nowadays girls are. Still somewhat shy. Not really so marvelous in the sack. In spite of big tits. Married of course. The husband works at night. He bosses the talk show I referred to . . ." And on: "I like companionship. We spend a lot of time together. Then when the insurance adjuster came . . ."

"What adjuster was that?" said Sammler.

"I put in a claim on a piece of luggage damaged at the airport. The fellow came over when Fanny was visiting me, and he fell in love with her—bang! Like that. He was a swinger, too, with chimpanzee teeth. Said he was a dropout from the Harvard School of Business. A real yellow face, and sweating. Awful. He looked like an oil filter that should have been changed five thousand miles ago."

"Ah, did he?"

"So I encouraged his interest in Fanny. That was good for my claim. Would I give him her phone number? I certainly did."

"With her permission?"

"I didn't think she'd mind. Then he phoned and said, 'This is Gus, honey. Meet me for a drink.' But her husband had picked up the phone. He works nights. And next time Gus came to see me I said, 'Boy, Gus, her husband is really sore. Stay away. He's tough, too.' Then Gus said . . ."

Was there no Eighteenth Street station? There was Twenty-third, Thirty-fourth. At Forty-second you changed to the IRT.

"Gus said, 'What am I afraid of? Look, I carry a gun.' He pulled out a pistol. I was flabbergasted. But it wasn't much of a gun either. I said, 'A thing like that? You couldn't shoot through a telephone book with it.' And before I knew it, he had the telephone book on a music stand and was aiming at it. That crazy sonofabitch. He was only five feet from it, and he fired. I never heard such a roar. The whole building heard. But I was right. The bullet went in only two inches. Couldn't pierce the Manhattan directory."

"Yes, a poor weapon."

"You know something about weapons?"

"Something."

"Well, you could just about wound a guy with that gun. Probably wouldn't kill unless you shot him in the head at short range. What a lot of lunatics around."

"Quite so."

"But I'm getting about two hundred bucks from insurance, which is more than the suitcase is worth, a piece of trash."

"Yes, clever business."

"Next day Gus came again and wanted me to write a recommendation for him."

"To whom?"

"To his superior in the adjuster's office."

At Ninety-sixth Street they ascended together into the full blast of Broadway. Feffer accompanied Sammler to his door.

"If you need assistance, Mr. Sammler . . ."

"I won't invite you up, Lionel. The fact is I'm feeling tired."

"It's spring. I mean it's the temperature change," said Feffer. "Even youth is susceptible to that."

Mr. Sammler in the elevator, extracting the Yale key from his change purse. He pushed into the foyer. In honor of spring, Margotte had set forsythia in Mason jars. One jar was overturned at once. Sammler brought a roll of paper towels from the kitchen, ascertaining as he went through the house that his niece had gone out. Soaking up the spilt water, watching the absorbent paper darken, he then lifted the telephone onto the maple arm of the sofa, sat on the bandanna covers, and dialed Shula. No reply. Perhaps she had turned off her telephone. Sammler had not seen her for several days. Now a thief, she very likely was in hiding. If Eisen was actually in New York, she had an added reason for locking herself away. Sammler could not imagine, however, that Eisen would actually want to molest her. He had other irons in the fire, he had other fish to fry (how fond old Sammler was of such expressions!).

Carrying the paper towels, the sopping and the dry, back to the kitchen, Sammler cut himself several slices of salami with the large chef's knife (Margotte seemed to have no small knives, she pared onions, even, with these great blades). He made a sandwich. Colman's English

Mustard, still a favorite. Margotte's low-calorie cranberry juice. Unable to find clean glasses, he sipped from a paper cup. The feel of wax was disagreeable but he was on his way out of the house and had no time for washing and drying. He went at once across Broadway to Shula's apartment. He rang, he rapped, he raised his voice and said, "Shula, it's Father. Open. Shula?" He wrote a note and slipped it under the door. "Call me at once." Then, descending in the black elevator (how rusty and black it was!), he looked into her mailbox, which she never locked. It was full, and he sorted through the mail. Throwaway stuff. Personal letters, none. So she was evidently away, hadn't taken out her letters. Maybe she had caught a train to New Rochelle. She had a key to the Gruner house. Sammler had refused the offer of a key to her apartment. He didn't want to walk in when she was with a lover. Such a lover as she would have was surely to be dreaded. Undoubtedly she had one now and then. Perhaps for her complexion, when it was bad. He once had heard a woman say this. And Shula was proud of her clear skin. How could you know what people—individuals—were *really* doing!

When he returned, he asked Margotte, "You haven't seen Shula, have you?"

"No, Uncle Sammler, I haven't. You had a call, though, from your son-in-law."

"Eisen has called?"

"I told him you were at the hospital."

"What did he seem to want?"

"Why, to see the family. Though he said they don't come to see him when they're in Israel, not Elya and not you. He really sounded hurt."

Margotte's sympathies, so readily available, so full, made others feel stony-hearted.

"And Elya, how is he?" she said.

"Not well, I'm afraid."

"Oh, I must go and visit poor Elya."

"Perhaps you should, but very briefly."

"Oh, I wouldn't tire him. As for Shula, she's afraid to see Eisen. She thinks she did him a terrible injury when you forced her to leave."

"I never did. She was glad to go. He seemed glad, too. Did Eisen inquire for her?"

"Not a word. Didn't even mention her name. He talked about his work. His art. He's hunting for a studio."

"Yes . . . Well, it won't be easy to find in this city of artists. Lofts. But then of course he fought at Stalingrad, he could winter in a loft."

"He wanted to go to the hospital and do a drawing of Elya."

"A thing we should prevent, by any means."

"Uncle Sammler, would you join me for a cutlet? I'm cooking schnitzel."

"Thank you, I've eaten."

He went to his room.

With a reading glass held trembling in the long left hand, Sammler threw quivering transparencies on the writing paper. From the desk lamp, glassy nuclei of brightness followed the words he wrote.

> Dear Professor Doctor:
> Your manuscript is safe. The woman who borrowed it is my daughter. She meant no harm. It was only her thick-handed, clumsy way of helping me, advancing an imaginary project that obsesses her. She is pierced by an inspiration—H. G. Wells, the scientific future. She believes we share this inspiration. I am pierced sometimes from a different side by the vision

of her activities. Psychologically archaic—all the fossils in her mental strata fully alive (the moon, too, is a kind of fossil)—she dreams about the future. Yet everyone grapples, each in his awkward muffled way, with a power, a Jacob's angel, to get a final satisfaction or glory that is withheld. In any case, kindly ask the authorities to call off their search. I beg you. My daughter evidently believed you were lending her this document, though it may point to treachery aforethought that she did not give you her name and address. However, I would be glad to bring *The Future of the Moon* to you. I have been reading it with fascination, though on the scientific side my qualifications are nil. More than thirty years ago, I enjoyed the friendship of H. G. Wells whose moon-fantasy you undoubtedly know—Selenites, subterranean moon-ocean, and all of that. As correspondent for Eastern European periodicals, I lived in England for many years. Woburn Square. Ah, it was lovely. But I apologize for my daughter. I can well imagine the anguish of spirit she must have caused you. In women the keenest sense of wrongdoing seems to be in a different place. The notebook lies before me at this moment. It is marbled green cardboard and the ink is brown and iridescent, almost bronze. I can be phoned at any hour of the night at the Endicott number under the date above.

Your obedient servant,
Artur Sammler

"Margotte," he said, leaving his desk.

She sat alone, eating in the dining room, under an imitation Tiffany shade of gay red-and-green paper. The tablecloth was an Indonesian print. All was really very dark, in the awkward room. She herself looked dark there, cutting the yellow-crusted veal on her dish. He should, more often, sit down to meals with her. A childless widow. He was sorry for her, the small face with its heavy black bangs. He took a chair. "Look here, Margotte, we have a problem with Shula."

"Let me set a place for you."

"No, thank you, I have no appetite. Please sit down. I'm afraid Shula stole something. Not a theft, really. That would be nonsense. She took something. A manuscript by a Hindu scientist at Columbia. It was, of course, done for me. That idiocy about H. G. Wells. You see, Margotte, this Indian book is about colonizing the moon and the planets. Shula took away the only copy."

"The moon. How fascinating, Uncle."

"Yes, industries on the moon. Manufacturing centers on the moon. How to build cities."

"I can see why Shula wanted it for you."

"But it must be returned. Why, it's stolen goods, Margotte, and detectives have been called in. And I can't find Shula. She knows she has done wrong."

"Oh, Uncle Sammler, would you call it a crime? Not by Shula. Poor creature."

"Yes, poor creature. To whom would this not apply, if you start to say poor creature?"

"I would never have said it about Ussher. I wouldn't say it about you, either."

"Really? Well, all right. I accept the correction. However, that Indian must be notified. Here I have a letter for him."

"Why not a telegram?"

"Useless. Telegrams are no longer delivered."

"That's what Ussher used to say. He said the messengers just threw them down the sewer."

"Mailing won't do. It might take three days for the letter to arrive. All these local communications are in decay," said Sammler. "Even Cracow in the days of Franz Josef was more efficient than the U.S. postal system. And Shula may be picked up by the police, that's what I'm afraid of. Could we send the doorman in a cab?"

"What's the matter with the telephone?"

"Yes, certainly, if I could be sure we would talk to Dr. Lal himself. A direct explanation. I hadn't thought of that. But how to get his number!"

"Couldn't you just take the manuscript to him?"

"Now that I know I have the only copy, I hesitate, Margotte, to go into the street with it, and especially at night, when people are being mugged. Suppose it were snatched out of my hands?"

"And the police?"

"They have given little satisfaction. I wish to avoid them. I did think perhaps of the security officers at Columbia, or even the Pinkerton people, but I would rather hand it over personally to Dr. Lal to make sure no charges will be brought against Shula. The Indian temperament is so excitable, you know. If he doesn't meet any of us, become personally acquainted, he will let the police advise him. Then we would need a lawyer. Don't suggest Wallace. In the past, Elya always had Mr. Widick take care of such matters."

"Well, perhaps handing him a letter is best. Better than the telephone. Maybe I should carry the letter to him, Uncle. Personally."

"Ah, yes, a woman. Coming from a woman, it might have a softening effect."

"Better than a doorman. It's still light. I can get a cab."

"I have a little money in my room. About ten dollars."

Then he heard Margotte on the telephone, making inquiries. He suspected that things were being done the least efficient way. But Margotte was prompt to help when difficulties were real. She didn't start discussions about Shula —the effects of the war or Antonina's death or puberty in a Polish convent or what terror could do to the psyche of a young girl. Elya was right. Ussher, too. Margotte was a good soul. Not persisting mechanically in her ways when the signal was given. As others did, jumping into their routines. Tumbling into their grooves.

In the bathroom there was a great rush of water. She was taking a shower, the usual sign that she was preparing to go out. If she had three occasions to leave the house, she took three showers in a day. He next heard her walking very rapidly in her bedroom, shoeless, but thumping quickly, opening closets and drawers. In about twenty minutes, dressed in her black basic and wearing a black straw hat, she was at his door and asking for the letter. She was a dear thing.

"You know where he is?" said Sammler. "Did you talk to him?"

"Not personally, he was out. But he's staying at Butler Hall, and the switchboard knew all about it."

Gloves, though the evening was warm. Perfume, quite a lot. Bare arms. Bruch might have liked those arms. They had a proper little heaviness of their own. She was at times a pretty woman. And Sammler saw that she was glad to have this errand. It saved her from an empty night at home. Ussher had been fond of late-late shows. Margotte rarely turned on the television set. It was often out of repair. Since Ussher's death, it had begun to look old-fashioned in its wood cabinet. Maybe it wasn't wood, but a woodlike wig of some dark and grained material.

"If I meet Dr. Lal—and should I wait for him at Butler Hall? Shall I bring him back with me?"

"I was planning to go again to the hospital," said Sammler. "You know, it's very bad for Elya."

"Oh, poor Elya. I know it's one thing on top of another. But don't make yourself too tired. You just got in."

"I'll lie down for fifteen minutes. Yes, if Dr. Lal wants to come, by all means, yes. Let him come."

Before she went, Margotte wanted to kiss the old man. He did not move away, although he felt that people were seldom in a fit state for kissing and that mostly it was done, in defilement, as a reminder of beatitude. But this kiss of Margotte's, reaching upward, getting on her toes and swelling her plump strong legs, was an appropriate one. She seemed grateful that he chose to live with her rather than with Shula, that he liked her so much, and that he turned to her also in trouble. Through him, moreover, she was going to meet a distinguished gentleman, a Hindu scientist. She was perfumed, she was wearing eye make-up.

He said, "I should be home by about ten."

"Then, if he is there, dear Uncle, I'll bring him back and he can wait here with me. He'll be so eager for his manuscript."

He saw her soon in the street. Touching the frieze curtain, he watched her going toward West End Avenue, up the pale width of the sidewalk, alert for a taxi. She was small, she was strong, and had a sort of compact female pride. Somewhat shaking, as women do when they hurry. Gotten up strangely. And altogether odd. Females! The drafts must blow between their legs. Such observations originated mainly in kindly detachment, in farewell-detachment, in earth-departure-objectivity.

In daylight still, the white Spry sign across the Hudson began to flash against pale green and also down into the dark water; while in the sunset copper the asphalt belly of the street was softly disfigured, softly rank, with its manhole covers. And the cars always packed tightly into the street. Machines for going away.

Removing shoes and socks, Mr. Sammler raised a long foot to the sink. Wasn't he too old for such movements? Evidently not. In the privacy of his room he was actually less stiff in the limbs. He bathed the feet and did not dry them thoroughly, for it was a warm evening. Evaporation relieved the smarting. As evolutionary time went we had not long been bipeds, and the flesh of the feet suffered for it, especially in spring when organisms experienced a peculiar expansion. Tired and breathing quietly, Sammler lay down. He left his feet uncovered. He brought the coolness of the sheet over his flat, slender chest. He turned away his lamp to shine on the drawn curtain.

The luxury of nonintimidation by doom—that might describe his state. Since the earth altogether was now a platform, a point of embarkation, you could think with a very minimum of terror about going. Not to waive another man's terror for him (he was thinking of Elya with the calibrated metal torment in his throat). But often he felt himself very nearly out of it. And everything soon must change. Men would set their watches by other suns than this. Or time would vanish. We would need no personal names of the old sort in the sidereal future, nothing being fixed. We would be designated by other nouns. Days and nights would belong to the museums. The earth a memorial park, a merry-go-round cemetery. The seas powdering our bones like quartz, making sand, grinding our peace for us by the aeon. Well, that would be good—a melancholy good.

Ah. Before he had let go the curtain, when Margotte disappeared, before sitting to remove the shoes, before turning to wash his feet, he had seen, come to think of it, the moon not too remote from the Spry sign, and round as a traffic signal. This moon image or circular afterimage was still with him. And we know now from photographs the astronauts took, the beauty of the earth, its white and its blue, its fleeces, the great glitter afloat. A glorious planet. But wasn't everything being done to make it intolerable to abide here, an unconscious collaboration of all souls spreading madness and poison? To flush us out? Not so much Faustian aspiration, thought Mr. Sammler, as a scorched-earth strategy. Ravage all, and what does death get? Defile, and then flee to the bliss of oblivion. Or bolt to other worlds.

He recognized by these thoughts that he was preparing to meet Govinda Lal. They would possibly discuss such matters. Dr. Lal, whose field seemed to be biophysics, and who might, like most experts, turn out to be a nonindividual, gave signs, in his writing anyway, of wider thoughtfulness. For after each technical section he offered remarks on the human aspects of future developments. He seemed aware, for instance, that the discovery of America had raised hopes in the sinful Old World of a New Eden. "A shared consciousness," Lal had written, "may well be the new America. Access to central data mechanisms may foster a new Adam." Well, it was very odd what Mr. Sammler found himself doing as he lay in his room, in an old building. Settling, the building had cracked its plaster, and along these slanted cracks he had mentally inscribed certain propositions. According to one of these he, personally, stood apart from all developments. From a sense of deference, from age, from good manners, he sometimes affirmed himself to be *out* of it, *hors d'usage*, not a man of the times. No force of nature, nothing paradoxical or demonic, he had no drive for smashing through the masks of appearances. Not "Me and the Universe." No, his personal idea was one of the human being conditioned by other human beings, and knowing that present arrangements were not, *sub specie aeternitatis, the* truth, but that one should be satisfied with such truth as one could get by approximation. Trying to live with a civil heart. With disinterested charity. With a sense of the mystic potency of humankind. With an inclination to believe in archetypes of goodness. A desire for virtue was no accident.

New worlds? Fresh beginnings? Not such a simple matter. (Sammler, reaching for diversion.) What did Captain Nemo do in 20,000 *Leagues Under the Sea*? He sat in the submarine, the *Nautilus*, and on the ocean floor he played Bach and Handel on the organ. Good stuff, but old. And what of Wells' Time Traveler, when he found himself thousands of years in the future? He fell in square love with a beautiful Eloi maiden. To take with one, whether down into the depths or out into space and time, something dear, and to preserve it—that seemed to be the impulse. Jules Verne was quite right to have Handel on the ocean floor, not Wagner, though in Verne's day Wagner was avant-garde among the symbolists, fusing word and sound. According to Nietzsche the Germans, insufferably oppressed by being German, used Wagner like hashish. To Mr. Sammler's ears, Wagner was background music for a pogrom. And what should one have on the moon, electronic compositions? Mr. Sammler would advise against that. Art groveling before Science.

But Sammler was preoccupied by different matters, far from playful. Feffer, wishing to divert him, had told him the tale of the insurance adjuster who pulled out the pistol. It was no diversion. Feffer had said that with that rotten gun you would have to shoot a man at close range, and in the head. Killing point blank. This shooting in the head was what Sammler had been attempting to shut out, screen off. Hopeless. Diversion shriveled up. He was obliged to give in, to confront certain insufferable things. These things were not subject to control. They had to be endured. They had become a power within him which did not care whether he could bear them or not. Visions or nightmares for others, but for him daylight events, in full consciousness. Certainly Sammler had not experienced things denied to everyone else. Others had gone through the like. Before and after. Especially non-Europeans had a quieter way of taking such things. Surely some Navaho, Apache must have fallen into the Grand Canyon, survived, picked himself up, possibly said nothing to his tribe. Why speak of it? Things that happen, happen. So, for his part, it had happened that Sammler, with his wife and others, on a perfectly clear day, had had to strip naked. Waiting, then, to be shot in the mass grave. (Over a similar new grave Eichmann had testified that he had walked, and the fresh blood welling up at his shoes had sickened him. For a day or two, he had to lie in bed.) Sammler had already that day been struck in the eye by a gun butt and blinded. In contraction from life, when naked, he already felt himself dead. But somehow he had failed, unlike the others, to be connected. Comparing the event, as mentally he sometimes did, to a telephone circuit: death had not picked up the receiver to answer his ring. Sometimes, when he walked on Broadway today, and heard a phone ringing in a shop when doors were open, he tried to find, to intuit, the syllable one would hear from death. "Hello? Ah, you at last." "Hello." And the air of the street visibly vapored with lead, and also with a brass tinge. But if there were live New York bodies passing as there had once been dead ones piled on top of him, if there were this crowd strolling, lounging, dragging, capering (a Broadway rabble to which he belonged)—if there were this, there was also enough to feed every mouth: baked goods, raw meat, smoked meat, bleeding fish, smoked fish, barbecued pork and chicken, apples like ammunition, antihunger orange grenades. In the gutters, along curbs was much food, eaten, as he saw at three a.m., by night-emerging rats. Buns, chicken bones, which, once, he would have thanked God to have. When he was a partisan in Zamosht Forest, freezing, the dead eye like a ball of ice in his head. Envying fallen sticks from his nearness to their state. In a moldered frozen horse blanket and rag-wrapped feet. Mr. Sammler carried a weapon. He and other starved men chewing at roots and grasses to stay alive. They drifted out at night to explode bridges, unseat rails, kill German stragglers.

Sammler himself, shooting men. There was Feffer's mad insurance adjuster, clutched by impulse or desire for display, firing at the telephone book on the music stand. That had something comically fanatical about it. Putting a bullet through a million close-printed names—a parlor game. But Sammler was driven through the parlor and back to Zamosht Forest. There at very close range he shot a man he had disarmed. He made him fling away his carbine. To the side. A good five feet into snow. It landed flat and sank. Sammler ordered the man to take off his coat. Then the tunic. The sweater, the boots. After this, he said to Sammler in a low voice, *"Nicht schiessen."* He asked for his life. Red-headed, a big chin bronze-stubbled, he was scarcely breathing. He was white. Violet under the eyes. Sammler saw the soil already sprinkled on his face. He saw the grave on his skin. The grime of the lip, the large creases of skin descending from his nose already lined with dirt—that man to Sammler was already underground. He was no longer dressed for life. He was marked, lost. Had to go. Was gone. "Don't kill me. Take the things." Sammler did not answer, but stood out of reach. "I have children." Sammler pulled the trigger. The body then lay in the snow. A second shot went through the head and shattered it. Bone burst. Matter flew out.

Sammler picked up as much as he could—gun, shells, food, boots, gloves. Two shots in winter air; the sound would carry for miles. He hurried, looking back once. The red hair and thick nose he could see from the bushes. Regrettably there was no chance to get the shirt. The stinking woolen socks yes. He had wanted those badly. He was too weak to carry his loot far. He sat down under winter-creaking trees and ate the German's bread. With it, he took snow into his mouth to help the swallowing, which was difficult. He had no saliva. The thing no doubt would have happened differently to another man, a man who had been eating, drinking, smoking, and whose blood was brimming with fat, nicotine, alcohol, sexual secretions. None of these in Sammler's blood. He was then not entirely human. Rag and paper, a twine-wound bundle, and those objects might have been blown where they liked, if the string had snapped. One would not have minded much.

At that minimum we were. Not much there for human appeal, for the pleading of a distorted face and sinews spreading into the throat.

When Mr. Sammler hid later in the mausoleum, it was not from the Germans but from the Poles. In Zamosht Forest the Polish partisans turned on the Jewish fighters. The war was ending, the Russians advancing, and the decision seems to have been taken to reconstruct a Jewless Poland. There was therefore a massacre. The Poles at dawn came shooting. As soon as it was light enough for murder. There was fog, smoke. The sun tried to rise. Men began to drop, and Sammler ran. There were two other survivors. One played dead. The other, like Sammler, found a break and rushed through. Hiding in the swamp, Sammler lay under a tree trunk, in the mud, under scum. At night he left the forest. He took a chance with Cieslakiewicz next day. (Was it only a day? Perhaps it was longer.) He spent those summer weeks in the cemetery. Then he appeared in Zamosht, in the town itself, wild, gaunt, decaying, the dead eye bulging—like a whelk. One of the doomed who had lasted it all out.

Scarcely worth so much effort, perhaps. There are times when to quit is more reasonable and decent and hanging on is a disgrace. Not to go beyond a certain point in hanging on. Not to stretch the human material too far. The nobler choice. So Aristotle thought.

Mr. Sammler himself was able to add, to basic wisdom, that to kill the man he ambushed in the snow had given him pleasure. Was it only pleasure? It was more. It was joy. You would call it a dark action? On the contrary, it was also a bright one. It was mainly bright. When he fired his gun, Sammler, himself nearly a corpse, burst into life. Freezing in Zamosht Forest, he had often dreamed of being near a fire. Well, this was more sumptuous than fire. His heart felt lined with brilliant, rapturous satin. To kill the man and to kill him without pity, for he was dispensed from pity. There was a flash, a blot of fiery white. When he shot again it was less to make sure of the man than to try again for that bliss. To drink more flames. He would have thanked God for this opportunity. If he had had any God. At that time, he did not. For many years, in his own mind, there was no judge but himself.

In the privacy of his bed he turned very briefly to that rage (for reference, he did it). Luxury. And when he himself was nearly beaten to death. Had to lift dead bodies from himself. Desperate! Crawling out. Oh heart-bursting! Oh vile! Then he himself knew how it felt to take a life. Found it could be an ecstasy.

He got up. It was pleasant here—the lamplight, his own room. He had gathered a very pleasant sort of intimacy about himself. But he got up. He wasn't resting, and he might as well go to the hospital. His nephew Gruner needed him. That thing was fizzing in his brain. Soil was scattered on *his* face. Look hard. You must see some grains. So, rising, Sammler smoothed back the bedding, the coverlet. He never left a bed unmade. He drew on clean socks. Up to the knee.

Too bad! Too bad, that is, to be pounded back and forth so abnormally on the courts, like a ball between powerful players. Or subject to wild instances. Oh merciless! Thank you, no, no! I did not want to fall into the Grand Canyon. Nice not to have died? Nicer not to have fallen in. Too many inside things were ruptured. To some people, true enough, experience seemed wealth. Misery worth a lot. Horror a fortune. Yes. But I never wanted such riches.

After the socks his ten-year-old shoes. He kept having

them resoled. Good enough for getting around Manhattan. He took excellent care of his things, he stuffed his good suit with tissue paper, put in shoe trees at night even though this leather was puckered with age and wear, streaming with wrinkles. These same shoes Mr. Sammler had worn in Israel, in the summer of 1967. Not Israel only but also Jordan, the Sinai Desert, and into Syrian territory during the Six-Day War. His second visit. If it was a visit. It was an expedition. At the beginning of the Aqaba crisis he had suddenly become excited. He could not sit still. He had written to an old journalist friend in London and said he was obliged to go, he absolutely must go, as a journalist, and cover the events. There was an association of Eastern European publications. All Sammler really wanted was credentials, a card to enable him to wire cables, a press pass to satisfy the Israelis. The money was supplied by Gruner. And so Sammler had been with the armies on the three fronts. It was curious, that. At the age of seventy-two on battlegrounds, wearing these shoes and a seersucker jacket and soiled white cap from Kresge's. Tankmen spotted him as an American because of the jacket, shouting, "Yank!" Coming up to them, he spoke to some in Polish, to others in French, English. He thought of himself at moments as a camel among the armored vehicles. No Zionist, Mr. Sammler, and for many years little interested in Jewish affairs. Yet, from the start of the crisis, he could not sit in New York reading the world press. If only because for the second time in twenty-five years the same people were threatened by extermination: the so-called powers letting things drift toward disaster; men armed for a massacre. And he refused to stay in Manhattan watching television.

Perhaps it was the madness of things that affected

Sammler most deeply. The persistence, the maniacal push of certain ideas, themselves originally stupid, stupid ideas that had lasted for centuries, this is what drew the most curious reactions from him. The stupid sultanism of a Louis Quatorze reproduced in General de Gaulle—Neo-Charlemagne, someone said. Or the imperial ambition of the Czars in the Mediterranean. They wanted to be the dominant naval power in the Mediterranean, a stupid craving of two centuries, and this, under the "revolutionary" auspices of the Kremlin, was still worked at, in the same way—worked at! Did it make no difference that soon floating dominion by armed ships would be as obsolete as Ashurbanipal, as queer as the dog-headed gods of Egypt? Why, no, it made no difference. No more than the disappearance of Jews from Poland made a difference to the anti-Semitism of the Poles. This was the meaning of historical stupidity. And the Russians also, with their national tenacity. Give them a system, let them grasp some idea, and they would plunge to the depths with it, they would apply it to the end, pave the whole universe with hard idiot material. In any case, it had seemed to Sammler that he must reach the scene. He would be there, to send reports, to do something, perhaps to die in the massacre. Through such a thing he could not sit in New York. That! Quivering, riotous, lurid New York—Feffer's gas city! And Sammler himself went to an extreme, became perhaps too desperate, carried away, beginning to think of sleeping pills, poison. It was really the tangled nervous system, the "nerve-spaghetti." These were his old Polish nerves raging. It was his old panic, his peculiar affliction. He would not read a second day's reports on Shukairy's Arabs in Tel Aviv killing thousands. He told Gruner that. Gruner said, "If you feel so strongly about it, I think you should go." Now Sammler thought that he had been guilty of exaggeration. He had lost his head. Still he had been right to go.

Sammler, from keeping his own counsel for so long, from seven decades of internal consultation, had his own views on most matters. And even the greatest independence was insufficient, still not enough. And there were mental dry courses in his head, of no interest to anyone else, perhaps—wadis, he believed such things were called, small ravines made by the steady erosion of preoccupations. The taking of life was one of these. Just that. His life had nearly been taken. He had seen life taken. He had taken it himself. He knew it was one of the luxuries. No wonder princes had so long reserved the right to murder with impunity. At the very bottom of society there was also a kind of impunity, because no one cared what happened. Under that dark brutal mass blood crimes were often disregarded. And at the very top, the ancient immunities of kings and nobles. Sammler thought that this was what revolutions were really about. In a revolution you took away the privileges of an aristocracy and redistributed them. What did equality mean? Did it mean all men were friends and brothers? No, it meant that all belonged to the elite. Killing was an ancient privilege. This was why revolutions plunged into blood. Guillotines? Terror? Only a beginning—nothing. There came Napoleon, a gangster who washed Europe well in blood. There came Stalin, for whom the really great prize of power was unobstructed enjoyment of murder. That mighty enjoyment of consuming the breath of men's nostrils, swallowing their faces like a Saturn. This was what the conquest of power really seemed to mean. Sammler tied his shoelaces—continued dressing. He brushed at his hair. Trancelike. At several removes from the self in the glass, opposite. And for the middle part of society there was envy and worship of this power to kill. How those middle-class Sorels and Maurrases adored it—the hand that gripped the knife with authority. How they loved the man strong enough to take blood guilt on himself. For them an elite must prove itself in this ability to murder. For such people a saint must be understood as one who was equal in spirit to the fiery twisting of crime in the inmost fibers of his heart. The superman testing himself with an ax, crushing the skulls of old women. The Knight of Faith, capable of cutting the throat of his Isaac upon God's altar. And now the idea that one could recover, or establish, one's identity by killing, becoming equal thus to any, equal to the greatest. A man among men knows how to murder. A patrician. The middle class had formed no independent standards of honor. Thus it had no resistance to the glamour of killers. The middle class, having failed to create a spiritual life of its own, investing everything in material expansion, faced disaster. Also, the world becoming disenchanted, the spirits and demons expelled from the air were now taken inside. Reason had swept and garnished the house, but the last state might be worse than the first. Well, now, what would one carry out to the moon?

He brushed the felt hat with an elbow, backed into the vestibule, locked and tested the door, buzzed for the elevator, and descended. Mr. Sammler, back walking the streets, which now were dark blue, a bluish glow from the street lamps. Stooped, walking quickly. He had only two hours, and if he couldn't catch the Eighty-sixth Street Crosstown to Second Avenue, he would be forced to take a cab. West End was very gloomy. He preferred even fuming, heaving, fool-heaped, quivering, stinking Broadway. With the tufts above his glasses silken, graying, tangled, rising as he faced the phenomenon. No use being the sensitive observer, the tourist (was there any land stable enough to tour?), the philosophical rambler out on Broadway, inspecting the phenomenon. The phenomenon had in some way achieved a sense of its own interest and observability. It was aware of being a scene of perversity, it knew its own despair. And fear. The terror of it. Here you might see the soul of America at grips with historical problems, struggling with certain impossibilities, experiencing violently states inherently static. Being realized but trying itself to realize, to act. Attempting to make interest. This attempt to make interest was, for Mr. Sammler, one reason for the pursuit of madness. Madness makes interest. Madness is the attempted liberty of people who feel themselves overwhelmed by giant forces of organized control. Seeking the magic of extremes. Madness is a base form of the religious life.

But wait—Sammler cautioning himself. Even this madness is also to a considerable extent a matter of performance, of enactment. Underneath there persists, powerfully too, a thick sense of what is normal for human life. Duties are observed. Attachments are preserved. There is work. People show up for jobs. It is extraordinary. They come on the bus to the factory. They open the shop, they sweep, they wrap, they wash, they fix, they tend, they count, they mind the computers. Each day, each night. And however rebellious at heart, however despairing, terrified, or worn bare, come to their tasks. Up and down in the elevator, sitting down to the desk, behind the wheel, tending machinery. For such a volatile and restless animal, such a high-strung, curious animal, an ape subject to so many diseases, to anguish, boredom, such discipline, such drill, such strength for regularity, such assumption of responsibility, such regard for order (even in disorder) is a great mystery, too. Oh, it is a mystery. One cannot mistake this for thorough madness, therefore. One thing, though, the disciplined hate the undisciplined to the point of murder. Thus the working class, disciplined, is a great reservoir of hatred. Thus the clerk behind the wicket finds it hard to forgive those who come and go their apparent freedom. And the bureaucrat, glad when disorderly men are killed. All of them, killed.

What one sees on Broadway while bound for the bus. All human types reproduced, the barbarian, redskin, or Fiji, the dandy, the buffalo hunter, the desperado, the queer, the sexual fantasist, the squaw; bluestocking, princess, poet, painter, prospector, troubadour, guerrilla, Che Guevara, the new Thomas à Becket. Not imitated are the businessman, the soldier, the priest, and the square. The standard is aesthetic. As Mr. Sammler saw the thing, human beings, when they have room, when they have liberty and are supplied also with ideas, mythologize themselves. They legendize. They expand by imagination and try to rise above the limitations of the ordinary forms of common life. And what is "common" about "the common life"? What if some genius were to do with "common life" what Einstein did with "matter"? Finding its energetics, uncovering its radiance. But at the present level of crude vision, agitated spirits fled from the oppressiveness of "the common life," separating themselves from the rest of their species, from the life of their species, hoping perhaps to get away (in some peculiar sense) from the death of their species. To perform higher actions, to serve the imagination with special distinction, it seems essential to be histrionic. This, too, is a brand of madness. Madness has always been a favorite choice of the civilized man who prepares himself for a noble achievement. It is often the simplest state of availability to ideals. Most of us are satisfied with that: signifying by a kind of madness devotion to, availability for, higher purposes. Higher purposes do not necessarily appear.

If we are about to conclude our earth business—or at least the first great phase of it—we had better sum these things up. But briefly. As briefly as possible.

Short views, for God's sake!

Then: a crazy species? Yes, perhaps. Though madness is also a masquerade, the project of a deeper reason, a result of the despair we feel before infinities and eternities. Madness is a diagnosis or verdict of some of our greatest doctors and geniuses, and of their man-disappointed minds. Oh, man stunned by the rebound of man's powers. And what to do? In the matter of histrionics, see, for instance, what that furious world-boiler Marx had done, insisting that revolutions were made in historical costume, the Cromwellians as Old Testament prophets, the French in 1789 dressed in Roman outfits. But the proletariat, he said, he declared, he affirmed, would make the first non-imitative revolution. It would not need the drug of historical recollection. From sheer ignorance, knowing no models, it would simply do the thing pure. He was as giddy as the rest about originality. And only the working class was original. Thus history would get away from mere poetry. Then the life of humankind would clear itself of copying. It would be free from Art. Oh, no. No, no, not so, thought Sammler. Instead, Art increased, and a sort of chaos. More possibility, more actors, apes, copycats, more invention, more fiction, illusion, more fantasy, more despair. Life looting Art of its wealth, destroying Art as well by its desire to become the thing itself. Pressing itself into pictures. Reality forcing itself into all these shapes. Just look (Sammler looked) at this imitative anarchy of the streets—these Chinese revolutionary tunics, these babes in unisex toyland, these surrealist warchiefs, Western stagecoach drivers—Ph.D.s in philosophy, some of them (Sammler had met such, talked matters over with them). They sought originality. They were obviously derivative. And of what—of Paiutes, of Fidel Castro? No, of Hollywood extras. Acting mythic. Casting themselves into chaos, hoping to adhere to higher consciousness, to be washed up on the shores of truth. Better, thought Sammler, to accept the inevitability of imitation and then to imitate good things. The ancients had this right. Greatness without models? Inconceivable. One could not be the thing itself—Reality. One must be satisfied with the symbols. Make it the object of imitation to reach and release the high qualities. Make peace therefore with intermediacy and representation. But choose higher representations. Otherwise the individual must be the failure he now sees and knows himself to be. Mr. Sammler, sorry for all, and sore at heart.

Before lighting out, before this hop to the moon and outward bound, we had better look into some of this. As for the Crosstown and at this time of night, it was a perfectly safe bus to take.

Dr. Gruner had private nurses around the clock. Sammler entered and found the uniformed woman sitting by the bed. The patient was sleeping. Sammler in a careful whisper introduced himself. "His uncle—oh, yes, he said you'd probably come," said the nurse. She didn't make it sound like a pleasant prediction. Under her starched cap the dyed dry hair was puffed out. The face itself, middle-aged, was fleshy, healthy, bossy. The eyes had an expression of sovereignty. Patients would be brought along the way that they must go: recovery or death.

"Is he asleep for the night, or is he taking a nap?" said Sammler.

"He may be waking up soon, but that's a guess. Miss Gruner is in the visitors' room."

"I'll stand a bit," said Sammler, not invited to sit.

There were many flowers, baskets of fruit, candy boxes,

best sellers. The television set was running, soundlessly. The nurse listened with an earpiece. Reflected light flickered on the wall behind the bed. Elya's hands were turned downward at his sides, as though he had arranged himself symmetrically before dropping off. The hairy hands were clean, strong, venous, with polished nails. The nails had the same shine as the shot glass from which Gruner had sipped his mineral oil. The Nujol bottle was there, too, and beside it the *Wall Street Journal.* Bald dignity. The cord of the electric razor was plugged in above. He always was clean-shaven. The priests of Apis the Bull, as described by Herodotus, with shaven heads and bodies. And with the sleeping mouth bulged out on one side as if Elya, who liked to say that he had grown up in Greenpoint among hoodlums, might have been dreaming about racketeers and gunfire. Under his chin the bandage was like a military collar. Sammler thought of him as a man who badly, even desperately, needed confirmation, support, and touch. Gruner was a toucher. His habit, even in passing through a room, was to touch, to take people's arms, even perhaps getting medical information about their muscles, glands, weight, or the growth of their hair. He also implanted his opinions, his hopes in their breasts, and then if he said, "Well, isn't it so?", it was indeed so. Like a modern General of the Army, an Eisenhower, he made his logistical preparations. This shrewdness was very childish. But easy to pardon. Especially at such a time. At such a time, how could he sleep?

Sammler backed through the door softly and went to the visitors' room. There Angela sat smoking but not in her usual sensual and elegant style. She had been crying, and her face was white and hot. Her figure was heavy, breasts a burden, knees bulging pale against the taut silk of the stockings. Was it only because of her father that she was weeping? Sammler sensed a combined cause for those tears. He sat opposite her and laid the Augustus John hat, mole-gray, on his lap.

"Sleeping still?"

"Yes," said Sammler.

Angela's large lips, as though to cool herself, were open; she breathed through her mouth. Hot, the slope face with close-textured skin seemed very tight. The heat rose also into the whites of the eyes. "Does he *really* understand the situation?"

"I wonder. But he is a doctor, and I think he does."

Angela cried again, and Sammler was even more convinced of a second cause for her tears. "And there's nothing else wrong with him," said Angela. "He's perfectly well except for that thing—that one tiny damned thing. And you think he knows, Uncle?"

"Yes, probably."

"But acting so normal. Talking about the family. He was so glad to see you and hoped you'd come back tonight. And he still keeps worrying about Wallace."

"One can see why."

"Wallace has been such a headache. At six, seven, he was such a beautiful gifted little boy. He put together mathematical things. We thought we had another Einstein. Daddy sent him to MIT. But next thing we knew he was a bartender in Cambridge, and he beat some drunk almost to death."

"I've heard."

"And now he's bugging Daddy to get him a plane. At such a time! A flying saucer would be more like it. Of course I share some of the blame for Wallace." Sammler knew that the conversation would take a tiresome psychiatric-pediatric turn, and that he would have to endure a certain amount of explanation.

"Of course I was resentful when they brought the kid home from the hospital. I asked Mother to put his crib in the garage. I'm sure he felt rejection, from the first. I never liked him. He was too gloomy. He just wasn't like a child. He had terrible fits of rage."

"Well, everybody has a history," said Sammler.

"I think I decided in adolescence that my brother was going to be a queer. I thought it was my fault, that I was so slutty that he became frightened of girls."

"Is that so? Well, I remember your confirmation," said Sammler. "You were quite studious. I was impressed that you were studying Hebrew."

"Just a front, Uncle. I was a dirty little bitch, really."

"I wonder. In retrospect, people exaggerate so."

"Neither Father nor I ever liked Wallace. We pushed him off on Mother, and that was like condemning him for life. Then it was one thing after another, his obese stage, his alcoholic stage. Well, now have you heard? He thinks there's money hidden in the house."

"Do you think so, too?"

"I'm not sure. There have been hints from Daddy about it. Mother too before she died. She seemed to believe that now and then Daddy would—he'd step out of line, as she used to say."

"To help out famous families from Dutchess County, as Wallace tells me?"

"Is that what he says? No, Uncle, what I heard was that Daddy did favors for the Mafia characters he grew up with. Top people in the Syndicate. He knew Lucky Luciano very well. You probably never heard of Luciano."

"Just vaguely."

"Luciano came out to New Rochelle now and then. And if Daddy did those things and they paid him in cash, it must have been embarrassing. He probably didn't know what to do with that money. But that's not what's weighing on my mind."

"No. Speaking of New Rochelle, you haven't seen Shula, have you, Angela?"

"I haven't. What is she up to?"

"She brought me a very interesting book. However, it wasn't hers to bring."

"I assume she's hiding from Eisen. She thinks he's come to claim her."

"A flattering fear. If only he were capable of coming on such a mission. If he didn't beat her, it would answer many needs. It would be a mercy. No, I don't think he wants her at all. He doesn't like it that she poses as a Catholic. That was his pretext. Although he did say he got along well with Pope Pius at Castel Gandolfo. And now Eisen is not the friend of Popes, he is an artist. I don't think he has much genius, though he's crazy enough to want great glory." But Angela didn't want to hear this now. Apparently she thought Sammler was trying to turn the subject in a theoretical direction—to discuss the creative psychotic.

"Well, he's been here."

"You saw Eisen? He's been annoying Elya? Did he go in?"

"He wanted to make drawings—to sketch him, you know."

"I don't like it. I wish he wouldn't bother Elya. What the devil does he want? Keep him away."

"Well, maybe I shouldn't have let him in. I thought he might entertain Daddy."

Sammler was about to answer, but several beats of comprehension passed through his head and made him see matters differently. Of course. Ah, yes. Angela was having her own troubles with Dr. Gruner. Angela was not one of your great weepers, not like Margotte with her high annual tearfall. If Angela was looking so wan that even the frosted hair, usually so glossy and powerful, seemed to bristle dryly and Sammler thought he saw the dark follicular spots on her scalp, it was because she had been wrangling with her father. Under stress, Sammler believed, the whole faltered, and parts (follicles, for instance) became conspicuous. Such at least was his observation. Elya must be furious with her, and she was trying to divert his attention. Visitors. Obviously this was why she had taken Eisen straight in. But Eisen was not diverting. He was one of those smiling gloomy maniacs. Very gloomy, really. A depressing fellow. The smart silk suit he had worn ten years ago in Haifa when he and his father-in-law had gone out in the street, to a café, to discuss Shula, might have made a satisfactory coffin lining. Eisen certainly deserved to be cared for, and that was one of the uses of Israel, to gather in these cripples. But now Eisen had broken out, had heard the jolly frantic music of America and wanted to get into the act. He made a beeline for the rich cousin. The rich cousin was in the hospital with some kind of fiddle-peg in his neck. Odd what an instinct they all had for molesting a dying man.

"Did Elya find Eisen amusing? I doubt it."

Angela wore a playful cap, matching the black and white shoes. Now that her head was lowered Sammler saw the large button of kid leather set in the radial creases.

"A while he did, I think," she said. "Eisen made sketches of Daddy. But then he tried to sell them to him. Daddy would hardly glance at them."

"Not surprising. I wonder where Eisen got the money to come to America."

"I don't know, maybe he saved up. He's put out with you, Uncle."

"I'm sure of that."

"For not coming to see him in Israel. You were there for the war. He says you cut him."

"That doesn't concern me much. I wasn't there to pay my respects to a son-in-law or to make social visits."

"He complained to Daddy about you."

"Horrible!" said Sammler. "Everybody hitting away with these stupidities. At this time!"

"But Daddy takes an interest in all kinds of things. If everything suddenly stopped, it would be abnormal. Of course it's bad to aggravate him. For instance, he's angry with me."

"I suppose there is really no good way for Elya to do this thing."

"I'd say that he should stop talking to Widick. You know his fat lawyer, Widick?"

"Of course, I've met the man."

"Four or five times a day on the telephone. And Daddy asks me to leave the room. They're still buying and selling, trading on the stock market. Also I assume they discuss his will, or he wouldn't send me outside."

"Evidently, Angela, in spite of the case you make against Mr. Widick, you've crossed your father yourself, in some way. And you seem to want me to ask about it?"

"I think I should tell you."

"It doesn't sound good."

"It isn't. It was when Wharton Horricker and I went to Mexico."

"I believe Elya likes Horricker. He wouldn't have objected to that."

"No, he hoped that Wharton and I would get married."

"Won't you?"

Angela held a lighted cigarette in forked fingers before her face. Actions normally graceful, now distressingly heavy. She shook her head, her eyes filling, reddening. Ah, trouble with Horricker. Sammler had guessed something of the sort. It was a little hard for him to understand why she should always have so much trouble. Perhaps he put it to himself that she enjoyed so many privileges, what more did she want? She had the income from half a million to live on: tax-exempt Municipals, as Elya would repeat. She had this flesh, these sex attractions and talents —*volupté* she had. She brought back the French sex vocabulary Sammler had learned at the University of Cracow reading Emile Zola. That book about the fruit market. *Le Ventre de Paris.* Les Halles. And that appetizing woman there who was also something good to eat, a regular orchard. *Volupté, seins, épaules, hanches. Sur un lit de feuilles. Cette tiédeur satinée de femme.* Excellent, Emile! And—all right!—orchards suffering when there were earth tremors could drop all their pears; this too Sammler could sympathetically understand. But Angela was always unusually involved in difficulty and suffering, tripping on invisible obstructions, bringing forth complications of painful mischief which made him wonder whether this *volupté* was not one of the sorest strangest burdens that could be laid on a woman's soul. Saw the woman (by her own erotic account), as if in the actual bedroom. By invitation he was there, a perplexed bystander. Evidently she believed it necessary that he should know what went on in

America. He did not need quite so much information. But better a surplus than ignorance. Both the U.S.A. and the U.S.S.R. were, for Sammler, utopian projects. There, in the East, the emphasis was on low-level goods, on shoes, caps, toilet-plungers, and tin basins for peasants and laborers. Here it fell upon certain privileges and joys. Here wading naked into the waters of paradise, et cetera. But always a certain despair underlining pleasure, death seated inside the health-capsule, steering it, and darkness winking at you from the golden utopian sun.

"So you've had a quarrel with Wharton Horricker?"

"He's angry with me."

"Aren't you angry with him?"

"Not exactly. I seem to be in the wrong."

"Where is he now?"

"He's supposed to be in Washington. He's doing something statistical on antiballistic missiles. For the Senate bloc against the ABM. I don't understand the thing."

"It's a pity to have such trouble now, to have a double difficulty."

"I'm afraid Daddy has found out about this."

In Angela's expression as in Wallace's there was something soft, a hint of infancy or of baby reverie. The parents must have longed overmuch for babies and so inhibited something in their children's cycle of development. Angela's last glance, before she began to sob, astonished Sammler. Open lips, wrinkled forehead, the skin expressing utter surrender, traits of the original person. An infant! But the eyes did not give up their look of erotic experience.

"Found out about what?"

"A thing that happened at Acapulco. I didn't think it was so very serious. Neither did Wharton. At the time, it was just a kick. I mean it was funny. We had a party with another couple."

"What sort of party was it?"

"Well, it was a sex thing for the four of us."

"With other people? Who were they?"

"They were perfectly all right. We met them on the beach. The wife suggested it."

"An exchange?"

"Well, yes. Oh, it is done now, Uncle."

"I hear it is."

"You are disgusted with me, Uncle."

"I? Not really. I knew all this long ago. I regret it when things become so stupid, that's true. It seems to me that things poor professionals once had to do for a living, performing for bachelor parties, or tourist sex-circuses on the Place Pigalle, ordinary people, housewives, filing-clerks, students, now do just to be sociable. And I can't really say what it's all about. Is it maybe some united effort to conquer disgust? Or to show that all the repulsive things in history are not so repulsive? I don't know. Is it an effort to 'liberalize' human existence and show that nothing that happens between people is really loathsome? Affirming the Brotherhood of Man? Ah, well—" Sammler steadied and restrained himself. He did not want to know the details of this incident in Acapulco, didn't want to hear that the man in the case was a municipal judge from Chicago, or a chiropractor or CPA or a dope-pusher or that he made perfume or formaldehyde.

"Wharton went along, he did his share, but afterward he turned sullen. Then on the plane, flying back, he told me how angry he was about it."

"Well, he's a fastidious young man. You can see from his shirts. I assume he was well brought up."

"He acted no better than the rest of us."

"If you expected to marry Wharton, it was certainly poor judgment to do this."

Sammler badly wanted to get this conversation over. Elya had told him not to worry about the future, a hint that he was provided for; but there were also practical considerations to bear in mind. What if he and Shula had to depend on Angela? Angela had always been generous—she spent easily. When they went to a gallery or to lunch, she, naturally, paid for cabs, paid the check, left the tip, everything. But it would not do to go too deeply with Angela into this life of hers. The facts were too bad, too bald, abominable, pitiful. To a degree such behavior was based on theory, on generational ideology, part of a liberal education, and was therefore to an extent impersonal. But Angela would later regret these confessions—regret, and resent his disapproval. On the whole he received her confidences in a disinterested way. He was not unsympathetic, unfeeling; he was (she had said it herself) objective, nonjudging. As they faced Elya's death, he decided that under no circumstances and on no account would he become involved in a perverse relationship with Angela in which he had to listen for his supper. His disinterestedness would never become one of her comforts, part of the furniture of her life. Not even his anxiety over Shula's future could force him into such a position. A receiver of sordid goods? His whole heart rose against this.

"Daddy is asking very pointed questions about Wharton."

"He has heard about this episode?"

"That's right, Uncle."

"Who would tell him such things? It seems unusually cruel."

"I don't know whether you understand about that fat

Widick, the lawyer. He and Wharton are related somewhere along the line. He's a bastard."

"That's not my impression at all. Normally fraudulent, perhaps, but that is simply business."

"He's a shit. Daddy thinks the world of Widick. He won the big case for him against the insurance company. I told you they talk four or five times a day on the phone. And Widick hates me."

"How do you know that?"

"I feel it. I get the spoiled-daughter look from him. There have always been people around who thought that Daddy had a bad thing about me, made me financially too independent. You know—pampered me and let me hang too loose."

"Hasn't he been exceptionally indulgent?"

"Not just for my sake, Uncle Sammler. You don't just act for yourself, and he's also lived through me. You can believe it."

Men, thought Sammler, often sin alone; women are seldom companionless in sin. But although Angela might be trying to force this interpretation on her father's kindness, it was possible that Elya too had his own lustful tendencies. Who was Sammler to say no? Things in general were desperate. The arterial bulge in Elya's brain must have cast its shadow earlier—spatters before the cloudburst. Sammler believed in premonitions, and death was a powerful instigator of erotic ideas. Sammler's own sex impulses (perhaps even now not altogether gone) had been very different. But he knew how to respect differences. He didn't measure others by himself. Now Shula had no *volupté*. She had something else. Of course she was not a rich man's daughter, and money, the dollar, was certainly a terrific sexual additive. But even Shula, though a scavenger or magpie, had never actually stolen before. Then suddenly she too was like the Negro pickpocket. From the black side, strong currents were sweeping over everyone. Child, black, redskin—the unspoiled Seminole against the horrible Whiteman. Millions of civilized people wanted oceanic, boundless, primitive, neckfree nobility, experienced a strange release of galloping impulses, and acquired the peculiar aim of sexual niggerhood for everyone. Humankind had lost its old patience. It demanded accelerated exaltation, accepted no instant without pregnant meanings as in epic, tragedy, comedy, or films. He had an idea even that the very special development of the significance of prisons since the eighteenth century had some relation to this shrinking ability to endure restraint. Punishment must be fitted, closely tailored to the state of the spirit, adapted to the need of the soul. Where liberty had been promised most, they had the biggest, worst prisons. Then another question: Had Elya performed abortions to oblige old Mafia friends? As to that, Sammler had no opinion. He simply couldn't say. Elya had never wanted to be a physician. He disliked the practice of medicine. But he had done his duty. And even doctors nowadays made sexual gestures to their patients. Put women's hands on their parts. Sammler had heard of this. Physicians who rejected the Oath, who joined the Age. Also Shula, Shula stealing, was contemporary—lawless. She was experiencing the Age. In so doing, she drew her father along with her. And possibly Elya, with the screw in his throat, had not wished to be left behind either, and had delegated Angela to experience the Age for him.

Be all that as it might—life once had nearly ended. Someone ahead, carrying the light, stumbled, faltered, and Mr. Sammler had thought it was over. However, he was still alive. He had not come through, for the connotation of coming through was that of an accomplishment and little had been accomplished. He had been steered from Cracow to London, from London to the Zamosht Forest, and eventually into New York City. One result of such a history was that he had formed a habit of condensation. He was a specialist in short views. And in the short view, Angela had offended her dying father. He was angry, and she wanted Sammler to intercede for her. Maybe Elya would cut her out of his will, give his money to charity. He had made large contributions to the Weizmann Institute. That Think-tank, they called it, at Rehovoth. Or perhaps she was afraid that he himself, Sammler, who was so close to Elya, would become his heir.

"Will you talk to Daddy, Uncle?"

"About this . . . thing of yours? That would be up to him. I wouldn't introduce the subject. I don't think he's just become aware of your style of life. I can't say what he's gotten out of it—vicariously, as you suggest. But he's not stupid, and giving a young woman like you a capital of half a million dollars to live in New York City, he would have to be very dumb to think you were not amusing yourself."

Great cities are whores. Doesn't everyone know? Babylon was a whore. *Ô La Reine aux fesses cascadantes.* Penicillin keeps New York looking cleaner. No faces gnawed by syphilis, with gaping noseholes as in ancient times.

"Daddy has such respect for you."

"What use should I make of that respect?"

"All the oldest, deepest, worst sexual prejudices are mobilized against me."

"Lord only knows what's in his mind," said Sammler. "Perhaps it's only one pain among many."

"He's said cruel things to me."

"This Mexican event is not the first," said Sammler. "Surely your father has always known. He hoped you would marry Horricker and stop this sexual nonsense."

"I'll see if he's awake," said Angela, and rose. Her soft and heavy self was dressed in one of its costumes. Her legs, exposed to the last quarter of the thigh, were really very strong, almost clumsy. Her face was at this moment baby-pale, and soft under the little leather cap. As she detached herself from the plastic seat, and the evening was quite warm, an odor was released. Both low comic and high serious. Goddess and majorette. The Great Sinner! What a vexation for poor Elya. What overvaluation. What an atrocious mixture of feelings. Angela was displeased with Sammler. She walked away.

As she was going, he remembered where he had last seen a cap like hers. It was in Israel—the Six-Day War he had seen.

He had seen.

It was almost as if he had attended—among other spectators. Arriving in fast cars at a point before Mount Hermon, where a tank battle was taking place, he was one of a press group watching a fight, below. Down in the flat valley, as in Vista-Vision. Where they were standing, Mr. Sammler and the others, Israeli press officers and journalists, were safe enough. The battle was two miles or more beyond them. The tank columns were maneuvering in dust. Bombs were spilling from planes as remote as insects. You saw the wings when they spun into the light, then heard detonations, and shrubs of smoke rose briefly. Remotely, you heard machinery—distant tank treads. You heard tiny war sounds. Then two more cars came tearing up, joined the group, and cameramen leaped out. They were Italians, *paparazzi,* someone explained, and had brought with them three girls in mod dress. The girls might have come from Carnaby Street or from King's Road in their buskins, miniskirts, false eyelashes. They were indeed British, for Mr. Sammler heard them talking, and one of them had on just the sort of little cap that Angela wore, of houndstooth check. The young ladies had no idea where they were, what this was about, had been quarreling with their lovers, who were now lying in the road on their bellies. Photographing battle, the shirts fluttering on their backs. The girls were angry. Carried off from the Via Veneto, probably, without knowing clearly where the jet was going. Then, bare to the waist, a runt but muscular, a Swiss correspondent with small twisted kinky-blond beard and his chest hung with cameras began to complain to the Israeli captain that it was improper for these girls to be at the front. Sammler heard him give this protest through his teeth, which were bad and tiny. The place where they were standing had been bombed earlier. One could not see why. There seemed no military reason for it. But the ground was full of large holes, still black with fresh bomb soot.

"Put them at least in those holes," the Swiss insisted.

"What?"

"Foxholes, foxholes. Another shell may come. You can't have them walking on the road, like this. You can't have it, don't you understand?" He was an unbearable little man. His war was being ruined by these stupid girls in costume. The Israeli officer gave in. He made the girls get into the burnt holes. All you could see of them then was heads and shoulders. Not quite frightened out of their anger, but beginning to be. Somewhat stunned by now, in the paint of great amorousness, one beginning to sob a little, and another puffing up and growing red. Becoming middle-aged—a scrubwoman. Frills of glistening black rising about the girls, the cordite-shining grass.

Other things as strange were occurring. Father Newell, the Jesuit correspondent, was there. He wore the full battle dress of the Vietnam jungles—yellow, black, and green daubs and stripes of camouflage. Representing a newspaper in Tulsa, Oklahoma, was it, or Lincoln, Nebraska? Sammler still owed him ten dollars, his share of the taxi they had hired in Tel Aviv to drive to the Syrian front. But he didn't have Father Newell's address. He might have tried harder to find it. On his way home from Southeast Asia, the priest was a tourist in Athens, looking at the Acropolis, when he heard of the fighting and went at once. The big jungle boots were as ample as galoshes. Father Newell sweated in his green battle clothes. His hair cropped Marine-style, his eyes also green and the cheeks splendid meat-red. Down below the tanks raced and the smoke puffed yellow from the ground. Few sounds rose.

Mr. Sammler in the waiting room now stirred and stood up. Wallace, entering from the general light of the corridor into the lamplight of the visitors' room, was already speaking to him. "Dad is sleeping, Angela says. I don't suppose you've had a chance to talk to him about the attic?"

"I have not."

Wallace was not alone. Eisen entered at his back.

Wallace and Eisen knew each other. How well? A curious question. But quite long, at any rate. They had met when Wallace, after his attempted horse tour of Central Asia and his arrest by the Russian authorities, had visited Israel and stayed with Cousin Eisen. Wallace had then prepared a full set of notes (going to work at once) for an essay arguing that the modernization Israel was bringing to the Middle East was altogether too rapid for the

Arabs. Pernicious. Wallace, of course, was bound to oppose Elya's Zionism. But Eisen, never comprehending, unaware of Wallace's sudden passion (soon vanishing) for Arab culture, brought him coffee in bed while he was working. Because Wallace was just out of a Soviet prison, thanks to Gruner and Senator Javits, and Eisen knew what it was to be in Russian hands. He had made Wallace rest, he waited on him. On his mutilated feet he had learned to move rapidly. Ingenious adaptation. The shuffle of his toeless feet in Haifa had put Sammler's teeth on edge. He couldn't have endured two hours alone with handsome, curly, smiling Eisen. But Wallace, with his great-orbited eyes and long lashes, reaching a skinny hairy arm from the bed and, without looking, accepting coffee in trembling fingers, coddled himself ten days in Eisen's bed after the jails of Soviet Armenia. The Russians had sent him to Turkey. From Turkey he went to Athens. From Athens, like Newell the Jesuit later, he flew to Israel. Tenderly, devotedly, Eisen had waited on him.

"Ah, here is my father-in-law."

Was it with pleasure at seeing him that Eisen beamed, or was it because the event (Eisen in New York for the first time in his life) was so splendid? He was gay but stiff, cramped under the arms and between the legs by his new American clothes. Wallace must have taken him to one of those execrable mod male shops, like Barney's. Perhaps to one of the unisex establishments. The madman wore a magenta shirt with a persimmon-colored necktie as thick as an ox tongue. The gloom of his never-ending laughter, the shining of his excellent teeth unharmed by the Stalingrad siege and unaffected by starvation when he hobbled over the Carpathians and the Alps. Teeth like that deserved a saner head.

"How nice to find you here," said Eisen to Sammler in Russian.

Sammler answered in Polish, "How are you, Eisen?"

"You wouldn't stop to visit me in my country, so I came to see you in yours," said Eisen.

In this reproach, a familiar and traditional Jewish opening, there was at least a vestige of normalcy. Not so in the next statement. "I have come to America to make myself a new career." *Karyera* was the word he employed. Dressed in the cramping narrow gray-denim garments, obviously old stock from the Ivy League period that had been palmed off on him, in magenta, persimmon, and tomato colors (the red Chelsea boots mounting to the ankles), his unbarbered curls fusing head and shoulders and brutally eliminating the neck, he was obviously getting a new image, revising his self-conception. No longer a victim of Hitler and Stalin; deposited starved to the bones on Israel's sands; lice, lunacy, and fever his only assets; taken from internment in Cyprus; taught a language and a trade. But you could not tell recovery where to stop. He had gone on to become an artist. Rising from negligibility, expendability, something that waited to be slaughtered with a trenching tool (Eisen said he had watched this before escaping from Nazi-occupied territory into the Russian zone—men too insignificant to waste bullets on, having their heads smashed by shovel blows); but rising and rising to heights of world mastery. By the divinity of art. Speaking, inspired, to mankind. Making signs in the universal language of charged pigments. Hurray, Eisen, flying from peak to peak! Though his colors were grayer than slate, blacker than coal, redder than disease, and his life studies were double dead, the bus that brought him in from Kennedy was a limousine; the expressways greeted him like a glorious astronaut, and he faced his *Karyera* with the moist laughing teeth, in most desperate ecstasy. (To pair with the Russian *Karyera,* you wanted the Russian *Extass!*)

He and Wallace were already doing business together. Eisen was designing labels for the trees and the bushes. They showed Sammler sample cards: QUERCUS and ULMUS, in thick blotchy letters of Gothic black. Other labels in the foreign cursive style Eisen had learned in the *Gymnasium* were neater. Poor Eisen had been a schoolboy when the war broke out and had no higher education. Sammler did his best to say something appropriate and harmless though he was repelled by everything that Eisen set on paper.

"These have got to be modified here and there," said Wallace. "But the idea is surprisingly right. For a greenie, you know."

"You are going into this business, really?"

Wallace said firmly, even with a slight jeer (forming about a dimple) at the old man's doubts, "Definitely, really, Uncle. In fact I'm going to test-fly some planes tomorrow, in Westchester. I'm going back this evening to spend the night at the old place."

"Is your pilot's license still good?"

"Why, of course it's good."

"Well, it must be an agreeable feeling of excitement—a new enterprise, with friends and relatives. What have you got there, Eisen?"

A heavy green baize bag hung from cords wound about Eisen's wrist. "Here? I have brought work of mine in a different medium." Eisen said. He clinked down the weight on the glass tabletop; the baize fell back.

"You've made some paperweights."

"Not paperweights. You could use them for that purpose, Father-in-law, but they are medallions." You couldn't offend Eisen because he took such pleasure in his accomplishments. As if he were inhaling some aromatic rarity, he began to close his eyes and to show those peerless bones, his teeth, and with both hands smoothed back the curls over his ears. "I have invented a new process in the foundry," he said. In technical Russian he began to explain, but Sammler said, "You are losing me, Eisen. I am not familiar with the vocabulary."

The metal was crude-looking, partly bronze but also pale yellow, tinged with sulfides like fool's gold. And Eisen had made the usual Stars of David, branched candelabra, scrolls and rams' horns, or inscriptions flaming away in Hebrew: *Nahamu!* "Comfort ye!" Or God's command to Joshua: *Hazak!* With a certain interest Sammler watched these crude, lunky pieces being laid out. After each, a pause, while the face of the connoisseur was intently examined for the beautiful reaction obviously due. These iron pyrites, belonging at the bottom of the Dead Sea.

"And what is this, Eisen, a tank, I take it, a Sherman tank?"

"Metaphor for a tank. Nothing is literal in my work."

"No one simply hallucinates any more," said Mr. Sammler in Polish. The remark was unnoticed.

"Shouldn't these be ground smoother?" said Wallace. "And what is this word?"

"*Hazak, hazak,*" said Sammler. "The order God gave before Jericho, to Joshua. 'Strengthen thyself.' "

"*Hazak, v'ematz,*" said Eisen.

"Yes, well . . . Why does God speak such a funny language?" said Wallace.

"I brought these medallions to show to Cousin Elya."

"Nonsense," said Sammler. "Elya's sick. He can't handle this rough heavy metal."

"No, no, I'll hold up one piece at a time. I want him to see what I accomplished. Twenty-five years ago I came to the Eretz a broken man. But I wouldn't die. I couldn't shut my eyes—not before I did something like a human being, something important, beautiful."

Sammler ventured no comment. After all, his heart was not so hard to touch. Moreover, he had been trained in the ancient mode of politeness. Almost as, once, women had been brought up to chastity. Well-schooled in murmuring over the trash Shula found in wastebaskets, he made the necessary sounds and passes of the hand, but then he said again that Elya was very ill. These medallions might tire him.

"I differ," said Eisen. "On the contrary. How can art hurt?" He began to stow the clinking pieces in the baize bag.

Wallace then said to someone behind Sammler, "Yes, he is." The private nurse had come in.

"Who is?"

"You, Uncle. This is Mr. Sammler here."

"Is Elya asking for me?"

"You're wanted on the telephone. You are Uncle Sammler?"

"Miss? I am Artur Sammler."

"A Mrs. Arkin. She wants you to call home."

"Oh, Margotte. Did she phone Elya's room? I hope she didn't wake him."

"The call was to the floor, not to the room."

"Thank you. Oh, yes, where is the public phone?"

"Do you need dimes, Uncle?" Sammler picked two

warm coins out of Wallace's palm. Wallace had been clutching his money.

Margotte tried extraordinarily hard to speak firmly. "Uncle? Now listen. Where did you leave Dr. Lal's manuscript?"

"I left it on my desk."

"Are you sure?"

"Of course I am sure. On my desk."

"Is there no other place you might have put it? I know you aren't absent-minded, but the strain is unusual."

"It isn't on the desk? Is Dr. Lal with you?"

"I sat him down in the living room."

Among the pots of soil. What must this Lal be feeling!

"And does he know it's gone?"

"I couldn't very well lie to him. I had to tell him. He wanted to wait here for you. We raced back from Butler Hall, of course. He was so anxious."

"Now, Margotte, we must keep our heads."

"He is in such distress. Really, Uncle, no one has the right to expose a person to such things."

"My apologies to Dr. Lal. I regret more than I can say . . . I can imagine how upset he is. But Margotte, only one person in the world could have taken that notebook. You must find out from the elevator man. Has Shula been there?"

"Rodriguez lets her in as one of the family. She *is* one of the family."

Rodriguez had a giant ring of keys, practically a hoop. He fetched it at need from a nail in the brick wall of the cellar.

"Really, Shula is too stupid. Enough is enough. I've been too easy with her. The embarrassment is terrible. Being the father of the woman-lunatic who ambushes this unhappy Indian. You spoke to Rodriguez?"

"It was Shula."

"Ah."

"Dr. Lal had a report from the detective who visited her today, at noon. I think the man threatened her."

"As I feared."

"He said the manuscript must be back by ten a.m. tomorrow; otherwise he would come with a warrant."

"To search? Arrest?"

"I don't know. Neither does Dr. Lal. But she got very excited. What she said was that she would go to her priest. She would go to Father Robles and complain to the Church."

"Margotte, you had better check with that priest. A search warrant in that apartment? She has been filling it with trash for twelve years. If the police put down their hats, they'll never find them again. But I would say she has gone to New Rochelle."

"Do you think so?"

"If she's not with Father Robles, that's where she is." Sammler knew her ways; knew them as the Eskimo knows the ways of the seal. Its breathing-holes. "She is protecting me now, because the stolen property is in my hands. She must have been terrified by the detective, poor thing, and then waited till we had both gone out." Spying on my door like the black man. Feeling that she was not included by her father among his most serious concerns. Determined to regain the top priority. "I have let her go too far with this H. G. Wells nonsense. And now someone has been hurt."

This unlucky Lal, who must have been sick of earth

to begin with if he had such expectations of the moon.

And partly he was right, for humankind kept doing the same stunts over and over. The old comical-tearful stuff. Emotional relationships. Desires incapable of useful fulfillment. Over and over, trying to vent and empty the breast of certain cries, of certain fervencies. What positive balance was possible? Was this passional struggle altogether useless? It was the energy bank also of noble purposes. Barking, hissing, ape-chatter, and spitting. But there were times when Love seemed life's great architect. Weren't there? Even stupidity might at times be hammered out as a golden background for great actions. Mightn't it? But for these weaknesses and these tenacious sicknesses, were there true cures? Sometimes the idea of cures seemed to Sammler itself pernicious. What was cured? You could rearrange, you could orchestrate the disorders. But cure? Nonsense. Change Sin to Sickness, a change of words (Feffer was right), and then enlightened doctors would stamp the sickness out. Oh, yes! So, then, philosophers, men of science, of brilliant intellect, understanding this more and more clearly, are compelled to sue for divorce from all these human states. Then they launch outward, moonward, their flying arthropod hardware.

"I shall go to New Rochelle with Wallace," said Sammler. "She is certainly there. To be sure, we will check with Father Robles. If he knows where she is . . . I'll call back."

Because she was not an American he felt a certain solidarity with Margotte. From her he did not have to conceal his (foreign) mortification. And she had shown delicacy in remembering not to ring Elya's room.

"What shall I do with Dr. Lal?"

"Apologize," he said. "Reassure. Comfort him, Margotte. Tell him I'm sure the manuscript is safe. Explain Shula's respect for the written word. And please ask him to keep the detectives out of this."

"Wait a minute. He is here. He would like to say a word."

An Eastern voice enriched the wire.

"*Is* this Mr. Sammler?"

"It is."

"Dr. Lal, here. This is the second robbery. I cannot tolerate much more. Since Mrs. Arkin has appealed for patience, I can hold off just a very little longer. But very little. Then I must have the police detain your daughter."

"If only it would help to put her behind bars! Believe me, I am sorrier than I can say. But I am perfectly sure the manuscript is safe. I understand you have no other copy."

"Three years of composition."

"That is distressing. I had hoped it was more like six months. But I can see how much careful preparation it would need." Normally Sammler shunned flattery, but now he had no choice. Moisture formed upon the black instrument, against his ear, and on his cheek was a red pressure mark. He said, "The work is brilliant."

"I am glad you think so. Judge how it affects me."

I can judge. Anyone can clutch anyone, and whirl him off. The low can force the high to dance. The wise have to reel about with leaping fools. "Try not to be too anxious, sir. I can recover your manuscript, and will do it tonight. I don't use my authority often enough. Believe me, I can control my daughter, and I shall."

"I had hoped to publish by the time of the first moon

landing," said Lal. "You can imagine how many bad paperbacks will be out. Confusing to the public. Meretricious."

"Of course." Sammler sensed that the Indian, probably passionate, resisting great internal pressure, was after all being decent, allowing for the frailty of an old man, the tightness of the situation. He thought, The fellow is a gentleman. Inclining his head within the soundproof metal enclosure, the dotted voile of insulation, Sammler yielded to Oriental suggestion: "May the sun brighten your face. Single you out among the multitude (imagining Hindus always in crowds: like mackerel-crowded seas) many years yet." Sammler was determined that Shula should hurt no one but himself. He had to put up with it, but no one else should.

"I shall be interested in your comments on my essay."

"Of course," said Sammler, "we will have a long talk about it. Please stand by. I will phone as soon as there is some news. Thank you for bearing with me."

Both parties hung up.

"Wallace," said Sammler, "I think I shall be driving to New Rochelle with you."

"Really? Then Dad did say something about the attic?"

"It has nothing to do with the attic."

"Then why? Is it something about Shula? It must be."

"Why, yes, in fact. Shula. Can we leave soon?"

"Emil is out there with the Rolls. Might as well use it while we can. What is Shula up to? She called me."

"When?"

"Not long ago. She wanted to put something in Dad's wall safe. Did I know the combination. Naturally I couldn't say I knew the combination. I'm not supposed to know."

"Where was she calling from?"

"I didn't ask. Of course you've seen Shula whispering to the flowers in the garden," said Wallace. Wallace was not observant and took little interest in the conduct of others. But for that very reason he prized highly the things he did notice. What he noticed he cherished. He had always been kind and warm to Shula. "What language does she speak to them, is it Polish?"

The language of schizophrenia, very likely.

"I used to read *Alice in Wonderland* to her. Those talking flowers. The garden of live flowers."

Sammler opened the patient's door and saw him sitting up, alone. Dr. Gruner in his large black spectacles was studying, or trying to study, a contract or legal document. He would sometimes say that he should have been a lawyer, not a doctor. Medical school had not been his choice but his mother's. Of his own free will he had probably done little. Consider his wife.

"Come in, Uncle, and shut the door. Let's make it fathers only. I don't want to see children tonight."

"I understand that feeling," said Sammler. "I've had it often."

"It's a pity about Shula, poor woman. But she is only wacky. My daughter is a dirty cunt."

"A different generation, a different generation."

"And my son, a high-IQ moron."

"He may come around, Elya."

"You don't believe it for a minute, Uncle. What, a ninth-inning rally? I ask myself what I spent so many years of my life on. I must have believed what America was telling me. I paid for the best. I never suspected that I wasn't getting the best."

Had Elya spoken in excitement, Sammler would have tried to calm him. He was, however, speaking factually and he sounded utterly level. In the goggles he looked particularly judicious. Like the chairman of a Senate committee hearing scandalous testimony without loss of composure.

"Where is Angela?"

"Gone to the ladies' to have a cry, I suppose. If she isn't Frenching an orderly, or in a daisy chain. When she goes around the corner, you never know."

"Oh, too bad. You ought not to be quarreling."

"Not quarreling. Just making things plainer, spelling them out. I figured this Horricker to marry her, but he'll never do it now."

"Is that certain?"

"Did she tell you what happened in Mexico?"

"Not in detail."

"That's just as well, if you don't know the details. The joke you made was right on the head, about the billiard table in hell, about something green where it's hot."

"It wasn't aimed at Angela."

"Of course I knew my daughter with twenty-five thousand tax-free dollars must be having herself a time. I expected that, and as long as she was handling herself maturely and sensibly I had no objections. All that, theoretically, is fine. You use the words 'mature' and 'sensible,' and they satisfy you. But then you take a close look, and when you take a close look, you see something else. You see a woman who has done it in too many ways with too many men. By now she probably doesn't know the name of the man between her legs. And she looks . . . Her eyes—she has fucked-out eyes."

"I'm sorry."

Something very odd in Elya's expression. There were tears about, somewhere, but dignity would not permit them. Perhaps it was self-severity, not dignity. But they did not come out. They were rerouted, absorbed into the system. They were subdued, converted into tones. They were present in the voice, in the color of the skin, in the lights of the eye.

"I must go, Elya. I'll take Wallace with me. I'll be back tomorrow."

Emil in the Rolls Royce may have had an enviable life. The silver limousine was his faucet. He had all that power to turn on. Also, he was outside the wretched, anxious rivalry, rancor, hatred, and warfare of ordinary drivers of lesser cars. Double-parked, he was not molested by cops. As he stood beside the grand machine, his buttocks, given a rectilinear projection by the formal breeches, were nearer to the ground than most people's. He seemed also to have a calm, serious spirit; heavy creases in the face; lips that turned inward and never showed the teeth; midparted hair like a cowl descending to the ears; a heavy Savonarola nose. The Rolls still carried MD on the license plates.

"Emil drove for Costello, for Lucky Luciano," said Wallace, smiling.

In the light of the padded gray interior, Wallace was beard-stippled. The large dark eyes in the big orbits wished to offer courteous entertainment. When you considered how profoundly Wallace was absorbed and preoccupied by business, by problems of character, by death, you recognized how generous and how difficult this was—how much trying, shaking, rousing, what an effort was required. Arranging a kindly smile for the old uncle.

"Luciano? Elya's friend? Yes. Eminent Mafia. Angela mentioned him."

"Connections from way back."

They drove out on the West Side Highway, along the Hudson. There was the water—how beautiful, unclean, insidious! and there the bushes and the trees, cover for sexual violence, knifepoint robberies, sluggings, and murders. On the water bridgelight and moonlight lay smooth, enjoyably brilliant. And when we took off from all this and carried human life outward? Mr. Sammler was ready to think it might have a sobering effect on the species, at this moment exceptionally troubled. Violence might subside, exalted ideas might recover importance. Once we were emancipated from telluric conditions.

In the Rolls was a handsome bar; it had a small light, within the mirror-lined cabinet. Wallace offered the old man liquor or Seven-Up, but he wanted nothing. Enclosing the umbrella between high knees, he was reviewing some of the facts. Outer-space voyages were made possible by specialist-collaboration. While on earth sensitive ignorance still dreamed of being separate and "whole." "Whole"? What "whole"? A childish notion. It led to all this madness, mad religions, LSD, suicide, to crime.

He shut his eyes. Breathed out of his soul some bad, and breathed in some good. No, thank you, Wallace, no whisky. Wallace poured some for himself.

How could the ignorant nonspecialist be strong with

strength adequate to confront these technical miracles which made him a sort of uncomprehending Congo savage? By vision, by archaic inner-preliterate purity, by natural force, nobly whole? The children were setting fire to libraries. And putting on Persian trousers, letting their sideburns grow. This was their symbolic wholeness. An oligarchy of technicians, engineers, the men who ran the grand machines, infinitely more sophisticated than this automobile, would come to govern vast slums filled with bohemian adolescents, narcotized, beflowered, and "whole." He himself was a fragment, Mr. Sammler understood. And lucky to be that. Totality was as much beyond his powers as to make a Rolls Royce, part by part, with his own hands. So perhaps, *perhaps!* colonies on the moon would reduce the fever and swelling here, and the passion for boundlessness *and* wholeness might find more material appeasement. Humankind, drunk with terror, calm itself, sober up.

Drunk with terror? Yes, and fragments (a fragment like Mr. Sammler) understood: this earth was a grave: our life was lent to it by its elements and had to be returned: a time came when the simple elements seemed to long for release from the complicated forms of life, when every element of every cell said, "Enough!" The planet was our mother and our burial ground. No wonder the human spirit wished to leave. Leave this prolific belly. Leave also this great tomb. Passion for the infinite caused by the terror, by *timor mortis,* needed material appeasement. *Timor mortis conturbat me. Dies irae. Quid sum miser tunc dicturus.*

The moon was so big tonight that it caught the eye of Wallace, drinking in the back seat, in the unlimited luxury of upholstery and carpets. Legs crossed, leaning back, he pointed moonward past Emil, above the smooth parkway north of the George Washington Bridge.

"Isn't the moon great? They're buzzing away, around it," he said.

"Who?"

"Spacecraft are. Modules."

"Oh, yes. It's in the papers. Would you go there?"

"Would I ever! In a minute," said Wallace. "Out—out? You bet I'd go. I'd fly. In fact, I'm already signed up with Pan Am."

"With whom?"

"With the airlines. I believe I was the five-hundred-twelfth person to phone for a reservation."

"Are they already taking reservations for moon excursions?"

"They most certainly are. Hundreds of thousands of people want to go. Also to Mars and Venus, jumping off from the moon."

"How very odd."

"What's odd about it? To go? It isn't odd at all. I tell you, the airlines get bales of applications. What about you, would you take the trip, Uncle?"

"No."

"Because of your age, maybe?"

"Possibly age. No, my travels are over."

"But the moon, Uncle! Of course you wouldn't physically be able to do it; but a man like you? I can't believe such a person wouldn't be raring to go."

"To the moon? But I don't even want to go to Europe," Mr. Sammler said. "Besides, if I had my choice, I'd prefer the ocean bottom. In Dr. Piccard's bathysphere. I seem to be a depth man rather than a height man. I do not personally care for the illimitable. The ocean, however deep, has a top and bottom, whereas there is no sky ceiling. I think I am an Oriental, Wallace. Jews, after all, are Orientals. I am content to sit here on the West Side, and watch, and admire these gorgeous Faustian departures for the other worlds. Personally, I require a ceiling, although a high one. Yes, I like ceilings, and the high better than the low. In literature I think there are low-ceiling masterpieces—*Crime and Punishment,* for instance—and high-ceiling masterpieces, *Remembrance of Things Past.*"

Claustrophobia? Death is confinement.

Wallace, continuing to smile, softly but definitely differed; yet took a subtle interest in Uncle Sammler's views. "Of course," he said, "the world looks different to you. Literally. Because of the eyes. How well do you see?"

"Partially only. You are right."

"And yet you described that Negro man and his thing."

"Ah, Feffer told you that. Your partner. I should have known he'd rush to tell. I hope he's not serious about snapping photographs on the bus."

"He thinks he can, with his Minox. He is sort of a nut. I suppose that when people are young and full of enthusiasm, you say, 'All that youth and enthusiasm,' but as they grow older you just say, about the same behavior, 'What a nut.' He was very excited by your experience. What actually did the man do, Uncle? He exhibited himself. Did he drop his trousers?"

"No."

"He opened them. And then he took out his tool. What was it like? I wonder . . . Did it occur to him that your eyesight wasn't good enough to see?"

"I don't know what occurred to him. He didn't say."

"Well, tell me about his thing. It wasn't actually black,

was it? It must have been a purple kind of chocolate, or maybe the color of his palms?"

Wallace's scientific objectivity!

"I don't wish to talk about it, really."

"Oh, Uncle, suppose I were a zoologist who had never seen a live leviathan but you knew Moby Dick from the whaleboat? Was it sixteen, eighteen inches?"

"I couldn't say."

"Would you guess it weighed two pounds, three pounds, four?"

"I have no way to estimate. And you are not a zoologist. You just this minute became one."

"Uncircumcised?"

"That was my impression."

"I wonder if women really prefer that kind of thing."

"I assume they have other interests in addition."

"That's what they say. But you know you can't trust them. They're animals, aren't they."

"Temporarily there is an animal emphasis."

"I'm not taken in by the gentle-dainty-lady line. Women are lustful. They're raunchier than men in my opinion. With all respect for your experience and knowledge of life, Uncle Sammler, this is a field where I wouldn't be inclined to take your word. Angela would always say that if a man had a thick dick—excuse me, Uncle."

"Angela is perhaps a special case."

"You prefer to think she's off the continuum. What if she's not?"

"I'd like to drop the subject, Wallace."

"No, it's really too interesting. And this is pure objectivity, not a dirty conversation. Now, Angela gives a good report on Wharton Horricker. It seems he's a long, strong fellow. She says, however, that he takes too much exercise, he's too muscular. It's hard to get tender emotions from a man who has such steel cable arms and heavy thick weight-lifting pectorals. An iron man. She says it interferes with the flow of tender feeling."

"I hadn't thought about it."

"What does she know about tender feeling? Just some guy between her legs—Everyman is her lover. No, Anyman. They say that fellows that beef themselves up like that—'I was a ninety-pound weakling'—that such fellows are narcissistic pansies. I don't judge anybody. What if they are homosexuals? That's nothing any more. I don't think homosexuality is simply a different way of being human, I actually think it's a disease. I don't know why homosexuals fuss so much and proclaim themselves so normal. Such gentlemen. Of course they have *us* to point at—and we're not so great. I believe this boom in faggots was caused by modern warfare. One result of 1914, that slaughter in the trenches. The men were getting blasted. It was obviously healthier to be a woman than a man. It was better to be a child. Best of all is to be an artist, combining child, woman, or dervish—do I mean a dervish? A shaman? A necromancer is probably what I mean. Plus millionaire. Many a millionaire wants to be an artist, or a kid or woman and a necromancer. What was I talking about? Oh, Horricker. I was saying that in spite of all that physical culture and weight lifting he was not a queer. But that he did have a fantastic image of male strength. A person making a determined self-effort. Angela's job seemed to be to take him down a few pegs. She's weepy about him today, but she's a pig, and he'll be forgotten tomorrow. I think my sister is a swine. If he's got too much muscle, she's got too much fat. What about that fat bust interfering with the flow of tender feeling? What did you say just now?"

"Not a word."

"Sometimes at night, last thing before sleeping, I go through a whole list of people and call them all swine. I find it's marvelous therapy. I clear my mind for the night. If you were in the room, you'd only hear me saying, 'Swine, swine, swine!' Not the names. Each name is mental. Don't you agree that she'll forget Horricker by tomorrow?"

"I think she may. But I trust she's not too lost."

"She's a female-power type, the *femme fatale*. Every myth has its natural enemies. The enemy of the distinguished-male myth is the *femme fatale*. Between those thighs, a man's conception of himself is just assassinated. If he thinks he's so special she'll show him. Nobody is so special. Angela represents the realism of the race, which is always pointing out that wisdom, beauty, glory, courage in men are just vanities and her business is to beat down the man's legend about himself. That's why she and Horricker are finished, why she let that twerp in Mexico ball her fore and aft in front of Wharton, with who-knows-what-else thrown in free by her. In a spirit of participation."

"I didn't know that Horricker had such a presumptuous image of himself."

"Let's get back to that other matter. What else did the man do, did he shake the thing at you?"

"Not at all. But the subject is becoming unpleasant. He was warning me not to defend the poor old man he robbed. Not to inform the police. I had already tried to inform them."

"You, naturally, would feel sorry for those people he robs."

"It's ugly. Not that I have such a tender heart."

"You've probably seen too much. Weren't you invited to testify at the Eichmann trial?"

"I was approached. I didn't feel up to it."

"You wrote that article about that crazy character from Lodz—King Rumkowski."

"Yes."

"I often think a man's parts look expressive. Women's too. I think they're just about to say something, through those whiskers."

Sammler did not answer. Wallace sipped his whisky as a boy might sip Coca-Cola.

"Of course," Wallace said, "the blacks speak another language. A kid pleaded for his life—"

"What kid?"

"In the papers. A kid who was surrounded by a black gang of fourteen-year-olds. He begged them not to shoot, but they simply didn't understand his words. Literally not the same language. Not the same feelings. No comprehension. No common concepts. Out of reach."

I was begged, too. Sammler however did not say this.

"The child died?"

"The kid? After some days he died of the wound. But the boys didn't even know what he was saying."

"There is a scene in *War and Peace* I sometimes think about," said Sammler. "The French General Davout, who was very cruel, who was said, I think, to have torn out a man's whiskers by the roots, was sending people to the firing squad in Moscow, but when Pierre Bezhukov came up to him, they looked into each other's eyes. A human look was exchanged, and Pierre was spared. Tolstoy says you don't kill another human being with whom you have exchanged such a look."

"Oh, that's marvelous! What do you think?"

"I sympathize with such a desire for such a belief."

"You only sympathize."

"No, I sympathize deeply. I sympathize sadly. When men of genius think about humankind, they are almost forced to believe in this form of psychic unity. I wish it were so."

"Because they refuse to think themselves entirely exceptional. I see that. But you don't think this exchange of looks will work? Doesn't it happen?"

"Oh, it probably happens from time to time. Pierre Bezhukov was altogether lucky. Of course he was a person in a book. And of course life is a kind of luck, for the individual. Very booklike. But Pierre was exceptionally lucky to catch the eye of his executioner. I myself never knew it to work. No, I never saw it happen. It is a thing worth praying for. And it is based on something. It's not an arbitrary idea. It's based on the belief that there is the same truth in the heart of every human being, or a splash of God's own spirit, and that this is the richest thing we share in common. And up to a point I would agree. But though it's not an arbitrary idea, I wouldn't count on it."

"They say that you were in the grave once."

"Do they?"

"How was it?"

"How was it. Let us change the subject. We are already on the Cross County Highway. Emil is very fast."

"No traffic, this time of night. I had my life saved, one time. It was before New Rochelle. I cut school and roamed the park. The lagoon was frozen, but I fell through the ice. There was a Japanese type of bridge, and I was climbing the girders, underneath, and tumbled off. It was December, and the ice was gray. The snow was white. The water was black. I was hanging on to the ice, scared shitless, and my soul felt like a little marble rolling away, away. A bigger kid came and saved me. He was a truant, too, and he crawled out on the ice with a branch. I caught hold, and he dragged me out. Then we went to the men's toilet in the boathouse, and I stripped. He rubbed me with his sheepskin coat. I laid my clothes on the radiator, but they wouldn't dry. He said, 'Jeez kid, you're gonna catch hell.' My dear mother raised hell all right. She pulled my ears because my clothes were wet."

"Very good. She should have done it oftener."

"You know something? I agree. You're right. The memory is precious. It's much more vivid than chocolate cake, and much richer. But Uncle Sammler, the next day at school when I saw the kid I made up my mind to give him my allowance, which was ten cents."

"He took it?"

"He sure did."

"I like such stories. What did he say?"

"Not a word. He just nodded his head and took the dime. He stuck it in his pocket and went back to his bigger pals. I guess he felt he had earned it on the ice. It was his fair reward."

"I see you have these recollections."

"Well, I need them. Everybody needs his memories. They keep the wolf of insignificance from the door."

And all this will continue. It will simply continue. Another six billion years before the sun explodes. Six billion years of human life! It lames the heart to contemplate such a figure. Six billion years! What will become of us? Of the other species, yes, and of us? How will we ever make it? And when we have to abandon the earth, and leave this solar system for another, what a moving-day that will be. But by then humankind will have become very different. Evolution continues. Olaf Stapledon reckoned that each individual in future ages would be living thousands of years. The future person, a colossal figure, a beautiful green color, with a hand that had evolved into a kit of extraordinary instruments, tools strong and subtle, thumb and forefinger capable of exerting thousands of pounds of pressure. Each mind belonging to a marvelous analytical collective, thinking out its mathematics, its physics as part of a sublime whole. A race of semi-immortal giants, our green descendants, dear kin and brethren, inevitably containing still some of our bitter peculiarities as well as powers of spirit. The scientific revolution was only three hundred years old. Give it a million, give it a billion more. And God? Still hidden, even from this powerful mental brotherhood, still out of reach?

But now the Rolls was in the lanes. You could hear the new spring leaves brushing and stirring as the silver car passed. After many years, Sammler still did not know the way to Elya's house in the suburban woods, the small roads twisted so. But here was the building, half-timbered Tudor style, where the respectable surgeon and his homemaking wife had brought up two children, and played badminton on this pleasant grass. In 1947 as a refugee Sammler had been astonished at their playfulness—adults with rackets and shuttlecocks. The lawn now was lighted by the moon, which seemed to Sammler clean-shaven; the gravel, fine, white, and small, made an amiable sound of grinding under the tires. The elms were thick, old—older than the combined ages of all the Gruners. Animal eyes appeared in the headlights, or beveled reflectors set out on the borders of paths shone: mouse, mole, woodchuck, cat, or glass bits peering from grass and bush. There were no lighted windows. Emil turned his brights on the front door. Wallace, as he hurried out, spilled his whisky on the carpet. Sammler groped for the glass and gave it to the chauffeur, explaining, "This fell." Then he followed Wallace over the rustling gravel.

As soon as Sammler entered, Emil backed away to the garage. That left only moonlight in the rooms. A house of misconceived purposes, as it had always seemed to Sammler, where nothing really functioned except the mechanical appliances. But Gruner had always taken care of it conscientiously, especially since the death of his wife, in a memorial spirit. Just as Margotte did for Ussher Arkin. That was fresh gravel in the drive. As soon as winter ended, Gruner ordered it laid down. The moon rinsed the curtains and foamed like peroxide on the nap of the white heavy carpets.

"Wallace?" Sammler believed he heard him below in the cellar. If he didn't turn on the lights, it was because he didn't want Sammler to know his movements. The poor fellow was demented. Mr. Sammler, forced by life, by fate, by what you like, to be disinterested, to think to the best of his ability on universal lines, was not about to stoop to policing Wallace in his father's house, to prevent him from digging out money—real or imaginary criminal abortion dollars.

Examining the kitchen, Sammler found no evidence that anyone had lately been here. The cupboards were shut, the stainless-steel sink and counters dry. As in a model exhibit. Cups on their hooks, none missing. But at the bottom of the garbage pail lined with a brown paper bag was an empty tuna-fish can; water-packed, Geisha brand, freshly fish-smelly. Sammler held it to his nose. Aha! Had someone lunched? Emil the chauffeur, perhaps? Or Wallace himself, straight from the can without vinegar or dressing? Wallace would have left crumbs on the counter, and the soiled fork, disorderly signs of eating. Sammler put back the cut tin circle, released the pedal of the pail, and went to the living room. There he felt the chain mail of the fire screen, for Shula was fond of fires. It was cool. But the evening was warm. This proved nothing.

He then went on to the second floor, recalling how he and she had played hide-and-go-seek in London thirty-five years ago. He had been good at it, talking aloud to himself. "Is Shula in this broom closet? Let me see. Where can she be? She is not in the broom closet. How mystifying! Is she under the bed? No. My, what a clever little girl. How well she hides herself. She's simply disappeared." While the child, just five years old, thrilling with game fever, positively white, crouched behind the brass scuttle where he pretended not to see her, her bottom near the floor, her large kinky head with the small red bow—a whole life there. Melancholy. Even if there hadn't been the war.

However, theft! That was serious. And theft of intellectual property—even worse. And in the dark he yielded somewhat to elderly weakness. Too old for this. Toiling along the banister in the fatiguing luxury of the carpet. He belonged at the hospital. An old relative in the waiting-room. Much more appropriate. On the second floor, the bedrooms. He moved cautiously in darkness. In the house-bound air were old odors of soap and eau de cologne. No one had lately ventilated the place.

A sound of water reached him, a slight movement in a full tub. A wallow. His hand reached in, wrist bent, sliding over the tile wall until he found the electric switch. In the light he saw Shula trying to cover her breasts with a washcloth. The enormous tub was only half occupied by her short body. The soles of her white feet, he saw, the black female triangle, and the white swellings with large rings of purplish brown. The veins. Yes, yes, she belonged to the club. The gender club. This was a female. That was a male. Much difference it could make to him.

"Father. Please. Please turn off the light."

"Nonsense. I'll wait in the bedroom. Wrap yourself up. Be quick about it."

He sat in Angela's old room. When she was a young girl. Or an apprentice whore. Well, people went to the wars. They took what weapons they had, and they advanced toward the front.

Sammler sat in a peach cretonne boudoir chair. Hearing no movements in the bathroom, he called, "I'm waiting," and she surged up from the water. He heard her feet, solid, rapid. In walking she always brushed objects with her body. She never simply walked. She touched things and claimed them. As property. Then she entered, quick-footed, wearing a man's woolen robe and a towel on her head, and she seemed to be gasping, shocked at being seen in the tub by her father.

"Well, where is it?"

"Daddy!"

"No. I am the one that is shocked, not you. Where is that document you have stolen twice?"

"It was not stealing."

"Other people may make new rules as they go along, but I will not, and you will not put me in that position. I was about to return the manuscript to Dr. Lal, and it was taken from my desk. Just as it was taken from his hands. Same method."

"That is not the way to look at it. But don't excite yourself too much."

"After all this, don't protect my heart or hint that I am an old man who may fall dead of apoplexy. You won't get away with anything like that. Now, where is this object?"

"It's really perfectly safe." She began to speak Polish. Severe, he denied her permission to speak that language. She was trying to invoke her terrible times of hiding—the convent, the hospital, the contagious ward when the German searching party came.

"None of that. Answer in English. Have you brought it here?"

"I've had a copy made. Daddy, I went to Mr. Widick's office . . ."

Sammler held himself in. Since he wouldn't allow her to speak Polish she was lapsing into something else, childishness. With small-girl softness, she lowered her mature, already fully middle-aged face. She was now meeting his look from one side, with only the one expanded childlike eye, and her chin shyly, slyly sinking toward the woolen robe.

"Yes? Well, what did you do in Mr. Widick's office?"

"He has one of those duplicating machines. I've used it for Cousin Elya. And Mr. Widick never goes home. He must hate home. He's always at the office, so I called and asked to use the machine, and he said, 'Sure.' I Xeroxed the whole thing."

"For me?"

"Or for Dr. Lal."

"You thought I might want the original?"

"If it's more convenient for you."

"Now, what have you done with these manuscripts?"

"I locked them in two lockers in Grand Central Station."

"In Grand Central. Good God. You have the keys, or have you lost the keys?"

"I have them, Father."

"Where are they?"

Shula was prepared for him. She produced two stamped and sealed envelopes. One was addressed to him, the other to Dr. Govinda Lal at Butler Hall.

"You were going to send these through the mails? The locker is for twenty-four hours only. These might take a week to arrive. Then what? And did you write down the numbers of the lockers? No. Then how would one know where they were if the letters got lost? You'd have to file a claim and prove ownership, authorship. Enough to drive a man out of his mind."

"Don't scold so hard. I did everything for you. You had stolen property in your house. The detective said it was stolen property, and anybody who had it was a receiver of stolen property."

"From now on, do me no such favors. It can't even be discussed with you. You seem to have no grasp of the matter."

"I brought it to you to show my faith in the memoir. I wanted to remind you how important it is. Sometimes you yourself forget. As if H. G. Wells were nothing so special. Well, maybe not to you, but to a great many people H. G. Wells is still important and very very special. I've been waiting for you to finish, and be reviewed in the papers. I wanted to see my father's picture in the bookshops, instead of all those foolish faces and unimportant stupid books."

The soiled rental keys in the envelopes. Mr. Sammler considered them. As well as exasperating, troubling, she was of course sadly amusing. If the lockers contained the manuscripts and not wads of paper in portfolios. No, he thought not. She was only a bit crazy. His poor child. A creature caused by him and adrift in a formless, boundless world. How had she come to be like this? Perhaps the inward, the intimate, the dear life—the thing that is oneself from earliest days—when it first learns of death is often crazed. Here magical powers must help, assuage, console, and for a woman, those marvelous powers so often are the powers of a man. As, Antony dying, Cleopatra cried she wouldn't abide in this dull world which "in thy absence is No better than a sty." And? A sty, and? He now remembered the end, fit for this night. "There is nothing left remarkable Beneath the visiting moon."

And he was supposed to be the remarkable thing, he who sitting on this glazed slipcover felt under him the tedium of its peach color and its fat red flowers. Such an article, meant to oppress and afflict the soul, was even now succeeding. He had remained touchable, vulnerable to trifles. But Mr. Sammler still received primordial messages too. And the immediate basic message was that she, this woman with her sexual female form plain in the tight wrapping of the woolen robe (especially beneath the waist, where a thing was to make a lover gasp), this mature woman should not now be asking that her daddy make sublunary objects remarkable. For one thing, *he* never bestrode the world like a Colossus with armies and navies, dropping coronets from his pockets. He was only an old Jew whom they had hacked at, shot at, but missed killing somehow, murdering everyone else with their blasts. In their peculiar transformation: a people changed into uniform, masked in military cloth and helmets, and coming with machinery for the purpose of murdering boys, girls, men, women, making blood run, burying, and finally exhuming and burning rotten corpses. Man is a killer. Man has a moral nature. The anomaly can be resolved by insanity only, by insane dreams in which delusions of consciousness are maintained by organization, in states of mad perdition clinging to forms of business administration. Making it "government work." All of that! But in this world he, now *he,* dear God! was to supply his unhinged, wavering-witted daughter with high aims. And of course in Shula's view he had been getting too delicate for earthly life, too absorbed in unshared universals, excluding her. And by extravagance, by animal histrionics, by papers pinched, by goofy business with shopping bags, trash-basket neuroses, exotic heartburn cookery she wished to implicate him and bring him back, to bind him and keep him in the world beside her. Some world! Some her! Their elevation would be joint elevation. She would back him, and he would accomplish great things in the world of culture. For she was *kulturnaya.* Shula was so *kulturnaya.* Nothing was more suitable than this philistine Russian word. *Kulturny.* She might creep down on her knees and pray like a Christian; she might pull that on her father; she might crawl into dark confession boxes; she might run to Father Robles and invoke Christian protection against his Jewish anger; but in her nutty devotion to culture she couldn't have been more Jewish.

"Very well, my photograph in bookshops. A fine idea. Excellent. But stealing . . . ?"

"It wasn't actually stealing."

"Well, what word do you prefer, and what difference does it make? Like the old joke: what more do I learn about a horse if I know that in Latin it is called *equus*?"

"But I'm not a thief."

"Very well. In your mind you're not a thief. Only in fact."

"I thought if you were really, really serious about H. G. Wells you would have to know if he predicted accurately about the moon, or Mars, and that you'd pay any price to have the latest, most up-to-date scientific information. A creative person wouldn't stop at anything. For the creative there are no crimes. And aren't you a creative person?"

It seemed to Sammler that inside him (*faute de mieux,* in his mind) was a field in which many hunters at cross-purposes were firing bird shot at a feather apparition assumed to be a bird. Shula had meant to set him a test. Was he the real thing or wasn't he? Was he creative, a force of nature, a true original, or not? Yes, it was a fitness test, and this was very American of Shula. Did an American exist who was not morally didactic? Was there any crime committed which didn't punish the victim for "the greater good"? Was there any sinner who did not sin *pro bono publico*? So great was the evil of helpfulness, and so immense the liberal spirit of explanation. The psychopathology of teaching in the United States. So, then, was Papa a true creative intransigent—capable of bold theft for the sake of the memoir? Could he risk all for H. G.?

"Truthfully, my child, have you ever read a book of Wells'?"

"Yes, I have."

"Tell me—but the truth, just between you and me."

"I read one book, Father."

"One? One book by Wells is like trying to bathe in a single wave. What was the book?"

"It was about God."

"*God the Invisible King*?"

"That's the one."

"Did you finish it?"

"No."

"Neither did I."

"Oh, Father—you?"

"I just couldn't read it. Human evolution with God as

Intelligence. I soon saw the point, then the rest was tedious, garrulous."

"But it was *so* intelligent. I read a few pages and was so thrilled. I knew he was a great man, even if I couldn't read the whole book. You know I can't read an entire book. I'm too restless. But you've read all his other books."

"No one could read them all. I've read many. Probably too many."

Smiling, Sammler emptied the envelopes and tossed the crumpled ball into Angela's wastepaper basket of gilded Florentine leather. Acquired by her mother on a tour. The keys he dropped into his pocket, leaning far to one side in the boudoir chair to get at the flap.

Shula, observing silently, was smiling also, holding her wrists with her fingers, forearms crossing on her bosom to keep the robe from falling open. Sammler, despite the washrag, had seen the brown-purple tips, enriched with salient veins. At the corner of her mouth, now that she had done her mischief, there was a chaste twist of achievement. The flat black kinked hair was covered up, towel-swathed, except, as always, for the kosher sidelocks escaping at her ears. And smiling as if she had eaten a plateful of divine forbidden soup, and what was to be done about it now that it was down? At the back, the white nape of her neck was strong. Biological strength. Below the neck there was a mature dorsal hump. A grown woman. But the arms and legs were not proportionate. His only begotten child. He never doubted that she performed acts originating far beyond, in the past, of unconscious ancestral origin. He was aware how true this was of himself. Especially in religious matters. She was a praying nut, but he, after all, was given to praying, too, often addressed God. Just now he asked to understand why he so much loved this fool woman with the thick, uselessly sensual cream skin, the painted mouth, and that towel turban.

"Shula, I know you did this for me—"

"You are more important than that man, Father. You needed it."

"But from now on, don't use me as an excuse. For your exploits . . ."

"We nearly lost you in Israel, in that war. I was afraid you wouldn't finish your lifework."

"Nonsense, Shula. What lifework! And killed? There? The finest death I could imagine. Besides, there was no danger. Ridiculous!"

Shula stood up. "I hear wheels," she said. "Somebody just drove up."

He had not heard. She had keen senses. Idiot ingenuous animal, she had ears like a fox. Rising so abrupt, standing silent to listen, queenly, dim-witted, alert. And the white feet. Her feet had not been disfigured by fashionable shoes.

"It probably is Emil."

"No, it's not Emil. I must get dressed."

She ran from the room.

Sammler went downstairs wondering where Wallace had gone. The doorbell began to chime and continued chiming. Margotte didn't know how to ring, when to stop pushing a button. He could see her, through the long narrow pane, in her straw hat, and Professor V. Govinda Lal was with her.

"We hired a Hertz car," she said. "The Professor couldn't bear to wait. We talked to Father Robles on the phone. He hadn't seen Shula in days."

"Professor Lal. Imperial College. Biophysics."

"I am Shula's father."

There were small bows, a handshake.

"We can sit in the living room. Shall I make a pot of coffee? Is Shula here?" said Margotte.

"She is."

"And my manuscript?" said Lal. *"The Future of the Moon?"*

"Safe," said Sammler. "Not actually in the house, but locked up safely. I have the keys. Professor Lal, please accept my apologies. My daughter has behaved very badly. Caused you pain."

Sammler under the foyer light saw the shocked and disappointed face of Lal: brown cheeks, black hair, neat, vivid, and gracefully parted, and a huge spreading beard. The inadequacy of words—the need for several simultaneous languages to address all parts of the mind at once, especially those parts left free by meager communication, functioning furiously on their own. Instead, as one were to smoke ten cigarettes simultaneously; while also drinking whisky; while also being sexually engaged with three or four other persons; while hearing bands of music; while receiving scientific notations—thus to capacity *engagé* . . . the boundlessness, the pressure of modern expectations.

Lal shouted, "Dear me! This is intolerable! Intolerable! Why am I sent this punishment!"

"Pour Dr. Lal a brandy, Margotte."

"I do not drink! I do not drink!"

In the dark setting of his beard the teeth were clenched. Then, aware of his own loudness, he said in more appropriate tones, "Normally I do not drink."

"But, Dr. Lal, you recommended beer on the moon. However—*I* am illogical. Go on, go on, Margotte, don't just look solicitous. Get the brandy. I'll have some if he won't. You know where the liquor is. Bring two glasses. Now, Professor, the anxiety will soon be over."

The living room was what they called "sunken." You had to descend. A well, a pool, a tank of carpet. It was furnished or decorated with professional completeness, densely arranged. This, if you allowed it to, gave pain. Sammler had known the late Mrs. Gruner's decorator. Or stultifier. Croze. Croze was petit, but had the strength of an art personality. He stood like a thrush. His little belly came far forward and lifted his trousers well above the ankles. His face had lovely color, his hair was barbered to the shapely little head, he had a rosebud mouth, and after you shook hands with Croze, your own hand was all day perfumed. He was creative. Capable of criminal acts, probably. All this was his creation. Here many boring hours had occurred, especially after family dinners. It wouldn't be a bad custom to send these furnishings into the tomb with the deceased, Egyptian style. However, here they all were, these spoils of silk, leather, glass, and antique wood. Here Sammler led the hairy Dr. Lal, a small man, very dark. Not black, sharp-nosed, the Dravidian type, dolichocephalic, but round-featured. Probably from Punjab. He had thin and hairy wrists, ankles, legs. He was a dandy. A macaroni (Sammler could not surrender the old words it had given him so much pleasure in Cracow to pick up from eighteenth-century books). Yes Govinda was a beau. He was also sensitive, intelligent, nervous, keen, a handsome, elegant, birdy man. One major incongruity: the round face enlarged by soft but strong beard. Behind, thin shoulder blades stuck through the linen blazer. He had a stoop.

"Where is your daughter, may I ask?"

"Coming down. I will ask Margotte to fetch her. She was frightened by your detective."

"He was clever to find her at all. Ingenious work. He did his job."

"No doubt, but with my daughter Pinkerton methods did not apply. Because of Poland, you see, and the war—police. She was hidden. So she panicked. Too bad you have had to suffer for it. But what can one do if she is somewhat . . . ?"

"Psycho?"

"That's putting it strongly. She's not entirely out of touch. She made a copy of your manuscript, and she took two lockers in Grand Central Station for copy and original. Here are the keys."

Lal's hand, long and thin, accepted them. "How can I be sure it's really there, my book?" he said.

"Dr. Lal, I know my daughter. I feel quite certain. Safe in fireproof steel. In fact, I'm glad she didn't bring the book on the train. She might have lost it—forgotten it on the seat. Grand Central is well lighted, policed, and even if one lock were to be picked by thieves, there would still be the other. Have no further anxiety. I see you are on edge. You can consider this disagreeable misadventure over. The manuscript is safe."

"Sir, I hope so."

"Let us have a sip of brandy. We have had some trying days."

"Agonizing. Somehow the kind of terror I anticipated in America. My first visit. I had an intuition."

"Has America been all like that?"

"Not altogether. But almost."

Noisy in the kitchen, Margotte was opening cans, taking

down bowls, slamming the icebox, clattering the flatware. Margotte's household doings were in continual transmission.

"I could take the train to New York," said Lal.

"Margotte can't drive. What will you do with the Hertz car?"

"Oh, damn! The car! Bloody machines!"

"I regret I can't drive," Sammler said. "Not to drive is the latest snobbery, I am told. But I am innocent of that. It is my eyesight."

"I'd have to come back for Mrs. Arkin."

"You might surrender your Hertz in New Rochelle, but I doubt that they are open at night. There must be a Penn Central timetable. However, it's close to midnight. We could ask Wallace to take you to the train, if he hasn't slipped out the back way—Wallace Gruner," he explained. "We are in the Gruner house. My relative—my nephew by a half-sister. But first let us have the supper Margotte is preparing. What you said before interested me, your presentiments about the U.S.? Twenty-two years ago, my own arrival was a relief."

"Of course in a sense the whole world is now U.S. Inescapable," said Govinda Lal. "It's like a big crow that has snatched our future from the nest, and we, the rest, are like little finches in pursuit trying to peck it. However, the Apollo flights are American. I have been employed by NASA. On other research. But this is where my ideas will count, if they are any use. . . . If I sound strange, excuse me. I've been distressed."

"With good reason. My daughter did you a real injury."

"I am beginning to feel easier. I don't think any hard feelings will remain."

Through the tinted lens and while breathing brandy

fumes, Sammler provisionally approved of Govinda Lal, who reminded him in some ways of Ussher Arkin. Very often, oftener than he consciously knew, and vividly, he thought of Ussher underground, in this or that posture, of this or that color or physical condition. As he thought of Antonina, his wife. So far as he knew the enormous grave had never been touched again. From which he himself, scratching dirt, pushing the corpses, came out choked with blood, and crept away on his belly. This preoccupation therefore was only to be expected.

Now Margotte was chopping onions in a bowl. Something to eat. Life in its lighted droplet cells continued its enactments. Poor Ussher in that plane at the Cincinnati airport. Sammler missed him and acknowledged that he had moved into the apartment with Margotte because of the contact with Ussher it afforded.

But he noted some of the same qualities, Arkin's qualities, in this very different, duskier, smaller, bushier Lal, whose wrist was no wider than a ruler.

Then Shula-Slawa came down the stairs. Lal, who saw her first, had an expression which made Sammler immediately turn. She had dressed herself in a sari, or something like it, had found a piece of Indian material in a drawer. It couldn't have been correctly wrapped. It also covered her head. Especially at the bust there was an error. (Sammler with increased concern this evening for the sensitivity of that area; if there was danger of exposure or of hurt, he felt it in his own organs.) He wasn't sure that she was wearing undergarments. No, there was no *Büstenhalter*. She was extremely white—citrus-thick skin, cream cheeks—and her lips, looking fuller and softer than ever, were painted a peculiar orange color. Like the Neapolitan cyclamens Sammler had admired in the botanical garden. Also, she wore false eyelashes. On her forehead was a Hindu spot made with the lipstick. Exactly where the Ash Wednesday smudge had been. The general idea was to charm and appease this angry Lal. Her eyes as she hurried, without looking, into the well of the room were heated, and in the old man's words to himself, kookily dilated, sensuality-bent. Though ladylike, she made too many gestures, coming forward too much, wildly overprompt, having too much by far to say.

"Professor Lal!"

"My daughter."

"Yes, so I thought."

"I am sorry. So terribly sorry, Dr. Lal. There was a misunderstanding. You were surrounded by people. You must have thought you were just letting me look at the manuscript. But I thought you were letting me take it home to my father. As I said, you remember? That he was writing the book about H. G. Wells?"

"Wells? No. But my impression is that he is very obsolete."

"Still, for the sake of science, of science, and for the sake of literature and history, because my father is writing this important history, and you see I help him in his intellectual cultural work. There's nobody else to do it. I never meant to make trouble."

No. Not trouble. Only to dig a pit and cover it with brushwood, and when a man fell into it to lie flat on the ground and converse with him amorously. For Sammler now suspected that she had run away with *The Future of the Moon* in order to create this very opportunity, this meeting. Were he and Wells really secondary, then? Was it really done to provoke interest? Wasn't that a familiar stratagem? To him, Sammler remembered, women used sometimes to act insolent to get his attention and say stinging things imagining that it made them fascinating. Was this why Shula had taken the book? Out of female seductiveness? One species: but the sexes like two different savage tribes. In full paint. Surprising and shocking each other in the bush. This Govinda, this light spry whiskered dark frail, flying sort of a man—an intellectual. And intellectuals she was mad for. They kept the world remarkable beneath that visiting moon. They kindled up her womb. Even Eisen, perhaps, to recover her esteem (among other reasons), had left the foundry and turned artist. Had probably lost track of the original motive, to show that he was, like her father, a man of culture. And now he was a painter. Poor Eisen.

But Shula was sitting very close to Lal on the sofa, almost taking him by the hand, by the arm, as if bent upon having a touch of his limbs. She was assuring him that she had reproduced his manuscript with great care. She worried lest the Xerox take away the ink and wipe the pages blank. She did page one dying of anxiety. "Such a special ink you use, and what if there should be a bad reaction. I would have died." But it worked beautifully. Mr. Widick said it was lovely copying. And it was in the two lockers. The copy was in a legal binder. Mr. Widick said you could even leave ransom money in Grand Central. Perfectly safe. Shula wanted Govinda Lal to see that the orange circle between the eyes had lunar significance. She kept tilting her face, offering her brow.

"Now, Shula, my dear," said Sammler. "Margotte needs help in the kitchen. Go and help her."

"Oh, Father." She tried, speaking aside in Polish, to tell him she wished to stay.

"Shula! Go! Go on now—go!"

As she obeyed, her cheeks had a hot and bitter look. Before Lal she wanted to show filial submission, but her behind was huffy as she went.

"I would never have recognized, never have identified her," said Lal.

"Yes? Without the wig. She often affects a wig."

He stopped. Govinda was thinking. Presumably about the recovery of his work from the locker. Yes. He felt his blazer pockets from beneath, making certain of the keys.

"You are Polish?" he said.

"I was Polish."

"Artur?"

"Yes. Like Schopenhauer, whom my mother read. Arthur, at that period, not very Jewish, was the most international, enlightened name you could give a boy. The same in all languages. But Schopenhauer didn't care for Jews. He called them vulgar optimists. Optimists? Living near the crater of Vesuvius, it is better to be an optimist. On my sixteenth birthday my mother gave me *The World as Will and Idea.* Naturally it was an agreeable compliment that I could be so serious and deep. Like the great Arthur. So I studied the system, and I still remember it. I learned that only Ideas are not overpowered by the Will—the cosmic force, the Will, which drives all things. A blinding power. The inner creative fury of the world. What we see are only its manifestations. Like Hindu philosophy—Maya, the veil of appearances that hangs over all human experience. Yes, and come to think of it, according to Schopenhauer, the seat of the Will in human beings is . . ."

"Where is it?"

"The organs of sex are the seat of the Will."

The thief in the lobby agreed. He took out the instrument

of the Will. He drew aside not the veil of Maya itself but one of its forehangings and showed Sammler his metaphysical warrant.

"And you were a friend of the famous H. G. Wells—that much is true, isn't it?"

"I don't like to claim the friendship of a man who is not alive to affirm or deny it, but at one time, when he was in his seventies, I saw him often."

"Ah, then you must have lived in London."

"So we did, in Woburn Square near the British Museum. I took walks with the old man. In those days my own ideas didn't amount to much so I listened to his. Scientific humanism, faith in an emancipated future, in active benevolence, in reason, in civilization. Not popular ideas at the moment. Of course we have civilization but it is so disliked. I think you understand what I mean, Professor Lal."

"I believe I do, yes."

"Still, you know, Schopenhauer would not have called Wells a vulgar optimist. Wells had many dark thoughts. Take a book like *The War of the Worlds*. There the Martians come to get rid of mankind. They treat our species as Americans treated the bison and other animals, or for that matter the American Indians. Extermination."

"Ah, extermination. I assume you have personal acquaintance with the phenomenon?"

"I do have some, yes."

"Indeed?" said Lal. "I have seen some of it myself. As a Punjabi."

"You *are* a Punjabi?"

"Yes, and in nineteen forty-seven studying at the University in Calcutta and present at the terrible riots, the fighting of Hindus and Moslems. Since called the great Calcutta killing. I am afraid I have seen homicidal maniacs."

"Ah."

"Yes, and slaying with loaded sticks and sharp iron bars. And the corpses. Rape, arson, looting."

"I see." Sammler looked at him. An intelligent and sensitive man, this was, with an expressive face. Of course such expressiveness was sometimes a sign of subjectivity and of inward mental habits. Not an outgoing imagination. He was beginning to think, however, that this Lal was, like Ussher Arkin, a man he could talk to. "Then it is not a theoretical matter to you. Nor to me. But excellent good-hearted gentlemen, Mr. Arnold Bennett, Mr. H. G. Wells, lunching at the Savoy . . . Olympians of lowerclass origin. So nice. So serious. So English, Mr. Wells. I was flattered to be chosen to listen to his monologues. I was also fond of him. Of course since Poland, nineteen thirty-nine, my judgments are different. Altered. Like my eyesight. I see you trying to observe what is behind these tinted glasses. No, no, that's quite all right. One eye is functioning. Like the old saying about the one-eyed being King in the Country of the Blind. Wells wrote a story around this. Not a good story. Anyway, I am not in the Country of the Blind, but only one-eyed. As for Wells . . . he was a writer. He wrote and wrote and wrote."

Sammler thought that Govinda was about to speak. When he paused, several waves of silence passed, containing tacit questions: You? No, you, sir: You speak. Lal was listening. The sensitivity of a hairy creature; the animal brown of his eyes; the good breeding of his attentive posture.

"You wish me to say more about Wells, since Wells is in a way behind all this?"

"Would you, kindly?" said Lal. "You have doubts about the value of Wells's writing."

"Yes, of course I have. Grave doubts. Through universal education and cheap printing poor boys have become rich and powerful. Dickens, rich. Shaw, also. He boasted that reading Karl Marx made a man of him. I don't know about that, but Marxism for the great public made him a millionaire. If you wrote for an elite, like Proust, you did not become rich, but if your theme was social justice and your ideas were radical you were rewarded by wealth, fame, and influence."

"Most interesting."

"Do you find it so? Excuse me, I am heavy-hearted this evening. Both heavy-hearted and talkative. And when I meet someone I like, I am apt to be garrulous at first."

"No, no, please continue this explanation."

"Explanation? I have an objection to extended explanations. There are too many. This makes the mental life of mankind ungovernable. But I have thought about the Wells matter—the Shaw matter, and about people like Marx, Jean Jacques Rousseau, Marat, Saint-Just, powerful speakers, writers, starting out with no capital but mental capital and achieving an immense influence. And all the rest, little lawyers, readers, bluffers, pamphleteers, amateur scientists, bohemians, librettists, fortune tellers, charlatans, outcasts, buffoons. A crazy provincial lawyer demanding the head of the King, and getting it, too. In the name of the people. Or Marx, a student, a fellow from the University, writing books which overwhelm the world. He was really an excellent journalist and publicist. As I was a journalist myself, I am a judge of his ability. Like many journalists, he made things up out of other newspaper articles, the European press, but he made them up extremely well, writing about India or the American Civil War, matters of which he actually knew nothing. But he was marvelously shrewd, a guesser of genius, a powerful polemicist and rhetorician. His ideological hashish was very potent. Anyhow, you see what I mean—people become authoritative and plebeians of genius elevate themselves first to nobility and then to universal glory, and all because they had what all poor children got from literacy: the ABCs, the dictionary, the grammar books, the classics. Until, soaring from their slums or their little petit-bourgeois parlors, they were addressing worldwide millions. These are the people who set the terms, who make up the discourse, and then history follows their words. Think of the wars and revolutions we have been scribbled into."

"The Indian press had much responsibility for those riots, certainly," said Lal.

"One thing in Wells's favor was that because of personal disappointments he at least did not demand the sacrifice of civilization. He did not become a cult-figure, a royal personality, a grand art-hero or activist leader. He did not feel disgraced by words. Many did and do."

"Meaning what, sir?"

"Well you see," said Mr. Sammler, "in the great bourgeois period, writers became aristocrats. And having become aristocrats through their skill in words, they felt obliged to go into action. Evidently it's a disgrace for true nobility to substitute words for acts. You can see this in the career of Monsieur Malraux, or Monsieur Sartre. You can see it much farther back in Hamlet when he feels that humiliation, Dr. Lal, saying, 'I . . . must like a whore unpack my heart with words.' "

" 'And fall a-cursing like a very drab.' "

"Yes, that is the full quotation. Or to Polonius, 'Words, words, words.' Words are for the elderly, or for the young who are old-in-heart. Of course this is the condition of a prince whose father has been murdered. But when people out of a contempt for impotence and paralyzed *talk* throw themselves into noble actions, do they know what they are doing? When they begin to call for blood, and advocate terror, or proclaim a general egg-breaking to make a great historical omelet, do they know what they are calling for? When they have struck a mirror with a hammer, aiming to repair it, can they put the fragments together again? Well, Dr. Lal, I am not sure what good this examination or rebuke can do. It is not as if I were certain that human beings can be controlled at any level of complexity. I would not swear that mankind was governable. But Wells was inclined to believe that it was. He thought, most of the time, that the minority civilization could be transmitted to the great masses, and that orderly conditions for this transmission were possible. Decent, British-style, Victorian-Edwardian, nonoutcast, nonlunatic, *grateful* conditions. But in World War Two he despaired. He compared humankind to rats in a sack, desperately struggling and biting. Indeed it was ratlike and sacklike. Indeed so. But now I have exhausted my interest in Wells. Yours too, I hope, Dr. Lal."

"Ah, you did know the man well," said Lal. "And how clearly you put things. You are a first-rate condenser. I wish I had your talent. I lacked it sorely when I wrote my book."

"Your book, what I had time to read of it, is very clear."

"I hope you will read it all. Excuse me, Mr. Sammler, I am confused. I don't know quite where Mrs. Arkin has brought me, or where we are. You explained, but I did not follow."

"This is Westchester County, not far from New Rochelle, and the house of my nephew, Dr. Arnold Elya Gruner. At the moment, he is in the hospital."

"I see. Is he very sick?"

"There is an escape of blood in the brain."

"An aneurysm. It can't be reached for surgery?"

"It can't be reached."

"Dear, dear. And you are dreadfully disturbed."

"He will die in a day or two. He is dying. A good man. He brought us from a DP camp, Shula and me, and for twenty-two years he has taken care of us with kindness. Twenty-two years without a day of neglect, without a single irascible word."

"A gentleman."

"Yes, a gentleman. You can see that my daughter and I are not very competent. I did some journalism, until about fifteen years ago. It was never much. Recently I wrote a Polish report on the war in Israel. But it was Dr. Gruner who paid my way."

"He simply let you be a kind of philosopher?"

"If that is what I am. I am familiar with many explanations of things. To tell the truth, I am tired of most of them."

"Ah, you have an eschatological point of view, then. How interesting."

Sammler, not much caring for the word "eschatological," shrugged. "You think we should go into space, Dr. Lal?"

"You are very sad about your nephew. Perhaps you would prefer not to talk."

"Once you begin talking, once the mind takes to this way of turning, it keeps turning, and it dips through all events. And perhaps it makes matters slightly more tolerable to let it turn. Though I can't see why they should be tolerable. It is really a frightful moment. But what can one do? The thoughts continue turning."

"Like a Ferris wheel," said fragile, black-bearded Govinda

Lal. "I should say that I have done work for Worldwide Technics, in Connecticut. Mine are highly sophisticated and theoretical assignments having to do with order in biological systems, how complex mechanisms reproduce themselves. Though it will not greatly signify to you, I am associated with the bang-bang hypothesis, related to the firing of simultaneous impulses, atomic theories of cellular conductivity. As you mentioned Rousseau, man may or may not have been born free. But I can say with assurance that he would not exist without his atomistic chains. I do hope you like my jokes. I enjoy your wit. If not mutual, that would be too bad. I refer to those chain structures of the cell. These are matters of order, Mr. Sammler. Though I have not the full blueprint to present. I am not yet that universal genius. Ha, ha! In earnest, however, biological science is in an extraordinary state of progress. Oh, it is lovely, it is so beautiful! To participate is a privilege. This chemical order, which is a fundamental of life, is of great beauty. Oh, yes, very great. And what a high privilege! It occurred to me as you were speaking of another matter that to desire to live without order is to desire to turn from the fundamental biological governing principle. Which is widely presumed to be there only to free us, a platform for impulse. Are we crazy, or what? From order, from governing principle, the human being can tear himself to express his immense privilege of sheer liberty or unaccountability of impulse. The biological fundamentals are like the peasantry, the whole individual considering himself to be a prince. It is the *cigale* and the *fourmi.* The ant was once the hero, but now the grasshopper is the whole show. My father taught me maths and French. The chief anxiety of my father's life was that his students would cut up the *Encyclopedia Britannica* with razors and take the articles with them for home perusal. He was a simple person. Because of him, I have loved French literature. First in Calcutta, and then in Manchester, I studied it until my scientific interests matured. But as to your question about space. There is, of course, much objection to these expeditions. Accusation that it is money taken from school, slum, and so on, of course. Just as the Pentagon money is withheld from social improvements. What nonsense! It is propaganda by the social-science bureaucracy. *They* would hog the funds. Besides, money alone does not necessarily make the difference, does it? I think not. The Americans have always been reckless spenders. Bad, no doubt, but there is such a thing as fruitful *gaspillage*. Wastefulness can be justified if it permits inventiveness, originality, adventure. Unfortunately, the results are mostly and usually corrupt, making vile profits, playboy recreations, and building reactionary fortunes. As far as Washington is concerned, a moon expedition no doubt is superb PR. It is show biz. My slang may not be current." The rich and Oriental voice was very pleasing.

"I am not a good authority."

"You know, however, what I have in mind. Circuses. Dazzlement. The U.S. becoming the greatest dispenser of science-fiction entertainments. As far as the organizers and engineers are concerned, it is a vast opportunity, but that is not of high theoretical value. Still, at the same time something serious happens within. The soul most certainly feels the grandeur of this achievement. Not to go where one can go may be stunting. I believe the soul feels it, and therefore it is a necessity. It may introduce new sobriety. Naturally the technology will impress minds more than the personalities. The astronauts may not seem so very heroic. More like superchimpanzees. Especially if they do not express themselves beautifully. But after all, this is the function of poets. If any. But even the technicians I venture to guess will be ennobled. But do you agree, sir, that we should go into space?"

"Well, why not? Up to a point, yes. Although I don't think it can be rationally justified."

"Why not? I can think of many justifications. I see it as a rational necessity. You should have finished my book."

"Then I would have found the irresistible proof?" Sammler smiled through the tinted glasses, and the blind eye attempted to participate. In the old black and neat suit, his stiff and slender body upright and his fingers, which trembled strongly under strain, lightly holding his knees. A cigarette (he smoked only three or four a day) burned between his awkward hairy knuckles.

"I simply mean you would be acquainted with my argument, which I base in part on U.S. history. After 1776 there was a continent to expand into, and this space absorbed all the mistakes. Of course I am not a historian. But if one cannot make bold guesses, one will have to surrender all to the experts. Europe after 1789 did not have the space for its mistakes. Result: war and revolution, with the revolutions ending up in the hands of the madmen."

"De Maistre said that."

"Did he? I don't know much about him."

"It may be enough to know that he agrees. Revolutions do end up in the hands of madmen. Of course there are always enough madmen for every purpose. Besides, if the power is great enough, it will make its own madmen by its own pressure. Power certainly corrupts, but that statement is humanly incomplete. Isn't it too abstract? What should certainly be added is the specific truth that having power destroys the sanity of the powerful. It allows their irrationalities to leave the sphere of dreams and come into the real world. But there—excuse me. I am no psychologist. As you say, however, one must be allowed to make guesses."

"Perhaps it is natural that an Indian should be supersensitive to a surplus of humanity. Calcutta is so teeming, so volcanic. A Chinese would be similarly sensitive. Any nation of vast multitudes. We are crowded in, packed in, now, and human beings must feel that there is a way out, and that the intellectual power and skill of their own species opens this way. The invitation to the voyage, the Baudelaire desire to get out—get out of human circumstances—or the longing to be a drunken boat, or a soul whose craving is to crack open a closed universe is still real, only the impulse does not have to be assigned to tiresomeness and vanity of life, and it does not necessarily have to be a death-voyage. The trouble is that only trained specialists will be able to take the trip. The longing soul cannot by direct impulse go because it has the boundless need, or the mind for it, or the suffering-power. It will have to know engineering and wear those peculiar suits, and put up with personal, organic embarrassments. Perhaps the problems of radiation will prove insuperable, or strange diseases will be contracted on other worlds. Still, there is a universe into which we can overflow. Obviously we cannot manage with one single planet. Nor refuse the challenge of a new type of experience. We must recognize the extremism and fanaticism of human nature. Not to accept the opportunity would make this earth seem more and more a prison. If we could soar out and did not, we would condemn ourselves. We would be more than ever irritated with life. As it is, the species is eating itself up. And now Kingdom Come is directly over us and waiting to receive the fragments of a final explosion. Much better the moon."

Sammler did not think that must necessarily happen. "Do you think the species doesn't want to live?" he said.

"Many wish to end it," said Lal.

"Well, if as you say we are the kind of creature which is compelled to do what it is capable of doing, it would follow that we must demolish ourselves. But isn't that up to the species? Could we say that at this point politics is anything but pure biology? In Russia, in China, and here, very mediocre people have the power to end life altogether. These representatives—not representatives of the best but Calibans or, in the jargon, creeps—will decide for us all whether we live or die. Man now plays the drama of universal death. Should all not die at once, together, like one great individual death, expressing freely all of man's passions toward his doom? Many *say* they wish to end it. Of course that may be only rhetoric."

"Mr. Sammler," said Lal, "I believe you intimate that there is an implicit morality in the will-to-live and that these mediocrities in office will do their duty by the species. I am not sure. There is no duty in biology. There is no sovereign obligation to one's breed. When biological destiny is fulfilled in reproduction the desire is often to die. We please ourselves in extracting ideas of duty from biology. But duty is pain. Duty is hateful—misery, oppressive."

"Yes?" said Sammler, in doubt. "When you know what pain is, you agree that not to have been born is better. But being born one respects the powers of creation, one obeys the will of God—with whatever inner reservations truth imposes. As for duty—you are wrong. The pain of duty makes the creature upright, and this uprightness is no negligible thing. No, I stand by what I first said. There is also an instinct against leaping into Kingdom Come."

The scene, for such a conversation, was itself curious—

the green carpets, large pots, silk drapes of the late Hilda Gruner's living room. Here Govinda Lal, small, hunched, dusky, with his rusty-gilt complexion, his full face and beard, was like an Oriental ornament or painting. Sammler himself came under this influence, like a figure in Indian color—the red cheeks, the spreading white hair at the back, the circles of his specs, and the cigarette smoke about his hair. To Wallace he had insisted that he was an Oriental, and now felt that he resembled one.

"As for the present state of affairs," said Govinda, "I see that personal dissatisfaction, which is so great, may contribute energy to the biggest job which fate has secretly prepared—earth-departure. It may be the compression preceding the new expansion. To hurl yourself toward the moon, you may need an equal and opposite inertia. An inertia at least two hundred fifty thousand miles deep. Or more. We moreover seem to have it. Who knows how these things work? You know the famous Oblomov? He couldn't get out of bed. This phantom of inertia or paralysis. The opposite was frantic activism—bomb-throwing, civil war, a cult of violence? You have mentioned that. Do we always, always to the point of misery, do a thing? Persist until exhausted? Perhaps. Take my own temperament, for instance. I confess to you, Mr. Sammler (and how glad I am that your daughter's peculiarities have brought us together—I think we shall be friends) . . . I confess that I am originally—originally, you understand—of a melancholy, depressed character. As a child, I could not bear to be separated from Mother. Nor, for that matter, Father, who was, as I said, a teacher of French and mathematics. Nor the house, nor playmates. When visitors had to leave, I would make violent scenes. I was an often-sobbing little boy. All parting was such an emotional ordeal that I would get sick.

I must have felt separation as far inward as my constituent molecules, and trembled in billions of nuclei. Hyperbole? Perhaps, my dear Mr. Sammler. But I have been convinced since my early work in biophysics of vascular beds (I will not trouble you with details) that nature, more than an engineer, is an artist. Behavior is poetry, is metaphorical order, is metaphysics. From the high-frequency tenths-of-millisecond brain responses in corticothalamic nets to the grossest of ecological phenomena, it is all the printing out, in mysterious code, of sublime metaphor. I am speaking of my own childhood passions, and the body of an individual is electronically denser than the tropical rain forest is dense with organisms. And all these existences are, it often suggests itself, poems. I do not even try to overcome this impression of universal poetry any more. But to return to the question of my own personality, I see now that I had set myself a task of distance from objects of closest attachment. In which, Mr. Sammler, outer space is an opposite—personally, an emotional pole. One is born between his mother's legs, afterward persisting outward. To see the sidereal archipelagoes is one thing, but to plunge into them, into a dayless, nightless universe, why that, you see, makes sea-depth petty, the leviathan no more than a polliwog—"

Margotte came in—short, thick, rapid, efficient legs, but drying her hands ineptly in both skirt and apron—saying, "We will all feel better when we eat something. For you, Uncle, we have lobster salad, and some Crosse and Blackwell onion soup and bauernbrot and butter, and coffee. Dr. Lal, I assume you are not a meat eater. Do you like cottage cheese?"

"If you please, no fish."

"But where is Wallace?" said Sammler.

"Oh, he went up with tools to fix something in the attic."

She smiled as she returned to the kitchen, smiled especially at Govinda Lal.

Lal said, "I am very much taken with Mrs. Arkin."

Sammler thought, She intended, sight unseen, that you should be taken with her. I can give you pointers on being happy with her. I'll lose my sanctuary, perhaps, but I can give that up if this is serious. With an outer-space perspective perhaps immediate urgencies and egoism are lessened and marriage would be a kindly association—*sub specie aeternitatis*. Besides, though small, Govinda was in certain ways like Ussher Arkin. Women do not like too much change.

"Margotte is an excellent person," said Sammler.

"That is my impression. And exceedingly, highly attractive. Has her husband been dead long?"

"Three years, poor fellow."

"Poor fellow indeed, to die young, and with such a desirable wife."

"Come, I am hungry," said Sammler. Already he was considering how to take Shula out of this. She was smitten with this Indian. Had her desires. Needs. Was a woman, after all. What could one do for a woman? Little, very little. Or, for Elya, with the spray bubbling in his head? Terrible. Elya reappeared strangely and continually, as if his face were orbiting—as if he were a satellite.

However, they sat down to a little supper in Elya's kitchen, and the conversation continued.

Now that Sammler had been charmed by Govinda and seen, or imagined, a resemblance to Ussher Arkin, and was affectionately committed, it went with his habit of mind to see him also in another aspect, as an Eastern curiosity, a bushy little planet-buzzing Oriental demon, mentally rebounding from limits like a horsefly from glass.

Wondering if the fellow might be a charlatan, in some degree. No, no, not that. One had no time to make *funny* observations, or paltry ones; one must be decisive and trust one's instincts. Lal was the real thing. His conversation was conversation, it was not a line. This was no charlatan, only an oddity. He was excellent, solid. His one immediately apparent weakness was to want his credentials known. He let fall names and titles—the Imperial College, his intimate friend Professor Waddington, his position as hunch-consultant with Professor Hoyle, his connection with Dr. Feltstein of NASA, and his participation in the Bellagio conference on theoretical biology. This was pardonable in a little foreigner. The rest was perfectly straight. Of course it amused Sammler that he and Lal spoke such different brands of foreign English, and it was also diverting that they were tall and short. To him height meant pituitary hyperactivity and maybe vital wastage. The large sometimes seemed to have diminished minds, as if the shooting up cost the brain something. Strangest of all in the eighth decade of one's life, however, was a spontaneous feeling of friendship. At his age? That was for your young person, still dreaming of love, of meeting someone of the opposite sex who would cure you of all your troubles, heart and soul, and for whom you would cure and fulfill the same. From this came a disposition for sudden attachments such as you now saw in Lal, Margotte, and Shula. But for himself, at his time of life and because he had come back from the other world, there were no rapid connections. His own first growth of affections had been consumed. His onetime human, onetime precious, life had been burnt away. More green growth rising from the burnt black would simply be natural persistency, the Life Force working, trying to start again.

However, while this little supper in the kitchen (laid on with Margotte's maladroit bounty) lasted, the sad old man experienced the utmost joy, too. It seemed to him that the others also felt as he did: Shula-Slawa in her misbound sari following the conversation with devoted eyes and mumming every word with soft orange-painted lips, leaning her head on her palm; Margotte, delighted of course; she was gone on this little Hindu; the occasion was intellectual, and moreover she was feeding everyone. Could any instant of life be nicer? To Sammler these female oddities were endearing.

Dr. Lal was saying that we did not get much from our brains, considering what brains were, electronically, with billions of instantaneous connections. "What goes on within a man's head," he said, "is far beyond his comprehension, of course. In very much the same way as a lizard or a rat or a bird cannot comprehend being organisms. But a human being, owing to dawning comprehension, may well feel that he is a rat who lives in a temple. In his external development, as a thing, a creature, in cerebral electronics he enjoys an adaptation, a fitness which makes him feel the unfitness of his personal human efforts. Therefore, at the lowest, a rat in a temple. At best, a clumsy thing, with dawning awareness of the finesse of internal organization employed in crudities."

"Yes," said Mr. Sammler, "that is a very nice way to put it, though I am not sure that there are many people so fine that they can feel this light weight of being so much more than they can grasp."

"I should be extremely interested to hear your views," said Lal.

"My views?"

"Oh, yes, Papa."

"Yes, dear Uncle Sammler."

"My views."

A strange thing happened. He felt that he was about to speak his full mind. Aloud! That was the most striking part of it. Not the usual self-communing of an aged and peculiar person. He was about to say what he thought, and *viva voce*.

"Shula is fond of lectures, I am not," he said. "I am extremely skeptical of explanations, rationalistic practices. I dislike the modern religion of empty categories, and people who make the motions of knowledge."

"View it as a recital rather than a lecture," said Lal. "Consider the thing from a musical standpoint."

"A recital. It is Dr. Lal who should give it—he has a musical voice. A recital—that is more inviting," said Sammler putting his cup down. "Recitals are for trained performers. I am not ready for the stage. But there isn't much time. So, ready or not . . . I keep my own counsel much too much, and I *am* tempted to pass on some of my views. Or impressions. Of course, the old always fear they have decayed unaware. How do I know I have not? Shula, who thinks her papa is a powerful wizard, and Margotte, who likes discussion of ideas so much, they will deny it."

"Of course," said Margotte. "It simply is not so."

"Well, I have seen it happen to others, why not to me? One must live with all combinations of the facts. I remember a famous anecdote about a demented man: Someone said, 'You are a paranoiac, my dear fellow,' and he answered, 'Perhaps, but that doesn't prevent people from plotting against me.' That is an important ray of light from a dark source. I can't say that I have felt any weakness in the head, but it may be there. Luckily, my views are short. I suppose, Dr. Lal, that you are right. Biologically, chemically, the subtlety of the creature is beyond the understanding of the creature. We have an inkling of it, and feel how, by comparison, the internal state is so chaotic, such a hodgepodge of *odi et amo*. They say our protoplasm is like sea water. Our blood has a Mediterranean base. But now we live in a social and human sea. Inventions and ideas bathe our brains, which sometimes, like sponges, must receive whatever the currents bring and digest the mental protozoa. I do not say there is no alternative to such passivity, which is partly comical, but there are times, states, in which we lie under and feel the awful volume of cumulative consciousness, we feel the weight of the world. Not at all funny. The world is a terror, certainly, and mankind in a revolutionary condition becoming, as we say, modern—more and more mental, the realm of nature, as it used to be called, turning into a park, a zoo, a botanical garden, a world's fair, an Indian reservation. And then there are always human beings who take it upon themselves to represent or interpret the old savagery, tribalism, the primal fierceness of the fierce, lest we forget prehistory, savagery, animal origins. It is even said, here and there, that the real purpose of civilization is to permit us all to live like primitive people and lead a neolithic life in an automated society. That is a droll point of view. I don't want to lecture you, however. If one lives in his room, as I do, though Shula and Margotte take such excellent care of me, one has fantasies about addressing a captive audience. Very recently, I tried to give a speech at Columbia. It did not go well. I think I made a fool of myself."

"Oh, but please continue," said Dr. Lal. "We are most attentive."

"A person's views are either necessary or superfluous," said Sammler. "The superfluous irritates me sharply. I am an extremely impatient individual. My impatience sometimes borders on rage. It is clinical."

"No, no, Papa."

"However, it is sometimes necessary to repeat what all know. All mapmakers should place the Mississippi in the same location, and avoid originality. It may be boring, but one has to know where he is. We cannot have the Mississippi flowing toward the Rockies for a change. Now, as everyone knows, it has only been in the last two centuries that the majority of people in civilized countries have claimed the privilege of being individuals. Formerly they were slave, peasant, laborer, even artisan, but not person. It is clear that this revolution, a triumph for justice in many ways—slaves should be free, killing toil should end, the soul should have liberty—has also introduced new kinds of grief and misery, and so far, on the broadest scale, it has not been altogether a success. I will not even talk about the Communist countries, where the modern revolution has been most thwarted. To us the results are monstrous. Let us think only about our own part of the world. We have fallen into much ugliness. It is bewildering to see how much these new individuals suffer, with their new leisure and liberty. Though I feel sometimes quite disembodied, I have little rancor and quite a lot of sympathy. Often I wish to do something, but it is a dangerous illusion to think one can do much for more than a very few."

"What is one supposed to do?" said Lal.

"Perhaps the best is to have some order within oneself. Better than what many call love. Perhaps it *is* love."

"Please do say something about love," said Margotte.

"But I don't want to. What I was saying—you see I am getting old. I was saying that this liberation into individuality has not been a great success. For a historian of great interest, but for one aware of the suffering it is appalling. Hearts that get no real wage, souls that find no nourishment. Falsehoods, unlimited. Desire, unlimited. Possibility, unlimited. Impossible demands upon complex realities, unlimited. Revival in childish and vulgar form of ancient religious ideas, mysteries, utterly unconscious of course—astonishing. Orphism, Mithraism, Manichaeanism, Gnosticism. When my eye is strong, I sometimes read in the Hastings *Encyclopedia of Religion and Ethics*. Many fascinating resemblances appear. But one notices most a peculiar play-acting, an elaborate and sometimes quite artistic manner of presenting oneself as an individual and a strange desire for originality, distinction, *interest*—yes, *interest!* A dramatic derivation from models, together with the repudiation of models. Antiquity accepted models, the Middle Ages—I don't want to turn into a history book before your eyes—but modern man, perhaps because of collectivization, has a fever of originality. The idea of the uniqueness of the soul. An excellent idea. A true idea. But in these forms? In these poor forms? Dear God! With hair, with clothes, with drugs and cosmetics, with genitalia, with round trips through evil, monstrosity, and orgy, with even God approached through obscenities? How terrified the soul must be in this vehemence, how little that is really dear to it it can see in these Sadic exercises. And even there, the Marquis de Sade in his crazy way was an Enlightenment philosophe. Mainly he intended blasphemy. But for those who follow (unaware) his recommended practices, the idea no longer is blasphemy, but rather hygiene, pleasure which is hygiene too, and a charmed and *interesting* life. An *interesting* life is the supreme concept of dullards.

"Perhaps I am not thinking clearly. I am very sad and torn today. Besides, I am aware of the abnormality of my own experience. Sometimes I wonder whether I have any place here, among other people. I assume I am one of you. But also I am not. I suspect my own judgments because my lot has been extreme. I was a studious young person, not meant for action. Suddenly, it was all action—blood, guns, graves, famine. Very harsh surgery. One cannot come out intact. For a long time I saw things with peculiar hardness. Almost like a criminal—a person who brushes aside flimsy ordinary arrangements and excuses, and simplifies everything brutally. Not exactly as Mr. Brecht said, *Erst kommt das Fressen, und dann kommt die Moral.* That is swagger. Aristotle said something like it and did not swagger or act like a bully. Anyway, by force of circumstances I have had to ask myself simple questions, like 'Will I kill him? Will he kill me? If I sleep, will I ever wake? Am I really alive, or is there nothing left but an illusion of life?' And I know now that humankind marks certain people for death. Against them there shuts a door. Shula and I have been in this written-off category. If you chance nevertheless to live, having been out leaves you with idiosyncrasies. The Germans attempted to kill me. Then the Poles also shot at me. I would have died without Mr. Cieslakiewicz. He was the one man with whom I was not written off. By opening the tomb to me, he let me live. Experience of this kind is deforming. I apologize to you for the deformity."

"But you are not deformed."

"I am of course deformed. And obsessed. You can see that I am always talking about play-acting, originality, dramatic individuality, theatricality in people, the forms taken by spiritual striving. It goes round and round in my head, all of this. I cannot tell you how often, for instance, I think about Rumkowski, the mad Jewish King of Lodz."

"Who is that?" said Lal.

"A person thrown into prominence in Lodz, the big textile city. When the Germans arrived, they installed in authority this individual. He is still often discussed in refugee circles. Rumkowski was his name. He was a failed businessman. Elderly. A noisy individual, corrupt, director of an orphanage, a fund-raiser, a bad actor, a distasteful fun-figure in the Jewish community. A man with a bit to play, like so many modern individuals. Have you ever heard of him?"

Lal had not heard of him.

"Well, you shall hear a little. The Nazis made him *Judenältester*. The city was fenced off. The ghetto became a labor camp. The children were seized and deported for extermination. There was famine. The dead were brought down to the sidewalk and lay there to wait for the corpse wagon. Amidst all this, Rumkowski was King. He had his own court. He printed money and postage stamps with his picture. He had pageants and plays organized in his honor. There were ceremonies to which he wore royal robes, and he drove in a broken coach of the last century, very ornate, gilded, pulled by a dying white nag. On one occasion he showed courage, protesting the arrest and deportation, in plain words the murder, of his council. For this he was beaten up and thrown out into the street. But he was a terror to the Jews of Lodz. He was a dictator. He was their Jewish King. A parody of the thing—a mad Jewish King presiding over the death of half a million people. Perhaps his secret thought was to save a remnant. Perhaps his mad acting was meant to amuse or divert the Germans. These antics of failed individuality, the *grand seigneur* or dictatorial absurdities—this odd rancor against the evolution of human consciousness, bringing forth these struggling selves, horrible clowns, from every hole and corner. Yes, this would have appealed to those people. Humor seldom failed to appear in their murder programs. This harshness toward clumsy pretensions, toward the bad joke of the self which we all feel. The imaginary grandeur of insects. And besides, the door had been shut against these Jews; they belonged to the category written off. This theatricality of King Rumkowski evidently pleased the Germans. It further degraded the Jews to have a mock king. The Nazis liked that. They had a predilection for such *Ubu Roi* murder farces. They played at Pataphysics. It lightened or relieved the horror. Here at any rate one can see peculiarly well the question of the forms to be found for the actions of liberated consciousness, and the blood-minded hatred, the killers' delight taken in its failure and abasement."

"Excuse me, but I have failed to make this connection," said Lal.

"Yes, I am sure I could be more lucid. It is part of the self-communing obsession that I have. But in the Book of Job there is the complaint that God requires far too much. Job protests that he is magnified unbearably—'What is man, that thou shouldst magnify him? And that thou shouldst set thine heart upon him? And that thou shouldst visit him every morning and try him every moment? How long wilt thou not depart from me, nor let me alone till I swallow down my spittle?' And saying 'I would not live always.' 'Now I shall sleep in the dust.' This too great demand upon human consciousness and human capacities has overtaxed human endurance. I am not speaking only of moral demand, but also of the demand upon the imagination to produce a human figure of adequate stature. What is the true stature of a human being? This, Dr. Lal, was what I meant by speaking of the killers' delight in abasement in parody—in Rumkowski, King of rags and shit,

Rumkowski, ruler of corpses. And this is what preoccupies me with the theatricality of the Rumkowski episode. Of course the player was doomed. Many other players, with less agony, have also a sense of doom. As for the others, the large mass of the condemned, I assume, as they were starving, that they felt less and less. Even starving mothers could not feel for more than a day or two the children torn from them. Hunger pains put out grief. *Erst kommt das Fressen,* you see.

"Perhaps my sense of connection is faulty. Please tell me if it seems so. My aim is to bring out . . . though the man was perhaps crazy from the start; perhaps shock even made him saner; in any case, at the end, he voluntarily stepped into the train for Auschwitz . . . to bring out the weakness of the outer forms which are at present available for our humanity, and the pitiable lack of confidence in them. The early result of our modern individuality boom. In such a figure we have the very worst of cases. The most monstrous kind of exaggeration. We see the disintegration of the worst ego ideas. Such ego ideas taken from poetry, history, tradition, biography, cinema, journalism, advertising. As Marx pointed out . . ." But he did not say what Marx had pointed out. He thought, and the others did not speak. His food had not been touched. "I understand that old man was very lewd," he said. "He fingered the young girls. His orphans, perhaps. He knew all would die. Then everything seemed to come out as an efflorescence, a spilling of his 'personality.' Perhaps when people are so desperately impotent they play that instrument, the personality, louder and wilder. It seems to me that I have seen this often. I remember reading in a book, but can't remember where, that when people had found a name for themselves, Human, they spent a lot of time Acting Human, laughing and crying and getting others to laugh and cry, seeking occasions, provoking, taking such relish in wringing their hands, in drawing tears from their glands, and swimming and boating in that cloudy, contaminated, confusing, surging medium of human feelings, taking the passion-waters, exclaiming over their fate. This exercise was condemned by the book, especially the lack of originality. The writer preferred intellectual strictness, hated emotion, demanded exalted tears only, tears shed at last, after much resistance, from the most high-minded of recognitions.

"But suppose one dislikes all this theater of the soul? I too find it tiresome to have to meet it so often and in such familiar forms. I have read many disagreeable accounts of it. I have seen it described as so much debris of the ages, historical junk, dead weight, as bourgeois property, as hereditary deformity. The Self may think it wears a gay new ornament, delightfully painted, but from outside we see that it is a millstone. Or again, this personality of which the owner is so proud is from the Woolworth store, cheap tin or plastic from the five-and-dime of souls. Seeing it in this way, a man may feel that being human is hardly worth the trouble. Where is the desirable self that one might be? *Dov'è sia,* as the question is sung in the opera? That depends. It depends in part on the will of the questioner to see merit. It depends on his talent and his disinterestedness. It is right that we should dislike contrived individuality, bad pastiche, banality, and the rest. It is repulsive. But individualism is of no interest whatever if it does not extend truth. As personal distinction, enhancement, glory, it is for me devoid of interest. I care for it only as an instrument for obtaining truth," said Sammler. "But setting this aside for the moment, I think we may summarize my meaning in terms like these: that many have surged forward in modern history, after long epochs of namelessness and bitter obscurity, to claim and to enjoy (as people enjoy things now) a name, a dignity of person, a life such as belonged in the past only to gentry, nobility, the royalty or the gods of myth. And that this surge has, like all such great movements, brought misery and despair, that its successes are not clearly seen, but that the pain of heart it makes many people feel is incalculable, that most forms of personal existence seem to be discredited, and that there is a peculiar longing for nonbeing. As long as there is no ethical life and everything is poured so barbarously and recklessly into personal gesture this must be endured. And there is a peculiar longing for nonbeing. Maybe it is more accurate to say that people want to visit all other states of being in a diffused state of consciousness, not wishing to be any given thing but instead to become comprehensive, entering and leaving at will. Why should they be human? In most of the forms offered there is little scope for the great powers of nature in the individual, the abundant, generous powers. In business, in professions, in labor; as a member of the public; as an inhabitant of the cities, these strange pits; as experiencer of compulsions, manipulations; as endurer of strain; as father, husband obliging society by performing his quota of actions —the individual seems to feel these powers less, less and less. So it certainly seems to me that he wants a divorce from all the states that he knows.

"It was charged against the Christian that he wanted to get rid of himself. Those that brought the charge urged him to transcend his unsatisfactory humanity. But isn't transcendence the same disorder? Isn't that also getting rid of the human being? Well, maybe man should get rid of himself. Of course. If he can. But also he has something in him which he feels it important to continue. Something that deserves to go on. It is something that has to go on, and we all know it. The spirit feels cheated, outraged, defiled, corrupted, fragmented, injured. Still it knows what it knows, and the knowledge cannot be gotten rid of. The spirit knows that its growth is the real aim of existence. So it seems to me. Besides, mankind cannot be something else. It cannot get rid of itself except by an act of universal self-destruction. But it is not even for us to vote Yea or Nay. And I have not stated my arguments, for I argue nothing. I have stated my thoughts. They were asked for, and I wanted to express them. The best, I have found, is to be disinterested. Not as misanthropes dissociate themselves, by judging, but by not judging. By willing as God wills.

"During the war I had no belief, and I had always disliked the ways of the Orthodox. I saw that God was not impressed by death. Hell was his indifference. But inability to explain is no ground for disbelief. Not as long as the sense of God persists. I could wish that it did not persist. The contradictions are so painful. No concern for justice? Nothing of pity? Is God only the gossip of the living? Then we watch these living speed like birds over the surface of a water, and one will dive or plunge but not come up again and never be seen any more. And in our turn we will never be seen again, once gone through that surface. But then we have no proof that there is no depth under the surface. We cannot even say that our knowledge of death is shallow. There is no knowledge. There is longing, suffering, mourning. These come from need, affection, and love—the needs of the living creature, because it *is* a living creature. There is also strangeness, implicit. There is also adumbration. Other states are sensed. All is not flatly knowable. There would never have been any inquiry without this adumbration, there would never have been any knowledge without it. But I am not life's examiner, or a connoisseur, and I have nothing to argue. Surely a man would console, if he could. But that is not an aim of mine. Consolers cannot always be truthful. But very often, and almost daily, I have strong impressions of eternity. This may be due to my strange experiences, or to old age. I will say that to me this does not feel elderly. Nor would I mind if there were nothing after death. If it is only to be as it was before birth, why should one care? There one would receive no further information. One's ape restiveness would stop. I think I would miss mainly my God adumbrations in the many daily forms. Yes, that is what I should miss. So then, Dr. Lal, if the moon were advantageous for us metaphysically, I would be completely for it. As an engineering project, colonizing outer space, except for the curiosity, the ingenuity of the thing, is of little real interest to me. Of course the drive, the will to organize this scientific expedition must be one of those irrational necessities that make up life—this life we think we can understand. So I suppose we must jump off, because it is our human fate to do so. If it were a rational matter, then it would be rational to have justice on this planet first. Then, when we had an earth of saints, and our hearts were set upon the moon, we could get in our machines and rise up . . ."

"But what is this on the floor?" said Shula. All four rose about the table to look. Water from the back stairs flowed over the white plastic Pompeian mosaic surface. "Suddenly my feet were wet."

"Is it a bath overflowing?" said Lal.

"Shula, did you turn off the bath?"

"I'm sure and positive I did."

"I believe it is too rapid for bath water," said Lal. "A

pipe presumably is burst." Listening, they heard a sound of spraying above, and a steady, rapid tapping, trickling cascading, snaking of water on the staircase. "An open pipe. It sounds a flood." He broke from the table and ran through the large kitchen, the thin hairy fists laid on his chest, his head drawn down between thin shoulders.

"Oh, Uncle Sammler, what is it?"

The women followed. Necessarily slower, Sammler also climbed.

Wallace's theory that there were dummy pipes in the attic filled with criminal money had been put to the test. Sammler guessed, since Wallace was so mathematical, loved equations, spent nights working out gambling odds, that he had prepared a plumbing blueprint before taking up the wrench.

Treading carefully in dry places became pointless on the second floor. There the carpeted corridor was like a soaked lawn and sucked at Sammler's cracked shoes. The attic door was shut but water ran under it.

"Margotte," said Sammler. "Go down this instant. Call the plumber and the fire department. Call the firemen first and tell them you are calling in the plumber. Don't stand. Be quick." He took her arm and turned her toward the door.

Wallace had evidently tried to stuff his shirt into the break. When calculation failed, he fell apart. The garment lay underfoot and he and Lal were trying to bring together the open ends of pipe.

"There's something wrong with the coupling. I must have stripped the threads," said Wallace. He was astride the flowing pipe. Dr. Lal, trying to make the connection, was being sprayed, beard and chest. Shula stood close to him. If great eyes could be mechanical aids—if staring and proximity could lead to blending!

"Is there no shutoff? Is there no valve?" said Sammler. "Shula, don't get drenched. Stand back, my dear, you're in the way."

"I doubt we can accomplish anything by this means," said Lal. The water fizzed loudly.

"You don't think so?" said Wallace.

They spoke very politely.

"Well, no. For one thing there is too much water force. And as you see, this connecting metal cannot be advanced," said Lal. He lowered the pipe and stepped aside. At the waist his gray trousers were black with water. "Do you know the water system here?"

"In what sense do I know it?"

"I mean, is it city-supplied, or do you have a private source? If it is city water, the authorities will have to be called. However, if it is a driven well, the solution may lie in the cellar. If it is a well, there is a pump."

"The odd thing is I never knew."

"What of the sewage, is it municipal?"

"You got me there, too."

"If it is a well and there is a pump there is a switch also. I shall go down. Is there a flashlight?"

"I know the house," said Shula. "I'll go with you." In the sari, loosely bound, sandals dropping from her eager feet, she hurried after Lal, who ran down the stairs.

Sammler said to Wallace, "Aren't there any buckets? The ceilings will come down."

"There's insurance. Don't worry about ceilings."

"Nevertheless . . ."

Sammler descended.

Under the kitchen sink and in the broom closet he found yellow plastic pails and climbed back. He recognized that he had the peculiar anxieties of the poor relation. He had certainly disliked this house, always. Found it hard while eating benefactor's bread to be natural here. Besides, all this dense comfort, the rooms crowded with conversation-pieces, attractions, stood on a foundation of nullity. The work of Mr. Croze, with his rosebud mouth, visible nostrils, Oscar Wilde hairdo, suave little belly, and perfumed fingers, who sent, as Elya bitterly said once, as tough and cynical a business statement as he had ever seen. Elya conceded he was being fittingly furnished, done right by, but he didn't like being upgraded by Mr. Croze, who dealt in beautiful rewards, in suburban dukedoms for slum boys who made good! Still—a flood! Sammler could not bear it. Besides, it was a typical Wallace production, like the sinking of the limousine in Croton Reservoir, the horse pilgrimage into Soviet Armenia, the furnishing of a law office to work crossword puzzles in—protests against his father's "valueless" success. There was nothing new in this. Regularly, now, for generations, prosperous families brought forth their anarchistic sons—these boy Bakunins, geniuses of liberty, arsonists, demolishers of prisons, property, palaces. Bakunin had loved fire so. Wallace worked in water, a different medium. And it was very curious (Sammler with the two plastic buckets, which were as yellow and as light as leaves or feathers, had time on the stairs, while the water ran, to entertain the curiosity) that in speaking of his father that afternoon Wallace had said he was hooked like a fish by the aneurysm and jerked into the wrong part of the universe, drowning in air.

"You brought some pails. Let's see if we can't fit them under the pipe. Won't do much good."

"It may do some. You can open a window and spill the water into the gutters."

"Down the spout. O.K. But how long can we keep bailing?"

"Till the fire department comes."

"You called the firemen?"

"Of course. I made Margotte call."

"They'll file a report. That's what the insurance people will go by. I'd better put away these tools. I mean I want this to seem accidental."

"That these pipes just dropped apart? Opened by themselves? Nonsense, Wallace, pipes only burst in winter."

"Yes, I suppose that's right."

"So you thought they were full of thousand-dollar bills. Ah, Wallace!"

"Don't scold me, Uncle. There's loot here somewhere. There is, I swear. I know my father. He's a hider. And what good is the money to him now? He couldn't afford to declare it even if—"

"Even if he were going to live?"

"That's right. And it's like he's turning away from us. Or like a dog in the manger."

"Do you think that's a suitable figure of speech?"

"It wouldn't be suitable for you, but when I say it it doesn't make much difference. I'm a different generation. I never had any dignity to start with. A different set of givens, altogether. No natural feeling of respect. Well, I certainly fucked these pipes up good and proper."

Sammler was considering how much alike Wallace and Shula were, with their misdeeds. You had to stop and turn and wait for them. They would not be omitted. Sammler held the second bucket under the splashing pipe. Wallace had gone to empty the first from the dormer, turning back with grimy wet hands, bare-chested, the short black hairs neatly symmetrical like a clerical dickey. Arms were long, shoulders white, shapely to no purpose. And with a certain drop of the mouth, smiling at himself, transmitting to Sammler as he had done before the mother's sense of the graceful boy, the child's large skull and long neck, the clear-lined brows, crisp hair, fine small nose. But, as in certain old paintings, another world was also represented above, and one could imagine on a straight line over Wallace's head symbols of turbulence: smoke, fire, flying black things. Arbitrary rulings. A sealed judgment.

"If he would tell me where the dough is, it would at least cover the water damage. But he won't, and you won't ask him."

"No. I want no part of it."

"You think I should make my own dough."

"Yes. Label the trees and bushes. Earn your own."

"We will. In fact, that's all I want from the old man, a stake for the equipment. It's his last chance to show confidence in me. To wish me well. To give me like his blessing. Do you think he loved me?"

"Certainly he loved you."

"As a child. But did he love me as a man?"

"He would have."

"If I had ever been a man according to his idea. That's what you mean, isn't it?"

Sammler, having recourse to one of his blind looks, could always express his thought. Or if you had loved him, Wallace. These are very transitory opportunities. One must be nimble.

"I'm sorry that so late at night you have to be bailing. You must be tired."

"I suppose I am. Dry old people can go on and on. Still, I am beginning to feel it."

"I don't feel so hot myself. How is it downstairs, bad? A lot of water?"

No comment.

"It always turns out like this. Is that my message to the world from my unconscious self?"

"Why send such messages? Censor them. Put your unconscious mind behind bars on bread and water."

"No, it's just the mortal way I am. You can't hold it down. It must come out. I hate it too."

Lean Mr. Sammler, delicately applying the light pail to the pipe, while the rapid water splashed.

"I know that Dad had guys up here installing phony connections."

"I would have thought if it was a lot of money the false pipe would be a thick one."

"No, he wouldn't do an obvious thing. You have the wrong image of him. He has a lot of scientific cool. It could have been this pipe. He could have rolled the bills tight and small. He is a surgeon. He has the skill and the patience."

Suddenly the splashing stopped.

"Look! He's shut it off. It's down to a dribble. Hurray!" said Wallace.

"Dr. Lal!"

"What a relief. He found a turnoff. Who is that fellow?"

"Professor V. Govinda Lal."

"What is he a professor of?"

"Biophysics, I think, is his field."

"Well, he certainly uses his head. It never once occurred to me to find out where our water came from. There must be a well. Can you imagine that! And we've been here since I was ten. June 8, 1949. I'm a Gemini. Lily of the valley is my birth flower. Did you know the lily of the valley was very poisonous? We moved on my birthday. No party. The van got stuck between the gateposts on moving day. So it's not municipal water—I'm so astonished." With his usual lightness, he introduced general considerations. "It's supposed to be a sign of the Mass Man that he doesn't know the difference between Nature and human arrangements. He thinks the cheap commodities—water, electricity, subways, hot dogs—are like air, sunshine, and leaves on the trees."

"Just as simple as that?"

"Ortega y Gasset thinks so. Well, I'd better see what the damage is and get the cleaning woman in."

"You could mop up. Don't let the puddles stand all night."

"I don't know the first thing about mopping. I doubt that I ever even held a mop in my hands. But I could spread newspapers. Old *Times*es from the cellar. But just one thing, Uncle."

"What thing is that?"

"Don't dislike me on account of this."

"I don't."

"Well, don't look down on me—don't despise me."

"Well, Wallace . . ."

"I know you must. Well, this is like an appeal. I'd like to have your good opinion."

"Are you depressed, Wallace, when things go wrong like this?"

"Less and less."

"You mean you're improving," said Sammler.

"You see, if Angela inherits the house that ends my chances for the money. She'll put the place up for sale, being unmarried. She doesn't have any sentiment about the old homestead. The roots. Well, neither do I, when you come right down to it. Dad doesn't really like the place himself. No, I don't feel any black gloom about the water damage. Everything is replaceable. At exorbitant prices. But the estate will pay the bill, which will be a real gyp. And there's insurance. Possessive emotions are in a transitional phase. I really think they are." Wallace could turn suddenly earnest, but his earnestness lacked weight. Earnestness was probably Wallace's ideal, his true need, but the young man was incapable of finding his own essences. "I'll tell you what I'm afraid of, Uncle," he said. "If I have to live on a fixed income from a trust it'll be the end of me. I'll never find myself then. Do you want me to rot? I need to crash out of the future my father has prepared for me. Otherwise, everything just goes on being possible, and all these possibilities are going to be the death of me. I have to have my own necessities, and I don't see those anywhere. All I see is ten thousand a year, like my father's life sentence on me. I have to bust out while he's still living. When he dies, I'll get so melancholy I won't be able to lift a finger."

"Shall we soak up some of this water?" said Sammler. "Shall we start spreading around the *Times*?"

"Oh, that can wait. The hell with it. We'll get screwed anyway on the repairs. You know, Uncle, I think I'm just half as smart as a man needs to be to work out these things, so I never get more than halfway there."

"So you have no connection with this house—no desire for roots, Wallace."

"No, of course not. Roots? Roots are not modern. That's a peasant conception, soil and roots. Peasantry is going to disappear. That's the real meaning of the modern revolution, to prepare world peasantry for a new state of existence. I certainly have no roots. But even I am out of date. What I've got is a lot of old wires, and even wires belong to the old technology. The real thing is telemetry. Cybernetics. I've practically decided, Uncle Sammler, if this enterprise doesn't pan out, with Feffer, that I'll go to Cuba."

"To Cuba, is it? But you aren't a Communist, too, Wallace?"

"Not at all. I do admire Castro, however. He has terrific style, he's a bohemian radical, and he's held his own against Washington superpower. He and his cabinet ride in jeeps. They meet in the sugar cane."

"What do you want to tell him?"

"It could be important, don't make fun of me, Uncle Sammler. I have ideas about revolution. When the Russians made their revolution, everybody said, 'A leap forward into a new stage of history.' Not at all. The Russian Revolution was a delaying action—ah, my God, what a noise. It's the fire trucks. I'd better run. They could just bash down the door. They have an orgy, these guys, with their axes. And I have to have an alibi for the insurance."

He ran.

In the yard the rotating lights swept through the trees, dark red over the lawn, the walls and windows. The bell was slamming, bangalang, and deeper down the road, gulping passionate shrieks, approached the mortal-sounding sirens. More engines were arriving. From the attic window Sammler watched as Wallace ran out, his hands raised, explaining to the helmeted men as they sprang in the soft gum boots from the trucks.

Water, they had brought.

Mr. Sammler had some wakeful hours that night. A predictable result of worry over Elya. Of the flood. Also of the conversation with Lal which had compelled him to state his views—historical, planetary, and universal. The order probably should be reversed: first there were the views, planetary or universal, and then there were hidden dollars, water pipes, firemen. Sammler went out and walked in the garden, behind the house, up and down the drive. He was dissatisfied. He had explained, he had taken positions, he had said things he hadn't meant, meant things he hadn't said. Indoors, there were activities, discussions, explanations, arrangements, rearrangements. In the house of a dying man. It was the turn again of certain minor things which people insisted on enlarging, magnifying, moving into the center: relationships, interior decorations, family wrangles, Minox photographs of thieves on buses, arms of Puerto Rican ladies on the Bronx Express, *odi-et-amo* need-and-rejection, emotional self-examinations, erotic businesses in Acapulco, fellatio with friendly strangers. Civilian matters. Civilian one and all! The high-minded, like Plato (now he was not only lecturing, but even lecturing himself), wished to get rid of such stuff—wrangles, lawsuits, hysterias, all such hole-and-corner pettiness. Other powerful minds denied that this could be done. They held (like Freud) that the mightiest instincts were bound up in just such stuff, each trifle the symptom of a deep disease in a creature whose whole fate was disease. What to do about such things? Absurd in form, but possibly real? But possibly not real? Relief from this had become imperative. And that was why, during the Aqaba crisis, Mr. Sammler had had to go to the Middle East.

At this moment, walking in white moonlight on Elya Gruner's washed gravel, which had been cut with black tracks by the fire engines, he recognized and again identified his motives. He had gone back to 1939. He wanted to refer again to Zamosht Forest, to more basic human characteristics. When had things seemed real, true? In Poland when blinded, in Zamosht when freezing, in the tomb when hungry. So he had persuaded Elya to let him go, to send him, and he had renewed his familiarity with a certain sort of fact. Which, as he was older and more fragile, had made his legs tremble more; the more he tried to stiffen himself up the more he faltered. Few outer signs of this were given. But wasn't he too old? Did he have any business to fly to a war?

It was announced in Athens, on the plane, that this flight would not continue because the fighting had already begun in Israel. Grounded! He must get out. The Greek heat was dizzy, in the airport. The public music circled through Mr. Sammler's unwilling head. The sugary coffee, the sticky drinks, also were a trial to him. The suspense, the delay, gnawed him intolerably. He went into the city and visited airline offices, he asked a business friend of Elya's, in oil or gasoline, to help, he visited the Israeli consulate and obtained a seat on the first El Al flight. He waited again at the airport until four a.m. among journalists and hippies. These young people—Dutch, German, Scandinavian, Canadian, American—had been encamped at Eilath on the Red Sea. The Bedouins on the ancient route from Arabia into Egypt had sold them hashish. It was a jolly place. Now with their guitars they wanted to go back. Responding to a primary event. Though recognizing no governments.

The jet was packed. One could not move. For lean old

men, breathing was difficult. A television man beside Sammler offered him a pull from his whisky bottle. "Thank you," said Sammler, and accepted. He swallowed down Bell's scotch. Just then the sun ran up from the sea like a red fox. It was not round but long, not far but near. The metal of the engines, those shapely vats in which the freezing air was screaming—light into blackness, blackness into light—hung under the wings beside Sammler's window. Whisky from a bottle—he smiled at himself—made him a real war correspondent. An odd person to be rushing to this war, although no more odd than these Stone Age bohemians with their solemn beards. There were others besides who did not seem very useful in a crisis. Sammler would be filing his old-fashioned dispatches to Mr. Jerzy Zhelonski in London to be read by a very mixed Polish public.

Mr. Sammler had had no business, at his age, in a white cap and striped seersucker jacket, to be riding in a press bus behind those tanks to Gaza, to Al Arish and beyond. But he had managed it all himself. There was nothing accidental about it. In these American articles of dress he had perhaps passed for a younger man. Americans and Englishmen always looked a little younger. Anyway, there he was. He was one of the journalists. He walked about in conquered Gaza. They were sweeping broken glass. In the square, armor and guns. Just beyond, the cemetery walls, the domes of white tombs. In the dust, scraps of food baking, sour; odors of heating garbage and of urine. Broadcast Oriental jazz winding like dysentery through the bowels. Such deadly comical music. Women, oldish women only, went marketing; or set out to market; there couldn't have been much to buy. The black veils were transparent. You saw the heavy-boned mannish faces underneath—large noses, the stern mouths projecting over stonelike teeth. There was nothing to keep you in Gaza for long. The bus stopped for Sammler, and young Father Newell in his Vietnam battle dress greeted him.

Knowing modern warfare, the Father was able to point things out which Sammler might have missed when they passed the last of the irrigated fields and entered the Sinai Desert. Then they began to see the dead, the unburied Arab bodies. Father Newell showed him the first. Sammler might never have noticed, might have taken the corpse for nothing but a greenish gunnysack, stuffed tight, dropped from a truck on the white sand.

Driven off the road, sunk in the sand, wrecked on the dunes, many burnt—all these vehicles, the personnel carriers, tanks, trucks, the light cars smashed flat, wheels freed, escaped; and very thick about these machines, the dead. There were dug positions, emplacements, trenches, and in them, too, there were hundreds of corpses. The odor was like damp cardboard. The clothes of the dead, greenish-brown sweaters, tunics, shirts were strained by the swelling, the gases, the fluids. Swollen gigantic arms, legs, roasted in the sun. The dogs ate human roast. In the trenches the bodies leaned on the parapets. The dogs came cringing, flattening up. The inhabitants had run away from the encampments you saw here and there—the low tents, Bedouin-style, but made of plastic crate wrappings dumped from ships, pieces of styrofoam, dirty sheets of cellulose like insect moltings, large cockroach cases. Poor folk! Ah, poor creatures!

"Well, they did a job, didn't they," said Father Newell. "How many casualties, would you say?"

"I have no idea."

"This was a small Russian experiment, I believe," Father Newell said. "Now they know."

In the sun the faces softened, blackened, melted, and flowed away. The flesh sank to the skull, the cartilage of the nose warping, the lips shrinking, eyes dissolving, fluids filling the hollows and shining on the skin. A strange flavor of human grease. Of wet paper pulp. Mr. Sammler fought his nausea. As he and Father Newell walked together, they were warned not to step off the road because of mines. Sammler read out for the priest the Russian letters stenciled white on the green tanks and trucks: GORKISKII AUTOZAVOD, most of them said. Father Newell seemed to know a lot about gun calibers, armor thickness, ranges. In a lowered voice, out of respect for the Israelis who denied its use, he identified the napalm. See all that reddish, all that mauve out there? Salmon-pink with a green tinge in the clinkers was the sure sign. Positively napalm. It was a real war. These Jews were tough. He spoke to Sammler as one American to another. The long blue seersucker stripes, the soiled white cap from Kresge's, the little spiral book in which Sammler made his notes for Polish articles, also from Kresge's, accounted for this. It was a real war. Everyone respected killing. Why not the priest? He walked in the big American battle boots as if he were not altogether a priest. He was not a chaplain. He was a newspaperman. He was not what he was assumed to be. Nor was Sammler. What Sammler was he could not clearly formulate. Human, in some altered way. The human being at the point where he attempted to obtain his release from being human. Wasn't this what Sammler had been getting at in the kitchen, talking to Lal and the ladies of divorce from every human state? Petitioning for a release from God's attention? My days are vanity. I would not live always. Let me alone. To be visited every morning, to be called upon, to be magnified. Let me alone.

Walking the narrow road with Father Newell, picking up curious objects, shells, bandages, Arab comic books and letters, stepping aside for trucks stacked high with bread, weighing down the springs, projecting at the rear. But really the main subject could not be changed, the subject of the dead. Bristling in the green-brown and gravy-colored woolens. The suffocating wet cardboard fumes they gave off. In the superhot, the crack light, the glassy persistency and distortion of the desert light, these swollen shapes were the main thing to be seen. They were the one subject the soul was sure to take seriously. And this perhaps was what Sammler's instinct had directed him to do. To go to Kennedy, to get on a jet, to land in Tel Aviv, to have snapshots taken, to obtain a press card, to find a bus to Gaza, to visit the great sun wheel of white desert in which these Egyptian corpses and machines were embedded, to make his primary contact. Certain desires thus were met, for which he could not account. And this war was, as human affairs went, a most minor affair. In modern experience, so very little. Nothing at all. And the people involved in it, the boys, after fighting, played soccer at Al Arish. They cleared a space, and they kicked and butted, they leaped up, they trotted on the sand. Or in the shade of the hangars they took out their books and read biology or chemistry, philosophy, preparing for exams perhaps. Then he and Father Newell were called over to look at captured snipers on the bed of a truck, trussed up and blindfolded. Below these eye rags, the desperate faces, as if it were *not* a most minor affair. One saw those, and then the next things, and then other things. And evidently Mr. Sammler had his own need for these sights, for which he mastered the trembling of his legs or the wish to cry which flashed through him when he saw the snipers' bandaged faces. He was taken down to the sea by some men. They entered the water to refresh themselves. He too went in and stood. In a broad band along the beaches the foam mixed with heat-shimmer for many miles, in varying deep curves of seething white between the sand and the great blue. For a little while, in the water, he did not smell rotting flesh, but soon had to tie a handkerchief over his face. The handkerchief quickly absorbed the smell. It tainted his clothing. His spittle tasted of it.

Via London, ten days later, he flew home. As if he had been on some sort of mission: self-assigned: fact-finding. He observed that modern London was very playful. He visited his old flat in Woburn Square. He noted that the traffic was very thick. He saw that there were more drunkards in the streets, that the British advertising industry had discovered the female nude, and that most posters along the escalators of the Underground were of women in undergarments. He found his acquaintances as old as himself. Then BOAC brought him back to Kennedy Airport, and soon afterward he was in the Forty-second Street Library reading, as always, Meister Eckhardt.

"Blessed are the poor in spirit. Poor is he who has nothing. He who is poor in spirit is receptive of all spirit. Now God is the Spirit of spirits. The fruit of the spirit is love, joy, and peace. See to it that you are stripped of all creatures, of all consolation from creatures. For certainly as long as creatures comfort and are able to comfort you, you will never find true comfort. But if nothing can comfort you save God, truly God will console you."

Mr. Sammler could not say that he literally believed

what he was reading. He could, however, say that he cared to read nothing but this.

On the lawn before the half-timbered house the ground was damp, the grass was fragrant. Or was it the soil itself that smelled so fresh? In the clarified, moon-purged air, he saw Shula coming, looking for him.

"Why aren't you in bed?"

"I'm going."

She gave him Elya's own afghan to cover himself with, and he lay down.

Feeling what a strange species he belonged to, which had organized its planet to such an extent. Of this mass of ingenious creatures, about half had gone into the state of sleep, in pillows, sheeted, wrapped, quilted, muffled. The waking, like a crew, worked the world's machines, and all went up and down and round about with calculations accurate to the billionth of a degree, the skins of engines removed, replaced, million-mile trajectories laid out. By these geniuses, the waking. The sleeping, brutes, fantasists, dreaming. Then they woke, and the other half went to bed.

And that is how this brilliant human race runs this wheeling globe.

He joined the other sleepers for a while.

The washstand in the small lavatory off the den was dark onyx, the fittings gold, the faucets dolphins, the soap dish a scallop, the towel thick as mink. Mirrors on four walls showed Mr. Sammler to himself in more aspects than he wanted. The soap was spermy sandalwood. The blade was dull and had to be honed on the porcelain. Very likely ladies occasionally slipped in to trim their legs with this razor. Sammler did not want to look for another blade upstairs. The master bedroom was seriously water-damaged. The ladies had pulled the twin mattresses from the beds to a dry corner. Dr. Lal had slept in the guest room. Wallace? Perhaps he had spent the night on his head, like a yogi.

Suddenly Sammler stopped shaving, paused and stared at himself, his dry, small, "cured" face undergoing in the mirror a strong inrush of color. Even the left, the swelled, the opaque guppy eye, took up some light from this. Where were they all? Opening the door, he listened. There was no sound. He went into the garden. Dr. Lal's car was gone. He looked in the garage, and that was empty. Gone, fled!

He found Shula in the kitchen. "Everyone has left?" he said. "Now how do I get to New York?"

She was pouring coffee through the filter cone, having first boiled the grounds, French style.

"Took off," she said. "Dr. Lal wasn't able to wait. There was no room for me. He rented a two-seater. A gorgeous little Austin Healy, did you see it?"

"And Emil, where is he?"

"He had to take Wallace to the airport. Wallace has to fly—to test-fly. For his business, you know what I mean. They're going to take pictures and so on."

"And I am stuck. Is there a timetable? I've got to be in New York."

"Well, it's nearly ten o'clock now and there aren't so many trains. I'll phone. And then Emil should be back soon, and he can drive you. You were sleeping. Dr. Lal didn't want to disturb you."

"Extremely inconsiderate. You knew and Margotte knew that I had to get back."

"The little car was very pretty. Margotte didn't look right in it."

"I am annoyed."

"Margotte has thick legs, Father. You've probably never even noticed. Well, they won't show in the car. Dr. Lal will call later in the day. You'll see him all right."

"Whom, Lal? Why? The document is there, isn't it?"

"There?"

"Don't irritate me by repeating questions. I am already irritated. Why didn't you wake me? The document *is* in the locker, isn't it?"

"I locked it up myself, with the quarter, and took out the key. No, you'll see him because Margotte is out for him. Maybe you didn't notice that either. I really need to talk to you about this, Father."

"Yes, I'm sure you do. I did notice, yes, to tell the truth. Well, she's a widow, and she's had enough of mourning, and she needs somebody like that. We aren't much comfort to her. I don't know what she sees in that bushy black little fellow. It's just loneliness, I suppose."

"I can see what she sees. Dr. Lal is very distinguished. You know it. Don't pretend, after the way you talked in the kitchen. It was beautiful."

"Well, well. What will I do? This thing of Elya's is very bad, you know."

"Very?"

"The worst. And I should have realized that returning might present problems."

"Father, just leave it to me. And you haven't finished shaving. No, go on, and I'll bring you a cup of coffee."

He went, thinking how he had been feinted out of position. Outgeneraled. Like Pompey or Labienus by Caesar. He should not have left the city. He was cut off from his base. And now how was he to reach Elya, who needed him today? Picking up the phone in the den to call the hospital, he heard the busy signal Shula was getting from the Penn Central. Patience, waiting, now were necessary—things Mr. Sammler had no talent for. But he had studied, he had trained himself. One began with external composure. So he sat down on the hassock, looking at the sofa, and at the silken green luxurious wool of Elya's own afghan he had slept under. It was a lovely morning, too. The sun came in as he sipped the coffee Shula brought him. Glass tables on legs and semicircular struts of brass spattered the Oriental rug with light, brought out the colors and the figures.

"Busy signal," she said.

"Yes, I know."

"There's a telephone crisis, anyway, all over New York. The experts are working on it."

She went into the garden, and Sammler again tried dialing the hospital. All lines were busy in that dreary place, and he hung up the repetitious croaking instrument. Thinking of the colossal number of conversations, all those communings. Utilizing the invisible powers of the universe. Out in the garden, Shula was also engaged in conversation. It was warm. Tulips, daffodils, jonquils, and a paradise of gusts. Evidently she asked the flowers how they were today. No answers required. Brilliant instances sufficed. She herself was a brilliant instance of something organically strange. His glimpse of the entire Shula last night now made him feel her specific weight, as she trod the grass. The entire female body was evoked, white skin everywhere, the thighs, the trunk, the actual feet, the belly with its organs, together with the kinky hair straggling from the scarf. All visible and almost palpable. And even about plants, who knew the whole truth? On educational TV one night he and Margotte watched a singular botanist who had attached a polygraph machine—a lie-detector—to flowers and recorded the reactions of roses to gentle and violent stimuli. Stridency made them shrink, he said. A dead dog cast before them caused aversion. A soprano singing lullabies had the opposite effect. Sammler would have guessed that the investigator himself, his pale leer, his wild stern police nose would distress roses, African violets. Even without nerves these organisms were discerning. We with our oversupply of receptors were in a state of nervous chaos.

Amid the tree shadows, pliant, and the window-frame shadows, rigid, and the brass and glass reflections, semi-steady, Mr. Sammler wiped his shoes with the paper towel Shula had placed under the coffee cup. The shoes were damp, still. They were soggy, unpleasantly so. Margotte also had her plants, and Wallace was about to found a plant business. It would be too bad if the first contacts of plants were entirely with the demented. Maybe I'd better have a word with them myself. Mr. Sammler was heavy-hearted and tried to divert himself. The heaviness was brutally persistent, however.

He came to the point. First, how apt it was that Wallace should flood the attic. Why, it was a metaphor for Elya's condition. In connection with that condition there arose other images—a blistering of the brain, a froth or rusty scum of blood over that other plant which lay in one's head. Something like convolvulus. No, like fatty cauliflower. The screw on the artery could not reduce the pressure, and where the vessel was varicose and weaker than cobweb it would open. A terrible flood! One might try to think of mitigating things— That, oh well! Life! Everyone who had it was bound to lose it. Or that this was Elya's moment of honor and that he called upon his best qualities. That was all very well, until death turned its full gaze on the individual. Then all such ideas were nothing. The point was that he, Sammler, should be at the hospital, now; to do what could be done; to say what might be said, and what should be said. Exactly what should or might be said Sammler did not know. He could not find the precise thing. Living as he did, in this inward style, working out his condensations or contractions, one became uncommunicative. To explain or expand his thoughts tired and vexed him, as he had learned last night. But he did not feel uncommunicative toward Elya. On the contrary, he wanted to say everything possible. He wanted to go to the hospital and *say* something! He loved his nephew, and he had something that Elya needed. All concerned ought to have had it. The first place at Elya's bedside belonged to Wallace or to Angela, but they were not about to take it.

Elya was a physician and a businessman. With his own family, to his credit, he had not been businesslike. Nevertheless, he had the business outlook. And business, in business America, was also a training system for souls. The fear of being unbusinesslike was very great. As he was dying Elya might conceivably draw strength from doing business. He had in fact done that. He kept talking to Widick. And Sammler had nothing with a business flavor to offer him. But at the very end business would not do for Elya. Some, many, would go on with business to the last breath, but Elya was not like that, not so limited. Elya was not finally ruled by business considerations. He was not in that insect and mechanical state—such a surrender, such an insect disaster for human beings. Even now (now perhaps more than ever) Elya was accessible. In fact Sammler had not seen this in time. Yesterday, when Elya began to speak of Wallace, when he denounced Angela, he, Sammler, ought to have stayed with him. Any degree of frankness might have been possible. In the going phrase, a moment of truth. Meaning that most conversation was a compilation of lies, of course. But Elya's was not one of those sealed completed impenetrable systems, he was not one of your monstrous crystals or icicles. Feeling, or stroking the long green fibers of the afghan, Sammler put it to himself that because he and Antonina had been designated, part of a demonstration of the meaninglessness of this vivid shuffle with its pangs of higher intuition from the one side and the continual muddy suck of the grave underfoot—that because of this he himself, Artur Sammler, had put up obstinate resistance. And Elya, too, was devoted to ideas of conduct which seemed discredited, which few people explicitly defended. It was not the behavior that was gone. What was gone was the old words. Forms and signs were absent. Not honor but the word honor. Not virtuous impulse, but the terms beaten into flat nonsense. Not compassion; but what was a compassionate utterance? And compassionate utterance was a mortal necessity. Utterance, sounds of hope and desire, exclamations of grief. Such things were suppressed, as if illicit. Sometimes coming through in ciphers, in vague figures scrawled on the windows of condemned buildings (the empty tailor shop facing the hospital). At this stage of things there was a terrible dumbness. About essentials, almost nothing could be said. Still, signs could be made, should be made, must be made. One should declare something like this: "However actual I may seem to you and you to me, *we are not as actual as all that.* We will die. Nevertheless there is a bond. There is a bond." Mr. Sammler believed that if this was not said in so many words it should be said tacitly. In fact it *was* continually asserted, in many guises. And anyway, we know *what is what.* But Elya at this moment had a most particular need for a sign and he, Sammler, should be there to meet that need.

He again telephoned the hospital. To his surprise, he found himself speaking with Gruner. He had asked for the private nurse. One could get through? Elya must be molested by calls. With the mortal bulge in his head he was still in the game, did business.

"How are you?"

"How are you, Uncle?"

The actual meaning of this might have been, "Where are you?"

"How are you feeling?"

"There's been no change. I thought we would be seeing each other."

"I'm coming in. I'm sorry. When there's something important there is always some delay. It never fails, Elya."

"When you left yesterday, it was like unfinished business between us. We got sidetracked by Angela and such hopeless questions. There was something I was meaning to ask. About Cracow. The old days. And by the way, I bragged about you to a Polish doctor here. He wanted very much to see the Polish articles you sent from the Six-Day War. Do you have copies?"

"Certainly, at home. I have plenty."

"Aren't you at home now?"

"Actually I'm not."

"I wonder if you'd mind bringing the clippings. Would you mind stopping off?"

"Of course not. But I don't want to lose the time."

"I may have to go down for tests." Elya's voice was filled with unidentifiable tones. Sammler's interpretive skill was insufficient. He was uneasy. "Why shouldn't there be time?" Elya said. There's time enough for everything." This had an odd ring, and the accents were strange.

"Yes?"

"Of course, yes. It was good you called. A while ago I tried to phone you. There was no answer. You went out early."

Uneasiness somewhat interfered with Sammler's breathing. Long and thin, he held the telephone, concentrating, aware of the anxious intensity gathered in his face. He was silent. Elya said, "Angela is on her way over."

"I am coming too."

"Yes." Elya lingered somewhat on the shortest words. "Well, Uncle?"

"Good-by, for now."

"Good-by, Uncle Sammler."

Rapping at the pane, Sammler tried to get Shula's attention. Among the wagging flowers she was conspicuously white. His Primavera. On her head she wore a dark-red scarf. Covering up, afflicted always by the meagerness of her hair. It was perhaps the natural abundance, growth power, exuberance that she admired in flowers. Seeing her among the blond openmouthed daffodils, which were being poured back and forth by the wind, her father believed that she was in love. From the hang of her shoulders, the turn of the orange lips, he saw that she was already prepared to accept unrequited longing. Dr. Lal was not for her; she would never clasp his head or hold his beard between her breasts. You could seldom get people to long for what was possible—that was the cruelty of it. He opened the French window.

"Where is the timetable?" he said.

"I can't find it. The Gruners don't use the train. Anyway, you'll get to New York quicker with Emil. He's going to the hospital."

"I don't suppose he'd wait at the airport for Wallace. Not today."

"Why did you say that about Lal, that he was just a bushy black little fellow?"

"I hope you're not personally interested in him."

"Why not?"

"He's not at all suitable, and I'd never give my consent."

"You wouldn't?"

"No, no. He wouldn't make any kind of husband for you."

"Because he's an Asiatic? You wouldn't be so prejudiced. Not you, Father."

"Not the slightest objection to an Asiatic. There is much to be said for exotic marriages. If your husband is a bore, it takes years longer to discover it, in French. But scientists make bad husbands. Sixteen hours a day in the laboratory, absorbed in research. You'd be neglected. You'd be hurt. I wouldn't allow it."

"Not even if I loved him?"

"You also thought you loved Eisen."

"He didn't love me. Not enough to forgive my Catholic background. And I couldn't discuss anything with him. Besides, sexually, he was a very gross person. Things I wouldn't care to tell you about, Father. But he is extremely common and lousy. He's here in New York. If he comes near me, I'll stab him."

"You amaze me, Shula. You would actually stab Eisen with a knife?"

"Or with a fork. I often regret that I let him beat me in Haifa and didn't do anything back to him. He hit me really too hard, and I should have defended myself."

"All the more important that you should avoid future mistakes. I have to protect you from failures I can foresee. A father should."

"But what if I did love Dr. Lal? And I saw him first."

"Rivalry—a poor motive. Shula, we must take care of each other. As you look after me on the H. G. Wells side, I think about your happiness. Margotte is a much less sensitive person than you. If a man like Dr. Lal was mentally absent for weeks at a time, she'd never notice. Don't you remember how Ussher used to speak to her?"

"He would tell her to shut up."

"That's right."

"If a husband treated me like that, I couldn't bear it."

"Exactly. Wells also thought that people in scientific research made poor husbands."

"He didn't!"

"I seem to remember his saying that. Does Wallace really know the first thing about aerial photography?"

"He knows so many things. What do you think of his business idea?"

"He doesn't have ideas—he has delusions, brainstorms. However, he wouldn't be the first maniac to make money. And his scheme has charm, dealing in plant names . . . well, some of the plants do have beautiful names. Take one like Gazania Pavonia."

"Gazania Pavonia is darling. Well, come out in the sun and enjoy the weather. I feel much better when you take an interest in me. I'm glad you understand that I took the moon thing for you. You aren't going to give up the project, are you? It would be a sin. You were made to write the Wells book, and it would be a masterpiece. Something terrible will happen if you don't. Bad luck. I feel it inside."

"I may try again."

"You must."

"To find a place for it among my preoccupations."

"You should have no other preoccupations. Only creative ones."

Mr. Sammler, smelling of sandalwood soap, decided to sit in the garden to wait for Emil. Perhaps the soap odor would evaporate in the sun. He didn't have it in him to rinse again in the onyx bathroom. Too close in there.

"Bring your coffee out."

"I'd like that, Shula." He handed her the cup and stepped onto the lawn. "And my shoes are wet from last night."

Black fluid, white light, green ground, the soil heated and soft, penetrated by new growth. In the grass, a massed shine of particles, a turf-buried whiteness, and from this dew, wherever the sun could reach it, the spectrum flashed: like night cities seen from the jet, or the galactic sperm of worlds.

"Here. Sit. Take those things off. You'll catch cold. I can dry them in the oven." Kneeling, she removed the wet shoes. "How can you wear them? Do you want to catch pneumonia?"

"Is Emil coming straight back or waiting for that lunatic?"

"I don't know. Why do you keep calling him a lunatic? Why is Wallace a lunatic?"

To a lunatic, how would you define a lunatic? And was he himself a perfect example of sanity? He was certainly not. They were his people—he was their Sammler. They shared the same fundamentals.

"Because he flooded the house?" said Shula.

"Because he flooded it. Because now he's flying around with his cameras."

"He was looking for money. That's not crazy, is it?"

"How do you know about this money?"

"He told me. He thinks there's a fortune here. What do you think?"

"I wouldn't know. But Wallace *would* have such fantasies—Ali Baba, Captain Kidd, or Tom Sawyer treasure fantasies."

"But he says—no joking—there's a fortune of money in the house. He won't rest until he finds it. Wouldn't it be a little mean of Cousin Elya . . ."

"To die without saying where it is?"

"Yes." Shula seemed slightly ashamed, now that her meaning was explicit.

"It's up to him. Elya will do as he likes. I assume Wallace has asked you to help find this secret hoard."

"Yes."

"What did he do, promise a reward?"

"Yes, he did."

"I don't want you to meddle, Shula. Keep out of it."

"Shall I bring you a slice of toast, Father?"

He didn't answer. She went away, taking his wet shoes.

Above New Rochelle, several small planes snored and buzzed. Probably Wallace was piloting one of them. Unto himself a roaring center. To us, a sultry beetle, a gnat propelling itself through blue acres. Sammler set back his chair into the shade. What had been in the sun a mass of pine foliage now resolved itself into separate needles and trees. Then the silver-gray Rolls turned the corner of the high hedges. The geometrical, dignified, monogrammed radiator flashed its rods. Emil stepped out, looking upward. A yellow plane flew over the house.

"That must be Wallace for sure. He said he was going to fly a Cessna."

"I suppose it is Wallace."

"He wanted to try the equipment on a place he knows."

"Emil, I've been waiting to go to the station."

"Of course, Mr. Sammler. But right now there aren't many trains. How is Dr. Gruner, do you know?"

"I spoke to him," Sammler said. "No change."

"I'd be glad to take you to town."

"When?"

"Very soon."

"It would save time. I have to stop at home. You aren't going back to the airport for Wallace?"

"He was going to land at Newark and take the bus."

"Do you think he knows what he's doing, Emil?"

"Without a license they wouldn't let him fly."

"That's not what I mean."

"He's the type of kid who wants to put things together his own way."

"I'm not sure he'll ever know . . ."

"He finds out as he goes along. He says that's what Action painters do."

"I could have more confidence in the process. I don't think he should be flying about today. His feelings, whatever they are—rivalry with his father, grief, or whatever—may carry him away."

"If it was my dad, I'd be at the hospital right now. It's different, now. We old guys have to go along."

Lifting his cap to extend the shade over his eyes, he gazed after the speeding Cessna. He revealed his long, full-bottomed Lombard nose. He had the wolfish North Italian look. His skin was tight. Perhaps he had been, as Wallace insisted, Emilio, a fierce little driver for the Mafia. But he was now at the stage of life at which the once-compact person begins to show an elderly frailty. This appeared in the shoulders and at the back of the neck, where the creases were deep. He was connected with the very finest, the supreme land vehicle. No competition with aircraft. He leaned against the fender, arms folded, making sure that no button scratched the finish. He held the hair-fragrant cap and tapped himself. He lightly struck the descending terraces, the large wrinkles of his forehead.

"I figure he wants shots from every altitude. He's flying low, all right."

"If he doesn't hit the house, I'll be very pleased."

"He could rack up the perfect score, after flooding the joint. You wonder, will he want to top that?"

Mr. Sammler brought out the folded handkerchief to slip under the lenses before removing his glasses, covering his disfigurement from Emil. He was unable to stare up longer, his eyes were smarting.

"How can one guess?" said Sammler. "Yesterday he said that it was his unconscious self that opened the wrong pipe."

"Yes, he talks that way to me, too. But I've been eighteen years with the Gruners and know that character. He's very, very disturbed about the doctor."

"Yes, I think he is. I agree. But that little machine . . . Like an ironing board with an egg beater. Are you a family man, Emil—do you have children?"

"Two. Grown up and graduated."

"Do they love you?"

"They act like it."

"That's already a great deal."

He was beginning to consider that he might not reach New York in time. Even Elya's request for clippings might delay him too long. But—one thing at a time. Then Wallace's engine grew louder. The noise attacked one's skull. It gave Sammler a headache. The injured eye felt pressure. The air was parted. On one side nuisance, on the other a singular current, an insidious spring brightness.

Blasting, shining, clear yellow, the color of a bird's bill, the Cessna made another, lower pass at the house. The trees threshed under it.

"He's going to crash. He'll hit the roof next time."

"I don't think he can buzz it any closer while snapping pictures," Emil said.

"He must certainly be below the permissible point."

The plane, rising, banking, grew smaller; you could hardly hear it now.

"Wasn't he about to strike the chimney?"

"It looked close, but only from our angle," said Emil.

"They shouldn't let him fly."

"Well, he's gone. Maybe that's it."

"Shall we start?" said Sammler.

"I'm supposed to pick up the cleaning woman at eleven —I think the phone has been ringing."

"The cleaning woman? Shula's in the house. She will answer."

"She's not," said Emil. "When I drove up I saw her in the road, walking along with her purse."

"Going where?"

"I wouldn't know. To the store, maybe. I'll get the phone."

The call was for Sammler. It was Margotte.

"Hello, Margotte. Well—?"

"We opened the lockers."

"What did you find, what she said?"

"Not exactly, Uncle. In the first locker was one of Shula's shopping bags, and in it there was only the usual stuff. *Christian Science Monitor*s from way back, clippings, and some old copies of *Life*. Also a great deal of student-revolt literature. SDS. Dr. Lal was shocked. He was very upset."

"Come, what about the second locker?"

"Thank God! We found the manuscript there."

"Intact?"

"I think so. He's looking through it." She spoke away from the phone. "Are pages torn out? No, Uncle, he doesn't think so."

"Oh, I am very glad. For him, and for myself. Even for Shula. But where is the copy she made on Widick's machine? She must have misplaced or lost that. But Dr. Lal must be delighted."

"Oh, he is. He's just going to wait at the soda fountain. It's such a chaos in Grand Central."

"I wish you had knocked at my door. You knew I had to get to town."

"Dear Uncle Sammler, we thought of that, but there was no room in the car. Am I mistaken, or are you irritated? You sound annoyed. We could have dropped you at the station." What Sammler refrained from saying was that he and Lal might have dropped her, Margotte, at the station. Was he annoyed! But even now, with skull-pressure, eye-pangs, he did not want to be too hard on her. No. She had her own female vital aims. No sense of the vital aims of others. His tension now. "Govinda was so anxious to leave. He insisted. However, the trains are fast. Besides, I phoned the hospital and talked to Angela. Elya's condition is just the same."

"I know. I've spoken to him."

"Well, you see? And he has to have some tests, so you would only have to wait if you were here. Now I'm taking Dr. Lal home to lunch. There's so much he doesn't eat, and Grand Central is a madhouse. And it smells so of hot dogs. Because of him, I notice it now for the first time."

"Of course. Home is better. By all means."

"Angela talked to me in a very mature way. She was sad, but she sounded so calm, and so aware." Margotte's kind and considerate views of people were terribly trying to Sammler. "She said that Elya was asking for you. He very much wishes to see you."

"I might have been there now. . . ."

"Well, he's down below anyhow," she said. "So take your time. Have lunch with us."

"I need to stop at the house. But no lunch."

"You wouldn't be in the way. Govinda likes you so much. He admires you. Anyway, you are my family. We love you like a father. All of us. I know I am a pest to you. I was to Ussher, too. Still, we loved each other."

"Well, well, Margotte. All right. Now let's hang up."

"I know you want to get away. And you don't like long phone conversations. But Uncle, I'm insecure about my ability to interest a man like Dr. Lal on the mental level."

"Nonsense, Margotte, don't be a fool. Don't get on the mental level. You charm him. He finds you exotic. Don't have long discussions. Let him do the talking."

But Margotte went on talking. She was putting in more coins. There were bongs and chimes. He did not hang up. Neither did he listen.

Further tests for Elya he took to be a tactic of the doctors. They protected their prestige by appearing to make real moves. But Elya himself was a doctor. He had lived by such gestures and had to submit to them now and without complaint. That certainly he would do. Now what of Elya's unfinished business? Before the vessel wall gave out did he really want to go on about Cracow? To talk about Uncle Hessid, who ground cornmeal and wore a derby and fancy vest? Sammler could recall no such individual. No. Elya with strong family feelings he could not gratify, wanted Sammler there to represent the family. His thin, lean presence, his small ruddy face, wrinkled on the one side. It was even more than piety for kinship which the age, acting through his children ("high-IQ moron, fucked-out eyes"), had leveled with derision and knocked flat. And Gruner called upon Sammler as more than an old uncle, one-eyed, growling peculiarly in Polish-Oxonian. He must have believed that he had some unusual power, magical perhaps, to affirm the human bond. What had he done to generate this belief? How had he induced it? By coming back from the dead, probably.

Margotte had much to say. She did not notice his silence.

By coming back, by preoccupation with the subject, the dying, the mystery of dying, the state of death. Also, by having been inside death. By having been given the shovel and told to dig. By digging beside his digging wife. When she faltered he tried to help her. By this digging, not speaking, he tried to convey something to her and fortify her. But as it had turned out, he had prepared her for death without sharing it. She was killed, not he. She had passed the course, and he had not. The hole deepened, the sand clay and stones of Poland, their birthplace, opened up. He had just been blinded, he had a stunned face, and he was unaware that blood was coming from him till they stripped and he saw it on his clothes. When they were as naked as children from the womb, and the hole was supposedly deep enough, the guns began to blast, and then came a different sound of soil. The thick fall of soil. A ton, two tons, thrown in. A sound of shovel-metal, gritting. Strangely exceptional, Mr. Sammler had come through the top of this. It seldom occurred to him to consider it an achievement. Where was the achievement? He had clawed his way out. If he had been at the bottom, he would have suffocated. If there had been another foot of dirt. Perhaps others had been buried alive in that ditch. There was no special merit, there was no wizardry. There was only suffocation escaped. And had the war lasted a few months more, he would have died like the rest. Not a Jew would have avoided death. As it was, he still had his consciousness, earthliness, human actuality—got up, breathed his earth gases in and out, drank his coffee, consumed his share of goods, ate his roll from Zabar's, put on certain airs—all human beings put on certain airs—took the bus to Forty-second Street as if he had an occupation, ran into a black pickpocket. In short, a living man. Or one who had been sent back again to the end of the line. Waiting for something. Assigned to figure out certain things, to condense, in short views, some essence of experience, and because of this having a certain wizardry ascribed to him. There was, in fact, unfinished business. But how did business finish? We entered in the middle of the thing and somehow became convinced that we must conclude it. How? And since he had lasted—survived—with a sick headache—he would not quibble over words—was there an assignment implicit? Was he meant to do something?

"I never want to annoy Lal," said Margotte. "He's gentle and small. By the way, Uncle, is the cleaning woman there?"

"Who? Cleaning?"

"You say charwoman. So is that the char? I hear the vacuum running."

"No, my dear, what you hear is our relative Wallace in his airplane. Don't ask me more. We'll see each other later."

He found his sodden shoes baking in the kitchen. Shula had set them on the open door of the electric oven and the toes were smoking. That, too! When he had cooled them, he labored to put them on with the handle of a tablespoon. The recovery of the manuscript helped him to be patient with Shula. She did not actually step over the line. The usefulness of these shoes, however, was at an end. They were ready for the dustbin. Not even Shula herself would want to retrieve them. And the immediate problem was not shoes, he could get to New York without shoes. Emil had already gone to fetch the charwoman. Taxis were listed in the Yellow Pages, but Sammler did not know which company to call, nor how much it might cost. He had only four dollars. Not to embarrass the Gruners you had to tip fifty cents at least. There was also fare to the city. Long-mouthed, silent, and with a hectic color, he tried to make the penny calculations. He saw himself, somewhere, eight cents short, trying to convince a policeman that he was not a panhandler. It would be better to wait. Perhaps Emil would meet Shula in the road, bringing her back with the char. Shula usually had money.

But Emil returned with the Croatian woman alone, and when he had shown her the water damage, he put on his cap, and, behaving to Sammler like a chauffeur, not at all treating him like a poor relation, he opened the silver door.

"Would you like the air conditioner, Mr. Sammler?"

"Thank you, Emil."

Examining the sky, Emil said, "It looks as if Wallace has all his pictures. He must be on his way to Newark."

"Yes, he's gone, thank God."

"I know the doctor wants to see you." Sammler was already seated. "What's the matter with your shoes?"

"I had trouble getting them on, and now I can't lace them. There's another pair at home. May we stop at the apartment?"

"The doctor talks about you all the time."

"Does he?"

"He's an affectionate fellow. I don't want to badmouth Mrs. Gruner, but you know how she was."

"Not demonstrative."

Emil shut the door, and very correct, walked behind the car and let himself into the driver's seat. "Well, she was very organized," he said. "As lady of the house, first class.

Like laid out with a ruler. Reserved. Fair. O.K. She ran the place like IBM—the gardener, the laundress, the cook, me. The doctor was grateful, being a kid from a rough neighborhood. She made him real Ivy. A gentleman." Emil backed the slow, silver high-bodied car, poor Elya's car, out of the drive. He gave Sammler the proper options of conversation or privacy. Sammler chose privacy and drew shut the glass panel.

Mr. Sammler's root feeling (a prejudice, if you like) was that women with exceedingly skinny legs could not be loving wives or passionate mistresses. Especially if with such legs they also had bouffant hairstyles. Hilda had been an agreeable person, cheerful, amiable, high-pitched, even at times breezy. But strictly correct. Often the doctor would demonstratively embrace her and say, "The world's best wife. Oh! I love you, Hil." He would clasp her from the side and kiss her on the cheek. This was permitted. It was allowed under a new dispensation which acknowledged the high value of warmth and impulsiveness. Undoubtedly Elya's feelings were strong, unlike Hilda's. But impulsive? There was in his conduct a strong element of propaganda. It came to him, perhaps, from the American system as a whole and showed his submissiveness. Everyone, to everyone, had a way of making propaganda for the good. Democracy was propagandistic in its style. Conversation was often nothing but the repetition of liberal principles. But Elya had certainly been disappointed in his wife. Sammler hoped that he had love affairs. With a nurse, perhaps? Or a patient who had become a mistress? Sammler did not recommend this for everyone, but in Elya's case it would have been beneficial. But no, probably the doctor was respectable. And it's a doomed man that woos affection so much.

It would soon be full spring. The Cross County, the Saw Mill River, the Henry Hudson thick with reviving grass and dandelions, the oven of the sun baking green life again. One was both sickened and strengthened by this swirling, this roughness and sweetness. Then—Mr. Sammler's elbow at rest on the gray cushion, and holding the back of one hand in the palm of the other—then there were the gray, yellow, homogeneous highways, from the engineering standpoint so impressive, from the moral, aesthetic, political something else. Staggering billions appropriated. But as someone had said about statesmen, the foremost of the Gadarene swine. Who had? He couldn't remember. Yet he was not cynical about these matters. He was not against civilization, nor against politics, institutions, nor against order. When the grave was dug, institutions and the rest had not been for him. No politics, no order intervened for Antonina. But there was no need to thrust oneself personally into every general question—to assail Churchill, Roosevelt, for having known (and surely they did know) what was happening and failing to bomb Auschwitz. Why not have bombed Auschwitz? But they didn't. Well, they didn't. They wouldn't. Emotions of justified reproach, supremacy in blame, made no appeal to Sammler. The individual was the supreme judge of nothing. Because he had to find things out for himself, he was necessarily the intermediate judge. But never final. Existence was not accountable to him. Indeed not. Nor would he ever put together the inorganic, organic, natural, bestial, human, and superhuman in any dependable arrangement but, however fascinating and original his genius, only idiosyncratically, a shaky scheme, mainly decorative or ingenious. Of course at the moment of launching from this planet to another something was ended, finalities were demanded, summaries. Everyone appeared to feel this need. Unanimously all tasted, and each in his own way, the flavor of the end of things-as-known. And by way of summary, perhaps, each accented more strongly his own subjective style and the practices by which he was known. Thus Wallace, on the day of destiny for his father, roared and snored in the Cessna snapping photographs. Thus Shula, hiding from Sammler, was undoubtedly going to hunt for treasure, for the alleged abortion dollars. Thus Angela, making more experiments in sensuality, in sexology, smearing all with her female fluids. Thus Eisen with his art, the Negro with his penis. And in the series, but not finally, himself with his condensed views. Eliminating the superfluous. Identifying the necessary.

Looking from the window, passing all in state, in an automobile costing upwards of twenty thousand dollars, Mr. Sammler still saw that together with the end of things-as-known the feeling for new beginnings was nevertheless very strong. Marriage for Margotte, America for Eisen, business for Wallace, love for Govinda. And away from this death-burdened, rotting, spoiled, sullied, exasperating, sinful earth but already looking toward the moon and Mars with plans for founding cities. And for himself . . .

He tapped the glass partition with a coin. The toll booth was approaching.

"It's O.K., Mr. Sammler."

Sammler insisted, "Here, Emil, take it, take it."

Measured by watch hands the trip was brief. In the off-hour, traffic moved quickly on the gray-and-yellow masterwork roads. Emil knew exactly how to drive. He was the faultless driver of the faultless car. He entered the city at One hundred twenty-fifth Street, under the ultrahigh railroad bridge that crossed the meat wholesalers' area. Sammler had some affection for this intricate bridge and the structural shadows it threw. Reflected in the shine of the meat trucks. The sides of beef and pork, gauze-wrapped, blood-spotted. Things edible would always be respected by a man who had nearly starved to death. The laborers, too, in white smocks, broad and heavy, a thickset personnel, butchers' men. By the river the smell was equivocal. You were not sure whether the rawness came from the tidewater or the blood. And here Sammler once saw a rat he took for a dachshund. The breeze out of this electric-lighted corner had the fragrance of meat dust. That was sprayed from the band saws that went through frozen fat, through marbled red or icy porphyry, and whizzed through bone. Try to stroll here. The pavements were waxed with fat.

Then a right turn, downtown on Broadway. The street rose while the subway was lowering. Up, the brown masonry; and down, the black shadow and steel tracks. Then tenements, the Puerto Rican squalor. Then the University, squalid in a different way. It was already too warm in the city. Spring lost the touch of winter and got the summer rankness. Between the pillars at One hundred-sixteenth Street Sammler looked into the brick quadrangles. He half expected Feffer to pass, or the bearded man in Levi's who had said he couldn't come. He saw growing green. But green in the city had lost its association with peaceful sanctuary. The old-time poetry of parks was banned. Obsolete thickness of shade leading to private meditation. Truth was now slummier and called for litter in the setting —leafy reverie? A thing of the past.

Except on special occasions (Feffer's lecture, twenty-four? forty-eight hours ago?), Sammler never came this way any more. Walking for exercise, he didn't venture this far uptown. And now, from Elya's Rolls Royce, he inspected the subculture of the underprivileged (terminology recently acquired in the *New York Times*), its Caribbean fruits, its plucked naked chickens with loose necks and eyelids blue, the wavering fumes of Diesel and hot lard. Then Ninety-sixth Street, tilted at all four corners, the kiosks and movie houses, the ramparts of wire-fastened newspaper bundles, and the colors of panic waving. Broadway, even when there was some urgency, hurrying to see Elya for possibly the last time, always challenged Sammler. He was never up to it. And why should there be any contest? But there was, every time. For something was stated here. By a convergence of all minds and all movements the conviction transmitted by this crowd seemed to be that reality was a terrible thing, and that the final truth about mankind was overwhelming and crushing. This vulgar, cowardly conclusion, rejected by Sammler with all his heart, was the implicit local orthodoxy, the populace itself being metaphysical and living out this interpretation of reality and this view of truth. Sammler could not swear that this was really accurate, but Broadway at Ninety-sixth Street gave him such a sense of things. Life, when it was like this, all question-and-answer from the top of intellect to the very bottom, was really a state of singular dirty misery. When it was all question-and-answer it had no charm. Life when it had no charm was entirely question-and-answer. The thing worked both ways. Also, the questions were bad. Also, the answers were horrible. This poverty of soul, its abstract state, you could see in faces on the street. And he too had a touch of the same disease—the disease of the single self explaining what was what and who was who. The results could be foreseen, foretold. So, then, brought down Broadway in high style,

Sammler visited his own (what did Wallace call it?) his own *turf*. As a tourist. And then Emil, by way of Riverside Drive, came round and set him down before the great, used, soiled mass of conveniences where he and Margotte lived. The time was half past twelve.

"It shouldn't take long. Elya asked for some papers."

There was a tightness at his heart. The remedy was fuller breathing, but he could not get his chest to rise and fall. Something had locked it. Margotte and Govinda were not back. The pin-up lamp burned needlessly in the foyer above the sofa with its maple armrests, the bandanna covers. There was a certain peace in the house. Or did it seem so because he had no time to sit down? He changed shoes, shook a few dollars from his jar, put the newspaper clippings into his wallet. On his desk was a bottle of vodka. Shula provided this out of the wages Elya paid her. It was excellent, Stolichnaya, imported from the Soviet Union. Sammler made use of it about once a month. He uncorked the bottle now and drank a glass. It went down burning, and he made a face. First aid for the old. Then he opened his door to the back stairs, slipping the latch lest one of the strong drafts there should come slamming and lock him out. He put his old shoes into the incinerator drop. He didn't want Shula arguing that she had done them no harm in the electric oven. They had had it.

For once the lobby television worked. Gray and whitish figures, unsteady on the vertical hold, wavered and fizzed. Sammler saw himself mortally pale on the screen. The shuddering image of an aged man. This lobby was like certain underground carpeted rooms in disused theaters—spaces to shun. It was less than two days ago that the pickpocket had forced him, belly-to-back, across this same brass-bolted rug into the corner beside the Florentine table.

Unbuttoning his puma-colored coat in puma silence to show himself. Was this the sort of fellow called by Goethe *eine Natur*? A primary force?

He stopped Emil from getting out of the car for him.

"I can work the door myself."

"We're off, then. Open the bar, pour yourself a drink."

"I hope the traffic will not be too thick."

"We'll go straight down Broadway."

"Turn on the TV."

"Thanks. No TV."

Again Sammler smelled the enclosed, fabric-scented air. He did not make himself comfortable. The tightness of heart was greater than before. It went on contracting; he thought it could not be worse, and then it was worse. The traffic was unusually heavy, jammed up at the lights. Delivery trucks were double-parked, triple-parked. The use of private cars in Manhattan had never seemed so irrational and harmful. He was swept by impatience toward the drivers of these large, purposeless machines but then the sweeping feelings swept beyond him. Conveyed in air-conditioned silence by the roarless power of the engine, he sat forward with his thighs upon the backs of his hands. Evidently Elya thought that he owed it to himself to maintain this Rolls. He couldn't have had much use for such a prestigious machine. It wasn't as if he were a Broadway producer, an international banker, a tobacco millionaire. Where did it take him? To Widick's law office. To Hayden, Stone Incorporated, where he had an account. On High Holy Days, he went to the temple on Fifth Avenue. On Fifty-seventh Street were his tailors, Felsher and Kitto. The temple and the tailors had been selected by Hilda. Sammler would have sent him to another tailor. Elya had a tall figure and wide stiff shoulders, too wide, considering the flatness of his body. His buttocks were too high. Like my own, for that matter. Sammler, in the sound-deadened cabinet of the Rolls, saw the resemblance. Felsher and Kitto made Elya too dapper. The trousers were too narrow. The virile bulge that appeared when he sat was inappropriate. He used matching ties and handkerchiefs by Countess Mara, and sharp, swaggering shoes which connected him less with medicine than with Las Vegas, with racing, broads, and singers in the rackets. Things equivocally related to his kindliness. Swaying his shoulders like a gunman. Wearing double-vented jackets. Playing gin and canasta for high stakes and talking out of the corner of the mouth. Detesting *Kulturny* physicians who wanted to discuss Heidegger or Wittgenstein. Real doctors had no time for that phony stuff. He was a keen spotter of phonies. He could easily afford this car, but had none of the life that went with it. No Broadway musicals, no private jet. His one glamorous eccentricity was to fly to Israel on short notice and stroll into the King David Hotel without baggage, his hands in his pockets. That struck him as a sporting thing to do. Of course, thought Sammler, Elya was also peculiar; surgery was psychically peculiar. To enter an unconscious body with a knife? To take out organs, sew in the flesh, splash blood? Not everyone could do that. And perhaps he kept the car for Emil's sake. What would Emil do if there were no Rolls? Now there was the likeliest answer of all. The protective instinct was strong in Elya. Undisclosed charities were his pleasure. He had many strategems of benevolence. I have reason to know. How very odd—astonishing, the desire to relieve and protect us. It was astonishing because Elya the surgeon also despised incompetence and weakness. Only great and powerful instincts worked so deeply and deviously, coming out on the side of things despised. But how could Elya afford to have rigid ideas of strength? He himself was a hooked man. Hilda had been far stronger than he. In the Mafioso swagger were pretensions of lawless liberty. But it was little Hilda with the rod-like legs and the bouffant hair and faultless hemlines and sweet refinements who was the real criminal. She had had her hook in Elya. And there had never been any help for Elya. Who was there to help him? He was the sort of individual from whom help emanated. There were no arrangements for return. However, it would soon be over. It was about to wash away.

As for the world, was it really about to change? Why? How? By the fact of moving into space, away from earth? There would be changes of heart? There would be new conduct? Why, because we were tired of the old conduct? That was not reason enough. Why, because the world was breaking up? Well, America, if not the world. Well, staggering, if not breaking.

Emil was driving more steadily again, below Seventy-second Street. The traffic had eased. There were no truck deliveries to impede it. Lincoln Center was approaching and, at Columbus Circle, the Huntington Hartford Building, which Bruch called the Taj Mahole. Wasn't that funny! said Bruch. At his own jokes he rolled with laughter. Ape-like, he put his hands on his paunch and closed his eyes, letting the tongue hang out of his blind head. What a building! All holes. But that was some lunch they put down for only three bucks. He raved about the bill of fare—Hawaiian chicken and saffron rice. Finally he had taken the old man there. It was indeed a grand lunch. But Lincoln Center Sammler had seen only from the outside. He was cold to the performing arts, and shunned large crowds. Exhibitions, electrical or nude, he had attended only because it amused Angela to keep him up to date. But he passed by the pages of the *Times* that dealt with painters, singers, fiddlers, or play actors. He saved his reading eye for better things. He had noted with hostile interest crews wrecking the nice old tenements and greasy-spoons, and the new halls rising.

But now, as they were nearing the Center, Emil stopped the car and pushed back the glass slide.

"Why are you stopping?"

Emil said, "There's something happening across the street." He looked, wrinkling his face deeply, as if this explanation must really be heeded. But why, at such a time, should he have stopped for anything? "Don't you recognize those people, Mr. Sammler?"

"Which? Has someone scraped someone? Is it a traffic thing?" Of course he lacked authority to tell Emil to drive on, but he gestured, nevertheless, with the back of his hand. He waved Emil forward.

"No, I think you'll want to stop, Mr. Sammler. I see your son-in-law there. Isn't that him, with the big green bag? And isn't that Wallace's partner?"

"Feffer?"

"That fat kid. The pink face, the beard. He's fighting. Can't you see?"

"Where is this? In the street? Is it Eisen?"

"It's the other fellow who's in trouble. The young guy, the beard. I think he's getting hurt."

On the east side of the slant street a bus had pulled to the curb at a wide angle, obstructing traffic. Sammler could see now that someone was struggling there, in the midst of a crowd.

"One of those is Feffer?"

"Yes, Mr. Sammler."

"Wrestling with someone—with the bus driver?"

"Not the driver, no. I think not. Somebody else."

"Then I must go and see what it is."

The craziness of these delays! Almost deliberate, almost intentional, they were breaking down every barrier of patience. They got to you at last. Why this, why Feffer? But he could see now what Emil meant. Feffer was pinned to the front of a bus. That *was* Feffer against the wide bumper. Sammler began to pull at the handle of the door.

"Not on the street side, Mr. Sammler. You'll be hit."

But Sammler, his patience utterly lost, was already hurrying through traffic.

Feffer, in the midst of the crowd, was fighting the black man, the pickpocket. There were twenty people at least, and more were stopping, but no one was about to interfere. Struggling in the criminal's grip, Feffer was forced back against the big cumbersome machine. His head was knocking on the windshield below the empty driver's seat. The man was squeezing him, and Feffer was scared. He resisted, he defended himself, but he was inept. He was overmatched. Of course. How could it be otherwise? His bearded face was frightened. Upturned, the broad cheeks flamed, and his wide-spaced brown eyes appealed for help. Or were thinking what to do. What should he do? Like a man groping in a stream for a lost object, while staring into air, mouth gaping in his beard. But he would not give up the Minox. One arm was held straight up, out of reach. The weight of the big body in the fawn-colored suit crushed him. He had had the bad luck to get his candid shot. The black man was snatching at the Minox. To get the tiny camera, to give Feffer a few kicks in the ribs, in the belly—what else would he have had in mind? Leaving, without haste if possible, before the police arrived. But Feffer, near panic, still was obstinate. Shifting his grip, the Negro grabbed and twisted his collar, holding him as he had held Sammler with his forearm against the wall. He choked Feffer with the neckband. The Dior shades, round and bluish, had not moved from the low-bridged nose. Feffer had caught the spouting red necktie in his fist, but could do nothing with it.

How shall we save this prying, stupid idiotic boy? He may be hurt. And I must go. There's no time. "Some of you," Sammler ordered. "Here! Help him. Break this up." But of course "some of you" did not exist. No one would do anything, and suddenly Sammler felt extremely foreign—voice, accent, syntax, manner, face, mind, everything, foreign.

Emil had seen Eisen. Sammler looked for him now. And there he was, smiling and very pale. He was evidently waiting to be discovered. Then he seemed delighted.

"What are you doing here?" said Sammler in Russian.

"And you, Father-in-law—what are you doing?"

"I? I am rushing to the hospital to see Elya."

"Yes. And I was with my young friend on the bus when he took the picture. Of a purse being opened. I saw it myself."

"What a stupid thing!"

Eisen held his green baize bag. It contained his sculptures or medallions. Those Dead Sea pieces—iron pyrites, or whatever they were.

"Let him give up the camera. Why doesn't he give it to him?" said Sammler.

"But how do we prevail upon him?" said Eisen in a tone of discussion.

"Get a policeman," Sammler said. He would have liked to say, too, "Stop this smiling."

"But I don't know English."

"Then help the boy."

"You help him, Father-in-law. I am a foreigner and a cripple. You're older, true. But I just got to this country."

Sammler said to the pickpocket, "Let go. Let him go."

The man's large face turned. New York was reflected in the lenses, under the stiff curves of the homburg. Perhaps he recognized Sammler. But nothing was said.

"Give him the camera, Feffer. Hand it over," Sammler said.

Feffer, with a stare of shock and appeal, looked as if he expected soon to lose consciousness. He did not bring down his arm.

"I say let him have that stupid thing. He wants the film. Don't be an idiot."

Feffer may have been holding out in expectation of a squad car, waiting for the police to save him. It was hard otherwise to explain his resistance. Considering the Negro's strength—his crouching, squeezing, intense animal pressing-power, the terrific swelling of the neck and the tightness of the buttocks as he rose on his toes. In straining alligator shoes! In fawn-colored trousers! With a belt that matched his necktie—a crimson belt! How consciousness was lashed by such a fact!

"Eisen!" said Sammler, furious.

"Yes, Father-in-law."

"I ask you to do something."

"Let them do something." He motioned with the baize bag to the bystanders. "I only came forty-eight hours ago."

Again Mr. Sammler turned to the crowd, staring hard. Wouldn't anyone help? So even now—now, *still!*—one believed in such things as help. Where people were, help might be. It was an instinct and a reflex. (An unexasperated hope?) So, briefly examining faces, passing from face to face to face among the people along the curb—red, pale, swarthy, lined taut or soft, grim or adream, eyes bald-blue, iodine-reddish, coal-seam black—how strange a quality their inaction had. They were expecting gratification, oh! at last! of teased, cheated, famished needs. Someone was going to get it! Yes. And the black faces? A similar desire. Another side. But the same. Though there was nothing to hear, Sammler had the sense that something was barking away. Then it struck him that what united everybody was a beatitude of presence. As if it were—yes—blessed are the present. They are here and not here. They are present while absent. So they were waiting in that ecstatic state. What a supreme privilege! And there was only Eisen to break up the fight. Which was, after all, an odd sort of fight. Sammler did not believe that the black man would choke Feffer into unconsciousness; he would only go on squeezing, screwing the collar tighter until Feffer surrendered the Minox. Of course, there was always a chance that he might strike him, pull a knife, stab him. But there was something worse here than this event itself, namely, the feeling that stole over Sammler.

It was a feeling of horror and grew in strength, grew and grew. What was it? How was it to be put? He was a man who had come back. He had rejoined life. He was near to others. But in some essential way he was also companionless. He was old. He lacked physical force. He knew what to do, but had no power to execute it. He had to turn to someone else—to an Eisen! a man himself very far out on another track, orbiting a very different foreign center. Sammler was powerless. To be so powerless was death. And suddenly he saw himself not so much standing as strangely leaning, as reclining, and peculiarly in profile, and as a *past* person. That was not himself. It was someone—and this struck him—poor in spirit. Someone between the human and not-human states, between content and emptiness, between full and void, meaning and not-meaning, between this world and no world. Flying, freed from gravitation, light with release and dread, doubting his destination, fearing there was nothing to receive him.

"Eisen, separate them," he said. "He's been choked enough. The police will come, and then there will be arrests. And I must go. To stand here is crazy. Please. Just take the camera. Take it. That will stop this."

Then handsome Eisen, shrugging, grinning, making a crooked movement of the shoulders, working them free from the tight denim, stepped away from Sammler as though he were doing a very amusing thing at his special request. He drew up the sleeve of his right arm. The dark hairs were thick. Then shortening his grip on the cords of the baize bag he swung it very wide, swung with full force and struck the pickpocket on the side of the face. It was a hard blow. The glasses flew. The hat. Feffer was not immediately freed. The man seemed to rest on him. Obviously stunned. Eisen was a laborer, a foundry worker. He had the strength not only of his trade but also of madness. There was something limitless, unbounded, about the way he squared off, took the man's measure, a kind of sturdy viciousness. Everything went into that blow, discipline, murderousness, everything. What have I done! This is much worse! This is the worst thing yet. Sammler thought Eisen had crushed the man's face. And he was now about to hit him again, with his medallions. The black man took his hands from Feffer and was turning. His lips came away from his teeth. Eisen had gashed his skin and the cheek was bleeding and swelling. Eisen clinked the weights from his wrist, spread his legs. "He'll kill that cocksucker!" someone in the crowd said.

"Don't hit him, Eisen. I never said that. I tell you no!" said Sammler.

But the bag of weights was speeding from the other side, very wide but accurate. It struck more heavily than before and knocked the man down. He did not drop. He lowered himself as though he had decided to lie in the street. The blood ran in points on his cheek. The terrible metal had cut him through the baize.

Eisen now heaved his weapon back over the shoulder, prepared to slam it straight down on the man's skull. Sammler seized his arm and twisted him away. "You'll murder him. Do you want to beat out his brains?"

"You *said*, Father-in-law!"

They quarreled in Russian before the crowd.

"You said I had to do something. You said you had to go. I must do something. So I did."

"I didn't say to hit him with these damned irons. I didn't say to hit him at all. You're crazy, Eisen, crazy enough to murder him."

The pickpocket had tried to brace himself on his elbows. His body now rested on his doubled arms. He bled thickly on the asphalt.

"I am horrified!" Sammler said.

Eisen, still handsome, curly, still with the smile, though now panting, and the peculiar set of the toeless feet, seemed amused at Sammler's ludicrous inconsistency. He said, "You can't hit a man like this just once. When you hit him you must really hit him. Otherwise he'll kill you. You know. We both fought in the war. You were a Partisan. You had a gun. So don't you know?" His laughter, his logic, laughing and reasoning at Sammler's absurdities, made him repeat until he stuttered. "If in—in. No? If out--out. Yes? No? So answer."

It was the reasoning that sank Sammler's heart completely. "Where is Feffer?" he said, and turned away.

Feffer, resting his forehead against the bus, was getting back his breath. Putting it on, no doubt. To Sammler this exaggeration was revolting.

Damn these—these *occasions!* he was thinking. Damn them, it was Elya who needed him. It was only Elya he wanted to see. To whom there was something to say. Here there was nothing to say.

Now he heard someone ask, "Where are the cops?"

"Busy. On the take. Writing tickets, someplace. Those shits. When you need 'em."

"There's plenty of blood. They better bring an ambulance."

The light upon the dull kinks, the porous carbon-cake of the man's head, still dropping blood, showed his eye shut. But he wished to get to his feet. He made efforts.

Eisen said to Sammler, "This is the man, isn't it? The man you told about who followed you? Who showed you his jinjik?"

"Get away from me, Eisen."

"What should I do?"

"Go away. Get away from here. You're in trouble," said Sammler. He spoke to Feffer, "What have you to say now?"

"I caught him in the act. Please wait awhile, he hurt my throat."

"Nonsense, don't put on agony with me. *This* is the man. *He's* badly hurt."

"I swear he was picking the purse, and I got two shots of him."

"*Did* you, now!"

"You seem angry, sir. Why are you so angry with me?"

Sammler now saw the squad car, the whirling roof light, and the policemen coming out at a saunter, pushing away the crowd. Emil drew Sammler away to the side of the bus and said, "You don't want any of this. We have to go."

"Yes, Emil, of course."

They crossed the street. Avoid getting mixed up with the police. They might detain him for hours. He should never have stopped at the flat. He should have gone directly to the hospital.

"I think I would like to sit in the front with you, Emil."

"Why, sure. Are you all shook up?" He helped him in. Emil's own hand was shaking, and Sammler himself had trembling arms and legs. An extraordinary weakness came up the legs from beneath.

The great engine ignited. Coolness poured from the air conditioner. Then the Rolls entered traffic.

"What was all that about?"

"I wish I knew," said Sammler.

"Who was that black character?"

"Poor man, I can't really say who he is."

"He took two mean wallops, there."

"Eisen is brutal."

"What did he have in that bag?"

"Pieces of metal. I feel responsible, Emil, because I appealed to Eisen, because I wanted so badly to get to Dr. Gruner."

"Well, maybe the guy has a thick skull. I guess you never saw anybody hitting to kill. You want to lie down in back for ten minutes? I can stop."

"Do I look sick? No, Emil. But I think I will shut my eyes."

Sammler was sick with rage at Eisen. The black man? The black man was a megalomaniac. But there was a certain—

a certain princeliness. The clothing, the shades, the sumptuous colors, the barbarous-majestical manner. He was probably a mad spirit. But mad with an idea of *noblesse.* And how much Sammler sympathized with him—how much he would have done to prevent such atrocious blows! How red the blood was, and how thick—and how terrible those crusted, spiny lumps of metal were! And Eisen? He counted as a war victim, even though he might anyhow have been mad. But he belonged in the mental hospital. A homicidal maniac. If only, thought Sammler, Shula and Eisen had been a little less crazy. Just a little less. They would have gone on playing casino in Haifa, those two cuckoos, in their whitewashed Mediterranean cage. For they used to get the cards out when they weren't scandalizing the neighborhood with their screams and slaps. But no. Such individuals had the right to be considered normal. They had liberty of movement, on top of it. They had passports, tickets. So then, poor Eisen flew across with his works. Poor soul, poor dog-laughing Eisen.

They all had such fun! Wallace, Feffer, Eisen, Bruch, too, and Angela. They laughed so much. Dear brethren, let us all be human together. Let us all be in the great fun fair, and do this droll mortality with one another. Be entertainers of your near and dear. Treasure hunts, flying circuses, comical thefts, medallions, wigs and saris, beards. Charity, all of it, sheer charity, when you consider the state of things, the blindness of the living. It is fearful! Not to be borne! Intolerable! Let us divert each other while we live!

"I'll park here and go up with you," said Emil. "They can give me a ticket if they like."

"The doctor is not back?" said Emil.

Obviously not. Angela sat alone in the hospital room.

"Then O.K. I'll be standing by if you want me."

"I seem to be smoking three packs a day. I'm out of cigarettes, Emil. I can't even concentrate on a newspaper."

"Benson and Hedges, right?"

When he left she said, "I don't like to send an elderly person on errands."

Sammler made no reply. The Augustus John hat was in his hand. He didn't lay it on the clean newmade bed.

"Emil is part of Daddy's gang. They're very attached."

"What's happening?"

"I wish I knew. He was taken down for tests, but two hours is a long time. I assume Dr. Cosbie knows his stuff. I don't like the man. I don't go for the magnolia charm. He acts as if he ran a military academy in the South. But I'm not one of the boys. Drill is not my dish. He's cross, cold, and repulsive. One of those good-looking men who don't realize that women dislike them. Take the straight chair, Uncle. You like those better. I have to talk to you."

Sammler drew the seat under him, and out of the light—he couldn't bear to face windows through which nothing but blue sky was visible. He saw trouble. Himself aroused, he was sensitive to all the signs. Another woman would have had a hectic color; Angela was candle-white. The amusing husky voice, copying Tallulah's perhaps, fell short of amusement. Her throat was prominent, it looked swollen, and the light brown brows, penciled out like wings, kept rising. She tried at times to give a look of appeal. She was angry, too. It was heavy going. Even wrinkling her forehead seemed difficult. Something was obstructed. With a low-necked satin blouse she wore a miniskirt. No, Sammler changed that, it was a microskirt, a band of green across the thighs. The frosted hair was pulled back tightly; the skin was full of female qualities (the hormones). On her cheeks large gold earrings lay. A big, shapely woman childishly dressed, erotically playing the kid, she was not likely to be taken for a boy. Sitting near her, Sammler could not smell the usual Arabian musk. Instead her female effluence was very strong, a salt odor, similar to tears or tidewater, something from within the woman. Elya's words had taken effect strongly—his "Too much sex." Even the white lipstick suggested perversion. But this was curiously without prejudice. Sammler felt no prejudice about perversion, about sexual matters. Nothing. It was too late in the day for that. Too much heat was on. Much larger powers of distortion were at work. The smash of Eisen's medallions on the pickpocket's face was still with Sammler. His own nerves, in the elementary way of nerves, connected this with the crushing of his eye under the rifle butt thirty years ago. The sensations of choking and falling—one *could* live through that again. If it was worth living through. He waited for the rubber bump of Elya's wheeled stretcher against the door.

"Has Wallace shown up? He was supposed to land at Newark."

"He didn't. I've got to tell you about Brother. When did you see him? I heard from Margotte about the pipes."

"In the flesh? I saw him last night. And this morning in the sky."

"Oh, so you watched him looping around, that idiot."

"Has he had an accident?"

"Oh, don't worry, he isn't hurt. I wish he had given himself a good bang, but he's like a Hollywood stunt man."

"He hasn't crashed, has he?"

"What do you think! It's already an item on the radio. He scraped his wheels off on a house."

"Dear Lord! Did he have to parachute? Was it your house?"

"He made a crash landing. It was some big place in Westchester. God alone knows why that creep should be out buzzing houses when we're in this predicament. It's enough to drive me mad."

"You don't mean that Elya heard this on the radio!"

"No, he didn't hear. He was already going down in the elevator."

"You say Wallace isn't hurt?"

"Wallace is in seventh heaven. Overjoyed. He had to have stitches in his cheek."

"I see. He'll have a scar. All this is terrible!"

"You have too much sympathy for him."

"I do admit that all this feeling sorry for people can be wearing. I also am provoked by him."

"You should be. They really ought to put my kid brother away. Lock him up in an asylum. You should have heard him babbling."

"Then you've spoken to him?"

"He had some guy to describe the beautiful landing. Then he took the phone in person. Something terrific. As if he had reached the North Pole by bicycle. You know we'll be sued for damages to the house. The plane is wrecked. Civil Aeronautics will take away his license. I wish they'd take him away, too. But he was very high. He said, 'Shouldn't we tell Dad?' "

"No!"

"Yes," said Angela. She was furious. With Dr. Cosbie, with Wallace, with Widick, Horricker. And she was bitter with Sammler, too. And he himself was far from normal. Far! The injured black man. The blood. And now, confronted by all that superfeminity, sensuality, he saw everything with heightened clarity. As he had seen Riverside Drive, wickedly illuminated, after watching the purse being picked on the bus. That was how he was seeing now. To see was delicious. Oh, of course! An extreme pleasure! The sun may shine, and be a blessing, but sometimes shows the fury of the world. Brightness like this, the vividness of everything, also dismayed him. The soft clearness of Angela's face, the effort of her brows—the full mixture of fineness and rankness he saw there. And the sun was squarely at the window. The streaked glass ran with light like honey. A barrage of sweetness and intolerable brightness was laid down. Sammler did not really want to experience this. It all rose against him, too dizzy, too turbulent.

"I can see that you and Elya went on talking about that event."

"He won't let it alone. It's cruel. Both to himself and to me. I can't stop him."

"What is there for you to do but give in? He's the one with the thing to do. There should be no arguments. Perhaps young Mr. Horricker should come up. Why doesn't he come? Show that he doesn't take it too much to heart. Does he, by the way?"

"He says so."

"Maybe he loves you."

"Him? Who knows. But I wouldn't ask him to come. That would be using Daddy's illness."

"You don't want him back?"

"Want him? Maybe. I'm not sure."

Was there a successor in view? Human attachments being so light, there were probably lists of alternates, preconscious reserves—men met in the park while walking the dog; people one had chatted with at the Museum of Modern Art; this fellow with the sideburns; that one with dark sexy eyes; the person with the child in a sanitarium, the wife with multiple sclerosis. To go with quantities of ideas and purposes there were quantities of people. And all this came from Angela's conversation. He heard and remembered everything, every drab fact, every crimson touch. He didn't want to listen, but she told him things. He had no wish to remember, but he remembered it all. And Angela really was a beauty. She was big, but a beauty, a healthy young woman. Healthy young women have their needs. Her legs were—her thighs nearly all shown down from the green ribbon of skirt—she was, beautiful. Horricker would suffer, knowing he had lost her. Sammler was still thinking things through. Tired, dizzy, despairing, he still thought. Still in touch. With reality, that is.

"Wharton is no kid. He knew what he was getting into, down in Mexico," said Angela.

"Ah, I don't understand any of that. I assume he's read some of those books you lent me—Bataille and other theorists—about transgression and pain and sex; lust, crime, and desire; murder and erotic pleasure. It didn't mean much to me, any of that stuff."

"I know it's not your kind of thing. But Wharton got his kicks out of that little broad. He liked her. Better than I liked the other man. I'd never see *him* again. But then on the plane Wharton perversely became jealous. Wouldn't let it alone."

"My only thought is that Elya might feel more at peace with you if he saw Horricker."

"I'm furious that Wharton should blab to Widick, and Widick to Father."

"I'm not prepared to believe that Mr. Widick would speak to Elya of this. He's decent enough in most ways. I don't know him well, of course. My main impression is of a stout lawyer. Not a villain. A big soft face."

"That fat sonofabitch. I'll curse him when I see him. I'll tear his hair out."

"Don't be so sure that it was some evil-doer. You may be wrong. Elya's extremely intelligent and quick to pick up hints."

"Who could it be, then? Wallace? Emil? But whoever dropped the hint, it began with Wharton, too weak to keep his mouth shut. Well, if he wants to visit Father that's all right. But I'm offended. I'm furious."

"You do have a feverish look, Angela. I don't want to agitate you. But in view of your father's preoccupation with all this, with Mexico, do you think you should arrive in such a costume?"

"This skirt, you mean?"

"It's very short. My opinion may be worthless, but it seems bad judgment to wear that kind of sexual kindergarten dress."

"Now it's my clothes! Are you speaking for him, or for yourself?"

The sunlight was yellow, sweet. It was horrible.

"Oh yes, I know I may be out of order, with bad puritanical attitudes from the sick past which have damaged civilization so much. I did read your books. We've discussed all this. But really, how do you expect your father not to be excited, to feel bitter, when he sees this provoking Baby Doll costume?"

"Really? My skirt? It never occurred to me. I dressed quickly and ran out. This is a strange thing to take up with me now. Everybody wears these skirts. I don't think I care for the way you put it."

"Undoubtedly I could have put it better. I don't want to be disagreeable. There are other things to think about."

"That's right. And I'm under a terrible burden. It is terrible."

"I'm sure of it."

"I'm in despair, Uncle."

"Yes, you must be. Of course you are. Yes."

"Yes, what? It sounds as if there's something more."

"There is. I'm in a state, too, about your father. He's been a great friend to me. I am sick, too, about him."

"We don't have to beat around the bush, Uncle."

"No. He's going to die."

"That's coming out with it all right," she said. She was for plain speaking, was this too plain?

"It's as terrible to say as to hear."

"I'm sure you love Daddy," she said.

"I do."

"Apart from the practical reasons, I mean."

"Of course Shula and I have been supported by him. I never concealed my gratitude. I hope that has been no secret," said Sammler. As he was dry and old, the beating of his heart, even violent beating, would not be evident. "If I were practical, if I were very practical, I would be careful not to antagonize you. I think there are reasons other than the practical ones."

"Well, I hope we're not going to quarrel."

"That's right," said Sammler. She was angry with Wallace, with Cosbie, Horricker. He did not want to add himself to the list. He needed no victory over Angela. He only wanted to persuade her of something, and didn't know whether even that was feasible. But he was certainly not about to make war on suffering females. He began to talk. "I'm feeling very jumpy, Angela. There are certain damaged nerves you don't hear from for years, and then they act up, they flare up. They're burning now, very painfully. Now I'd like to say something about your father, as long as we're waiting for him. On the surface, I don't have much in common with Elya. He's a sentimental person. He makes a point, too much of a point, of treasuring certain old feelings. He's on an old system. I've always been skeptical of that myself. One might ask, where is the new system? But we don't have to get into that. I never had much natural liking for people who make open declarations of affection. Being a 'Britisher' was one of my foibles. Cold? But I still appreciate a certain restraint. I didn't care for the way Elya courted everyone, tried to make contact with people, winning their hearts, engaging their interest, getting personal even with waitresses, lab technicians, manicurists. It was always too easy for him to say 'I love you.' He was forever saying it to your mother in public, embarrassing her. I don't intend to discuss her with you. She had her good points. But as I was a snob about the British, she was a German Jewess who cultivated the Wasp style (now outmoded, by the way), and I recognized it. She was going to refine your father, an *Ostjude*. He was supposed to be the expressive one, the one with the heart. Isn't that about right? So your father was assigned to be expressive. He certainly had his work cut out for him with your mother. I think it would have been easier to love a theorem in geometry than your poor mother. Excuse me, Angela, for going on like this."

She said, "It's like we're sitting on the edge of a cliff anyway, waiting here."

"All right, Angela. One might as well talk, then. Not to

add to your difficulties . . . I just saw something peculiarly nasty, on my way over. Partly my fault. I feel distressed. But I was saying that your father has had his assignments. Husband, medical man—he was a good doctor—family man, success, American, wealthy retirement with a Rolls Royce. We have our assignments. Feeling, outgoingness, expressiveness, kindness, heart—all these fine human things which by a peculiar turn of opinion strike people now as shady activities. Openness and candor about vices seem far easier. Anyway, there is Elya's assignment. That's what's in his good face. That's why he has such a human look. He's made something of himself. He hasn't done badly. He didn't like surgery. You know that. He dreaded those three- and four-hour operations. But he performed them. He did what he disliked. He had an unsure loyalty to certain pure states. He knew there had been good men before him, that there were good men to come, and he wanted to be one of them. I think he did all right. I don't come out nearly so well myself. Till forty or so I was simply an Anglophile intellectual Polish Jew and person of culture—relatively useless. But Elya, by sentimental repetition and by formulas if you like, partly by propaganda, has accomplished something good. Brought himself through. He loves you. I'm sure he loves Wallace. I believe he loves me. I've learned much from him. I have no illusions about your father, you understand. He's touchy, boastful, he repeats himself. He's vain, grouchy, proud. But he's done well, and I admire him."

"So he's human. All right, he's human." She was, perhaps, only half following him, though she looked straight at him, full-face, knees apart so that he saw the pink material of her undergarment. Seeing that pink band, he thought, "Why argue? What is the point?" But he replied.

"Well, everybody's human only in some degree. Some more than others."

"Some very little?"

"That's the way it seems. Very little. Faulty. Scanty. Dangerous."

"I thought everybody was born human."

"It's not a natural gift at all. Only the capacity is natural."

"Well, Uncle, why are you putting me through this? What have you got in mind? You're after something."

"Yes, I suppose I am."

"You're criticizing me."

"No, I'm praising your father."

Angela's gaze was dilated, brilliant, smeary, angry. No fights, for God's sake, with a despairing woman. Still, he was getting at something. He held his thin body rigid; the ginger-gray brows overhung the tinted dimness of the shades.

"I don't like the opinion I think you have of me," she said.

"Why should that matter on a day like this? Well, perhaps I do feel that today there ought to be a difference. Perhaps if we were in India or Finland we might not be in quite the same mood. New York makes one think about the collapse of civilization, about Sodom and Gomorrah, the end of the world. The end wouldn't come as surprise here. Many people already bank on it. And I don't know whether humankind is really all that much worse. In one day, Caesar massacred the Tencteri, four hundred and thirty thousand souls. Even Rome was appalled. I am not sure that this is the worst of all times. But it is in the air now that things are falling apart, and I am affected by it. I always hated people who declared that it was the end. What did they know about the end? From personal experience, from the grave if I may say so, *I* knew something about it. But I was flat, dead wrong. Anybody may feel the truth. But suppose it to be true—true, and not a mood, not ignorance or destructive pleasure or the doom desired by people who have botched everything. Suppose it to be so. There is still such a thing as a man—or there was. There are still human qualities. Our weak species fought its fear, our crazy species fought its criminality. We are an animal of genius."

This was a thing he often thought. At the moment it was only a formula. He did not thoroughly feel it.

"O.K., Uncle."

"But we don't have to decide whether the world is ending. The point is that for your father it *is* the end."

"Why are you pushing that, as if I didn't know. What do you want from me?"

Indeed what? From her, sitting there, breasts shown, diffusing woman-odors, big eyes practically merged; tormented, and at this moment strangely badgered by Caesar and the Tencteri, by ideas. Let the poor creature be. For now she was claiming to be a poor creature. And she was. But he could not let her be—not yet.

"As a rule these aneurysms cause instant death," he said. "With Elya there has been a delay, which gives an opportunity."

"An opportunity? What do you mean?"

"A chance to resolve some things. And it has made your father realistic—facing up to facts that were obscure."

"Facts about me, for instance? He didn't really want to know about me."

"Yes."

"What are you getting at?"

"You've got to do something for him. He has a need."

"What something am I supposed to do?"

"That's up to you. If you love him, you can make some sign. He's grieving. He's in a rage. He's disappointed. And I don't really think it is the sex. At this moment that might well be a trivial consideration. Don't you see, Angela? You wouldn't need to do much. It would give the man a last opportunity to collect himself."

"As far as I can see, if there is anything at all in what you say, you want an old-time deathbed scene."

"What difference does it make what you call it?"

"I should ask him to forgive me? Are you serious?"

"I am perfectly serious."

"But how could I— It goes against everything. You're talking to the wrong person. Even for my father it would be too hokey. I can't see it."

"He's been a good man. And he's being swept out. Can't you think of something to say to him?"

"What is there to say? And can't you think of anything but death?"

"But that's what we have before us."

"And you won't stop. I know you're going to say something more. Well, say it."

"In so many words?"

"In so many words. The fewer the better."

"I don't know what happened in Mexico. The details don't matter. I only note the peculiarity that it is possible to be gay, amorous, intimate with holiday acquaintances. Diversions, group intercourse, fellatio with strangers—one can do that but not come to terms with one's father at the last opportunity. He's put an immense amount of feeling into you. Probably most of his feeling has gone toward you.

If you can in some way see this and make some return . . ."

"Uncle Sammler!" She was furious.

"Ah. You're angry. Naturally."

"You've insulted me. You've been trying hard enough. Well, now you have—you've insulted me, Uncle Sammler."

"It was not the object. I only believe that there are things everyone knows, and must know."

"For God's sake, quit this."

"I shall mind my own business."

"You lead a special life in that dumpy room. Charming, but what's it got to do with anything! I don't think you understand people's business. What do you mean about fellatio? What do *you* know about it?"

Well, it hadn't worked. What she threw at him was what the young man at Columbia had also cried out. He was out of it. A tall, dry, not agreeable old man, censorious, giving himself airs. Who in hell was he? *Hors d'usage.* Against the wall. *A la lanterne!* Very well. That was little enough. He ought not perhaps to have provoked Angela so painfully. By now he himself was shaking.

The gray nurse at this moment came and called Sammler to the telephone. "You are Mr. Sammler, aren't you?"

He started. Quickly he got to his feet. "Ah! Who wants me? Who is it?" He didn't know what to expect.

"The phone wants you. Your daughter. You can take it outside, at the desk."

"Yes, Shula, yes?" her father said. "Speak up. What is it? Where are you?"

"In New Rochelle. Where is Elya?"

"We are waiting for him. What do you want now, Shula?"

"Have you heard about Wallace?"

"Yes, I've heard."

"He did a really great thing when he brought in that plane without wheels."

"Yes, magnificent. He's certainly marvelous. Now, Shula, I want you out of there. You are not to prowl around that house, you have no business there. I wanted you to come back with me. You are not supposed to disobey me."

"I wouldn't dream of it."

"But you did."

"I didn't. If we differ, it's in your interest."

"Shula, don't fool with me. Enough of my interests. Let them alone. You called with a purpose. I'm afraid I begin to understand."

"Yes, Father."

"You succeeded!"

"Yes, Father, aren't you pleased? In the—guess where? In the den where you slept. In the hassock you sat on this morning. When I brought in the coffee and saw you on it, I said, 'That's where the money is.' I was just about sure. So when you went away, I came back and opened it up, and it was filled—filled with money. Would you think that about Cousin Elya? I'm surprised at him. I didn't want to believe it. The hassock was upholstered with packages of hundred-dollar bills. Money was the stuffing."

"Dear God."

"I haven't counted it," she said.

"I will not have you lying."

"All right, I did count. But I don't really know about money. I don't understand business."

"Did you speak to Wallace on the phone?"

"Yes."

"And did you tell him about this?"

"I didn't say one single word."

"Good, very good, Shula. I expect you to turn it over to Mr. Widick. Call him to come and get it, and tell him you want a receipt for it."

"Father!"

"Yes, Shula."

He waited. He knew that, gripping one of those New Rochelle white telephones, she was marshaling her arguments, she was mastering her resentment at his ancient-father's stubbornness and stupid rectitude. At her expense. He knew quite well what she was feeling. "What will you live on, Father, when Elya is gone?" she said.

An excellent question, a shrewd, relevant question. He had lost out with Angela, he had infuriated her. He knew what she would say. "I'll never forgive you, Uncle." And what's more she never would.

"We will live on what there is."

"But suppose he doesn't leave any provision?"

"That's as he wishes. Up to him, entirely."

"We are part of the family. You are the closest to him."

"You will do as I tell you."

"Listen to me, Father. I have to look out for you. You haven't even said anything to me about finding this."

"It was damn clever of you, Shula. Yes. Congratulations. That was clever."

"It really was. I noticed how the hassock bulged under you, not like other hassocks, and when I felt around I heard the money rustle. I knew from the rustle, what it was. Of course I didn't say anything to Wallace. He'd squander it in a week. I thought I'd buy some clothes. If I was dressed at Lord and Taylor, maybe I'd be less of an eccentric type, and I'd have a chance with somebody."

"Like Govinda Lal."

"Yes, why not? I've made myself as interesting as I could within my means."

Her father was astonished by this. Eccentric type? She *was* aware of herself, then. There *was* a degree of choice. Wig, scavenging, shopping bags, were to an extent deliberate. Was that what she meant? How fascinating!

"And I think," she was saying, "that we should keep this. I think Elya would agree. I'm a woman without a husband, and I've never had children, and this money comes from preventing children, and I think it's only right that I should take it. For you, too, Father."

"I'm afraid not, Shula. Elya may already have told Mr. Widick about this hoard. I'm sorry. But we're not thieves. It's not our money. Tell me how much it was?"

"Each time I count, it's different."

"How much was it the last time?"

"Either six or eight thousand. I laid it all out on the floor. But I was too excited to count straight."

"I assume it's much, much more, and I can't allow you to keep any."

"I won't."

Of course she would, he was certain of it. As a trash-collector, treasure-hunter, she would be unable to surrender it all.

"You must give Widick every cent."

"Yes, Father. It's painful, but I will. I'll hand it over to Widick. I think you're making a mistake."

"No mistake. And don't take off as you did with Govinda's manuscript."

Too late to be tempted. One more desire gone. He very nearly smiled at himself.

"Good-by, Shula. You're a good daughter. The best of any. No better daughter."

Wallace, then, had been right about his father. He had done favors for the Mafia. Performed some operations. The money did exist. There was no time to think about all this, however. He put up the phone and left the marble counter to find that Dr. Cosbie had been waiting for him. The one-time football star in his white coat held his upper lip pressed by the nether one. The bloodless face and gas-blue eyes had been trained to transmit surgeons' messages. The message was plain. It was all over.

"When did he die?" said Sammler. "Just now?"

While I was stupidly urging Angela!

"A little while back. We had him down in the special unit, doin' the maximum possible."

"You couldn't do anything about a hemorrhage, I see, yes."

"You are his uncle. He asked me to say good-by to you."

"I wish I had been able to say it also to him. So it didn't happen in one rush?"

"He knew it was startin'. He was a doctor. He knew it. He asked me to take him from the room."

"He asked you to?"

"It was obvious he wanted to spare his daughter. So I said tests. It's Miss Angela?"

"Yes, Angela."

"He said he preferred downstairs. He knew I'd take him anyway."

"Of course. As a surgeon, Elya knew. He certainly knew the operation was futile, all that torture of putting a screw in his throat." Sammler removed his glasses. His eyes, one a sightless bubble, under the hair of overhanging brows, were level with Dr. Cosbie's. "Of course it was futile."

"The procedure was correct. He knew it was."

"My nephew wished always to agree. Of course he knew. It might have been kinder though not to make him go through it."

"I suppose you want to go in and tell Miss Angela?"

"Please tell Miss Angela yourself. What I want is to see my nephew. How do I get to him? Give me directions."

"You'll have to wait and see him at the chapel, sir. It's not allowed."

"Young man, it is important and you had better allow me. Take my word for it. I am determined. Let us not have a bad scene out here in the corridor. You would not want that, would you?"

"Would you make one?"

"I would."

"I'll send his nurse with you," said the doctor.

They went down in the elevator, the gray woman and Mr. Sammler, and through lower passages paved in speckled material, through tunnels, up and down ramps, past laboratories and supply rooms. Well, this famous truth for which he was so keen, he had it now, or it had him. He felt that he was being destroyed, what was left of him. He wept to himself. He walked at the habitual rapid sweeping pace, waiting at crossways for the escorting nurse. In stirring air flavored with body-things, sickness, drugs. He felt that he was breaking up, that irregular big fragments inside were melting, sparkling with pain, floating off. Well, Elya was gone. He was deprived of one more thing, stripped of one more creature. One more reason to live trickled out. He lost his breath. Then the woman came up. More hundreds of yards in this winding underground smelling of serum, of organic soup, of fungus, of cell-brew. The nurse took Sammler's hat and said, "In there." The door sign read P.M. That would mean post-mortem. They were ready to do an autopsy as soon as Angela signed the papers. And of course she would sign. Let's find out what went wrong. And then cremation.

"To see Dr. Gruner. Where?" said Sammler.

The attendant pointed to the wheeled stretcher on which Elya lay. Sammler uncovered his face. The nostrils, the creases were very dark, the shut eyes pale and full, the bald head high-marked by gradients of wrinkles. In the lips bitterness and an expression of obedience were combined.

Sammler in a mental whisper said, "Well, Elya. Well, well, Elya." And then in the same way he said, "Remember, God, the soul of Elya Gruner, who, as willingly as possible and as well as he was able, and even to an intolerable point, and even in suffocation and even as death was coming was eager, even childishly perhaps (may I be forgiven for this), even with a certain servility, to do what was required of him. At his best this man was much kinder than at my very best I have ever been or could ever be. He was aware that he must meet, and he did meet—through all the confusion and degraded clowning of this life through which we are speeding—he did meet the terms of his contract. The terms which, in his inmost heart, each man knows. As I know mine. As all know. For that is the truth of it—that we all know, God, that we know, that we know, we know, we know."